CW01509144

What readers are saying about *Evil in High Places*

'Fans of historical thrillers will devour this'

'An author at the top of his game and this ranks as
one of his best novels to date'

'A gripping read with lots of excitement and action'

'Rory Clements is brilliant at evoking the feeling of the times
and weaving it into an exciting thriller detective story'

'This gripping thriller is full of tension and
keeps readers hooked'

'A pacy thriller . . . utterly compelling'

'Clements brings pre-war Munich to life . . . A perfect blend of
historical detail, espionage and intelligent plotting'

'Full of twists and turns as tight as the winding
bend up to Schloss Stark'

'I was gripped from first page to last'

'Rory Clements has written an excellent page-turner, to be
recommended to anyone who appreciates a good book'

'An exciting story with plenty of action . . . I look
forward to the next in the series'

'An excellent piece of historical fiction. Atmospheric,
detailed and gripping – this has it all'

'Captivating, atmospheric . . . a terrific historical thriller'

'Clements has produced another mystery thriller masterpiece'

'A tense, well-written story . . . I kept turning the pages'

'Another solid thriller from a master storyteller . . .
Thoroughly recommended'

'A corker with murder and intrigue . . . An excellent book'

'This reads like a noir, hard-boiled detective and all'

'Another great thriller . . . highly recommended'

Rory Clements

EVIL IN HIGH PLACES

PENGUIN
VIKING

VIKING

UK | USA | Canada | Ireland | Australia
India | New Zealand | South Africa

Viking is part of the Penguin Random House group of companies
whose addresses can be found at global.penguinrandomhouse.com

Penguin Random House UK,
One Embassy Gardens, 8 Viaduct Gardens, London SW11 7BW

penguin.co.uk

Penguin
Random House
UK

First published 2025

001

Set in 13.5/16pt Garamond MT Std
Typeset by Jouve (UK), Milton Keynes
Printed and bound in Great Britain by Clays Ltd, Elcograf S.p.A.

The authorised representative in the EEA is Penguin Random House Ireland,
Morrison Chambers, 32 Nassau Street, Dublin D02 YH68

A CIP catalogue record for this book is available from the British Library

HARDBACK ISBN: 978–0–241–72818–5
TRADE PAPERBACK ISBN: 978–0–241–72817–8

Penguin Random House is committed to a sustainable future
for our business, our readers and our planet. This book is made from
Forest Stewardship Council® certified paper.

For Imogen
with love

I

Bavaria, 1936

When Elena Lang went missing, Sebastian Wolff couldn't work out what all the fuss was about.

'She's a film star,' he told his boss. 'She's probably overslept – in someone else's hotel room. That's how the business works.'

'You're a cynic, Wolff.'

'Perhaps, but I'm a murder detective, not a missing persons drudge.'

'What you are, Wolff, is my subordinate. You'll do what I tell you to do, and today I'm ordering you to find Elena Lang.'

'At your service as always, chief.'

That was an hour ago at the Police Presidium in Ettstrasse, central Munich. Now here he was in the south of the city at Geiselgasteig, home of the Bavaria Film AG studios, accompanied by his assistant, Sergeant Hans Winter.

Seb knew why he was here. He spoke English, and the film's director was English, as was the company behind the production. Oh, and there was the small matter of the Olympics. Nothing must detract attention from the big event. That meant no murders, no missing people, no scandals.

Seb and his sergeant approached the front gate of the studios.

'Did you see her latest, captain?' Winter asked.

'What?'

'Elena Lang's new film, *Rapture*.'

'Nice title. I suppose you took that girl of yours.'

Winter nodded and looked sheepish.

Seb laughed. 'Was it good?'

'I suppose so, if you like historical romances. Malwine liked it, so did the audience: they stood up and cheered and applauded. I thought it was all rather foolish and soppy.'

'Foolish and soppy, Winter? That's the whole point of the cinema, isn't it? An hour or two of foolishness to escape from the cares of reality. That, and your arm around your girl. So her name's Malwine, is it? You hadn't told me that before.'

'You didn't ask. She's named after Bismarck's sister. Her father, Herr Schmidt, is something senior at BMW and he's a great German patriot.'

'Isn't everyone these days?'

Winter gave him a warning look as if to say, *Be careful, captain. You might be safe with me, but there are less friendly ears in the new Germany.*

Seb shrugged. 'And what do they think of you, these great patriots?'

'They were polite when I met them, but I think they disapprove. I fear they might suspect. Her father talks about Versailles and the betrayal of the Fatherland. Also his loathing of Jews. And, whenever he says that, he peers at me closely to see my reaction. I don't know how to talk to the man.'

Winter's words did not need comment. Wolff knew that his sergeant lived in constant fear that his part-Jewish ancestry would be discovered. 'You can tell me all about Malwine and her family over a beer later. On the plus side, she's certainly smartened you up.'

A new suit and tie, polished shoes. At the age of thirty-one, Hans Winter was finally beginning to look respectable.

When they first met, back in June of the previous year, his hair was badly cut, his suit was shabby, and his tie was stained. Not a good advertisement for the Bavarian Political Police.

'For the moment,' Seb continued, 'we'd better find the missing Elena Lang.'

The entrance to the lot was in a quiet street, bounded by woodland to the east. Behind the fence, studio buildings that looked no more enticing than aircraft hangars dominated the scene. It all seemed very bland, but this was where the magic was created. Further to the west, beyond the lot, the Isar flowed serenely towards the centre of the city.

Two tall SS men in long leather coats, their shoulders back and rigid, eyes fixed to the front, stood to attention at the gate. Why the SS were needed here was beyond Seb. Behind the guards, a pair of even taller soldiers, dressed in the bright red of the famous old Prussian Infantry No. 6 regiment, hurried across the damp paved area, each with a glass of beer in one hand and a cigarette in the other.

'Who on earth are they?' Winter said, mystified.

'Actors playing Potsdam Giants. Obviously not the Elena Lang film – that's a modern thriller.' Seb showed his Kripo badge to the SS men and Winter did the same with his BPP warrant.

'You gentlemen here about herself, I suppose.'

'Indeed, officer. Any idea where she might be?'

'Legs apart somewhere, I've no doubt.' He grinned, without relaxing his strict posture, then immediately looked sheepish. 'Please don't tell anyone I said that, detective.'

'Don't worry. The thought had already crossed my mind.'

The SS man's gaze drifted to the gatehouse. 'If you go over there and sign in, they'll put a call through so someone can come to collect you, gentlemen.'

*

3

Two minutes later, a young woman arrived. Small and dark-haired. 'Herr Wolff?'

Seb nodded. 'That's me. And this is Sergeant Winter of the Bavarian Political Police. He is presently on attachment to the Criminal Police.' He wasn't going to mention that the BPP were Munich's very own version of the Gestapo. Nor was he going to add that Winter had actually been foisted on him because Wolff wasn't trusted and needed watching. Their relationship had not started well but had progressed to some kind of understanding, even warmth. They knew each other's secrets: Seb's loathing of the Nazis; Winter's Jewish blood.

The woman looked Winter up and down critically, then turned her gaze back to Seb.

'Very pleased to meet you both. I'm Olivia Sands – Alan Harcourt's assistant. I believe you speak English. Mr Harcourt would prefer it that way.'

'As you wish.' He caught Winter's eye and shrugged. 'I'll give you the gist, sergeant.'

'Follow me, if you would, gentlemen,' Miss Sands said. 'Mr Harcourt is presently in the editing suite but will meet us in his office in a short while.'

'Perhaps you could fill us in on what you know about the movements of Fräulein Lang.'

'Of course.' She smiled, her face open and welcoming. 'And I shall arrange some coffee if you like.'

'Thank you.'

They were escorted to a first-floor office in a building deep inside the studio complex. The room was in chaos. A desk, four chairs, a very bright reading lamp, papers on every surface, tins full of film reels, drawings of what looked like potential movie scenes pinned to the four walls. The whole place smelt of tobacco smoke and sweat.

Without compunction, Olivia Sands swept piles of documents from two chairs on to the floor. 'Your seats, detectives. Let me organise that coffee and hopefully Mr Harcourt will arrive soon.'

'Before you go, you were going to tell us about the movements of Elena Lang,' Seb said as he took his seat.

'Oh, dear, where to begin?'

'When was she last seen?'

'That would be Friday. We didn't work Sunday, but we did have a shoot on Saturday morning and she wasn't here. Mr Harcourt was annoyed but he wasn't too worried because he had other scenes to complete without her. Hardly the first time she's missed a morning shoot.'

'So she was last seen on the lot four days ago?'

'Correct.'

'And she's been staying in central Munich at the Vier Jahreszeiten?'

'Also correct. And, before you ask, yes, we have checked and checked again with the hotel management. Her bed hasn't been slept in since Thursday evening and she hasn't eaten in the restaurant.'

'How does she normally make her way from the hotel to the studio?'

'A car is there for her at six every morning.'

'And the driver is trustworthy?'

'Viktor has been with the studio for many years. If you want to talk to him, I'll make him available.'

'Thank you. And when did you first alert the police?'

'Yesterday morning, ten o'clock. I placed a call to the Police Presidium myself, but I didn't think it had been taken very seriously, so I called again in the afternoon. Since then Mr Harcourt has spoken to various friends – particularly Adolf Wagner. And now, like magic, things are happening.'

Adolf Wagner. Gauleiter – regional governor – of Munich and Upper Bavaria and, perhaps most telling of all, a close friend of his namesake, Adolf Hitler.

A phone call from the one-legged Wagner to Deputy Police President Thomas Ruff would have got things moving. Ruff was Seb's immediate boss, a bureaucrat terrified of his own shadow since the Night of the Long Knives purge less than two years ago, and the murder of Ruff's own commanding officer.

'Why wait all that time before you called us?'

Miss Sands shrugged. 'This is not untypical behaviour for an actress, I'm afraid. Anyway, it was the weekend. Miss Lang knows people in the area and might well have been visiting one of them, so no one was terribly surprised. We were all irritated but not worried for her safety.'

'But there's something different this time. Something's unnerved you.'

'Well, even when actors and actresses miss shoots, we usually have a pretty good idea where they are. You may not be surprised to learn that thespians don't tend to shun the limelight. Often as not, if an actress is missing, an actor will be, too – and vice versa.'

'You say she has friends in the area. I would like details of them.'

'I don't know any of them myself but I will certainly ask around.'

'Tell me, if it's not impertinent, why did Mr Harcourt choose to make this film in Bavaria rather than England?'

'There aren't many mountains in London and anyway he loves Bavaria – he directed in this studio back in the twenties and made friends, particularly among the senior men in the local Nazi movement. People like Wagner. When he approached various people about this new film, they were happy to offer him studio space at an exceptionally good price, as well as privileged access to various locations, particularly the Alps, which are central to the story. The film is tentatively titled *Evil in High Places*.'

'So Mr Harcourt knows Bavaria well?'

'Indeed. And his German language skills actually aren't bad. When I asked you to speak English, that is simply the way he prefers it.'

A door slammed somewhere below and then heavy footsteps on the stairway announced the imminent arrival of the celebrated film director Alan Harcourt. Seb had seen some of his films; he had made his name in the silent era but was proving even more popular with his talkies, specialising in high-suspense thrillers.

He knew how to make an entrance: his figure filled the doorway, shrouded in smoke. He was holding a large cigar in his left hand. A bear of a man, breathing fire. His gaze pivoted between the two new men and landed on Seb. 'I take it you're in charge,' he said in English, his voice a growl.

Seb stood up and bowed perfunctorily. 'Yes, sir. Captain of Detectives Wolff.'

'We're filming in the mountains tomorrow and she has to be there. This cannot be rearranged. I am on an unbreakable deadline because I have to be back in England by the twenty-fourth. Do you understand?'

'Yes, sir.'

'So what are you doing about it?'

'I'm talking to you, Mr Harcourt. And then I'll talk to anyone else who knows Fräulein Lang and try to find clues to her movements and present whereabouts.'

'Damn it, man, if anyone on set knew her whereabouts, we wouldn't need you here.'

'Do you have a better idea, Mr Harcourt?'

'Yes. My idea is that you get out there and find the bitch.'

Seb wasn't fazed. He was used to difficult people. As a non-Nazi in a city full of Nazis, he had to go along with their games, treat arrogance as a social disorder and get on with his job as best he could. 'My feelings entirely, Mr Harcourt. First, though, I'd like to ask you a couple of questions, then talk to her co-stars if they're on the lot.'

'Ask *me* questions? What use would that be? Damn it, I was told you were the best detective in Munich – what must the others be like?'

'Miss Sands tells me that Fräulein Lang has friends in Bavaria. Perhaps you could furnish me with some of their names.' Seb saw the irritation in Harcourt's eyes but pressed on regardless. 'By the way, sir, do you have any reason to believe that something might have happened to her? That her disappearance might not be entirely voluntary?'

'You mean has she been abducted or killed? My God, I would happily kill her myself. She's just a pain in the bloody neck. Wish I'd never cast the bloody woman. Been nothing but trouble since day bloody one.'

'What sort of trouble, sir, if you don't mind my asking?'

'Actors and actresses are there to do exactly as the director says. She has ideas of her own. Turns up late, has the temerity to try changing the script, suggests angles. Sulks.'

'How does she get on with the male star of the film?'

'Gary Tate? Oh, I don't think she has anything to do with him off set.' Harcourt snorted at the very thought. 'She's not really his type.'

Seb took this to imply that Gary Tate was probably more attracted to his own sex, but that would have to remain unsaid, German laws being strict on such matters.

'Talk to him if you must,' Harcourt continued. 'But just get on with it. Time is everything. He's still here, but I've dismissed the others. Can't have them drinking endless cups of coffee and smoking tobacco fields of cigarettes at my expense – we're on a damned budget.'

'Where will I find Mr Tate?'

'Stage Two.'

'One more question, sir: you didn't quite tell me if you believe Fräulein Lang is still alive?'

Harcourt shrugged. 'She damned well better be because I'll be hard pressed to finish the film without her.' His enormous face mutated into something close to a sneer. 'But, then again, she's insured to the hilt, so maybe her death wouldn't be such a bad option.'

With that, he turned and disappeared, leaving nothing but a Harcourt-shaped halo of smoke.

2

'I'm sorry,' Olivia Sands said, reverting to German. 'I didn't quite get around to the coffee.'

'Don't worry. Just take us to Stage Two and see if you can drum up the names of Elena Lang's friends and acquaintances.'

'Of course. And let me apologise for Mr Harcourt. I'm sure he's desperately worried about Elena, but he's under a lot of pressure. This film means a great deal to him – I think he sees it as his riposte to *The Thirty-Nine Steps*.'

'Ah, yes, I read the book,' Seb said. He had borrowed it from the skipper on the *Eastern Star*, the British freighter where he worked for four years. It was one of the books that helped with his struggle to learn English. 'I believe it's been made into a film.'

'Very successfully, by Alfred Hitchcock – which has upset Harcourt no end. They are great rivals. But no matter. Come along.'

They found Gary Tate in one of the vast buildings which housed the film sets. He was in his dressing room, feet up on the counter in front of a large, brightly lit mirror, cigarette in his mouth, gazing vacantly at the ceiling.

'Mr Tate?'

'Is that you, Olivia?' He didn't bother to turn or look at her.

'I have two gentlemen here from the Munich police. They'd like to talk to you.'

'Are you serious? Just because that bloody tart has gone off somewhere for a shag?'

Seb stepped forward. 'Miss Lang's disappearance is being taken extremely seriously.'

Tate sighed, slowly removed his feet from the make-up bench with its mass of jars and bottles of slap and powder and hair-styling items, and turned around to face his visitors. He raised his right arm in a desultory, mocking fashion. 'Heil Hitler,' he said.

'Heil Hitler, Mr Tate,' Seb said, hastily followed by Winter. 'This is Captain Wolff and Sergeant Winter.'

'*Guten Tag, meine Herren.*'

'Good day to you, too, Mr Tate. And English is fine. We just have a couple of questions for you.'

'Fire away.'

'Do you have any inkling where Miss Lang might be?'

'Well, definitely not with me. Maybe she's working her way through the local SS brigade. Ask the fellows at the gate. They might know.'

'I'll take that as a "no". My next question is whether you know the names of any of her friends in Munich or the wider Bavaria?'

'Why would I? On set we work together to make a film. When the day's over, she goes her way, I go mine.'

'Where are you staying, Mr Tate?'

'That's three questions; you said two. Oh, the Vier Jahres-zeiten. Just like madame. On occasion, we've even shared a car to the studio.'

'With the studio driver, Viktor?'

'With Viktor.'

Seb could not fail to be struck by Gary Tate's remarkable good looks. Dark hair, bright eyes, flawless skin. Perfect and yet somehow rugged, just right for the silver screen. He had one of those faces that almost seemed to be smiling even when he wasn't. Seb guessed his age to be about thirty. He spoke quickly to Hans Winter in German to outline the conversation and ask whether he had any questions of his own.

'When did Herr Tate last see Fräulein Lang? Did he see her at the hotel on Friday after the shoot?'

Seb put the question to the actor and once again the answer was a curt 'no'.

'Did you share the car back to the hotel?'

'We did. But I didn't see her again.'

'All right, thank you for your time, Mr Tate,' Seb said. 'We may be in touch.'

'Don't hurry back.'

The Vier Jahreszeiten Hotel was on Maximilianstrasse, to the north of the old city. A man and a woman stood at the front desk, both in the hotel's smart livery. Seb made a point of approaching the woman.

'How can I help you, sir?'

Seb flashed his Kripo badge. 'Captain of Detectives Wolff, Police Presidium.'

The woman's arm shot up. 'Heil Hitler, Captain Wolff.'

'Heil Hitler, fräulein. And this is Sergeant Winter of the Bavarian Political Police.'

The woman tensed and threw another salute. Seb understood her nervousness. Everyone knew that the BPP were the local secret police and everyone feared them because they had the power to throw you in Dachau concentration camp without trial. This was something Seb had discovered for himself the previous summer, though only for one uncomfortable night. Others stayed a great deal longer; some died. There was no appeal.

'We are investigating the disappearance of one of your

guests, the film actress Elena Lang. Have you ever had dealings with her?'

'Yes, sir. She's an honoured guest.'

'And what is your name?'

'Ingol, sir.'

'Fräulein Ingol, perhaps you could take me to Miss Lang's room?'

'Yes, sir.' She turned to her desk colleague. 'Herr Schell, would you cover for me here while I show these two officers to Miss Lang's room?'

Schell clicked his heels. 'Of course.'

Seb nodded at Winter. 'Sergeant, you stay here with Herr Schell and see if he has any idea where Miss Lang might be.'

Elena Lang's accommodation was a suite of four large rooms including a bathroom, sitting room, dining room and bed-chamber. It occurred to Seb that few people in Munich had access to such space in their own homes; he certainly didn't. The apartment he shared in Ainmüllerstrasse with his mother and son would fit into the two reception rooms alone.

The suite was immaculate and smelt of flowers; everything was in its place.

'Is this how Miss Lang left the room?'

'No, sir. I hope I'm not speaking out of turn, but Miss Lang isn't the sort of person to tidy up after herself. But then she doesn't need to and we don't expect it of our guests, for our chambermaids are skilled in their work and attend to the smallest details of cleanliness.'

Seb looked in the wardrobe, which was full of women's clothes – dresses, blouses, shoes. He opened drawers, in which smaller items were folded perfectly and divided by tissue paper. The bed was vast – big enough to sleep four adults.

He opened the drawers of the bedside tables. In one he found a well-thumbed script for the film she was supposed to be making, *Evil in High Places*. Also a couple of books – an Agatha Christie, *Murder on the Orient Express*, and *The Riddle of the Sands* by Erskine Childers. Both books in the original English.

The concierge saw what he was looking at. 'I believe Miss Lang speaks good English, for I've observed her talking with British members of the film crew.'

There were four telephones in the suite, one on each of the bedside tables and in each of the other rooms.

A wide leather-topped desk in the sitting room was graced with a writing pad, fountain pen, inkwell and Vier Jahreszeiten-headed notepaper. Again, nothing to indicate her whereabouts. 'Where are Miss Lang's suitcases?'

'The porters bring them downstairs and put them into storage when they're unpacked. I'm sure they're empty.'

'I would like to see them anyway.'

'Of course, captain. I'll take you to them when you're finished here.'

'Oh, I'm finished here.' The rooms were almost completely devoid of anything personal save for the books, script and clothes. Clearly Miss Lang travelled light.

They rode down in the lift together. 'Has Miss Lang had any visitors while she has been here?'

The concierge looked uneasy. 'You mean apart from the film crew?'

'I mean including the film crew – and others.'

'There have been people, yes, but mostly they stay in the bar with her or they eat together in the restaurant.'

'But not always?'

'I'm not sure it's my place to say, sir.'

'She's entertained men in her room?'

The young woman nodded, her face reddening.

'I would like the names of these men, Fräulein Ingol.'

'We don't have their names. The only visitors I knew were the Englishman Mr Harcourt and his assistant Miss Sands, but they remained downstairs in the bar.'

'And has Miss Lang gone missing before?'

'She didn't always stay the night here, but I wouldn't say she was missing as such. We never had any cause for concern until now. The comings and goings of guests is no business of the hotel or its staff.'

'Tell me about telephone calls. She must have made and received calls. Have there been messages?'

'I'm not sure, but it is possible – likely even. My colleague Herr Schell would be able to tell you.'

'Let's see what he has to say.'

Schell was talking to Hans Winter at the desk. 'Anything, sergeant?' Seb asked.

'Possibly. There was a message for Miss Lang on Thursday evening.'

He turned his attention to the male concierge. 'Tell me about it, Herr Schell.'

'The caller asked to speak to Miss Lang, but she wasn't here. The woman on the phone said to please ask Miss Lang to call Sophie.'

'And that was all?'

'Yes, but I'm sure I recognised the woman's voice, for she's been here many times before. I believe it was Sophie von Stark, sir.'

'Sophie von Stark? Of the von Stark family?'

'Yes, captain.'

'Did she leave a number to call?'

'No, sir.'

Seb wrote his own name and numbers on a piece of paper

and slid it across the counter. 'If either of you hears anything else in regard to Miss Lang's whereabouts, call me without delay – any time, day or night.'

'Yes, captain,' Schell said.

'And do you now wish to inspect Miss Lang's suitcases?' Fräulein Ingol asked.

'Show them to Sergeant Winter.' He had more important things to do: somehow, he had to talk to Sophie von Stark. But that might not be so easy. Such people were not accessible.

'What am I looking for, captain?' Winter asked.

Seb rolled his eyes. 'Clues, Winter.' As a member of the political police, Winter had little experience of detective work, but he was learning.

3

The von Starks. A noble family of extreme wealth going back hundreds of years. Older than the Rothschilds or the Krupps, they had been among the most aristocratic of German dynasties since the time of the Fuggers, the Welsers and the Tuchers, though perhaps not quite as wealthy as the Fuggers. But then no one was, for Jakob Fugger of Augsburg was the wealthiest man who ever lived.

The von Starks had made their money through mining, various manufacturing industries, slave-trading and money-lending. It was said that they had financed the winning side in every European war since 1500 – the reason for this being that they tended to finance both sides of a conflict.

The twentieth-century von Starks had not been slow to support the Nazi movement and were already reaping their reward with major contracts for shipbuilding and other great engineering projects from Hamburg in the north to Munich in the south and all points east and west.

You could not just make a phone call to such people. Which castle or palace would you call? Sophie was the daughter of the family. She and her brother, Werner, would one day inherit their parents' riches. They lived in another world.

However, there was one man who might just be able to help Seb make contact.

Seb left his Lancia outside the hotel and strode westwards along Maximilianstrasse. He had business at the Residenz, once the great city-centre palace of the kings of Bavaria and now the home of Seb's uncle Christian Weber – his mother's younger brother and boss of the city council.

It was a short walk, no more than five minutes, but far enough to feel the chill in the air. He sensed snow in the offing, something that would definitely please the organisers of the Olympics and the Nazi hierarchy who had staked so much on its success.

They wanted to show themselves in a good light. That meant temporarily removing anti-Jewish slogans, refraining from beating people up in the street, smiling at the foreign press – anything to prove that they weren't the thugs depicted in the American newspapers.

As far as Seb was concerned, that was going to be difficult to pull off. He didn't like the present government, but that wasn't unusual. His job was to solve crimes and bring murderers to court; their politics meant nothing to him. It didn't matter who was in charge of the country; life had to go on and people needed the protection of an impartial police force.

Uncle Christian received him in the Black Hall, as he always did. Seb suspected he did so simply because he liked the name. Because it intimidated visitors even before they arrived at the Residenz.

The room wasn't black but it was ornate and impressive, like the rest of the immense palace, which Uncle Christian had acquired through corruption on an industrial scale and, more importantly, his close friendship with Adolf Hitler. Christian Weber was one of the select band known as the Old Fighters, those who had marched alongside the Führer in the attempted coup of 1923. Their mutual loyalty and friendship had stood the test of time.

Seb was usually made to wait, but this time his uncle was with him inside a couple of minutes, his pork belly straining against his SS-Oberführer uniform.

'Boy, what can I do for you this time? You never come to see me unless you want something.'

'Some advice, uncle, that's all.'

'My advice? Marry that girl of yours. Why didn't you do it last summer? I'd have turned it into the event of the year and you'd have made your mother the proudest woman in Bavaria.'

'That's a story for another day, uncle.' It was a good question, though. Why hadn't he married Hexie Schuler? He had posed the question, she had said yes, and here they were seven months later, still unwed and no date set.

'What is it, boy? What can I do for you today?'

'I need to talk to Sophie von Stark, but I've no idea how to get in touch with her.'

'God in heaven, why would you need to talk to her? Bit above your station, isn't she?'

'I'm looking for the film star Elena Lang. There has been no sign of her since Friday. Last hint of a contact I have for her is that Sophie left a message at the Vier Jahreszeiten desk asking Miss Lang to call her.'

'Don't mess with the von Starks. Be very, very careful. They haven't survived for five hundred years by being squeamish about doing away with enemies.'

Seb wanted to laugh but restrained himself. 'I just want to speak to her, that's all. You know everyone in Bavaria, so it occurred to me you might just know how to contact her.'

'Come with me.'

Weber, generally known as 'The Pig', turned and strode through half a dozen glittering chambers until he came to a large office. Two secretaries, both in smart skirts and white blouses and both remarkably pretty with braided blonde hair, immediately rose from their desks and stood to attention.

'Maria, find the number for Schloss Stark.'

'Yes, sir.'

Two minutes later she was calling through to the castle, asking whether the honourable Sophie von Stark was in residence and explaining that a senior detective with the Munich police would very much like to talk to her regarding the whereabouts of Fräulein Elena Lang.

The secretary turned to her boss. 'The man who answered said he was in the estate office and would go and inquire.' She held the phone to her ear for another five minutes, then nodded and said, 'Very well. Heil Hitler and thank you.' She put the phone down.

'Well?' Weber demanded.

'The lady is not in a position to talk to the detective on the phone, but Captain Wolff will most likely be received if he would care to attend Schloss Stark in person.'

'So they're here in Bavaria?'

'It appears so, sir.'

Weber clapped his nephew on the back. 'Boy, there's your answer. Don't say I don't do anything for you. Do you know Schloss Stark?'

'Not far from Garmisch-Partenkirchen, between Grainau and Ehrwald.'

'Off you go, then. And give my love to your dear mother when next you see her.'

4

Seb met up with Hans Winter at the Police Presidium in Ettstrasse and told him his plan.

'Should I come with you, captain?'

'No, you stay in Munich. Talk to Olivia Sands again, press her for details of possible friends or acquaintances of Miss Lang. I take it there was nothing in her luggage?'

'Nothing.'

'Leave messages for me if you find any leads. I'll try to call through. Failing contact, we'll meet here tomorrow morning at eight o'clock.'

Usually, Schloss Stark would be an easy drive in Seb's red Lancia Augusta – probably no more than an hour and a half – but, with the weather closing in and the temperature dropping, it was not so pleasant. As he neared the mountains, the roads became icy and he was worried about the state of his tyres.

Even at this time of year, however, the Bavarian countryside would always look beautiful to Seb. He particularly loved the brooding backdrop of the Alps as he drove south towards Garmisch-Partenkirchen – 'Gapa', as it had been nicknamed since the twin towns had become one on the orders of the Führer.

Part of him felt irritated to be making such a long journey when a phone call would have served just as well: did Sophie von Stark know where her friend Elena Lang was, yes or no? It would have taken no more than a minute. Another part of him was happy to make the drive, which seemed a great deal better for the soul than sitting in his office at Ettstrasse. And, yes, he was interested to meet Sophie von Stark, the daughter of this most discreet – even secretive – of families.

Never had she or her brother had their picture in the newspapers; never was the smallest detail of their golden lives revealed to the public. If he passed her in the street, he would be none the wiser.

So he was curious. How could he not be?

Gapa was busier than he had ever seen it, even at the height of the tourist season. Olympic flags and swastikas seemed to be draped from every house, hotel and public building. SS troops and Hitler Youth helpers were out in force on all the streets. Bars, hotels and guest houses were packed with pleasure-seekers and competitors. Young people carrying skis and skates walked and talked together.

The twin towns were straining at the seams, and the fears that hosting the winter Olympics would cost a great deal more than the income it would generate were looking to be unfounded.

The big problem was still the lack of snow on the lower slopes. Plenty at the top of the Alpspitze and Zugspitze peaks that rose above the town, but the pistes became grad-ually more bare and green as they descended through the trees from Kreuzeck towards the Olympic centre in the valley. The ski jumps and designated slalom and downhill courses were unusable.

Seb knew there was talk of putting the opening ceremony back by two days in the desperate hope that snow would arrive, but that plan would bring organisational problems of its own.

Passing through the Garmisch portion of the twin town, he turned westwards on the road that skirted the northern flanks of the village of Grainau and the exquisite Lake Eibsee.

The meadows still looked green instead of white, the dozens of scattered hay-barns – so emblematic of this fertile valley – somewhat sad without their winter coats.

This was where Seb began to get the best view of the Zugspitze, Germany's highest mountain at almost 3,000 metres. Once past Eibsee, closely following the Loisach River beneath the Ammergauer Alps, the road narrowed as it approached the border. To his right he saw it, Schloss Stark, standing in majesty on a rocky crag overlooking the valley and stream.

The castle guarded the area like a sentinel. It told the world that its inhabitants were in charge, that anyone who strayed from the path would pay a heavy price. This was architecture as a statement of power and wealth.

There was no signpost to Schloss Stark, but it could not be missed. Seb took the only road that could lead there. The ascent was steep in places, but the Lancia dealt with it surprisingly easily; with no passengers or luggage aboard, the 1.2-litre engine was more than capable even with less-than-perfect tyres.

Many old castles in Germany had fallen into ruin over the centuries, as once-rich noble families failed to keep up with the economic currents. But the von Starks had never encountered any such problems and their alpine home – one of several they owned around Germany and elsewhere – was clearly in pristine condition, its light-coloured walls of Wetterstein limestone intact, its arched windows full of light.

He was stopped at the gatehouse, which had a tall, pointed tower and was almost as impressive as the castle itself, though on a much smaller scale.

Winding down the window, he found himself facing a middle-aged man in green-and-silver livery.

'Heil Hitler. How can I help you, sir?'

'Heil Hitler. Captain Wolff, Munich Kripo.' He pushed his badge under the gatekeeper's nose. 'To see the Fräulein von Stark.'

'Ah, yes, sir, you're expected. Please drive on. You'll be met at the main entrance.'

Seb thanked the man, wound up the window and continued up the road for another kilometre until he came into the shadow of the castle itself. Close up, it was very different to the impression he'd got from the valley. Yes, the walls were still light grey – just like the stone of the mountains it faced, and from which it was made – but in the lee of the building it seemed dark and foreboding and he couldn't quite understand why. He felt overpowered, almost intimidated, as countless others must have done over the centuries.

A footman attired in the same green-and-silver livery as the gateman was waiting for him at the door. Four other men, all in SS uniform, were leaning against the ramparts, watching him. What, he wondered, were *they* doing here?

He and the footman exchanged the tedious salute, then Seb was ushered into the ornate and high-ceilinged entrance hall. Every surface seemed to be either gilded or painted with scenes from Teutonic mythology: knights in armour, serpents, naked maidens. It felt like being trapped inside a Wagnerian opera.

'Wait here, please, captain.'

A massive, circular chandelier of wrought iron – like some sort of medieval wheel of war – hung above his head. It menaced rather than merely impressed, for if it fell it would crush a man with the force of a pneumatic hammer. Instinctively, Seb stepped out of its range.

The servant returned. 'Fräulein von Stark will see you in the Paradise Hall now, sir.'

Seb followed the man through a series of golden corridors to a vast, even more ornate hall. The ceiling was painted with an idealised yet sinister version of the Garden of Eden with the snake taking prime position, curled menacingly around a naked Eve.

A young woman was standing in the centre of the room. She was small, slender, fair-haired and dressed casually in a woollen skirt, woollen stockings and a thick blue pullover. In her hand she had a glass of white wine. So this was the aristocratic daughter of the great von Stark dynasty. Was he supposed to bend the knee and kiss her hand or give the Hitler salute? He really had no idea how to conduct himself.

The servant bowed to her and indicated Seb. 'This is Captain Wolff of the Munich Police Department, ma'am.'

She extended her tiny pale hand, palm down. Kiss it? Shake it? He took it in his own right hand and was about to lower his head to plant his lips on it when she shook his hand and all was well. No sign of a Hitler salute, which was a relief and a little surprising.

'Captain Wolff, how good of you to come all this way. I'm afraid we were all skiing up on the Zugspitze when you called. Pray tell me, what is this about my good friend Elena?'

'She's been missing since Friday and I believe you called the hotel for her. I was wondering whether she had got back to you?'

Sophie von Stark looked puzzled. She didn't smile but nor did she appear unfriendly. There was something neutral and reserved about her which he couldn't quite fathom. Perhaps she was simply unaccustomed to dealing with people outside her charmed circle.

'Yes,' she said, 'I remember leaving a message at the Vier Jahreszeiten, but I heard nothing back, which is most unlike her. She has the very best of manners. Where do you think she is, captain?'

'I wish I knew. Mr Harcourt the film director is extremely worried, for obvious reasons. Do you know Fräulein Lang well?'

'Oh, indeed, Elena and I are the very best of friends. We've known each other for years. How awful that she is missing. You don't think anything dreadful has happened to her?'

'I have no reason to think so.' But he was beginning to have dark thoughts, wondering whether a murder detective might actually be the proper man for this job after all. 'Can you think of anyone else who might know her whereabouts?'

'I'm sure she has lots of acquaintances, for she's a much loved figure.'

'Any names in particular?'

'Oh, I'd have to give that some thought.'

Seb smiled. 'It would be a great help to me.'

Her eyes met his. 'I suppose my present guests know her. We've all been skiing together.'

'Perhaps I could talk to them?'

She hesitated, then shrugged her slight and elegant shoulders. 'Why not? I'd hate to think your long journey here a total waste of time. We're having a little après-ski get-together. Perhaps you'd like to join us for a drink and some cake?'

'Thank you.'

'Come through to the drawing room. It's much warmer. We must find the divine Elena as quickly as possible, for our own peace of mind as much as for Mr Harcourt's splendid film.'

5

The room was much smaller than the hall and had a log fire in a stone hearth. It was more like a cosy drawing room in a great house than a cold, cheerless castle. The walls were full of remarkable works of art. Seb's eye was immediately drawn to a small but exquisite portrait of a dark-haired young woman. Though not a scholar, he knew straight away that it was by the Austrian master Gustav Klimt – the light, the decorative swirls, the gold leaf.

'Do you like it?' Sophie von Stark inquired.

'I do. Very much.'

'One of our more recent acquisitions. I adore it. Now let me introduce you to everyone.'

His eyes were pulled away from the portrait and back to the daunting group that awaited him.

Besides Sophie, there were four men and another woman. All wore ski-wear – the men in corduroy trousers tucked into long woollen socks, with pullovers, thick checked shirts and knitted ties.

Dear God, the other woman was none other than the blue-eyed English valkyrie Unity Mitford, towering over Sophie by about thirty centimetres. Seb despised her. Uncle Christian had told him to avoid her at all costs, but Seb hadn't needed the warning. She was the fourth of the six celebrated – *notorious* – Mitford sisters, all daughters of a British nobleman. But, more worryingly, she had become good friends with the Führer, dining with him regularly at his favourite restaurants in Munich or taking tea and pink-iced cakes with him at his apartment in Prinzregentenplatz.

She had made her presence felt last year when Seb was investigating the murder of an aristocratic young English-woman. Unity had done her damnedest to bring about the conviction and execution of a young Jewish man whom she loathed; Seb had done his best to prove that the man was innocent, and in doing so he knew the anti-Semitic Miss Mit-ford would never forgive him.

Seb's beloved Hexie had told him that Unity had designs on marrying Hitler. And Hexie should know, because she worked at the counter of the photographic shop owned by Hitler's constant companion Heinrich Hoffmann.

There was no better place for picking up gossip in the whole of Germany. And the source of much of the gossip was Hoffmann's young daughter Henriette, who just hap-pened to be married to Baldur von Schirach, the man in charge of the Hitler Youth.

Very little that happened in the higher reaches of the Nazi Party escaped Henriette's keen eyes and ears, and she loved to pass on what she learnt.

The heads of the après-ski group all turned in Seb's direction.

Unity immediately stepped forward, addressing Seb in English. 'It's Herr Wolff the clever detective, isn't it?'

'Miss Mitford, what a pleasure.'

'Is that all?'

'Ah, yes. Heil Hitler, Miss Mitford.' He thrust out his arm in the approved manner. Were you really supposed to go through this charade every time you met someone indoors? How long until the dreadful man with the ridiculous mous-tache was voted out of office?

'That's much better. Heil Hitler, Herr Wolff. Try not to

forget again. I would hate to have to report you.' She wasn't smiling. Seb wasn't convinced she was able to, but he knew that she would indeed denounce him without a qualm.

Hexie had told him that there were those in Munich who avoided any sort of social gathering where Unity might be in attendance, for a misplaced word would inevitably find its way to the political police and the offender could expect a dawn visit.

'I'm looking for Fräulein Elena Lang the film actress,' he said. 'Perhaps you know her, Miss Mitford.'

'Of course I do. I know everyone.'

'She's missing. I was hoping that someone here might have an idea where I could find her. Or, if not, perhaps point me in the direction of someone who might.'

'Elena missing? That's impossible. Have you tried the Bavaria Film Studios? She's making a movie, you know – with that English director, Harcourt.'

'It's Mr Harcourt who has asked us to locate her. Her disappearance is holding up filming.'

'Then you'd better find her, hadn't you? Do your job, Wolff.' With that she turned her back on him and resumed her conversation in English with a rather delicate-looking man.

Sophie von Stark took Seb's elbow and guided him towards the other three men. 'This is my brother, Werner Freiherr von Stark,' she said, indicating the first of the three men, a slim man in his mid-twenties, about the same height as Seb and perhaps a little older than his sister. The siblings had similar features, their skin glowed, and their fair hair, though tousled from the skiing, had a rich sheen.

Seb began to go through the Hitler salute again, but Werner reached out and pulled down his arm. 'That's quite enough of that nonsense,' he said.

Presumably, the von Starks considered themselves above

such commonplace practices as the Hitler salute. People bowed to them, not the other way around.

'So you're from the Police Presidium?'

'Indeed, sir.'

'And you can't find Elena. That's rather alarming.' He turned to his neighbour, a man Seb recognised as Unity's friend – or was it minder? – the SS officer Fritz Mannheim, a junior adjutant in the Führer's personal bodyguard. 'Do you have any idea, Fritz?'

'None at all.' He threw out his right arm. 'Heil Hitler, Inspector Wolff.'

Seb returned the salute. He didn't bother correcting the bespectacled Mannheim by mentioning that since their last meeting he had been promoted from criminal inspector to captain of detectives.

Sturmbannführer Mannheim, like the von Stark siblings, was in his twenties. Ostensibly, he was Unity Mitford's boyfriend, but no one really believed that. Some thought he was deputed to accompany Unity to keep her safe; others believed he was spying on her for SS chief Himmler.

The other man at Werner's side was tall and athletic and aged about forty. Like Unity, he was fair-haired and, like her, he did not smile or display the slightest semblance of warmth when introduced. In fact, he looked at Seb with suspicion and a hint of animosity. His name was Paul Jena and, though they hadn't met, Seb was well aware of who he was. Were those SS men outside something to do with him? It seemed likely.

Paul Jena was an SS-Gruppenführer – major general – presently assigned to the SS central office at Karlstrasse 10, Munich, and the SS-Junker School at Bad Tölz. He was one of the most powerful men in Bavaria, known as an old friend of various senior members of the Nazi regime.

While the von Starks smelt of extreme wealth, Jena exuded

power. It was impossible to live and work in Munich without being aware of him; he was a man to be avoided.

'You have lost Elena Lang, Herr Wolff? You'd better find her quickly or there will be consequences. We cannot have world-famous film stars disappearing.'

'Indeed not.' It really wasn't worth Seb's while to point out that *he* hadn't lost Elena Lang.

'Oh, stop bullying the poor man!' It was the fifth member of the party speaking, the delicate one who had been conversing with Unity. He was clearly British. 'I'm Howard Jack,' he said, shaking Seb's hand. 'Bobo tells me you speak English like a native.'

Bobo. Unity's nickname among her close friends and family.

'I do speak English, yes. I worked aboard a British merchant ship for four years.'

'How wonderfully romantic. I must go down to the seas again and all that.'

'Masefield. "Sea-Fever".'

Jack beamed. 'Well done, officer, well done indeed. Are you a poet?'

'I'm afraid not. Are you, Mr Jack?'

'Oh, I scratch away to pass the time, as one does. Now let's find some cake and wine for you and remove you from the scowls of these ghastly Nazis.' He stuck his tongue out at Unity and she returned the insult.

Seb did not like this conversation. An upper-class Englishman might be able to get away with describing Nazis as ghastly or bullies to their faces, but it would do an ordinary German no good to be associated with such language. Important not to smile or let it be known that one approved, especially not in the presence of two SS officers, one of them a Gruppenführer.

A waiter was hovering and Jack summoned him over. Seb took a glass of wine but declined the cake.

'Perhaps you have some idea where I might find Elena Lang, Mr Jack.'

'Hmm, that's a tricky one. But let's see what we can do with a little magic, shall we?' He looked at his companions, then clapped his hands. 'Abracadabra,' he said, his voice loud and dramatic. 'Hey presto!'

And, almost instantly, there she was.

Elena Lang, in all her movie star glory, was striding out from a door at the end of the room, a glass of wine in her hand and a grin on her beautiful face.

They were all looking at Seb, awaiting his reaction. And then, as one, they all roared with laughter.

6

What had just happened? Some ridiculous practical joke at his expense. Was that the sort of thing these aristocrats did? Mock the little people?

Seb felt like hammering one or two of them to the ground with his fist or the butt of his Walther PPK, and yet what could he do but accept that he should be relieved that Elena Lang was alive and well?

'Well, you had me there,' he said, trying to smile, while realising the words were pathetically inadequate.

'It seems the joke's on you, detective.' The Englishman Howard Jack was grinning broadly. Unity at his side was clapping frantically and the others all seemed mighty pleased with themselves.

Seb couldn't bear to look at them. He could take a joke at his expense, but this was of a different order: this impinged on his honour as a professional police officer.

'So you've been here all along, Fräulein Lang?'

'I have. I'd done the big scenes and needed a few days' skiing with my lovely friends. I don't understand what all the fuss is about.'

'Mr Harcourt was worried. He'll be very pleased that you're safe and well.'

'Alan Harcourt is a monster and I really don't care a jot whether he's pleased or not.'

'I'll be expected to report back to him. May I tell him you'll be available for filming tomorrow?'

'I'll tell him myself. Perhaps you'll give me a lift, officer.'

'I'm leaving now.' He badly wanted to get out of this place and away from these people.

'Perfect.'

It was only when they were halfway down the hill from the castle to the main road that it occurred to him to ask Elena Lang where she wished to be taken. 'The studio – or the Vier Jahreszeiten perhaps?'

'No, I have a hotel in Garmisch. The Alpspitze. Harcourt and the others will be coming here this evening for tomorrow's mountain sequences.'

'You know, I rather think he was hoping to have you on set today, Fräulein Lang.'

'My name is Elena. Perhaps I can use your name, too.'

'Sebastian – Seb to my family and friends.'

'Then Seb it is. And, yes, I know Harcourt was expecting me today, but I had a point to make. He treats me like a slave, there to do his bidding, as if I have no say in how I should play my role. I despise him.'

Seb knew the feeling was mutual, yet he found himself taking Elena's part. His brief encounter with the cigar-chomping bear that was Alan Harcourt had left him cold. But their relationship, however fraught, was their business. 'What about the others on set? Your co-star, Gary Tate?'

'He's a tailor's dummy.'

Seb waited for her to continue, but her summation was limited to those four damning words. *He's a tailor's dummy*. As far as Elena Lang was concerned, he was a nobody.

'And Harcourt's assistant, Olivia Sands?'

'Yes, I like her. She tries to smooth things, keep us from each other's throats. The film would be a great deal better if she were the director. If Leni Riefenstahl can make films, why not Olivia? Why not me? I could do it.'

34

Seb liked her. She was easy to talk to, not haughty like the others at Schloss Stark. As a detective he was used to making fast judgements about people, and he sensed a warmth and honesty to Elena Lang. He would have liked to know her better, would gladly have taken her back to Munich if it meant more time in her company.

'Tell me about yourself, Seb. The way you were chatting to Howard you clearly speak good English – that must be unusual for a Munich detective.'

Once again, Seb explained about his years aboard a British ship. 'I had a son and my mother to support in the worst of the great inflation. I walked to Hamburg and secured a berth on a freighter called the *Eastern Star*.'

'And the war before that – were you old enough to fight?'

He nodded. That was something he didn't like to talk about. He had been a machine-gunner, forced to take count-less human lives – not a thing for light conversation.

'I understand,' she said gently. 'None of you talk about it, do you? But, tell me, are you religious?'

'Catholic, lapsed.'

'And the war did that, yes?'

'Many of us came to the conclusion that God had no interest in saving us.'

She smiled a little sadly. 'And they were right. The scientist in me asks, how could there be all this, the universe? How could it be? The actress says, how could it *not* be? How could there be nothing? And, you know what, Seb – neither prop-osition makes sense. There is no answer.'

'The scientist in you?'

She laughed. 'I should be working in a laboratory some-where, not preening for the camera. Science was always going to be my life.'

'That's remarkable. How did you end up a movie star?'

'By accident. I grew up in Vienna. My father was an international trader and my mother was – still is – a doctor. My brother Constantin – he's ten years older than me – is a professor of medicine at Harvard. I had plans to go to Göttingen to study physics, but it was not to be. I was spotted by a family friend who works in the film industry and liked my looks. I went along to an audition just for the hell of it, and here I am. Mostly I love it but one day my looks will fade, and I'll give it all up and return to academia. And there you have it, Seb Wolff: that is my life story in half a dozen short sentences. Make of it what you will.'

He would have liked to know more about her, but the journey to Garmisch was short, no more than twenty minutes, and soon they were in the bustling town, pulling up at the Alpspitze, one of the best and most expensive hotels in the resort. This would be where many of the visiting politicians and the top Olympic officials would be staying. Here, or the equally renowned Alpenhof.

'What of all your luggage in Munich?'

'Oh, I'll call them and they'll send it on. I'll also call Olivia, so she knows I'll be here for tomorrow's shoot.'

He kept the engine running, waiting for Elena to climb out, but she just sat there. It occurred to him that she expected him to get out and open the door for her and then carry her valise into the lobby like a porter. So be it. He began to open his own door, but she reached out and held his arm.

'Please, just wait with me a moment, Seb.' Her eyes were fixed ahead, her hand tense on Seb's arm. Her other hand was in her lap, knotted into a fist.

'Is something wrong, Elena?'

'Someone wants me dead.'

The words cut through the cool air. 'What do you mean?'

'What I say, Seb. Someone intends to kill me.'

'Is this something to do with Alan Harcourt?'

'It's not that simple. I don't know my killer's name. I suppose, if I had any sense, I would just go – back to Vienna, or maybe Hollywood. But I doubt I'd be safer there.'

'Tell me more.'

'I can't.'

She was serious. This was no joke, no mocking the little people.

'Can I help you? Do you want police protection? I could arrange it.'

She turned and smiled at him. 'I like you very much, Seb Wolff. I have only known you half an hour, and I trust you. Do you have a girl?'

'Yes, I have a girl. Her name is Hexie. Hexie Schuler.'

'She's a lucky one.'

'I'm not sure she'd agree, but what about you, Elena? Who's trying to hurt you? Who are you scared of?'

'Seb, you really don't want to know. I shouldn't have said anything. Go home to your Hexie.'

She leant over and kissed him on the cheek, then opened the car door, dragged out her valise and disappeared into the front lobby of the Alpspitze Hotel.

7

Back in Munich, his first port of call was his office in the Police Presidium. Sergeant Winter wasn't there, but he had left a note to say that he had had no luck in his search for Elena Lang and that he would be back in the morning.

Winter probably had a date with Malwine, his new love. Probably the *only* love he had ever had. Hans Winter was not the most attractive of men, but if she had fallen for him, that was good news.

Seb couldn't help feeling sorry for the sergeant. He had been born and brought up in Dortmund, the child of a Lutheran family. Like millions of others, he believed that Hitler offered hope to his country and had happily signed up to all his beliefs, including a rabid hatred of Judaism.

After the Nazis came to power, he joined the Gestapo and blindly went along with the persecution of the Jews – until the fateful day he learnt that he, too, had Jewish blood.

He had secured a transfer to the Bavarian Political Police, clearly desperate to get as far away from his family and their secrets as he could. It was obvious to Seb now that Winter's increasing anti-Semitism was an attempt to camouflage his own heritage. But he took it to terrible extremes, even hounding an innocent Jew to death.

When he turned his sights on Seb, he was picking on the wrong man, for Seb had an old friend in Dortmund who discovered the truth about the sergeant. When Seb revealed this to him, it was as if a storm broke in Winter's mind. Everything he believed in, all the certainties, were swept away.

Then, somehow, he changed and was a better man for it. It seemed to Seb that, perhaps for the first time in his life, Hans Winter was able to tell right from wrong.

And now he had found love.

For the moment, however, Seb was less concerned with Winter than with the claim by Elena Lang that her life was in danger. He wanted to know more because, whether or not it was true, her fear was very real. He had seen terror in people's eyes many times in his thirty-five years – and he knew when it was genuine.

Sitting briefly at his desk, he admonished himself for not pressing her for more information and trying to find some way to protect her. That was what his heart told him; his head told him that she wasn't going to say any more, that she had already said too much.

He dialled the Alpspitze and asked to speak to Miss Lang. The desk clerk checked and said that she was in the bar having a pre-dinner drink with people from the film crew.

'Could you ask her to come to the telephone? Tell her it's Wolff from the Munich police.'

'Yes, sir.'

Two minutes later she was on the line. 'Hello, Seb.' Her voice was soft and cool, like her physical presence. He understood why cinema-goers had fallen in love with her.

'Elena, if you're in danger, I can help you.'

'I wish that were possible.' She laughed and he could imagine her beguiling smile. 'It's good of you to call, but really we should not talk about these things on an open telephone line.'

'You must have seen or heard something to make you think someone wishes you harm. Has there been an overt threat or is it just a suspicion?'

'Not now, Seb. Maybe you'll be in Garmisch for the

Olympics and we can talk then. My worry is that I have already made you a target simply by mentioning it.'

'Don't worry about me. It's my job to be in danger. That's what we police get paid for: we put our lives on the line to keep the public safe.'

'Go and have a drink with Hexie. Don't give me another thought. I'm probably just being foolish and paranoid. Good night, Seb.'

The phone went dead.

Did she really believe that *he* was in danger? He needed to discover more, but for the moment there was nothing to be done. He drove up to Schellingstrasse and parked outside the Schelling-Salon, the bar where he and Hexie often met. It was just around the corner from her workplace, the Hoffmann photographic shop.

She was at the bar with one of her colleagues, a cheerful young woman whom he had met a few times before. Hexie saw him as he entered and beckoned him over.

The room was packed, full of smoke and beer fumes, the sound of laughter and the clicking of billiard balls and, behind it all, some unidentifiable tune on an accordion.

He wove his way through the throng, then took Hexie's face in his hands and planted a kiss on her lips. 'You taste of beer,' he said.

'And you taste of someone who needs beer.'

'Then feel free to order me one.' He turned and kissed her companion on the cheek. 'Good evening, Carin. How are you?'

'About to go home for my supper, so I'll leave you two lovebirds to it. You can go and rip each other's clothes off somewhere.'

'We have good news, Seb,' Hexie announced. 'Hoffmann

has become so insanely rich with his monopoly on the Führer's photographs that he has given all of us tickets for the Games! He has even found us rooms in a Gapa guest house.'

'Perhaps he's not such a boorish swine after all.'

'We go there in the morning. I can't believe it. Isn't that exciting? I so want to see the downhill. It will be the event of a lifetime. We'll have tickets for the figure skating, too. We might see Sonja Henie!'

'I must say, I'd like to see some of it myself. But there's slim chance of that.'

Hexie and Carin were both dressed in traditional Bavarian dirndls with their hair braided, just the way Heinrich Hoffmann liked his female employees to present themselves to the world. When he was drunk and bleary-eyed, which was much of the time, Hoffmann would simply stand and look at them and say, 'Perfect examples of perfect Aryan maidens.'

Where he had got the idea that they were maidens was anyone's guess, but they didn't bother to contradict him and nor did they complain about wearing the bloody dirndls. Hexie went along with it because she liked the job.

Carin took her leave and disappeared into the night, while Hexie ordered a beer.

'So how was your day, Seb?' she said at last.

'Very strange. You?'

'Very boring. No good gossip. But all is well with the world now I have a beer in my hand and my man at my side. Anyway, tell me about your strange day.'

'I've been consorting with international movie stars, rich aristocrats and senior Nazis.'

'Lucky you. Anyone I might have heard of?'

'Elena Lang. Sophie von Stark.'

'Well, yes, that *is* impressive. Very glamorous. Tell me more.'

Seb told her the whole story. Finally, he came to the curious moment outside the Alpspitze Hotel when Elena spoke of her fears. Suddenly Seb realised that Hexie's face was drawn and severe; she wasn't amused any more.

'Have I said something?'

'You shouldn't be talking about this. Not here.'

'Hexie? What is this?'

'There's something you need to know, Seb.'

'What?'

'I don't want to talk about it with all these people around. This isn't amusing. You really could be putting us both in danger.' Her eyes scanned the room. The Salon was one of the few places in Munich where free-thinkers still liked to imagine they had the upper hand, but there were uniforms here, too: SS uniforms.

'You're very mysterious, Hexie Schuler.'

'And you have an unfortunate tendency towards recklessness, Sebastian Wolff.'

'Drink up and we can talk in the car.'

'So?' he said. 'What do you know that I don't?'

They were driving towards her new apartment near Stiglmaierplatz, which was more spacious and more convenient for her work than her former place in the south of the city.

'You really don't know much about Elena Lang, do you? You've no idea who she's been seeing, have you?'

'Then you'd better tell me.'

'Joseph Goebbels. She's been his mistress for months.'

Seb took his eyes off the road for a few moments to study her face. 'Who told you this?'

'Who do you think?'

'Your boss's talkative daughter.'

'Got it in one. I overheard her talking to Evie Braun last

month. It was the same day the film crew arrived in town. Evie and Henriette both thought the whole thing with Goebbels and Elena was hilarious, but I didn't and I really wished I hadn't heard it. Henriette and Evie are both untouchable. We're not.'

'What did they say?'

'Apparently the whole movie thing is a nightmare cooked up by Goebbels. He allowed Alan Harcourt the right to film at the Bavaria Studios and in the German Alps for practically nothing – on condition that he gave Elena Lang the lead role in the film.'

'Ahh . . .'

'Which might be fine, except that Elena and Harcourt loathe each other with a vengeance. At that stage Harcourt almost pulled out but he's desperate to make this film here.'

'Why would Elena accept the role if she hates Harcourt so much?'

Hexie shrugged. 'Perhaps the money was too good to refuse. You're her new friend – ask her.'

'Don't mention this to anyone else, Hexie.'

'Do you think I'm stupid? I didn't even tell you.'

No, she hadn't and that was most unlike her. Normally she couldn't wait to regale him with the latest gossip.

But this was not the sort of revelation that you would like to have traced back to you. Defaming the minister of propaganda was not good for an individual's health. That it might be true would not save you from any unpleasantness.

He was beginning to understand why Elena Lang was so scared and why she was adamant that she couldn't be protected.

When you dine with tigers, expect to be on the menu.

Hexie's new apartment was on the top floor of an old three-storey house.

'Are you coming in?'

'I need to eat.'

'I'm surprised you've still got an appetite now you know what you're dealing with.'

'I've barely eaten all day.' Should have had that cake when Sophie von Stark offered it, he thought.

'I've got food and I can cook. Pasta and my special tomato sauce? I've even got a little bit of Parmesan to sprinkle on top. Or we could nip around the corner to the Löwenbräu-keller if my cooking's not good enough for you.'

'Mutti will have cooked something.'

'Then be a good boy and go home to Mutti.'

He was tired and worried but that was no excuse; his reaction to Hexie's offer was rude and unnecessary. He put the back of his hand to her cheek. 'I'm sorry, that was unforgivable. I'll call home and tell Mutti I can't make it. Yes, I'd love whatever you have in mind. You're a fine cook. Spaghetti with your Sugo di Pomodoro would be wonderful.'

She was still in a huff, or pretending to be. 'Don't expect anything else. No sweet course for you.'

And that made him laugh, which was just what he needed after an exhausting day of twists and turns as tight as the winding bend up to Schloss Stark.

8

In the end he stayed the night with her. Before he left in the morning, she asked him what he was going to do.

'You mean about Elena Lang?'

'Of course. I'm certainly not talking about our endlessly delayed wedding.'

He was in no mood for an argument, but the fact was they both knew why they hadn't got around to marrying. It was because of Uncle Christian's insistence that he would make it the wedding of the year and would even invite his old friend Adolf as guest of honour, and that was something that neither Seb nor Hexie could stomach. They were beginning to wonder whether it was possible to slip over the border into Austria or Switzerland and exchange vows there.

'What can I do? What do you suggest?'

'You have to protect her. I don't know how because I'm not a cop. You're the man with the power to do something – that's obviously why she mentioned it to you. It was a cry for help.'

'I'll see what I can do.'

'You'll *see* what you can do?'

'I can't force her to accept help.'

Hexie shook her head, then kissed him on the lips. 'Do better, Seb Wolff. Do better.'

It was cold outside. The thermometer by the front door said zero degrees. Snow was surely coming; the opening ceremony of the Games might be saved after all. In public, people prayed for divine intervention by the Führer. In private, they prayed to the God of their forebears.

He beat Winter to Ettstrasse, but he didn't beat Thomas Ruff, deputy president of the Munich Police, who immediately summoned him up to his office on the fifth floor.

'Well done, Wolff, you found Fräulein Lang. The Gauleiter is mighty pleased.'

'Indeed, sir.'

'So all is well with the film. Mr Harcourt has asked for his thanks to be conveyed to you; the crew will be up in the mountains filming today. This is excellent news, for nothing must tarnish the good name of Bavaria or Germany. The headlines during the Games must all be about gold medals, wonderful ice-skating and the Führer's welcome speech. Not missing film stars – and definitely no criminals.'

'Yes, sir, I fully understand. Though there is one other thing I must mention.'

'Make it quick. I have another job for you.'

'Elena Lang confided in me that she has fears for her safety. She didn't explain why or who might wish her harm, but I believed her and so I offered her protection. She refused.'

Ruff blinked furiously, his shoulders stiff. 'Why would she have said these things to you, Wolff?'

'I wish I knew, sir, but I'm worried. How do you protect someone who refuses help?'

'Let me take advice and get back to you.'

Which meant he wasn't going to make a decision because this could be political dynamite. It occurred to Seb that Ruff probably knew that Elena Lang had been having an affair with Goebbels and that was the source of his fear.

Why this pathetic excuse for a man had ever joined the police was beyond Seb. Thomas Ruff should have been working in the back office of a town hall in a rural backwater, not in charge of the day-to-day running of one of the country's most important forces. He was directly answerable to men like Reichsführer-SS Heinrich Himmler and Reinhard Heydrich – and it clearly terrified him.

'In the meantime, we do have another small problem, which I trust you'll address with your customary efficiency and skill, Wolff. A man's body has been found in woodland along the Scharnitz Pass, not far from Mittenwald on the German side of the border.'

Seb saw the tension in his boss's neck as he began his customary pacing around the office. They both knew that the Scharnitz Pass was just a few kilometres from Garmisch-Partenkirchen and the Olympics, which meant that this might not be such a 'small problem'.

'Are we talking murder, sir?'

'I'm not certain but I fervently hope not. Gunshot wound to the head, so it could as well be suicide or a hunting accident. But it must be kept quiet. No word must reach the press, either local or international. This must be contained or there will be hell to pay – and you'll be the one paying it.'

'Do we know the man's identity?'

'Papers found on the body identify him as SS-Scharführer Theodor Krieger, resident in Farchant.'

An SS man. That didn't sound like good news.

'Where's the corpse?'

'Exactly where it was found by a woodsman two hours ago, guarded by a Mittenwald officer named Tischler. You'll go there now: make sure the woodsman and the local police all keep their mouths shut, then organise the removal of the body to Munich for autopsy. This will be done in total secrecy.'

'The local cops may already have spoken to others.'

'Fortunately, the officer understood the sensitive nature of the incident and had the sense to call through to Ettstrasse straight away. I'd just arrived here when the call was transferred to me. This can and will be kept quiet, Wolff. Our careers depend on it. So go there now and remember: secrecy, secrecy, secrecy.'

Preposterous. How could such a thing be kept secret? Word spread like wildfire in those rural areas. The place where Theodor Krieger's body had been found was barely five kilometres from Mittenwald, which was less than twenty kilometres from Garmisch-Partenkirchen, and in such regions that was only a shout away, the echo of an alpenhorn across the valley.

So, if anyone in Mittenwald knew about it, within a couple of hours everyone in Gapa would, too. Murder was always big news when it occurred locally – a story to make you gasp with horror, check your locks and embellish with awe down through the generations.

Hans Winter had arrived at Ettstrasse and was preparing coffee when Seb returned from the fifth floor. 'Come on, sergeant. We have work to do.'

'Can we have coffee first? I had a rough night.'

'Bring it with you.'

Seb realised that his little Lancia Augusta would not do, so he called through to the vehicle pound and secured a van for the journey. Ten minutes later, with a full tank and Winter's gullet scorched from the coffee, they were travelling south, roads icy but still no sign of snow.

'What's this about, captain?'

'A possible murder in the Scharnitz Pass beyond Mittenwald. Anyway, why are you feeling so rough? Too much beer, I suppose.'

'Malwine was giving me a hard time. She's older than me and I sense that she's keen to marry and have children. I feel the same way, but how is that possible? I'm terrified to apply for the necessary ancestry documents, so I cannot propose to her.'

Seb paused, unsure what to say. 'I take it you think the Nuremberg Laws apply to you?'

'I'm not sure. They're so complicated. All I know for certain is that I have two Jewish grandparents, which makes me a *Mischling*, but I fear it may be three or even four. But to reveal any of that would make me unemployable and even one Jewish grandparent would probably drive Malwine away. Her father would throw me out like the rubbish.'

Seb had read about the Nuremberg Laws when they were passed just five months earlier. They banned marriage and sexual relations between Jews and non-Jewish Germans. That was straightforward enough, though despicable.

Where it got complicated was on the matter of defining who would be classified as a Jew when there had been so much intermarriage down the generations.

The extreme hard-liners wanted those with two Jewish grandparents to be defined as Jews, but Hitler had decided on three.

None of it was much comfort to Hans Winter. Even a hint of Jewish blood would destroy his career in the political police and his hopes of marrying.

As they drove higher into the Scharnitz Pass, the ice was getting worse and the lack of grip on the roads was unsettling.

'I'm not sure how you're still working for the BPP, sergeant. Don't they require an Aryan certificate?'

'Yes, of course.'

'So you have one?'

'Yes, but it's not unassailable.'

'You mean it's forged.'

Winter nodded miserably. 'I don't trust it. Everyone's taking these things more seriously since Nuremberg.'

Seb shook his head. He was thoroughly ashamed of his own country, that it could bring in such legislation and call it *The Law for the Protection of German Blood and German Honour*. If such prejudice were legalised, it was an immutable mark of *dishonour* for Germany.

'What do I do?'

Seb knew what he would do in Winter's position: leave the country at the earliest opportunity and bide his time abroad until the present government was voted out of office. Perhaps Malwine would go with him; perhaps not. But Germany at this time was not a good place to have Jewish blood.

'Perhaps I should leave the BPP and find some other work? But I have no other skills that I can think of.'

'Drive trams? Serve beer?'

'The pay cut –'

'Then remain in the BPP as long as you can. Perhaps you'll be a good influence, speak out against persecution.' Even as he said it he knew it was a lie. The anti-Semitism in the Nazi regime was part of the woodwork, deeply ingrained; one man's voice would be nothing but a howl in the wilderness. 'I don't know, sergeant. It's your life and your career. You must decide.'

'I need the money, especially if I'm to be married. And the crazy thing is that I'm not Jewish: I don't feel Jewish, and I have no knowledge of the people or the religion. When I discovered, by chance, that my grandfather was a rabbi, it was like being told I was a Martian. It means nothing to me.'

'You were not a friend of the Jews when I met you. Have your feelings towards them changed at all?'

'Yes. I admit I didn't treat them well and I know I was

wrong. Just as I know I cannot cast off my ancestry. None of us can change the facts of our birth. So now I'm torn. I was baptised and brought up a Lutheran – and we all know what Luther said about Jews: burn their synagogues, smash their homes, seize their money and property, destroy their holy books and kill their rabbis. Should I therefore have killed my grandfather? I'm lost, Captain Wolff, utterly lost.'

'Do you not sometimes think you should leave the country, sergeant? For your safety?'

'But this is my country, captain. My job is to protect the people, uphold the rule of law and maintain the peace.'

The Schupo – the uniformed cop from the local Mittenwald gendarmerie – was waiting at the side of the road in a wooded area of the Scharnitz Pass, close to the Isar River and within three kilometres of Mittenwald. He must have been bitterly cold but held himself erect and did not bother with gloves. A tough man of the mountains, Seb decided, pulling the van on to the verge.

'Wolff, Munich Kripo,' he said, showing his badge. 'And this is Sergeant Winter, BPP.'

The Schupo clicked his heels and gave a brisk bow of the head as though receiving royalty. 'Anselm Tischler, Mittenwald Schutzpolizei.'

Seb was delighted to have avoided the Hitler salute. Many of these country people were not happy about the loss of their traditions to the new political philosophy. In particular, they hated the way they were expected to pull down their treasured flags of Bavarian blue and white and replace them with the red-and-black swastika.

'Where's the fellow who found the body?'

'I've told him to stay there and make sure no one interferes with it.'

'Is he trustworthy?'

'I've known Hubertus Hirt all my life.'

'Have either of you mentioned the body to anyone else?'

'Only your office in Munich, by telephone. I spoke personally with the deputy president of police.'

'No one in Mittenwald?'

'No, sir.'

'Good man. Let's see it, then.'

It did not take Seb long to work out that this was murder. Very few suicides managed to shoot themselves twice in the head and once in the heart, not to mention that there was no gun in evidence.

The body was half covered in leaves. It lay flat on its back, the remains of the head twisted right, arms outstretched as though nailed to a cross. According to his identification documents and wallet – which had no money in it – the deceased was indeed an SS trooper named Theodor Krieger, just as Ruff had been told. The corpse was clothed in a warm outdoor jacket, thick trousers and hiking boots – civilian attire, not military.

'*Grüss Gott*, Herr Hirt.' Seb gave the woodsman the traditional greeting of the region.

Hubertus Hirt nodded his head and said nothing. Seb noticed that he avoided eye contact, kept his gaze down towards the ground.

'When did you find the body?'

'Four and a half hours ago. Six in the morning.'

'And what were you doing up here?'

'This is where I work. I cut firewood for the people of Mittenwald and also care for the forest.' He spoke slowly, stuttered slightly.

'But it's dark at six in the morning.'

'Yes, sir.'

Seb was beginning to wonder whether the woodsman was simple. He turned to the Schupo. 'Does he understand the point I am making, Tischler? I can't work out why Hirt would be here so early. He couldn't do his job without light.'

'He lives up here, sir. There's a hut higher up the slope, about a kilometre from here. He finds it more convenient to stay here, where he works, than reside in Mittenwald.'

'That still doesn't explain why he was out and about so early. In summer, yes; in winter, surely not.'

'He heard shots, sir, and went to investigate.'

Now, at last, some sense. 'Perhaps you could ask him to explain the sequence of events.'

Tischler smiled at Hirt. 'Can you tell the detective what happened after you heard the shots, Hubertus?'

'I was already dressed and I was eating my oats. My dog was barking. I left my breakfast, lit a torch and went outside. I couldn't tell where the shots had come from, but I heard other noises from this direction, so I came here. And then I found the body.'

'What sort of noises?' Seb asked. 'Talking? Footsteps?'

'Perhaps. It was difficult to be sure. I didn't see anyone and I couldn't hear any words.'

'Do you have a gun of your own, Herr Hirt?'

The woodsman looked to the Schupo for guidance.

'Just answer Herr Wolff with the truth. You have nothing to hide.'

'I have a shotgun. I take birds for the table.'

'No other firearms?'

'No, sir.'

'And what did you do once you had discovered the body?'

'I rode my bike to Mittenwald and told Anselm what had happened.'

'Did you not look through the man's pockets to discover his identity?'

'His wallet was by his side, open. I saw that he had no money and assumed the killer had stolen it. I left it there.'

'Very good. You did exactly the right thing, Herr Hirt. But you know that you must not mention this to another soul. Not to your family or friends. No one. Do you understand?'

'Yes, sir. I will tell no one.'

'Tischler, this is absolutely clear, yes?'

'I'm sure Hubertus understands.'

'And what about you, Tischler? You have a family?'

'Yes, wife and three young children.'

'Have you mentioned a word of this to them?'

'No, sir.'

'Did they not hear you talking to Herr Hirt?'

'No, sir, they were not awake, and we spoke outside to be safe.'

'Then keep it that way. Not a single word. If I hear any gossip about this murder, I'll know that it can only have come from you or Hirt, and there will be a heavy price to pay.' He hated threatening these two decent men like this, but it was for their own good.

'You have my word of honour, captain.'

'Good. Then let us work together to move the body to our van.'

Hirt put up his index finger. 'I have a handcart close by for transporting logs.'

'Excellent. And one more thing, Herr Hirt – why would anyone apart from you be in these woods, in the dark, at such an hour?'

Hirt looked down at his feet.

'Have there been people in the woods at that time before?'

'I – I don't think so. No.'

Seb continued to look at him, but still the man wouldn't meet his eye. He had appeared to hesitate with his answer, but perhaps that was the stutter.

Seb took a few pictures of the crime scene with the office Leica. Then they lifted the corpse and carted it down to the van, concealing it inside.

On the way back to Munich, he stopped in Garmisch-Partenkirchen, outside a large and rather splendid-looking chalet with a sign declaring it to be the Hotel Postillion.

Winter gave his boss a questioning look.

'You know what this place is, sergeant? It's the temporary headquarters of the Bavarian Political Police. I want you to find accommodation here. This is where our investigation is going to be centred, so you have no need to come back to Munich with me.'

'What do you want me to do here? I can't make inquiries without mentioning the murder.'

'Use the BPP phone, put a call through to Deputy President Ruff and tell him what we've found. Make sure you're not overheard.'

'But then what?'

'Just listen, sergeant. Use your ears. Listen to your BPP colleagues, listen in the bars. Borrow a BPP car and go to Mittenwald. Someone knows something. Be a detective.'

Winter looked uncomfortable. The truth was, he was only here to report back to his bosses on Seb's trustworthiness or otherwise. Still, Seb had hopes that he might measure up and be of some use.

'And see what you can find out about the film crew at the Alpspitze Hotel. Don't talk to them; just watch and report back to me – about Elena Lang in particular. That shouldn't be such hard work, sergeant – watching a movie star.'

'Why do I need to do that?'

Seb raised an eyebrow. 'Don't act dumb, Winter. She was missing, wasn't she? I found her but I'm still interested in her welfare. Use your judgement, the common sense God gave you. And most of all make use of the BPP resources.'

'I don't think the BPP men like me these days. They don't see me as one of them since I've been assigned to you.'

'Just get on with it, Winter.'

'Should I go to the victim's home in Farchant? He has a wife and family; they won't even know he's dead yet.'

'No, I'll be back this afternoon. Meet me here at three and we'll go together.'

9

Professor Lindner did not spend long examining the body of Theodor Krieger. 'Wolff, I don't really need to cut this one open. Your initial conclusion of murder is perfectly accurate: three bullet holes. Two entry wounds in the back of the head, one through the chest into the heart.'

They were in the post-mortem lab in the university hospital in Munich. Lindner was as cool and distant as ever.

'Weapon?' Seb asked.

Lindner held up a bloody and dented bullet with a pair of tweezers. 'I removed this. From a brief examination I'd guess the gun was much the same as the one you are carrying under your jacket. Walther PP 7.65 police issue. Which doesn't mean that the assailant is a police officer. In my experience these guns are all over the place. Not hard to come by.'

'That doesn't give us much of a start, then.'

'Perhaps not, but there are a couple of pointers. One, the man was not bound, which suggests he might have gone into the woods voluntarily. This isn't certain, though, for anyone might be persuaded to walk there if he had a pistol trained on him.'

'And the other pointer?'

'More of a hunch really. I'm pretty certain the shots to the back of the head came first and the third one, to the heart, was simply making sure, like a good professional assassin. My gut feeling is that he was walking into those woods with a man or men he knew and was taken by surprise. He never realised what was coming. In which case you need to find out why two or more men would be venturing into the woods at such an ungodly hour. That's *your* job, Wolff. Detective work, not anatomy.'

'Possessions?'

'Holstered pistol with full magazine, dagger, handkerchief, peppermints – and you've already got his wallet.'

'The pistol suggests you're probably correct in assuming that he walked into the woods of his own volition. Otherwise his weapon would surely have been removed.'

'There you go, Wolff. Detective work.'

Seb drove home to his apartment in Ainmüllerstrasse in Schwabing, known as the artists' quarter, not that Seb was acquainted with any artists. He and his mother and son lived there because it was relatively cheap and because it was where they had always lived.

He wasn't thinking about the murder victim or Elena Lang; he was thinking about Hexie. Something she had said in bed last night, almost a throwaway line.

'You could always move in here, you know. It's big enough.'

'I thought you wanted to get married first.'

'Did I say that? I don't remember saying that.'

He didn't know how to reply.

'I know what this is about, Seb. You're worried about leaving your mother and your son. But Jurgen will soon be leaving home himself for his stint with the Reich Labour Service.'

'I would rather he were going to university.'

'But he's not, is he? And, after his labour service, he will become a Luftwaffe pilot.'

Seb nodded. It was all true and it cut deeply. At Jurgen's age, Seb had gone to war. He wanted things to be different for his son. Do well in the Abitur exams, study law, medicine, science or languages at a good university.

'The fact is, there's already a distance between you,' Hexie continued softly, 'and it's just going to get wider and deeper. Whether you like his decisions or not, he'll be making his own way in the world. As for your mother, well, you'll have to make a choice. You either live with her for the rest of her life – and that could easily be another thirty years – or you break away and live your own life, a thing that was denied you by early fatherhood.'

Everything she said was right. In his mind, he had been thinking that he would wait until March when Jurgen turned eighteen, or maybe the end of the school year, to decide his own next step. But now he realised that neither of those dates was very far away and the decision he had been putting off would soon have to be made.

He nodded. 'It makes sense – and it's what I want. It's just about finding the right moment to break it to Mutti. And, you know, if possible, I'd like to stay quite close to her.'

She smiled at him. He knew that it was not in her nature to make things difficult for him and that she understood his predicament. 'Fair enough,' she said. 'You pick the time and we'll find somewhere else, a place we choose together.'

'Thank you. Next time we both have a day off we'll have a look.'

Now he was home and his mother, Angela, was unhappy.

'You didn't come home. I had cooked *Leberkäse*.'

'I tried to call you, Mutti, but no one answered the phone.'

'Jurgen ate your portion.'

'Then it didn't go to waste.'

'Did that Hexie cook for you? Does she even know how to cook?'

'Yes, she cooked pasta and sugo. She's a good cook – almost as good as you, Mutti.'

His mother snorted with derision. She wasn't susceptible to flattery.

'Anyway, where's Jurgen today?'

'Didn't he tell you, Sebastian? He's gone to Garmisch-Partenkirchen. His troop is helping with the Olympics. Directing guests, doing anything required of them.'

'Good for them.' The idea that the Hitler Youth might actually be doing something useful for a change instead of marching, singing Nazi songs and shouting anti-Semitic slogans was a welcome bit of news.

Mutti gestured to the kitchen table. 'There's a letter for you.'

Seb was surprised. He rarely received letters. He picked it up but, instead of opening it, he shoved it in his jacket pocket.

'Sebastian, who's it from?'

'I don't know. I'll find out when I open it.'

'Why don't you open it now?'

Because some instinct told him that this might not be something he wanted to open under Mutti's watchful eyes. He had noticed the Berlin postmark and he knew that she would have seen it, too. 'I haven't got time. I just called in to say hello and apologise for last night.'

And, more than that, the truth was he hadn't forgotten that handwriting. It was the same as on the letters he'd received in 1918, in the trenches on the Western Front.

Before returning to the mountains, he called in at Ettstrasse to return the van, collect the Lancia and report to Deputy President Ruff.

'No doubt about it, I'm afraid, sir,' he said. 'Two bullets in the head, one in the heart. It's murder.'

'Your sergeant called and told me. God damn it, Wolff,

that's the last thing we need. Why does everything happen to me?'

'I'll investigate as quietly and quickly as I can.'

Ruff was wringing his hands. 'There's already great interest in this incident from on high simply because the victim was an SS man. Have you reported to the SD office in Gapa?'

'Not yet.'

'They'll provide you with more information about the victim, this Krieger.'

'How did the SS find out about the murder?'

'God in heaven, Wolff, sometimes I wonder about you. I had to tell them, of course. It was an SS man, for pity's sake! I thought we'd been through this. Do you have no concept of politics?'

'And where do I find the Sicherheitsdienst in Garmisch-Partenkirchen?'

'Villa Erika. They're based there for the duration of the Games. Get on with it, Wolff – and don't let me down.'

10

Finding the Villa Erika in Garmisch-Partenkirchen was not as easy as it might have been. The locals looked nervous when asked and claimed they had no knowledge of the place, but it was obvious to Seb that they were lying. Clearly its association with the SD was no secret.

The SD, or Sicherheitsdienst, was the intelligence department of the SS, and to some citizens it was more to be feared than the Gestapo.

From the outside, the Villa Erika looked like a warm, pleasant property, one of the better houses in town. Its roof sloped gently and the picket fence at the front spoke of homeliness. It was quite central but not particularly large, and in other times might serve as the home of a respectable bank manager or shopkeeper. Had the family given it up voluntarily or had it been requisitioned? Seb tried not to think about it; it was not his concern.

An office had been installed on the ground floor, just off the main entrance. An Untersturmführer, surely the lowest rank of the SS officer class, sat there, scribbling into a ledger or file. Seb introduced himself and said he had been instructed to report here.

'Ah, yes, Captain Wolff, wait a few moments.'

A minute later the officer returned and resumed his work. Seb watched him and wondered what he could possibly be doing in a peaceful ski resort: surely not cataloguing anti-Nazi comments; that was the BPP's job.

Five minutes later, the door opened again.

'Heil Hitler, captain. We meet once more.'

It was Paul Jena, the senior SS officer he had met the previous day at Schloss Stark. This time he was in black uniform and he used every centimetre of his height and athletic bearing to tell the world who was in charge here.

Beyond him, outside in the corridor, stood the four SS troopers Seb had also seen at the castle. Some sort of personal entourage for the self-important Gruppenführer Jena perhaps.

'Heil Hitler, Herr Gruppenführer.' If there was one place the salute should always be used, this was it. 'I was ordered to report here.'

'Indeed.' Jena turned to the junior officer. 'Leave us.'

The Untersturmführer jumped up, clicked his heels, saluted and scuttled from the room, closing the door after him.

'I was shocked to hear that SS squad leader Krieger has been murdered. Awful news. This is a very sad day.'

'Yes, sir. I conveyed the body back to Munich and have been briefed by pathologist Professor Lindner. Krieger was shot twice in the head from behind and once in the heart. It is likely that he didn't know that he was under threat.'

'And this was in the wood on the edge of the Scharnitz Pass?'

'Yes, sir.'

'This is terrible, terrible. We must catch the killer. *You* must catch the killer, captain.'

'I will do my utmost, Herr Jena.'

'I'm told you're the best detective in the region. I want you to know that you have my full support. Anything you need, any assistance – and you will have it. But, more than that, I summoned you here to repeat what you already know: that this inquiry must be conducted with the utmost delicacy. You'll inform Frau Krieger of her husband's fate, but she must be sworn to secrecy, even from her own family. You will undoubtedly also need to talk to other potential witnesses and suspects, but, again, you'll use your authority to silence them.'

'In some cases that might be difficult.'

'If you have the slightest doubt about potential witnesses maintaining silence, you have full authority to take them into protective custody in single cells at Stadelheim Prison. Be ruthless, Captain Wolff. There is no room for error. I've spoken to Propaganda Minister Herr Dr Goebbels, and he's adamant that nothing – *nothing* – must be allowed to detract from the friendly, happy Olympic Games.'

Seb nodded and clicked his heels because he knew it was required of him, but he was appalled. The thought of locking someone up without even a suspicion of criminal behaviour could never be justified. He had been brought up to believe in the rule of law. But this would be the way Paul Jena operated. Charm the big fish like Werner and Sophie von Stark; crush the small fry underfoot.

'You're uncertain?'

'No, sir.'

'Good man.' Jena smiled, but it lacked empathy or even amusement. 'I hope our little prank yesterday did not discomfort you too much.'

'I was just delighted to find Fräulein Lang alive and well. I was beginning to worry.'

'She is a fine specimen, is she not? You must have got to know her a bit better on the drive down.'

'We said very little. I was concentrating on the road.'

'But to have one of the world's most famous film stars at your side – that must have been quite an event for a humble police detective.'

'Indeed, I was honoured to have her in my car.'

'So she said nothing?'

'She thanked me for the lift.'

Jena nodded his head slowly, as though pondering the reply. 'Good,' he said at last, as though he still harboured doubts. 'And have you heard any gossip?'

'I'm not sure what you mean, general.'

'About Elena Lang.'

'No, sir. All I know is that presently she's making a film with Mr Harcourt.'

'You have a girlfriend, I believe. A certain Fräulein Herta Schuler, yes?'

How the hell did he know that? Was there a file on them somewhere? And why Herta – her baptismal name – when no one called her that? 'Yes, that's my fiancée, sir. Though all her friends call her Hexie.' He felt the damp chill of sweat on the nape of his neck.

'And she works at the Hoffmann shop. A place of loose tongues, I should imagine. Girls gossiping together. And Hoffmann likes a drink and his daughter is not known for her discretion.'

'Forgive me, Herr Gruppenführer, none of this means anything to me.'

'So you really have heard no rumours about Elena Lang?'

'No, sir.'

His head nodded again, and his eyes drilled into Seb's. 'Let's keep it that way. Ears and mouth shut, Wolff. That's the best recipe for good health.'

'One more thing, Herr Gruppenführer – will I have access to members of Krieger's SS troop?'

'No, I'll deal with that. I met the man once or twice at Karlstrasse, but in truth he never seemed quite one of us, if you get my meaning. From what I've been told by my fellow officers, he might have been dismissed from the service in the coming weeks. His death, though tragic, has removed that unpleasant duty.'

'May I ask why he faced dismissal?'

'Nothing solid, no evidence of misconduct, just a feeling that the man lacked honour, that he had criminal tendencies. But that does not lessen the importance of finding his killer. No one can be allowed to imagine that they can do harm to an SS squad leader and get away with it.'

Leaving the building, the icy blast hit him, but he was sweating profusely. Was he under surveillance by the SD? And what about Hexie? She had understood the sensitivity of her information about Elena Lang and Goebbels, but it would be a good idea to remind her. The idea of a Goebbels attack-hound such as Paul Jena breathing down their necks was not conducive to peace of mind.

He found Hans Winter at the Hotel Postillion. The poor man was disconsolate and seemed to have no idea what to do with himself.

'Come on, sergeant, we'll make a detective of you yet,' he said by way of encouragement, but it was a vain hope. The truth was he didn't believe for a moment that Winter had a gram of initiative in his bones. 'Let's go and inform the widow.'

They drove north out of Garmisch into the well-to-do village of Farchant, stopping at a shop to ask for directions to Frau Krieger's house. It was just two streets away.

Just before parking, Seb turned to Winter. 'I imagine your old BPP friends at the Postillion were overjoyed to see you, sergeant.'

'They are not my friends. They don't like me and the feeling is mutual.'

'And have you heard anything?'

'Only that the Communists have been sticking up anti-Nazi posters around town.'

'Not exactly big news.'

Petra Krieger was doing her weekly wash when they arrived. She stood at the door of her surprisingly large house in an apron, with her sleeves rolled up and her hands and forearms dripping.

'Yes?'

'I'm Captain Wolff of the Munich police and this is Sergeant Winter. Are you Frau Krieger?'

She frowned. 'Have I done something wrong?'

'May we come in, please?'

'I'm in the middle of the laundry.'

'This is important.'

She attempted to dry her hands on her apron, then stepped aside to permit them entry to her immaculate home. She gazed down at their feet.

'Would you like us to remove our shoes?'

'Of course.'

She provided them with slippers and they moved through to the front room, a space so spotless that Seb could not imagine that it was ever used. They sat down.

'Do you have children, Frau Krieger?'

'Three boys, seven, nine, eleven. They're at school.'

That was good. Better to have this conversation without children in the house. 'I'm afraid I have bad news. A body has been found and we believe it is your husband, Theodor.'

'What do you mean, *a body*?'

'A dead body. He had papers about his person identifying him as SS-Scharführer Theodor Krieger.'

'Theo is dead?'

'That is our belief. I'm sorry to be the bearer of such tragic news.'

'How did he die?'

'He was shot. Murdered.'

She sat there, her face unreadable. Not falling apart; in fact, showing barely any emotion at all, merely a vague curiosity.

'Frau Krieger?' Seb said. 'Do you understand what I'm saying?'

'You're saying that someone has killed Theo.' Her voice flat and distant.

This was not what Seb had anticipated. He turned to Winter. 'Perhaps you would be good enough to get a glass of water from the kitchen, sergeant.' In other circumstances, Seb might suggest that a neighbour or friend be fetched to give comfort to the widow, but that could not be done. No one outside this house was to be informed of the murder.

'Do you have a photograph of your husband?'

She didn't hesitate, simply rose from her chair, walked across the room to a sideboard and picked up a framed photograph. 'This is our wedding, almost thirteen years ago. Summer 1923. I was pretty then.'

Seb studied the photograph. There was no doubt that the man in the picture was the man found dead in the woods. And, yes, Frau Krieger had been more slender and attractive, but that was true of everyone, wasn't it, with the passing of the years?

A few moments later, Winter returned with the glass of water for Frau Krieger. She ignored it. Seb passed the photograph to Winter, who also looked at it closely, then nodded.

'I'm afraid there is no doubt, Frau Krieger. Your husband is dead. We'll arrange a viewing for you later so that you can confirm his identity.'

'Who did this to him? Does it have something to do with that bitch Schramm?'

'Schramm?'

'Traudl Schramm. The English Whore. Did she do this? First, she steals my husband, then she kills him.'

'Is she here in Farchant, this woman?'

'No, she lives and works in Garmisch-Partenkirchen or sometimes Munich, I believe. Near the SS central office at Karlstrasse 10. That's where Theo spends much of his time on his SS duties.' Petra Krieger snorted with scorn. 'When I say she works near there, I mean she spends all day on her back with her legs in the air, being taken by anyone who'll have her. Perhaps that's what she calls work.'

'You mentioned something about her being English?'

'That was her mother, but she has always lived in Bavaria. Everyone calls her the English Whore.'

'Do you know where she is working at the moment?'

'No, and nor do I care.'

Seb shrugged. It didn't matter; he'd find her easily enough. 'Do you have any other thoughts about who might have wished your husband harm?'

'Anyone with a brain.'

This was becoming even more strange. 'Frau Krieger, I must put it to you that you don't sound unhappy that your husband's been killed.'

Her face was as hard as cold iron. She said nothing.

'So there were problems in your marriage?'

She shrugged.

'What were your thoughts when he didn't come home last night?'

'He comes and goes as he wishes. He comes home at weekends sometimes, to beat me and the children, collect clean clothes and take food. Some weeks he gives us a few pfennigs to survive, maybe the odd Reichsmark. Other times he gives us nothing. We are less than dirt to him, and he is nothing to us, just a stone around our necks. Theo Krieger is a swine. The worst thing that happened to him was the war ending. He loved war. He loved killing. If he's now been killed, it's a fitting end. The devil is welcome to him.'

Seb exchanged glances with Winter. 'Frau Krieger, do you have the names of any enemies who might have wished him harm? Or friends for that matter – friends who might have betrayed him?'

'He had plenty of enemies and only one friend, a man equally despicable – Xaver Knorr. Krieger and Knorr – they called themselves "The Two Ks". I call them the two devils.'

'Where would we find Xaver Knorr?'

She rolled her eyes as though such questions were of no importance, especially when she had the laundry to finish. 'I have no idea. Dead, too, hopefully. Or perhaps taking his turn with Traudl Schramm – who knows?'

Seb turned to Winter. 'Do you have any questions, sergeant?'

'Was your husband always like this? If so, why did you marry him?'

'I wanted children. He was the only man who asked me. There were not many available men in 1923 because they mostly died in the war. Women like me, we took what we could get or lived as old maids. Anyway, he didn't hit me until a week after the wedding.'

'Frau Krieger,' Seb said, 'I must inform you that there is a political element to this case. The authorities do not wish to have your husband's death written up in the newspapers as a murder while the Games are under way. You're to tell your friends and family that your husband has died in a car accident.'

'If you say so – it makes no difference to me.'

'I cannot stress how important this is. If word were to get out that he was murdered, you would be in serious trouble. If I hear of any whispering, I'm authorised to have you taken into protective custody – prison. Do you understand?'

She laughed. 'So the swine can torment me from beyond the grave!'

'No, that's not what I'm saying.'

'And what do I tell the boys?'

'You tell them the same: that their father was killed in a road accident. Nothing more, nothing less. Don't try to elaborate. For the moment – at least until the conclusion of the Olympic Games – you cannot confide in anyone. Not your family, not your best friends. No one.'

'Will there be a widow's pension?'

'Sergeant Winter?'

'I will look into that on your behalf, Frau Krieger.'

'And now can I get back to my washing?'

'Not much love in that house. Theodor Krieger certainly won't be missed,' Winter said, as they drove the few kilometres back to Garmisch-Partenkirchen.

'We need to talk to Traudl Schramm and Xaver Knorr. Take the train back to Munich to see if police or BPP files list them. In the meantime, I'm going to have to find somewhere in town to stay, which might not be easy with the place full.' He did have an idea, though . . .

As he hoped, he found Hexie at the Waxenstein Guest House, just about to go out drinking with Carin.

'Seb, you didn't tell me you'd be here.'

'I'm working.'

'But you are working on protecting Elena, aren't you?'

'This is another case. Can't explain what, I'm afraid.'

Hexie rolled her eyes. 'Are you coming for a beer with us, then?'

'I'll meet you later. I take it you two are sharing a room?'

'No, we have a room each – isn't that amazing? I even have a view of the mountains. If ever I said an unkind word about Heinrich Hoffmann, I take it all back. And we have season tickets to all the events at a cost of one hundred and seventy Reichsmarks. Can you imagine that?'

A room each? That was just what Seb had hoped she would say. 'How big is this room of yours, Hexie? I need somewhere to stay, and everywhere in town is full.'

She put her hands on her hips and gave him her finest glare. 'So you won't move in with me in Munich, but you want to share my bed in Gapa?'

He shrugged. 'Well?'

'I'll have to think about that, won't I? You'll have to be very nice to me, Sebastian Wolff. We'll be drinking in the Kandabar. Bring your wallet.'

He had a good idea where he might find Traudl Schramm, but first there was something he could put off no longer. The letter was burning a hole in his pocket. He knew very well who it was from and the very thought of her made his heart beat faster.

Halfway down Ludwigstrasse in the centre of the Parten-kirchen side of the twin town, he found a café. It was crowded and the windows were steamed up, but there was a single vacant table, which he grabbed before ordering a coffee from the beleaguered waitress.

He took the letter with its Berlin frank and placed it in front of him. The sensible, more cautious half of him thought that he should screw it into a ball and throw it into a bin or, better still, burn it.

But he couldn't. He picked up a knife from the table and slid it into the envelope.

The letter was from Ulrike, as he knew it would be. Ulrike Brandt, his first love and the mother of Jurgen. He had not seen her or heard from her in over sixteen years. She had simply walked out one day, leaving the baby with Seb and his mother. A few days later a letter had arrived saying she was in Berlin, that she was sorry but that Jurgen would be better off without her.

She asked Seb not to look for her and left no forwarding address.

And that was that – the last he knew of the girl he loved, the girl he dreamt of every night in the trenches while he waited to be killed.

And now, after all these years, when he was happy with Hexie, when he had stopped dreaming of her, when Jurgen had accepted that he would never know his mother, there was this. It was almost too painful to look at, but he couldn't help himself.

My Dear Seb,

I hope this letter finds you. The only address I have is your mother's home but perhaps you are now married and have moved away. I am writing because I cannot get out of my head the fact that my little boy is almost eighteen and must be on the cusp of manhood.

You will, I know, have brought Jurgen up to be a fine human being with morality and decency in his bones. I suspect, too, that your mother will have ensured that he is a churchgoer with a strong faith. Between you, I am certain that you will have made a far better job of child-rearing than I could ever have done.

For all that, I am eternally grateful. And I am ashamed of myself that I have so far played such a small role in my son's life. We were both young and immature, but I fled when I'm sure you would have held firm.

I am older now, and steadier, and I would like the opportunity to get to know my boy, my darling Jurgen. I understand that he may despise me and shun me, and that will be his choice.

It is entirely possible that he now has a stepmother and half-brothers and half-sisters and that you are all settled in a warm and loving family home. But do you think it possible that he might have a small place in his heart for the foolish young girl who abandoned him?

I am an artist now and I am to have an exhibition in Munich after the Olympics. I will be there and I am hoping that we might meet, the three of us — you, me and Jurgen — sometime in the days leading up to the opening night, to which you are, of course, invited.

I have a room booked at a small guest house called the Isarbruck from the 7th. It is near the river and just south of the English Garden. Perhaps you would do me the kindness of coming to find me. I know we cannot fill in sixteen or more years, and yet I long to learn how life has treated the boys I loved.

Your Ulrike

Seb read the letter three times. He couldn't stop his eyes swimming with tears and kept his head low so that no one should see. Then he slipped the letter back into the envelope and put it in his pocket again.

He let out a deep sigh, blinked and irritably brushed his sleeve across his eyes. To think he had truly believed he'd got this woman out of his system. How could she still have this effect on him after all these years?

The waitress responded to his raised hand and came over. He handed her the cost of the coffee and a decent tip and thanked her.

She looked concerned. 'Is everything all right with you, sir?'

'Yes, yes, fräulein. A hard day, that's all.'

'Me, too, sir. I think the whole world is here.'

'Perhaps you could help me. I haven't quite worked out where everything is in Gapa. Could you tell me where the foreign press is stationed?'

'I don't know for certain, but I expect you'll find them in the Olympic Committee headquarters on the corner of Bahn-hofstrasse and Wettersteinstrasse. Just walk westwards from here along Schnitzschulstrasse in the direction of Garmisch. It's behind the ticket office. Someone there will help you.'

'Thank you.'

As Traudl Schramm's mother was said to be English, it seemed likely that her daughter might speak the language. In which case it made sense that such a person would be drafted in to use their translation skills for visitors from Britain, America or Canada. All hands on deck, as they used to say on the *Eastern Star*.

His hunch was right. She was working in the press room where interpreters and translators helped journalists. He found her camped at a desk with sports reporters from several London daily papers.

'Fräulein Schramm?' he said, having been pointed in her direction.

She was chatting to someone but turned on hearing her name. 'Yes?' she said in English.

'I need to talk to you,' Seb said in German. 'Is there somewhere quiet near here?'

'Who are you?'

'I will explain that in due course; suffice to say that this is official business.'

She was clearly in two minds whether to argue the point, but quickly decided that it would be best to obey. The words 'official business' tended to have that effect in the Third Reich. She was good-looking with regular features, auburn hair, sensual hooded eyes. He guessed she was in her mid-to-late twenties.

'Very well. There's a private office we can use.'

'No, let's go outside.' Seb wasn't confident that a private room used by the foreign press wouldn't be bugged by Himmler's goons. 'Follow me if you would.'

Outside, near the car park facing Wettersteinstrasse, she lit a cigarette, stuck it between her lips and folded her arms across her chest. She hadn't bothered with a coat and clearly felt the chill.

Seb took out his badge. 'Munich Kripo, Murder Team. My name is Wolff, captain of detectives. Do you know why I'm here?'

'I have no idea, but I'm sure you'll tell me.' If she was impressed or concerned by his identity, she wasn't about to show it.

'I'm informed that you've been engaged in a relationship with SS-Scharführer Theodor Krieger. Is that correct?'

She looked bored. 'What business is it of yours, Herr Wolff?'

'Just answer my question.'

She shrugged, and that was when he noticed the raw toughness in her eyes. Most people approached by a murder cop would have been either fearful or consumed with curiosity. Not Traudl Schramm.

'Well?'

'Yes, I know Theo. It's not a secret and I don't care if I'm the object of gossip and rumour. Is that enough information for you? Or would you also like to know that I'm a single woman and sometimes he stays the night – and who can blame him when he has that ice-tongued harpy at home?'

'How long has this affair been going on?'

'I thought you said Murder Team, not Morality Police.'

'Fräulein Schramm, I have to tell you that Theodor Krieger is dead, almost certainly murdered.' He had lowered his voice and he waited a few moments for the news to sink in, gazing into her eyes for some hint of a reaction, but he got none.

'Do you understand what I'm saying?'

'I think so.'

Two women in Krieger's life. Neither of them seemed to care greatly that he was dead. Seb moved on.

'I'm telling you this in the strictest confidence, for if any word of the crime were to get out, there would be a very severe response from the highest authorities in the land. Working in the press office, you perhaps understand more than most that every effort is being made to paint Germany and these Winter Olympics in a favourable light. Which means an absence of crime.'

He had spoken too soon, and he realised it. He should have waited for the initial words to sink in and *then* checked her reaction. The man with whom she was having an affair, perhaps even loved, was dead, the victim of murder; that was the big news. The need for secrecy could have followed in due course.

She removed the cigarette from her mouth. 'Are you saying Theo is dead?' It was as though she had not heard him properly.

'I'm afraid so, Fräulein Schramm.'

'Murdered?'

'Please lower your voice.'

'Where? When? I saw him less than twenty-four hours ago and he was fine then.'

'Do you live near here, Fräulein Schramm?'

'My apartment is two hundred metres away.'

'Can we go there? I cannot stress too highly the need for confidentiality. I'm sorry to have imparted this news to you in such a brutal fashion, but there are other factors at play in this terrible event.'

Her apartment couldn't have been more different from the large, scrubbed home of Petra Krieger. This place amounted to just one room, with a double bed, electric cooker, sink, sofa, small wooden table with two chairs, a wireless, a wardrobe and a wild scattering of female clothes on the bed and floor. Across the shared corridor was a communal bathroom and separate toilet.

Seb didn't bother to remove his shoes and nor did his hostess. He sat on the sofa and she sat on the edge of the bed.

He was surprised to see that her eyes were moist, but

perhaps that was a result of the cold air outside rather than emotion. After her initial reaction, he had not expected any tears to be shed for Theodor Krieger.

'You had better tell me everything, captain.'

'Krieger was killed not far from here, in the woods on the slopes of the Scharnitz Pass. He was shot at close range with a pistol, twice in the head and once in the heart. It seems likely that he was taken by surprise and would have known nothing about it. Death would have been virtually instantaneous.'

'Who did it?'

'That's what I'm trying to discover. I hoped you might be able to help me with possible suspects.'

'But why was he there?'

Seb shrugged. 'Again, I was hoping you might have some thoughts. You said you saw him less than twenty-four hours ago.'

'We went out to supper together, then came back here.'

'What time did he leave?'

'I was asleep and he didn't wake me. Perhaps eleven o'clock or midnight. I really don't know. I first knew he had gone when I woke at about two in the morning. But I just turned over and went back to sleep.'

'He didn't leave a note?'

That made her laugh. 'Not the sort of thing Theo would do. He would see such gestures as unmanly.'

'Do you have any idea who might have wished him harm?'

'The harpy, or one of her father's friends.'

'What does Frau Krieger's father have to do with this?'

'He's in Dachau, the treacherous pig. Theo hated him and denounced him for being a Bolshevik, for speaking against the Führer and spreading Communist propaganda. That above all is why Theo's wife hates him – for telling the truth

80

about her disgusting father. Ask *her* who killed him. She'll know.'

Seb stayed with Traudl Schramm for twenty minutes. He got the whole story of her affair with Theodor Krieger. It was simple enough, the same tale told countless times. Traudl was in a bar with friends, both male and female, and she caught Krieger's eye.

Drinks were taken; she was attracted to him. He was strong and rugged and looked exactly the way he would have wished to be seen: the powerful fighting man, a soldier. Ten or more years older than her with experience of the world. Strong, confident, merciless, virile.

He had spoken with pride of his time in the trenches, told her of the pleasure he had taken in bayoneting Frenchmen, ranted against those who betrayed Germany by capitulating to the Allies in 1918: the *November Criminals* – the Jews and Communists in Berlin who had conspired to bring about the country's humiliation. Or so the Nazis said.

'I liked that about him,' Traudl said. 'He was a true German. A National Socialist to the very core of his being.'

Traudl had been happy to accept him into her bed and her life; she was lonely after the break-up of a long engagement. She accepted his tale of a cold, distant wife without question. Whether she truly believed it did not matter. The important thing was that it made her feel that the affair was acceptable. She could go to the parish church of St Martin and take communion and even confession with an almost easy conscience. If Krieger's wife was cold, it was not a real marriage and so a man must fulfil his needs elsewhere. Everyone knew that.

As she concluded her simple tale of love and lust, Seb began speaking in English, which surprised her and she smiled for the first time.

'I believe you are half-English, Fräulein Schramm?'

'And you?'

'I served aboard a British freighter before joining the Munich police.'

'You speak the language well. My mother, God rest her soul, was born and brought up in Manchester and married my father before the war. They were truly in love. She taught English in the high school here but had a hard time when the war came. Those feelings have not altogether disappeared. There are still those with ill feeling towards the British, which is why I'm known by some as the English bitch – or worse.'

'That must be hard.'

'Oh, I've become used to it. And you know what, I love this country as much as anyone. I followed the Führer from the early days and joined the National Socialist Women's League in October 1931, the very month of its foundation. No one can call me traitor – unlike the harpy and her father. If it were me, I would happily put bullets in both their heads.'

The conversation had strayed from the murder of Theodor Krieger. Seb began speaking in German again. 'I'm still hoping for more information from you, Fräulein Schramm. Let us talk about Herr Krieger. Apart from his wife and her father, who were his enemies?'

'Why do you think he had enemies?'

'Doesn't everyone? No one who has lived any sort of life can have avoided upsetting one or two people along the way.'

'I know of no one else whom I would class as Theo's enemy.'

'What of Xaver Knorr?'

'Why do you mention him? He and Theo were always good friends.'

'You have met him, then?'

'Yes, two or three times. They were drinking together the night I first met Theo. They were like brothers.'

'Sometimes we are betrayed by those we trust the most.'

She simply shook her head and reached for her cigarettes.

'Where would I find Xaver Knorr?'

'God knows.'

'Is he in the SS?'

'No, he works for someone, an old woman and her husband. Does stuff around the house and estate for them, like a factotum. They're quite rich; that's all I know.'

'Here in Gapa?'

'Somewhere near Bad Tölz, I think, but I could be wrong. Let me add something – I said that Theo was good friends with Xaver and that was certainly true, and they did have a brotherly bond, but that doesn't mean they were similar. I think Xaver Knorr is not always the most law-abiding of men. To be honest, I never really liked him that much, but that's always the way, isn't it? We accept our lover's friends though we may not warm to them.'

'But, as far as you're concerned, Theo himself was always law-abiding?'

'Oh, yes. He was a man of honour, like all good soldiers. Upright and honest.'

Which was not what Gruppenführer Paul Jena had suggested. Krieger, he had said, was suspected of having 'criminal tendencies'. That was the expression, wasn't it?

'Fräulein Schramm, you asked me what Herr Krieger was doing up in the woods along the Scharnitz Pass, and I said I was hoping you might have an answer to that question. What does seem clear is that the trip there was arranged beforehand, because he went out at dead of night and left you sleeping. It was a strange place to be at such a time, and he wasn't alone. If you were to make a wild guess, what do you think they could have been doing there?'

'Maybe they were hunting. Theo was always a hunter.'

'Hunting what?'

'I don't know. Night creatures? Whatever animals roam the forests in the dark.'

It was a possibility, but somehow Seb doubted it. People didn't take handguns to hunt unless the prey was human.

Seb reiterated his order that she should not mention a word of this to anyone. 'This week you're working in an extremely sensitive area, Fräulein Schramm, surrounded by journalists from around the world. If any of them should ask you about this crime, what will you say?'

'I'll tell them I don't know what they're talking about.'

'And then what?'

'I'll get in touch with you immediately. I'm not stupid, Captain Wolff, and nor would I ever do anything to harm the movement.'

'One more thing. Are any of Herr Krieger's belongings here in your room?'

'He keeps a razor here and a toothbrush, a spare shirt, maybe a jacket, socks, a tie, I think. He comes and goes at will and sometimes leaves stuff. I'm not the tidiest or the most houseproud of women, so I don't keep tabs on such things. Actually, I like his things being here. I like the smell of him.'

'May I look around?'

'Feel free.'

He scoured the room, gently picking up items of female underwear in case something was concealed beneath. As he moved methodically around the little apartment, she sat on the edge of the bed, her head downcast, and he noticed that her body was shaking as she dragged ferociously at her cigarette. Maybe she wasn't so hard after all.

A man's jacket was hanging in the wardrobe. It had to be Theodor Krieger's. Seb tried the pockets and found an undeveloped – or unused – 35mm-film canister.

She wasn't looking so he didn't ask whether he could take it; he simply slipped it into his own pocket.

13

Seb made his way to the Kandabar and looked for Hexie and Carin, but they weren't there. It was seven o'clock. They had probably gone elsewhere to get a bite to eat.

But he saw another group and very much wished that he hadn't, for they had seen him, too: the people he had met at Schloss Stark, all smartened up and minus only Gruppen-führer Jena and Elena Lang.

The effete English poet Howard Jack waved to him and Seb waved back, hoping that would be an end to it, but then Jack wandered over in his direction.

'It's Captain Wolff, isn't it? Are you staying in Gapa for the Games?'

'Wouldn't miss them for the world.' A lie was easier than trying to come up with some convoluted excuse for his presence in town.

'You look as if you've been stood up. Come and join us, won't you? We all decided we just had to come out with hoi polloi for an alpine pub crawl. A celebration of the newly arrived young men and women from every corner of the earth. So fit, so strong, so beautiful. We're getting in the mood, soaking up the atmosphere, clapping along with the leather-clad boys as they slap their thighs and knees and shoes. I love it all. Mind you, not everyone's happy. Bobo Mitford simply can't stop scowling. She's beside herself with fury because all the anti-Jew posters and the *Stürmer* stands have been taken down and hidden away.'

'It's very kind of you, Mr Jack, but I won't join you. You're right, as it happens – my girlfriend has stood me up and I need to find her. She has the key to our room. Please give my apologies to your friends.'

'I understand completely, Captain Wolff, but the invitation stands if you can't find her. The delicious Elena Lang may be joining us later if she can escape Harcourt.' He winked at Seb. 'I saw the way you looked at her. I have an eye for these things. I know when a man and a woman have an interest in each other.'

Seb laughed. He very much doubted whether Howard Jack had any great understanding of what went on between men and women.

The Englishman put his hand on Seb's shoulder. 'I apologise for the horrible jape we played on you at Schloss Stark. You can guess whose idea that was, and she wouldn't drop it. Come on, captain, one beer. It'll annoy Bobo and delight the rest of us.'

What could he do? He badly needed a beer. 'All right,' he said, 'just the one.'

'Good fellow. I want to know all about your time at sea with the English sailors.'

This time Seb beat Unity to the Hitler salute, but it didn't stop her glaring at him. 'Haven't you heard, Wolff, we're all to say *Grüss Gott* during the Games? Don't want to upset the foreign wets.'

No, he hadn't heard. 'Forgive me, Miss Mitford. The salute just comes so naturally to me.'

'Don't try to make fun of me, Wolff, or you'll most assuredly regret it.'

'Oh, Bobo,' Jack said, 'do put a sock in it, darling. The poor man is doing his best in very trying circumstances.'

'Well, *you* should certainly be in Dachau, Howard.'

'I'm sure I should, but I can do what I want and say what I want and no one will lay a finger on me because I'm English, not German.' He took a deep drag of his cigarette and blew a smoke ring at Unity.

Neither Sophie nor her brother Werner von Stark bothered to join in the conversation. Fritz Mannheim, Unity's spectacle-wearing SS companion, gave Seb an enigmatic smile as though he knew something the others didn't. Was it possible that he had heard about the murder of Theodor Krieger? As a brother-in-arms, Jena might have told him.

'So tell me, Sebastian,' Jack said, 'are you a sportsman?'

'I adore skiing, but I've never raced other than with school-friends, so I doubt anyone would call me a sportsman.'

'I think we should arrange a little race along the down-hill course from Kreuzjoch. You, me, Bobo, Sophie, Werner, Fritz – and perhaps we could get Paul Jena and Elena Lang along. Not timed, just set off together. Last one down buys the drinks.'

'I'm sure you'd all thrash me,' Seb said, gulping his beer. He wanted to get away from these people as fast as possible.

Sophie von Stark, small, fair and quiet, was sitting on the other side of the table. It seemed to Seb that her flesh was almost translucent. Was that the result of being brought up with great wealth, never having to work, always eating the finest foods?

It was strange how anonymous she was in this place, despite her great power and riches. Many eyes turned to Unity Mitford, but no one gazed at Sophie or her brother. The family's policy of always shunning the limelight had been remarkably successful. No one knew these uber-wealthy people outside the small, charmed circle they inhabited.

Seb had a theory about this: firstly, it was to protect them against unwanted attention from beggars and extortionists.

But, secondly, it was to ensure that the family was largely forgotten and ignored, so that they should not be envied.

Any student of history would tell you that envy was the enemy of the high-born and the wealthy; it led to insurrection and revolution. Just ask the aristocrats of Russia or France. They had paid a heavy price for flaunting their treasures.

'I think you should leave Herr Wolff alone,' Sophie said. 'If he doesn't want to ski with us, that's his business.'

'We wouldn't want him accidentally falling off a precipice, would we?' Unity said. 'That would be awful.'

Howard Jack leant across and whispered in Seb's ear. 'Bobo's got another bee in her bonnet. It seems a certain young woman named Eva Braun will be joining the great leader to watch the skating. Bobo had hoped she'd have him all to herself; now it seems she's not going to get a look-in.'

Unity had heard him. 'If you ever mention that woman's name in my presence, Howard Jack, I will cut you dead and have you deported.'

Jack winked at Seb and grinned. 'Told you.'

Seb downed the last of his beer. Interesting that word of Hitler's relationship with Evie Braun was starting to get out. The door to the bar was opening and he caught the welcome sight of Hexie coming in. He stood up. 'Thank you for the beer, ladies and gentlemen, and perhaps we will have that race. For the moment, my girl has arrived and we have a table booked for supper.'

'Oh, you must introduce us!' Jack said.

'Another time, perhaps.'

He bowed his head briskly to each of them in turn, then moved across to the bar, where Hexie was waiting. It occurred to him that in his ten-minute sojourn with the group, Werner von Stark had not uttered a single word.

*

'Hexie, I want to get out of here, sharpish.'

'Why don't we eat here?'

'I'm trying to get away from that lot over there. Their company is excruciating. I told them we have a table booked elsewhere.'

'I recognise the one with the fat white fingers. The ghastly Unity, isn't it? But who are the others?'

'I'll explain all when we leave.'

'No, first a drink.'

'Very well, what do you want?'

'Oh, I don't know.' Hexie placed a finger on her lower lip. 'What do I want? Champagne perhaps? A vintage Bordeaux? I think you owe me the very best if I'm to share my bed with you tonight. Don't you think, Herr Wolff? Not that I can be bought, of course.'

'Beer, then,' Seb said. He signalled to a waitress clad in a low-cut dirndl, with a leather bag stuffed with notes and coins weighing down her waist. 'Will Carin want one?'

'I've lost her. Or, rather, she's lost me. We went to another bar first and she got talking to a member of the Canadian ice-hockey team. Couldn't tear herself away. He was very handsome and neither understood a word the other was saying, but that won't stop them from devouring each other. Come on, Seb, tell me – who are your new friends? Obviously, I recognise Mitford, but the others?'

'Are you really sure you want to know?'

'Go on.'

'They're the ones from Schloss Stark. The woman is Sophie von Stark and the one on the left is her brother, Werner. He doesn't say a lot. The little one is an upper-class English poet called Howard Jack. And then there's the Mitford minder, the one with the glasses, an SS officer named Mannheim. Perhaps you recognise him from the Osteria.'

'So what are they doing in a dive like this?'

'Slumming it, looking down their noses at the little people. People like us.'

'I can't believe it. I suppose their clothes look quite expensive – but it's just traditional Bavarian *Tracht*. Hardly high fashion or anything. I wouldn't have noticed them.'

'That's the whole point. They just go their own way and no one knows who they are. They inhabit another world, Hexie. Even now, they probably have several bodyguards stationed anonymously around the bar with concealed guns, but no one will ever know unless trouble starts, because they all exist in a tight cocoon. Normal mortals get only the tiniest of glimpses inside their glittering lives.'

'The opposite of your uncle Christian.'

'Exactly. He flaunts it and he'll lose it. These families last hundreds of years.'

'I think one of your new friends is heading our way.'

Seb looked around. Howard Jack had arrived. There was no escape.

'Still here, captain?'

'Fräulein Schuler decided she needed an aperitif.'

The Englishman put out his hand. 'Pleased to meet you,' he said in German.

'And you, Herr, er –'

'Jack. Howard Jack. And do you have another name apart from Schuler?'

'I'm sorry,' Seb said. 'This is Hexie.'

'Then that's what I shall call you. And you shall both call me Howard. Do you speak English, Hexie?'

'I get by when necessary. Seb helps me.'

'I saw you across the room and I thought, surely that beautiful woman can't have anything to do with our new policeman friend. But it seems you do. And I have to tell you, Hexie, I believe you are the prettiest girl I've seen in Bavaria. What on earth do you see in this miserable law officer? There's no justice.'

'He has his good points, though they can be hard to find. Anyway, you flatter me, Howard.'

'Nonsense. Look, I'm not going to detain you, but I have a little invitation for you both. Sophie and Werner and I would absolutely love you to come to our grand celebration for the opening of the Games.'

'I adore a party,' Hexie said, before Seb could get a word in.

'And the party will adore you. Everyone who's anyone will be there and it will be a fairytale riot. The top bananas from the Olympic Committee, the great and the good of Bavarian society and some dreadful Nazis in their glittering uniforms, all collar flashes and high, shiny boots. But we can ignore the Nazis, can't we?'

'Seb?'

'I really don't think –'

'Buses will be laid on for those without cars, such as the skiers and skaters, and you're welcome to hop aboard – or you can come in your own car. Your names will be at the gatehouse. Oh, and the film crew have been invited: Elena Lang, Gary Tate, Alan Harcourt, all the stars. I promise you it will be a party to die for.'

'Then we must go, mustn't we, Seb? Can we?'

'Let's think about it. See how it fits in with our plans.'

'But what would I wear?' Hexie said. 'I don't have fine clothes with me.'

'Come exactly as you are, darling Hexie, and you'll be gazed upon by one and all. Come as Gretel or Snow White and you'll not feel out of place. Or, even better, get your lovely man to buy you something special. The men will adore you, while Bobo and the stuffier matrons will hate you for putting them in the shade.'

'I don't have evening wear either,' Seb said.

Howard Jack sized him up. 'Don't worry, I'll have something sent over to you. Where are you staying?'

'The Waxenstein Guest House.'

The Englishman beamed and blew them a kiss as he took his leave. 'You'll look divine, both of you.'

14

They ate a quick supper of cheese *Spätzle* at the restaurant of the guest house. Outside, the rain had turned to light snow. Perhaps the Führer's weather miracle might still materialise.

'Surely we can go to that party, Seb? Think of it – dancing and drinking with the rich and famous at Schloss Stark! It's the chance of a lifetime – something to tell our children and grandchildren.'

'Let's see how tomorrow goes. I *am* working, Hex.'

'How about this for a deal? I let you stay in my bed; you take me to the party.'

Seb had no way to refuse. He knew her well enough to realise she had made up her mind.

Also, he had another favour to ask of Hexie. He leant across the table. 'I have a 35mm film in my pocket. I want it developed and prints made. How can I get that done quietly? No fuss.'

She thought for a moment. 'I don't know anyone in Gapa. There must be facilities here for the press, but they'll be rushed off their feet.'

'What about back in Munich?'

'Hoffmann's closed the shop for the duration of the Games, but there is a man we use if our own darkroom is out of action for any reason – sickness or holiday.'

'Could you call him? Tell him it's confidential. Would he go along with that? I can send Hans Winter to him on the train.'

'So that's yet another favour you're demanding of me.'

'I'll pay you back.'

'I know you will – because I'm going to find a suitable dress for Schloss Stark tomorrow and you're contributing.'

'You drive a hard bargain, Hexie Schuler. And what's all this stuff about children and grandchildren? Where did that come from?'

She patted her belly. 'Didn't I tell you?'

'Are you serious?'

'Three months. It's not showing yet. The doctor says it will be arriving the first week in August. Isn't that exciting? I've been longing to tell you but I wasn't sure how you'd take the news.'

He reached over and clasped her hand. He was aware the blood had drained from his face, and yet he had to smile and be thrilled.

'I've been thinking of names. If it's a boy, it will have to be Adolf – or perhaps Hermann. No, Adolf, of course. Or *both* if it's twins. Adolf and Hermann, just think of it – two boys for the greater good of Germany.'

He frowned and looked into her eyes and then he knew. 'You are a bad woman, Hexie Schuler.'

She laughed so loudly that heads turned. 'And you're very easy to goad, Seb Wolff.'

Was he pleased that she wasn't pregnant? He wasn't quite sure. They should be married; they should be considering starting a family. But this wasn't the moment to be thinking of such things.

He looked at the Swiss cuckoo clock on the wall. He needed to telephone Ettstrasse to see if there was any word from Sergeant Winter.

Hexie stood up, still holding his hand. 'Come on, bedtime. You look exhausted.'

'First a quick telephone call.'

'It can wait.'

He allowed himself to be led away and up the stairs. All the time, he was churning inside. The letter from Ulrike was still there in his pocket. He knew very well that he should tell Hexie about it – be completely open – even though she would be horrified by its contents.

But he also knew that he *wouldn't* tell her about it. Not tonight anyway. Somehow, he had to find a way to ease it to her gently.

And then there was the other, equally difficult problem: how to tell Jurgen that his mother was coming to Munich?

15

Seb managed to drag himself away to the phone while Hexie brushed her teeth. There was a message at Ettstrasse for him from Hans Winter. He had gone back to Munich to search the Police Presidium files for anything on the dead man, Theodor Krieger, or his friend Xaver Knorr, but his efforts were in vain, so now he was going to the political police archives at the Wittelsbach Palace.

He would stay overnight at home and be in the office from 8 a.m. until 9 a.m. if Seb could telephone then.

Seb cursed. It would have been more convenient if Winter had come back here to Garmisch so that he could take the film to be developed. For all he knew, it contained nothing but happy snaps of Krieger's three children, but it was worth a look.

They woke to the brilliant light of a snow-filled sky. The whole world seemed cloaked in white silence.

'Looks like the prayers to Adolf have paid dividends,' he muttered.

'Hmm?' Hexie said, not really awake.

'It's snowing, really snowing, just in time for the opening ceremony. Come on, let's get some breakfast. I've got work to do.'

He called the Presidium in Munich at eight o'clock sharp from a public phone booth. Winter was there as promised.

'Find anything, sergeant?'

'They have both been up to something – Krieger and

Knorr. They were being watched for potential illicit currency dealing until a month ago, but then the inquiry stopped. No explanation, but you have to wonder whether Krieger pulled strings to have the investigation halted.'

'Do you have any evidence that that's what happened?'

'No, just my own suspicions. Even the most junior SS men wield power over the BPP.'

'Do you have an address for Xaver Knorr?'

'I do. He works for a family called Sachs. Moritz and Selma Sachs. They live a little south of Bad Tölz, on the outskirts of the village of Liliendorf. The house is called Valhalla. Very Nordic.'

'See if you can get a car from the pound and come back here as soon as possible. A blizzard is whipping up, but the ploughs will keep the roads open. As quickly as you can, sergeant. I've got a task for you.'

'Before you go, Ruff wants a word with you, captain. Hold on to the line and I'll have you transferred.'

Two minutes later, he was through to the deputy president of police.

'What's going on, Wolff?'

'I'm investigating the murder of Theodor Krieger.'

'What's there to investigate? The wife's behind it – revenge for her own ill-treatment and the denunciation of her father.'

Seb was astonished by the remark. 'You've heard about her father, then?'

'If you must know I had dinner with Heinrich Deubel last night.'

'I see.' Deubel was the commandant at the Dachau concentration camp, where Petra Krieger's father was being held. But surely Ruff should not have been discussing such matters with Deubel. The order from on high had been clear: no one – absolutely no one – was to be informed of the murder.

98

'Look, damn it, Wolff, I know what you're thinking, but Deubel is a solid man and can be trusted. He's SS – and the SS cannot be kept out of this inquiry. Anyway, they of all people are not going to go to the press! And by talking to him I've saved you a great deal of time and effort.'

'Petra Krieger is a houseproud mother, sir. Yes, she's angry but, I promise you, she didn't take her husband into the woods at dead of night and shoot him with a police-issue pistol. I doubt she knows a butt from a muzzle.'

There was a moment's silence on the line. Then Thomas Ruff exploded. 'How dare you, Wolff! If you ever talk to me in such a condescending way again, you'll be in white gloves waving traffic by day's end. And you know very well I'm not saying she actually pulled the trigger. She hired someone or conspired with one of her father's friends. Haul her in and interrogate her properly.'

Had this really stemmed from a friendly dinner with the Dachau commandant or had someone got to Ruff? Perhaps Winter was right: someone had intervened in the BPP surveillance of Krieger and Knorr. *Keep calm*, Seb told himself. *Don't give in.*

'I should tell you, sir, that on the evening before the murder, Krieger was with his mistress, Traudl Schramm, in her apartment in Gapa. He left of his own accord and went off into the night, probably around midnight and almost certainly for an assignation of a criminal nature. That's where I need to look – and Krieger's SS friends know it. If you doubt me, talk to Paul Jena.'

There was another silence on the line.

'Herr Ruff?'

'Did you say Jena?'

'Indeed. SS-Gruppenführer Jena.'

'Are you saying he has spoken to you?'

99

'You told me to go to the SD office in Gapa, so we met there. He mentioned the possibility that Krieger was a crook and that he had been in danger of being dismissed from the SS. With that in mind, there's every possibility that Krieger's death had nothing to do with a wife's desire for vengeance and everything to do with certain racketeers with whom he consorted.'

Seb could feel the tension and anger from ninety kilometres away. His hapless boss was trapped. He could almost hear the man's teeth grinding.

'Shall I proceed with my investigation or do you really want me to arrest Frau Krieger?'

'To hell with it, Wolff. Do it your own way but get it done quickly and quietly. And keep me informed every step of the way.'

The call ended. Outside, the street was cloaked in white. A queue of four people waited for the phone, but Seb found himself rooted to the spot.

Not for the first time, the conversation with his boss had been acrimonious. It suddenly occurred to him that both he and Ruff were guilty of the same sin: closing their minds.

Perhaps Ruff was right (and Traudl Schramm for that matter). Perhaps the dead man's wife wasn't so innocent. The desire for vengeance was the most ancient and powerful of driving forces.

So, yes, that still needed investigating. Perhaps there were even more lines of inquiry that he had not yet considered.

For the moment, he had to wait for Winter and pass on the film to him. And then he wanted to get to the house at Liliendorf to talk to Xaver Knorr. He returned from the phone booth to the guest house and joined Hexie in her room.

'I've got things to do – mostly see Hans Winter, but he won't be here for a couple of hours. Shall we go shopping together for this 24-carat gold-trimmed evening gown you're demanding?'

'You forgot the diamond and ruby sequins. And, no, I'll do that after lunch. This morning, if you have nothing else to do, you can take me to the opening ceremony. It should be quite a spectacle and the snow is really blowing up.'

'My pleasure. But, first, a long breakfast with lots of coffee and pastries.'

'And you agree now that we can go to Schloss Stark this evening?'

He nodded. 'Anything for you, Hexie Schuler.' He didn't need to mention it, but there was another reason he had decided it would be a good idea to go to the castle: he still harboured fears for Elena Lang, and she would be there.

The streets were thick with snow. The air was brisk and white and the mountains were no longer visible. This was the weather and scenery Seb had always associated with Gapa. Apart from the war and his time traversing the North Sea, he had been coming here most winters since his teens, even if only for a few hours at a time.

What he loved less today was that the roads were closed off by oppressive ranks of uniformed men with boots, helmets, long leather coats with swastika armbands, and rifles with bayonets attached. The whole area from the Kainzenbad railway station to the ski stadium had been sealed by the Leibstandarte-SS, the official bodyguard of Adolf Hitler. He would be arriving by special train from Munich.

Seb and Hexie had to skirt their way around the forbidden route. The occasion might be joyous, but the threat of assassination was taken seriously and so the

Führer was surrounded by strict security. Even the slopes above the town were patrolled by BPP men, either on foot or skis.

The patrols had been intensified because of the assassination two days earlier of the leader of the Swiss Nazi Party. Wilhelm Gustloff had been shot dead in Davos by a Jew named David Frankfurter. It had focused the minds of the senior Nazis back home in Germany.

Hexie had her ticket in her purse. Seb merely produced his Munich police badge and was immediately admitted to the magnificent Olympic Stadium.

It was a quarter to eleven; a band was playing and the stands were packed, the flags of the competing nations fluttering alongside the Olympic flag. And the snow came down and settled on roads and roofs alike.

A few minutes later, a roar went up on all sides as the top men of the German and International Olympic committees arrived on the balcony of the main building. And then there they were, the big noises of the Nazi movement: Frick, Hess, Goebbels, and Hitler himself.

He wore a long coat of soft leather and had removed his hat so that all his adoring people should see him clearly. He saluted them and they saluted back. Behind him, in steel helmet, a stormtrooper stood guard, looking nothing like the image of peace and goodwill that Hitler and Goebbels were keen to portray.

At Hitler's side was Henri de Baillet-Latour, president of the International Olympic Committee, who had also removed his hat and wore plus fours beneath a warm overcoat. Then the competing teams marched into the arena, many giving the Olympic salute with arm outstretched, palm down, which looked uncomfortably like the Hitler salute. Others avoided saluting at all.

'That's the British team, isn't it?' Hexie demanded. 'Why do they wear black armbands?'

'Their king died two weeks ago.'

'They still had a king?'

'They did – and now they have another one.'

'That's so nineteenth century.'

The last team into the stadium was the German one. They were met with a peal of thunderous Sieg Heils. Then Baillet-Latour made his speech, the flame was lit, and Hitler declared the Games open.

A little way along the balcony stood the hawk-eyed Goebbels, waving and smiling as he took in the scene of his propaganda triumph. Snow dusted his bare head and shoulders.

Finally, a volley of cannon fire echoed off the hillsides and across the valley, its roar muffled by the snow.

It suddenly occurred to Seb that he had his police pistol in a shoulder holster under his jacket. He was not more than thirty metres away from Hitler. With one well-aimed shot he could change the course of history.

The moment passed and the Walther remained unfired.

'That was splendid,' Seb said, his arm around Hexie's shoulders. 'One could almost be proud of one's country. Peace and understanding among nations.'

'Careful, Seb.'

'Did I say something wrong?'

'You said *almost*. And you sounded sarcastic.' She leant forward and pointed across the crowd. 'Why look, isn't that Jurgen?'

Seb followed her outstretched arm and saw his son with a group of Hitler Youth lads, all standing in line, legs akimbo, shoulders wide, hands clasped behind their backs. 'Ah, yes.'

'We must go and say hello.'

'I'm pretty sure he wouldn't appreciate that.'

Jurgen stood out for his obvious athleticism, his strong features and fair hair. Some might see him as the ideal of Aryan adolescence. Seb just saw him as his son and fervently wished he would give up the Hitler Youth militia nonsense and concentrate on more important things. But that was easier said than done. How do you quit an organisation when all your friends are members?

Instinctively Seb's hand went to his pocket, where the letter from the boy's mother still resided. What was he going to say to him? He would have to choose the moment very carefully. In particular, he must do it before informing Hexie and Mutti.

Another roar went up from the crowd and Seb looked back up to the balcony, where a new face had made an appearance. The great movie actress herself – Elena Lang. As she waved to the adoring crowd, Joseph Goebbels turned to her and applauded, as though they had never met.

Seb looked at Hexie, and they both raised their eyebrows.

16

They made their way out through the milling crowd just as Hitler left for Munich on his special train.

'Shopping now, I suppose?'

'Really, Seb, I don't need you. In fact, you'd be hopeless, so I'll find Carin and she can help me.'

That suited Seb because he really couldn't afford the time. He had a heavy workload today. Together, he and Hexie trudged through the thick snow back to the guest house. Hans Winter was already there, waiting.

Seb kissed Hexie farewell, then took Winter along the road to the Kandabar, which was already doing a brisk trade. 'Let's have a beer while we work out our next move.'

They settled down in one of the less noisy corners. Seb went over his conversation with Ruff. 'We have to cover both bases. If the road's clear enough, I'm going to drive up to Liliendorf and see if I can find Xaver Knorr. I think another visit to Frau Krieger is also in order. And you, sergeant, will go to Dachau and grill Frau Krieger's father. It would be a good idea to call ahead in case he's out on a work detail. See if they can have him ready for you.'

'Do we have his name?'

'Friedrich Brauer. Question him hard, but no violence. I won't stand for that, whatever the Gestapo boys in Dortmund taught you. Trust your instinct: Is he lying? Is he concealing something? Could he have got word out to a co-conspirator, ordering the murder? Or is he an innocent man caught up by forces beyond his control?'

Winter took all this in, nodding in agreement. 'What if . . .' he said at last.

'Yes?'

'I just had a foolish idea, that's all.'

'Go on.'

'No, I can't. You'll think I'm crazy.'

'Spit it out.'

Winter took a deep sigh. 'You really want to hear it, captain?'

'I want you to get to the point so we can carry on with our inquiries,' he said. In the forefront of his mind, nagging at his brain, was the terrifying possibility that Elena Lang was in mortal danger. This murder of an SS trooper was an unwelcome distraction.

'It's just that I can't see how I'll learn anything from Friedrich Brauer simply by talking to him,' Winter said. 'He'll deny everything.'

'If you've got a better idea, tell me.'

'I could go into Dachau undercover. The Gestapo used this tactic to effect more than once in the main jail in Dortmund. Prisoners talk to each other, boast about crimes which they would never admit to the forces of law. One of our men would go in undercover, as a prisoner.'

It really was a stupid idea. 'You've lost your mind, sergeant.'

Winter shrugged, as if to say that, yes, he knew it was stupid. 'I thought you'd say that, captain, but no one would recognise me there. Neither the guards nor the inmates.'

'And you're willing to take the risk? I'm impressed that you should put yourself up for such a mission, but I still say it's crazy.'

'I'd like to try it.'

'It never occurred to me that you had such courage, sergeant.'

'And now you're mocking me.'

Seb smiled. 'Perhaps I am.'

'The idea terrifies me, captain. But it might work.'

'You certainly look like an undesirable, so you should fit in well.'

That made Winter laugh and it eased the tension. 'Thank you, sir.'

'You don't really think you could carry it off, do you?'

'Perhaps. I won't know unless I try it.'

'It could be very dangerous. You'll recall that I've been in there myself.' He met Winter's eyes with a wry smile, for it was Winter who had consigned Seb to Dachau for the 'crime' of not saluting the Führer. That had been their first encounter and matters had become worse between them, until, finally, they had come to an uneasy understanding.

'I'm sorry about that, captain. Truly I am.'

'Oh, it's all forgotten.' But of course it wasn't and never would be. 'I must remind you, however, that it's not a pleasant place. Punishment is meted out at the will of the guards. You will have no appeal, no recourse to justice. And then there are the other inmates to worry about. They might not like you, especially if they suspect you of being an informer. Are you serious about this, sergeant?'

He nodded. 'I am.'

'Then I suppose I can't stop you. Good luck, and may your God go with you.'

Winter nodded his appreciation. 'I will do my duty.'

What Seb didn't know was that Hans Winter had another motive entirely for offering to enter the circles of hell.

There was a time last year when an innocent man died because Hans Winter had lacked courage. It occurred to Seb that Winter saw this as a chance of atonement, a chance to prove his manhood.

Men of Winter's generation, those who had missed the war, sometimes felt inferior to their elders who had fought for Germany. It was understandable why such men should wish to test themselves by fire.

'What will you do if an inmate recognises you?'

'That seems unlikely, but, if it happens, I'll withdraw.'

'What if a guard reveals the truth?'

'The guards won't know. Only the commandant. I'll be treated like every other detainee.'

Seb was shaking his head. But then this was a difficult investigation, and if Winter could clear up just one line of inquiry, it would be a huge step forward. One that would leave Seb free to concentrate his efforts on whoever was threatening Elena Lang. And it was possible the Dachau idea might just work. A long shot, but, as Winter said, it had worked before. 'You'd certainly need cooperation from Commandant Deubel. Do you know him?'

'No, but I believe the boss does.'

'You're right – Deputy President Ruff could fix this for you. One last time, are you sure?'

'I'm positive, captain.'

'Then do it. But I want you out as soon as possible.'

'Thank you. I won't let you down.'

'Three days, preferably sooner. And you'll need to work out a cover story.'

'I was thinking I should be a political prisoner, like Brauer.'

'Good idea. Be a Communist. Do you think you can pull that off?'

'In Dortmund we dealt with the Communists every day. I know all about them.'

'Then go and talk to Ruff. And, on your way, I have another little task for you.' Seb took the film canister out of his pocket, along with the address of the photographic lab

Hexie had suggested. 'I want this developed. Hexie has called ahead and this man has agreed to process it as a matter of urgency. I'll pick up the pictures when I'm next in Munich. Remind him that this is confidential. He's not to tell anyone.'

'What's in the film?'

'Your guess is as good as mine, sergeant. But I very much want to know. By the way, I have been meaning to ask you – are you still making reports on me to your old chums in the political police?'

'I have to. I wouldn't be assigned to you otherwise – they don't like you and they're not convinced you're a Nazi.'

'And what do you tell them?'

Winter laughed. 'I tell them you're a pussycat, sir.'

'Very funny.'

Seb knew the truth: it was the influence of his rich uncle and his success as a detective that kept him out of Dachau. Or worse. There were men in the political police who would take great pleasure in killing him.

Ten minutes later, Seb placed a call to Ruff and explained his new thinking. This conversation was a little easier than the last one.

'So you now agree with me that vengeance is a likely motive and that Friedrich Brauer is worth investigating?'

'One must keep an open mind.'

'That's what I like to hear. And I will call Herr Deubel and ask him to cooperate with Sergeant Winter's proposal. It is a fine idea. Well done to both of you.'

Seb picked up the Lancia Augusta. Despite the snow, it started first time. Good Italian engineering.

The scattered farming village of Liliendorf was no more than twenty-five kilometres away, but it took him over an hour to get there, his windscreen wipers working overtime in the driving snow, his headlights unable to pick out the road more than fifty metres ahead. When he arrived in the village, he asked for directions to a house called Valhalla, home of the Sachs family.

The first man he approached simply spat on the ground and turned away. Next, Seb went into a bakery, one of only two shops in the little lakeside community, and asked again. The young woman scowled at him and asked why he wanted to know, so he showed her his Kripo badge.

'Carry on through the village, one kilometre on your right down a long drive. Make sure you arrest them and sling them in prison. Even better, throw them out of the country.'

'Why, what have they done?'

'It's not what they've done. It's who they are.'

Ah, thought Seb, they must be Jews.

The house was an imposing villa, but the name Valhalla was perhaps stretching it a bit. This was not in the league of Schloss Stark, but Seb liked it. The occupants must be quite well-to-do. It was coated in fresh snow, long icicles hanging from the guttering.

He parked in front of the building, ducked through the snow and hammered at the front door. A woman answered. She was small, grey-haired, a little overweight, probably in her fifties and wearing black. Seb instantly tried to work out whether this was the mistress of the house or a servant and took a chance on the former.

'Frau Sachs?'

'Yes. How can I help you?'

'My name is Wolff from the Munich police department. Captain Wolff. I believe you have an employee called Xaver Knorr.'

'Why, yes, that's correct. Xaver does a great deal of work for us. He hasn't done anything wrong, has he?'

'Let's hope not. Is he here?'

'I don't believe so, but I could find out for you if you would care to wait. He comes and goes, you see.'

'So this is not his residence?'

'No, he has a house in the village. Would you like to come indoors out of the cold, captain?'

'Thank you.' Seb stepped into the entrance hall, which was surprisingly bare of any sort of furnishing or ornament.

Frau Sachs seemed to notice his interest. 'We're packing up and moving to Weimar. A lot of our property is already in storage.'

'I understand.' Perhaps they hoped a cultural town like Weimar might be more welcoming than the small-minded anti-Semites who inhabited villages like Liliendorf, the sort of people who put up banners stating *Jews not welcome here*.

'Perhaps you would like a cup of coffee?'

'That's very kind of you.'

'First, let's see if Xaver's about. I'm afraid my husband is in his study writing and doesn't like to be disturbed.'

The house was beautiful. Seb thought it must have been very homely when fully furnished, the sort of property where a well-off family might raise several children and then decide it was a bit too big for just two people. Seb followed Selma Sachs out to the back, which gave way to snow-covered lawns and several outbuildings. All very neat and well cared for.

They went around the outbuildings, one of which was a large hay-barn, and looked out over snowy hillside pastures and a frozen lake that stretched towards the village. 'We have quite a lot of land,' the woman said. 'Xaver is a sort of estate manager for us. In the past, he looked after the livestock, and he's always found staff when we needed them for harvests, planting, that sort of thing.'

'How long has he been with you?'

'It must be twelve years now. He makes his own hours, which suits us so long as all the work is done.'

'Do you trust him?'

She stopped and turned to Seb. 'I don't understand.'

'Is he honest?'

'May I ask what you're investigating, officer?'

'I'm afraid you can't. I just want to know your opinion of the man. Is he a faithful servant? Have you ever had cause to doubt him?'

'No. He's been wonderful, a great help to us. I don't know how we could have managed without him in recent years.'

'Does he do work both inside and outside the house?'

'He looks after everything for us, mostly outside. We usually have a maid come in every day for indoor work. She's been off sick for a while, though; we're looking for someone new.'

'Someone older perhaps?'

Frau Sachs nodded with a sad smile. 'Yes, someone a little older, over forty-five.'

'Don't worry, Frau Sachs, I'm not here to enforce the new race laws.' Jews were now forbidden to employ a German woman under the age of forty-five in their home.

'I can't understand it, I'm afraid.'

Nor could Seb.

'You know, officer, we've employed many local people over the years and we've treated them well, with good pay. I thought the villagers liked us, for they were always happy to accept our money. But now they won't come near us and we're shunned. That's why we've decided to move to Weimar.'

'But Xaver Knorr has stood by you?'

'Yes. We depend on him. My husband isn't ageing well and isn't capable of physical work. Nor am I the person I once was. We ran this place as a home but also a small farm.

Moritz was an art dealer, so I did most of the work here, helped by others. Now our livestock has had to be sold and in a week or two we'll be gone.'

'How long have you lived here?'

'Since I married Moritz. He was born in this house. It's been in his family for almost a hundred years. My husband was an infantry officer in the Army Group Rupprecht and fought bravely for Germany. Iron Cross first class. But that seems to make no difference to people's opinion of us. To them his heroism for the Fatherland means nothing. We are not German in their eyes.'

'I'm sorry.'

'Thank you. That's very kind of you.'

'I hope Weimar treats you better. Now where is this man Knorr?'

They looked in the hay-barn, the tack room, the old byre and then they went around the house, Frau Sachs calling out Knorr's name as they went. In all the rooms, Seb was struck by the absence of furniture and ornaments. It was all rather sad. Finally, they ended up back in the kitchen and she put the coffee on.

'I would like Herr Knorr's address in the village.'

'Yes, I can give you that.'

As the coffee brewed, the door opened and a small, frail man in his sixties appeared, his grey head bowed and his hands shaking.

'This is my husband, officer. Moritz, this is a police detective from Munich. He wishes to talk to Xaver about some matter.'

'Really? What has he done?'

'I'm sorry, but as I told your wife, it's not a matter I can discuss. I'll look for him at his home.'

'Been up to his tricks, has he?'

'What do you mean, sir?'

'Always was a sly one, that fellow. You can see it in his eyes. You'd never listen, though, would you, mother?'

Selma Sachs gently eased her husband from the room. 'Go back to your writing, Moritz, and leave this to me.'

The old man shuffled off, shaking his head.

'What did he mean by that? Why did he call Knorr sly? And what are these tricks?'

'My husband imagines things, officer. He thinks I'm his mother. He sits all day and writes nonsense. He's not well. The doctor says it's his heart and early senility.'

'Do you have children?'

'Yes, three of them. Two sons and a daughter. But they're grown up and have moved away. We don't see them as often as we'd like.'

'Just to go back a step. Your husband might not be his old self, but he seemed to have strong opinions about Xaver Knorr.'

'It's nothing, really. He confuses him with someone else. I deal with the house and estate now, and I promise you that Xaver is perfectly honest.' She was pouring coffee. 'Sugar? Cream?'

'Black will be fine, thank you. One more question and then I'll leave you alone. Have you ever met any friends of your man Knorr?'

'In the past he's brought in people from the village to help, for instance when we had cattle he would have assistance moving them up to the summer pasture, also to cut the hay, but I don't remember anyone in particular – just casual labour. Local men looking to earn a few more marks.'

'A man called Theodor Krieger? Does that name mean anything to you?'

'No, sir. I don't think I've ever heard that name.'

The coffee was hot but Seb drank it anyway. He took his leave of Selma Sachs with Xaver Knorr's address in his pocket.

As Seb drove away, it occurred to him that Frau Sachs had been remarkably accommodating and very quick to allow him into her house and explain about the move to Weimar.

As if it were all rehearsed.

17

Xaver Knorr's house was a decent property with a plot of land for outbuildings of its own. He wasn't home so Seb spoke to a neighbour who was fighting a losing battle shovelling snow from his path.

'Try the bar.'

'Which is where?'

'Just across the road, opposite the church. You can't miss it.'

The bar was smoky and small, a place for locals, not tourists. It reeked of farmyards and bonfires, and snow had been brought in on boots. Apart from the barman, the only occupants were three customers sitting together around a corner table. One of the men was in knee-length leather shorts in defiance of the weather; the other two were in long working men's trousers.

Seb approached them. 'Is one of you gentlemen Xaver Knorr?'

They all looked at each other, then one spoke up. He had a long-stemmed pipe in his hand, cropped hair and a broad Bismarck moustache. 'Who wants to know?'

Seb produced his badge. 'Wolff, captain of detectives, Munich.'

'Good to meet you, Herr Wolff.' The man continued, 'What do you want Herr Knorr for?'

'That's my business. Are you Knorr?'

'Maybe I am, maybe I'm not. Let me know what this is about, and I might think of telling you.'

Seb turned to the other two, who were smirking.

'Which one of you is it?'

'He's not very friendly, is he, this fancy cop?' It was the one with the Bismarck moustache again. 'And what's he doing so far from Munich? We don't like big-city types, do we, boys?'

Seb made his mind up. Bismarck moustache was Xaver Knorr. 'It's you. Come on, let's have you outside.'

'The way I see it, there's three of us and one of you. Must think you're tough, detective.'

'Take it easy,' Seb said. He could see that this could easily spin out of control. The three men had obviously had a lot to drink and had decided to make this difficult. 'I just want a few words with you in private.'

'I've got no secrets from my friends here. Think of them as my legal counsel.'

Hopes of a peaceful solution to this confrontation were evaporating. These men were enjoying the sport. This was fun for them; mock the cop, try to intimidate the outsider, see if they could break his nerve.

That wasn't going to happen.

'You have two choices, Knorr. You'll come and talk with me in a private place or I'll haul you to the Police Presidium for formal questioning, followed by a few days or weeks in protective custody.'

'Are you threatening me?'

Seb pulled out his Walther PPK and pointed it at Knorr. 'Damned right I am. Get out of that chair and come with me.'

'You wouldn't shoot an unarmed man.'

'Try me.' These three men had been drinking heavily and clearly had no respect for authority. It was always better to head off trouble before it started, so if that meant putting a bullet in a hand or foot, Seb wouldn't hesitate. He had fired enough lethal shots in the war not to be fazed by inflicting a couple of painful flesh wounds.

Knorr was powerfully built, but Seb reached forward and grabbed him by his coat collar, pulling him from the chair. Knorr lost his balance and fell towards the floor, crunching his shoulder and crying out. His pipe flew from his hand and skidded across the stone flags, tipping out burning tobacco and ash.

The bartender gazed across but said nothing, all the while polishing a glass. He was clearly used to trouble and knew it was wise not to get involved.

'Get up,' Seb ordered.

The other two men were rising from their chairs as though ready to come to their friend's assistance. 'Not you, just him.' Seb ranged his pistol at each of them in turn. He yanked Knorr to his feet, then dragged him towards the door.

'You two. Stay where you are or you'll be in Dachau by nightfall. And you' – he pointed the gun at the bartender – 'keep out of this or I'll close the place down.'

The bartender put his hands in the air. 'Nothing to do with me, chief.'

Knorr was clutching his shoulder and trying to shake off Seb's grip, but Seb had the upper hand now and opened the door, allowing a gust of snow to blow in. He pulled him out into the street and pushed him up against the wall.

'Any more trouble from you, Knorr, and I'll shoot your balls off. Do you understand?'

'Go fuck your mother.'

Seb smacked the gun into the side of the man's head. He stumbled again. The blow hadn't been hard enough to cause serious damage, but it might just knock some sense into his beer-addled brain.

'Tell me about Theodor Krieger.'

'What? What are you talking about?' He had his hand up to his temple, his mouth twisted into a grimace.

'You heard me.' Seb swung the Walther back in a short arc as though he would hit again. Knorr flinched.

'What about him? What do you want to know about Theo?'

'When did you last see him?'

'Why? What's he done? Where is he?'

'You tell me, Knorr. Tell me everything you know about your friend Krieger. What are you both up to?' He lifted his chin towards the bar-room door. 'Your friends in there – are they part of it? I bet they are. You start talking or I'll haul you all in, alive or dead. And either way I'll be congratulated by my colleagues.'

'I've nothing to say to you.'

The snow was sliding down the back of Seb's neck and he didn't like it. Knorr's house was no more than a hundred metres away and the Lancia was parked outside.

Seb hit Knorr again. This time a fist into the stomach, so that he doubled over with a gasp. Seb didn't enjoy doing it. It wasn't in his nature to beat up suspects, but his instinct told him that, with just him against three, the odds weren't good. That's why he had pulled out the gun and why he was giving Knorr a light going-over. There was no other way of dealing with this little problem.

'Come on, you're going home.' Seb pushed him from behind, the pistol levelled at the back of Knorr's head. The man tried to resist but slid on the snow and lost his footing. Behind them, the bar door opened and the other two men came out. This time they had weapons: one, a hammer; the other, a knife.

Seb had been expecting them. He fired a shot between the feet of the one in front, catching the edge of his boot. The man leapt in the air, and they both backed off.

'I won't miss again.'

*

Knorr's front door was unlocked. Seb pushed him inside and slammed the door shut behind them. The main room was a large kitchen living area, warmed by a *Kachelofen* wood-burner tiled in blue and white. Apart from that, the place was not exactly homely or comfortable.

'Sit down.'

Knorr was almost subdued now, and he did what he was told.

Seb found a glass near the sink and filled it with water, then handed it to Xaver Knorr. 'Drink this. Then we're going to have a conversation and you're going to answer all my questions.'

With somewhat surprising obedience, Knorr sipped the water.

'First,' Seb said, 'is anyone else in this house?'

'Why would there be?'

'Just answer the question.'

'No, there's no one else.'

'Do you have a wife?'

'No.'

'A mistress?'

'If I had, I wouldn't tell you.'

'Do you often go into the woods in the Scharnitz Pass?'

That pulled Knorr up short. He didn't like the question. It meant something to him and he was struggling to find a suitable answer.

'Well?'

'I've never been there. Why would I go there?'

'You and Theo and maybe your other friends. A boys' day out. Perhaps a little picnic? Shoot some wildlife for the pot or its fur, maybe a feather for your hat? A little trip across the pass into Austria perhaps? You tell me, Knorr: why *do* you go to the Scharnitz Pass?'

'I don't.'

'Old smugglers' route, I suppose. What are you bringing in? What does Austria have that the Third Reich doesn't?'

'Are you going to tell me what this is about?'

'I suspect you already know. This is about your partner in crime, Theodor Krieger. Remember him? Oh, and I'm sure you know his wife, Petra, and his mistress, Traudl. They certainly know you and I'm not sure either of them likes you very much.'

'Has something happened to Theo? Is that what you're saying?'

'Did you have a falling-out? Disagreement among thieves?'

'I'm not a thief and I've never had a falling-out with Theo. We're old friends from schooldays. He's a brother to me. If something's happened to him . . . please, let me know.'

For a brief moment, Seb began to wonder. Was this man genuine? Yes, he was undoubtedly a thug, but maybe he really didn't know anything about Krieger's death on the hillside.

'Drink the water. Sober up. I've got bad news for you.'

Knorr was clutching the glass, but he didn't drink. His eyes met Seb's for the first time since the bar. He was silent, expectant.

'Krieger's dead. His body was found in the woods on the Scharnitz Pass. But you already knew that, didn't you?'

The man's mouth opened but no words came out. If he was acting, he was good at it. Perhaps he should be in that film they were making.

'If you genuinely had nothing to do with his death, I'm sorry to have to give you this news.'

'Dear God, Theo dead?'

Seb nodded slowly. Let it sink in; let the man mull it over.

'How?'

'How do you think? Take a wild guess.'

'Murdered?'

'Right first time.'

'Who did it?'

'I was hoping you could help me with that.'

'How was he killed?'

'Shot.'

'When did this happen?'

'Early yesterday. You were meeting around midnight for your little jaunt into the woods – don't you remember?'

'I didn't see him yesterday. We had no arrangement to meet.'

'Traudl Schramm suggested he was meeting you.' It was a simple lie but worth trying. Something had to give, because this was going nowhere.

'Does Traudl know?'

Seb nodded.

'His wife's behind it. The bitch. She hired someone to do this.'

'We're keeping all lines of inquiry open. I'm looking for a killer and I'm looking for a motive. You're a suspect, Herr Knorr, and so you would do well to tell me everything you know about Theodor Krieger. The sooner we find the man with the gun, the sooner you'll be in the clear. But, before we go any further, I have to tell you one thing: you will not mention this murder to anyone, not to your friends in the bar, not to your closest relative or lover. Do you understand?'

'You can't keep a thing like this secret.'

'We can and we will. A few kilometres from here, the Winter Olympics have just been declared open by the Führer and he's made it clear that nothing – absolutely nothing – will detract from the peace and harmony of the Games. There will be no murders, no robberies, nothing of an unpleasant nature.'

In his last conversation with Ruff, Seb had been told that, at the exact time Hitler was declaring the Games open in Garmisch-Partenkirchen, two warplanes were crashing into each other over Munich, killing several people on the ground, injuring many and causing massive destruction.

It was chaos, a huge incident. In the normal course of events, it would be a big story, one of the most sensational of the year. Everyone in Munich would know, but, with the Olympics under way, it wouldn't be a story at all. Perhaps three or four paragraphs consigned to the bottom of page twelve in the newspapers.

'Theo's friends have to know.'

'No, there will be complete silence. Anyone who mentions the death of Krieger, let alone the fact that he was murdered, will be locked up for a very long time.'

Knorr was silent, his jaw clenched tight.

'I'm glad you understand. Now tell me: who killed Theodor Krieger?'

18

As Hans Winter entered the Dachau shunt room, he was shaking. He hadn't expected it to be like this. For the sake of keeping his identity secure, the guards were not to be told that he was a member of the BPP, which meant that he had been subject to abuse ever since he was handed over to them.

The only person at the camp who knew his true identity was the commandant, Heinrich Deubel. To everyone else, he was Hans Winter, Communist. There was no time for false identification to be produced.

'He's a Jew,' one of the guards said, looking Winter up and down.

'He's just scrawny.'

'No, he's a Jew. Let's take a look at his prick. Clothes off, Winter.'

Winter dropped his trousers, removed his shirt, tie and jacket, and stood there in his underpants and socks. The room was bitter.

'What did I tell you to do, Winter?'

'To undress.'

'To undress, sir.'

'Yes, sir.'

'Then do it before I kick you in your worthless ball-sack. Or do you want me to remove the rest of your clothes for you?'

Winter removed his socks, then stepped out of his pants. The guards stared at him, then grinned at each other. The smaller of the two grabbed hold of his penis, held it tight for a few seconds, then pulled back the foreskin. It was deliberately rough and Winter recoiled.

'Well, well, there's a surprise. A Commie who's not a Jew.' Finally, he released the member.

'Not an impressive object, is it? I've seen bigger slugs in my mother's windowbox.'

'Now your wristwatch: take it off. All your possessions will be kept here until you've atoned for your sins and become a good German. But that will be explained to you in due course. For the moment, you'll follow me to the showers for delousing.'

There was no heating, and the walk, barefoot on concrete, was intensely cold. First, his head was shaved in silence by another inmate wielding a blunt razor, then he was herded into a freezing shower where he shivered so desperately he thought his heart might pack up.

After five minutes, he was ordered out. He wasn't given a towel, but was marched back to the shunt room, naked and colder than he had ever been. He was given a thin shirt, a rough canvas suit and wooden clogs. The outfit was totally inadequate for the weather.

One of the guards handed him a toothbrush, razor, bar of soap, tin cup and tin plate. 'Look after them; you won't get replacements.'

'Yes, sir.'

'This is unusual but orders have come down that you're to be assigned to Barrack A, Dormitory 4. Why should that happen, Winter? Are you something special? A gang leader? Why should the commandant care which barrack you're in?'

'I don't know, sir.'

The guard slapped his face with both hands and grinned. 'No matter; enjoy your stay at the Hotel Dachau. The food's shit and the beds are hard, but apart from that it's just like the Vier Jahreszeiten.'

Winter had been assigned one of the top bunks right next to Friedrich Brauer's. Before arriving, the camp commandant had given him a bit of background on the man.

'It seems he was denounced by his son-in-law for passing around Communist leaflets at his place of work, and also sticking up Red posters in Grainau, Farchant and Gapa. He worked on the railways and the station master confirmed that he was a troublemaker, always trying to foment strikes and go-slows. Very anti-Hitler. We're working the bastard hard, and he's not getting out any time soon.'

'Could he have arranged a murder from inside the camp?'

'There are occasional visits, but I have none recorded for Brauer. Inmates are released when their behaviour warrants it, so it would be possible to carry out messages on another's behalf.'

Winter's arrival in the dormitory – which had bunks for fifty-four men in tiers of three, all in a single structure – coincided with the prisoners' return from their day's work. They were all exhausted and hungry, and no one was interested in conversation. Winter was sitting on the edge of his bunk, legs hanging over the side. Brauer looked up at him.

'Who are you?'

'Winter. Hans Winter. Number 7482.'

'What are you doing on Blindorf's bunk, 7482?'

'The guard told me to come here. Who's Blindorf?'

One of the other inmates intervened. 'He was taken out of line, Friedrich. I think he's being released. That's what the guard said.'

'Bollocks. Blindorf is in for the long haul. Why would he be out before me?'

Winter said nothing. He knew the truth: Blindorf had been moved to the punishment bunker for the duration of Winter's stay, thus freeing up the bunk next to Brauer's.

'Lucky bastard if he *is* out,' Brauer said. He looked up at Winter. 'What you in for? Red triangle – political, then.'

'Fighting for political freedom against the Nazi swine.'

'Marxist?'

'Red through and through, like my father before me.'

'You're not Bavarian. Where are you from?'

'Dortmund.'

'Well, welcome to Bavaria. Come on, get your plate and cup and you can sample the delights of Dachau cuisine. Have you got any money?'

'No. It was taken away in the shunt room.'

'But you've got people outside – people who can pay for better food to be sent in?'

'No.'

'More fool you. You're stuck with Dachau slop.'

'Where do we go?'

'Follow me. Then it's evening roll-call. You'll enjoy that.'

Seb got no useful information from Xaver Knorr. Half a dozen names of mutual acquaintances and friends, but no evidence of enmity that might lead to death. Knorr seemed certain that Krieger's widow and her father were somehow responsible for the murder.

Driving back through worsening conditions, Seb turned right at the village of Farchant and stopped outside the Krieger home.

Petra Krieger took a long time answering the door.

'Have I caught you at a bad time, Frau Krieger?'

'I was tired. All the washing and cooking. The kids are out with their friends, so I took the chance for a lie-down.'

'And who can blame you. May I come in?'

'I've got to go out soon.'

'I won't keep you long.'

She stepped aside and allowed him in. They went to the cold, pristine front room. He didn't bother to sit down. 'I just wanted to bring you up to date with our investigations into your husband's murder. I'm afraid we haven't found the killer so far, but I have spoken to a couple of people. First, your husband's mistress, Traudl Schramm. Also his friend Xaver Knorr.'

He smiled at her and said no more. The silence was palpable until she was forced to break it.

'What did they say? Denied everything, I suppose.'

'They both accused you of organising or being in some way implicated in your husband's death as an act of vengeance.'

'They would say that.'

'Are you suggesting they've been lying?'

'The English Whore would say anything to do me down.'

'Tell me about your father. I believe he's in Dachau. You didn't mention that before.'

'I didn't think it was relevant, captain. Yes, my bastard of a husband denounced him to the BPP, and he was hauled away and consigned to the camp without trial.'

'What crime is he alleged to have committed?'

'The crime of politics. He does not like the Nazi regime.'

'He must be very angry with your husband.'

'I'm sure he is, but I've not had a chance to talk with him. Dachau is a difficult journey from Farchant.'

'Not so difficult. Straightforward train journey to Munich, then one change to Dachau. Anyway, your father. There must be other like-minded men, friends of your father, who would happily kill your husband for what he did.'

'My father is a peaceful man. He has no such friends.'

'You keep a very tidy house, Frau Krieger. Where did your husband store his papers?'

'We have another little room by the kitchen.'

'Then please show me.'

She looked alarmed. 'What do our papers have to do with this?'

'I won't know until I look at them. You want to find the killer, surely?'

'Of course, but our papers are private.'

'I'll decide what's private. Come on.'

As he moved towards the door, he heard a noise, something like a door clicking shut. 'Is there someone else in the house, Frau Krieger?'

She stiffened uncomfortably. 'No, I told you, the boys are with friends.'

'Let's go and have a look, shall we? Perhaps you have a burglar.'

'Captain Wolff, I'm very busy. I have to go out and I have to get supper ready for my children. I'm behind with my chores because of my little sleep. Could we not do all this at some other date?'

'It won't take a moment. Better safe than sorry.'

The man was hiding in a wardrobe in the Kriegers' bedroom. He was wearing socks and underwear and had his other clothes and shoes clutched in his arms. Seb looked at him; the man stared back, wide-eyed.

'I think I've found the culprit, Frau Krieger,' Seb said. 'For some reason he seems to have got undressed. Not usual behaviour for the burglars I've encountered in the past.'

Her body stiffened, half embarrassed, half indignant. 'Why shouldn't I take a lover? Theodor slept with everything in a skirt.'

'What's your name?' Seb demanded of the man as he stepped gingerly from the wardrobe.

'Feld, sir. Horst Feld.'

'What have you told him, Frau Krieger?'

'Nothing. I have said nothing.'

'Feld? Do you know what has happened to this lady's husband?'

'No, sir. He must be with his troop.'

'Are you married?'

'No, sir.'

'I imagine you would like to marry Frau Krieger if she were free.'

'Perhaps, sir. I don't know. I love her very much.'

He was a miserable creature, his vest straining from a beer belly that overhung his pants, and a face that had consumed too much sausage and cake.

'Get dressed and we'll talk some more. Now then, Frau Krieger, your papers?'

19

The last meal of the day at Dachau was vegetable soup and black bread. The portions were quite generous, but it was bland, unseasoned and thin, with little in the way of nutritional value. Winter took no more than a few mouthfuls, then handed the rest to Brauer.

'How did they find you, Brauer, the BPP, I mean?'

'Same story as most people here – denounced. The BPP don't have to hunt us; there are more than enough enemies among our own families, friends and communities to hand us over, either because they hate us or in hope of an easy life in return. The dawn knock at the door . . . Is that how it was for you, Winter?'

'Just like that. I was denounced, too – by my nephew. Fully fledged Hitler Youth. If I could find a way to do it, I would have the little swine killed. One less Nazi in the world would be a bonus, don't you think?'

'Put your anger away, Winter, or you won't survive here.'

'That's easy for you to say, but this was my sister's boy. I had always been good to him. I tried to be something of a father to him after his own father – my brother-in law – died on the road.' Winter surprised himself by the ease with which he lied.

'I wish your story was unique, but it's not.'

'Surely you want to find out who shopped you and exact some revenge?'

'Don't assume to know what I want, Winter. And be careful how you speak to people here. Who's to say there aren't spies among us?'

'I can't help it, Brauer. I'm eaten up by this hunger, this thirst for retribution. But what can I do, stuck here?'

The bell went.

'Roll-call,' Brauer said. Everyone moved at once. No one sauntered. Double pace or accept the blows, that was the rule. 'It's going to be a cold one in this snow,' he continued, as they ran to put their cups and plates back in the barrack-room. 'One hour standing to attention is considered merciful. Four hours is the record since I've been here.'

In the event, it was almost two hours of cold, shivering pain. An older man two rows in front of Winter swayed for five minutes, then collapsed. A guard came over and beat him with his crop, ordering him to get to his feet. Only after a minute of this did he realise he was getting no reaction from the old man: he was dead.

Winter was shocked. In the Gestapo in Dortmund and even here in Munich in the BPP, he had sent men to this place. What sort of swine did that? The merciless Hans Winter of old was becoming a stranger to him, as though they were two different people.

He might have troubles of his own outside this camp, but now they seemed trivial compared with the fate of these three thousand or so men – some strong, many weak, some young, some old, others sick. All overworked, malnourished, denied justice and scared. He wouldn't be here for long, but what did the future hold for the other poor bastards?

When they were finally allowed to return to their dormitories, they had just enough time to brush their teeth in the two basins shared by fifty-four men; then, at eight thirty sharp, they crawled into their pathetic beds and the lights were extinguished.

Their bedding was hopelessly deficient. As the temperature

dropped each man shivered, none could sleep properly. Some whimpered, others groaned from the biting cold.

Winter lay on his bunk with his eyes open, his hands and feet frozen, his body shaking, while those around him struggled to sleep. In the end, they all managed to get a sleep of sorts, some snoring and farting, others escaping into dreams of a long-lost home. The dreams, even the nightmares, were always preferable to this place, where the monsters were real.

Beside him, Friedrich Brauer lay on his back, breathing deeply, his breath vaporising. There was nothing to dislike about the man, nothing to suggest he had organised his son-in-law's murder. He would try to converse with him more tomorrow, just in case he had missed something – just in case Brauer was a good deceiver.

He had clearly managed to live a covert life in the world of forbidden politics; perhaps he was still cautious.

In the meantime, Winter had a secret task of his own to perform, one that he had not even mentioned to Captain Wolff. It wasn't simple courage that had brought him to this place; it was desperation.

He was looking for a Jew. And he had seen a couple of likely candidates in the eating hall: the Star of David sewn on to the breast of their canvas jackets was the giveaway.

Very thoughtful of the Nazis to provide him with such a useful identification tool. Red triangle for political prisoners, green for common criminals, pink for homosexuals and the star for Jews.

Made it all so much easier.

A servant from Schloss Stark was waiting for Seb at the guest house. He had brought three evening suits of slightly different styles and waited while Seb tried them on and made a decision. He also provided a selection of shirts, white ties and black patent shoes.

Howard Jack had estimated his size with great accuracy.

Hexie looked on in amusement. 'How does it feel to be a millionaire, Seb?'

'Shame they didn't send gowns for *you*.'

'Oh, I'm sure they know better than to try that with a woman. Anyway, I found something delightful. Fine shops in Gapa. You'll see it soon enough.'

'I can't wait.'

It had been a long, wearying day. His conversation with Petra Krieger and her dull lover Horst Feld had almost robbed him of the will to live. They gazed at each other like turtle doves and answered his questions in monosyllables.

If either was capable of murder, they concealed it remarkably well. It was difficult to imagine them organising breakfast, let alone a major crime.

As for the family's papers, they showed nothing. Receipts, pay slips, rent notices, Krieger's SS documentation, his Nazi Party membership, birth and marriage certificates. Ordinary stuff.

The day's encounters had drained Seb, so the thought of making the journey to Schloss Stark and enduring hours of polite conversation and dancing was the last thing he wanted to do. And yet the detective in him badly needed to be there. He had to talk to Elena Lang again. Hexie was right: somehow he had to protect the woman.

'What now?' Hexie said. 'We have hours to wait.'

'I wouldn't mind some sleep, but actually I'm going to see if I can locate Jurgen. Just to say hello without embarrassing him. He'll probably be freezing in a tent somewhere nearby.'

*

After a long and confusing trip around the twin towns, he found Jurgen in the Kurpark, helping direct guests to the ballroom for the official celebratory banquet, a stiff and dull affair. The snow had eased off, leaving crisp air to breathe and oily slush to trudge through.

Father and son nodded to each other.

'I saw you at the opening ceremony,' Seb said.

'I saw you, too. What are you doing here, old man?'

'Working. Same as you.' He smiled, wishing there wasn't this awkwardness between them. Awkwardness? That was the least of it. At times it seemed outright hostility – an unbridgeable ravine. 'Could you get away for ten minutes or so? There's something I'd very much like to talk about.'

'Let me guess. I'm wasting my time in the Hitler Youth and I should be studying for university. Same old refrain.'

'No, not that. Please can you get away, just for a few minutes? It's important.'

Jurgen looked around and caught the eye of his troop leader. 'I'll ask.'

He sauntered over and, after a brief conversation, returned. 'All right, half an hour, no more. Are you going to buy me coffee?'

'There's a café near here.'

The café was about to close but the proprietor said he'd stay open for a little while longer and, yes, they could have coffees and they had a few cakes left.

'Just black coffee.'

'With cream and sugar for me,' Jurgen said. 'So what is it, old man? What's so important that you drag me away from my work?'

Seb really didn't know how to go about this. He welled up merely thinking about it, so he said nothing, just took the letter from his pocket and placed it on the table and pushed it towards his son.

'What's this?'

'Read it.'

Jurgen's eyes met his father's and quickly turned away, clearly overcome by the emotion he saw there. He was looking at the handwritten envelope and must have noticed the Berlin postmark. Then, without another word, he took out the letter and read it slowly, his eyes vainly blinking away tears as he did so.

It could not have taken more than a minute or two to read, yet he studied it for five minutes before finally looking up at his father's face again.

Seb still didn't know what to say. The thought of the letter was too much for him to bear, so what must it be like for his son? Of all the relationships in the world, the mother/child is the most sacred and most deep. A man might feel great sadness at his father's death but when his mother dies he will howl with despair, however old he is.

At exactly the same moment, they got up from the table and fell into each other's arms.

What was there to say? There were no words. Not at the moment – perhaps later or another day.

20

It was difficult to imagine that the ancient walls of Schloss Stark had ever contained so much human life. The immense Paradise Hall where Seb had been received in echoing isolation was now alive and full. Its painted ceiling depicting the temptation of Eve glowed in the light of hundreds of candles. An orchestra played Strauss, but the music was almost drowned out by the constant hum of conversation and laughter.

It was indeed a fairytale, as Howard Jack had promised. The waiting staff were dressed in dazzling costumes, acting as characters from the tales of the Brothers Grimm.

Cinderella was there in her rags, with her broomstick. At her side, almost like a conjoined twin, there was another Cinderella in a ball gown and crystal shoes.

Rapunzel with her long, long hair. Hansel and Gretel in lederhosen and dirndl. The Frog King, The White Snake, The Maiden without Hands, Snow White, Rumpelstiltskin, The Golden Goose and dozens of others.

They swarmed like bees, handing out nectar and ambrosia in the form of vintage wines and morsels of caviar and smoked meats. They asked to be referred to by the name of their character, helpfully displayed about their person.

'Champagne, sir?'

How could he refuse? Hexie certainly wasn't going to. 'Thank you, Hansel,' he said.

The waiter smiled and handed over two glasses.

Hexie was wearing dark blue satin, off the shoulder, and

she did look gorgeous. Even Seb had surprised himself by enjoying the sensation of his reflection, puffed up in his beautifully tailored evening wear. He had expected to feel out of place among the rich, successful and powerful, but, no, he belonged here. Both he and Hexie belonged here. Why shouldn't they walk among these people with their heads held high?

Unless he was deceiving himself, he had the strong impression that no one was looking at them with anything other than admiration, probably wondering who they were among so many well-known faces.

'Hexie Schuler, you look ravishing. An absolute goddess. I knew you would.'

It was Howard Jack. He had spotted them as soon as they arrived and had woven his way through the crowds, as sinuous as the serpent in Eden.

'Thank you.'

'And even you, Seb Wolff, have managed to scrub up into something quite respectable. Well done.'

'That's down to you, Mr Jack. Thank you for organising the clothes.'

'My pleasure. I raided Werner's closet. I could see that he was about your size. Now who do you want to meet? Why look, there's Elena Lang with Harcourt and their entourage. Shall we go and say hello, hobnob with the stars of the flickering screen?'

Alan Harcourt had his customary cigar gripped in his left hand. He didn't recognise Seb, nor was he interested in him, but he instantly latched on to Hexie.

'You're an actress, aren't you? What have I seen you in lately?'

Hexie wasn't stupid. She knew when she was being flattered or wooed. '*The Princess of Persia*,' she said.

'And you were dazzling in it, my dear. Who's your agent? I must have you for my next film.'

She laughed out loud, having invented *The Princess of Persia* in a split-second moment of inspiration. 'My agent? Oh, I'm with Sebastian Wolff Associates. You must know them.'

'Of course I do. Remind me, are they based in Munich or Berlin?'

'Munich and New York. But Sebastian is right here at my side. Why don't you make a deal with him now? My engagements diary is rather full for the next year or two, but perhaps he could make space for us in your next film. What's it called?'

Harcourt's face darkened as he realised she was mocking him. Disappearing in a cloud of smoke, he turned his shoulder on her and went back to conversing with his male star Gary Tate.

Seb grinned at her. That was his Hexie. Took no prisoners.

And then Elena Lang was there, smiling at them both. 'Are you going to introduce me?' she said.

'Fräulein Lang, this is my fiancée, Hexie Schuler.'

The women shook hands. 'I'm very pleased to meet you. Captain Wolff has told me all about you. I think he is very much in love with you.'

'I quite like him, too. Sometimes.'

Seb had had enough of this. 'And tonight I'm just Sebastian or Seb, not Captain Wolff. I'm off work for a few hours.' He didn't believe it for a moment. There were secrets here. If there was a threat to Elena Lang, the chances were that someone in Paradise Hall knew about it.

Harcourt's assistant Olivia Sands slid into view and more introductions were made.

'I have to thank you, captain, for putting our minds at ease. It was all a panic over nothing.'

'Just doing my job, Miss Sands. And in truth it turned

out rather well for me, because here I am at this wonderful celebration.'

She smiled. 'Always good to have a policeman close at hand. Who knows when a riot might break out?'

'I'm not a policeman tonight. I refuse to be. But, tell me, is all going well with the film now you're in the mountains? Was the snowfall a godsend or a disaster? I wondered if your visibility might have been restricted.'

'It's been perfect. We were above the clouds up on Zugspitze. Blue skies there. But it's been exhausting work. Very cold. I believe we got some wonderful shots – fabulous close-ups with Elena and Gary. Mr Harcourt is thrilled. One more day up there – or two at the most – and we should have a wrap.'

'If there's any way I can help, just ask. I'm likely to be in Gapa for a day or two.' He bowed his head and turned away, leaving Olivia to talk with Hexie while he gave his attention back to Elena Lang. 'Might we have a brief word alone?'

'Here? I'm not sure how that will work.'

'What you said worried me greatly.'

'I was just being foolish. When you're on screen in a big film, you attract a lot of attention, and not all of it good. Sometimes it gets to me.'

'Are you sure that's all?'

She grimaced. 'This life, to an outsider, seems so glamorous, but the truth is a lot more mundane and rather grubby. I would like a quieter existence, alone with my books in a university library or with a Bunsen burner and test tubes in a lab.'

'But a threat *has* been made. You weren't making that up. Did someone threaten you to your face or by other means – a phone call, a letter?'

'Please, Seb, I was probably imagining it. I shouldn't have said anything.' She touched his arm. 'Hexie is even more beautiful than I imagined. I thought she was a lucky girl to have you. Now I know that you're the lucky one.'

'I'm not going to argue with that.' She was changing the subject and he felt powerless. How do you protect someone who won't be protected?

'So just enjoy the evening. Stuffy old Strauss will be finishing soon and then there will be dancing. Perhaps you'll reserve one for me if Hexie will allow it. For now, however, I must go and find Sophie and Werner to pay my respects. They're perfect hosts, aren't they?'

A low unanimous gasp filled the room and conversation descended to a murmur: a newcomer was arriving.

All eyes turned to the entranceway as the diminutive but instantly recognisable figure of Joseph Goebbels appeared with his entourage. Applause – clapping and shouts and cheers – broke out to welcome the propaganda minister. Many threw out their right arms in salute.

At his side, stern-faced but smiling, walked his glamorous wife, Magda. They were accompanied by Werner and Sophie von Stark, and Gruppenführer Jena in full SS uniform with a small unidentifiable woman in his wake. With them were the men in charge of the Games: Karl Ritter von Halt, president of the German Olympic Committee, and Henri de Baillet-Latour, president of the IOC, and the rest.

In close attendance were Unity Mitford and Fritz Mannheim, the latter also in full SS uniform.

Goebbels smiled and waved, then patted the air down to quiet the applause. Gradually, people looked away and the conversation restarted.

'Quite an entrance,' Hexie said.

'Indeed.'

'But did you notice the Mouse-Frau, Herr Wolff?' It was Howard Jack, suddenly at his shoulder again.

'I'm not sure what or who you're referring to, Mr Jack.'

'The Gruppenführer's little wife, of course. Frau Jena. No one knows her first name because he never introduces her. Such a sad creature.'

What could Seb say? He couldn't admonish an Englishman for his freedom of speech, nor was there any point in warning him that such talk could cause him problems, because it wouldn't. All Seb could do was smile non-committally.

'It's the same with all of them, all your top Nazis,' Jack continued. 'They have their mistresses or boyfriends but drag out the Mouse-Frauen when these big events take place. They just love the public veneer of respectability that a wife brings. Why, even Joe Goebbels has brought the missus out to play tonight, leaving poor Elena to fend for herself.'

'You are very indiscreet, Howard.'

'It's fun, isn't it? Enraging the Nazis.'

'You should be careful.'

'Indeed I should. I might get run over. In fact, it almost happened.'

'Really?'

'Didn't you hear? Darling Elena and I were walking near her hotel earlier this evening when one of those big bloody Mercedes lost control and shot up on the pavement. Missed her by half an inch. Elena was horribly shaken.'

'Dear God, could it have been deliberate?'

'Who knows? But I tell you this: the bastard didn't stop. Full-uniform bloody stormtrooper – they think they own the world. Elena could barely speak. It was a damned close call, detective.'

Seb and Hexie mingled and separated as they became involved with different groups. Seb smiled and nodded as people spoke to him, but really his mind was elsewhere. He was alarmed by Elena's near-miss. Accident? Murder attempt? Who could tell?

Mostly, however, he was thinking of Jurgen and the letter from Ulrike. The excitement of conflicting emotions coursing through the boy was plain to see. He couldn't take in the news, couldn't believe that he might really meet the woman who had brought him into the world.

When Seb and his son parted, the matter still hung in the air. 'This is very much up to you, Jurgen,' he said. 'You have the choice whether to meet her or not. I won't put pressure on you either way, but I know that if your grand-mama were to hear about this she would fight tooth and nail to stop you seeing your mother. My only advice is not to tell her. But I fear that she already suspects something, for she saw the postmark and probably recognised the hand.'

'Have you told Hexie?'

'No, only you.'

'Will you tell her?'

'I'll have to. But I doubt she'll be happy.'

Seb couldn't think of any other way to address this. He wanted to see Ulrike again, but would that be disloyal to Hexie? He didn't know.

The problem was made worse by the other difficulties crowding his brain: the mystery of Theodor Krieger's murder, his fears for Hans Winter undercover in Dachau, the unsettling matter of a threat to Elena Lang.

None of this was helped by the arrival of Joseph Goebbels. It merely served to remind him of the dangerous, toxic waters in which Elena swam.

In the early hours, the guests were invited to move out on to the battlements for a dazzling display of fireworks, shot skywards from across the valley into the dancing snowflakes.

Everyone had been given an umbrella on the way out to protect their expensive hairstyles and priceless gowns.

Seb stood apart, alone, his gaze fixed on the starbursts and blazing trails but not really seeing them for what they were.

Then they returned to Paradise Hall for more dancing to a very non-Nazi jazz band. Seb watched them for a while then looked around for Hexie. It was getting on for two in the morning and he wanted a couple of turns with her before they made their way back to the guest house.

Where had she got to?

A waiter dressed as some unidentifiable Grimm character passed by and Seb took a couple of canapés of crisp toast and caviar but turned down the offer of more champagne. Not a good idea to drive drunk in these conditions.

'Have you seen Elena?' Olivia Sands had appeared at his side.

'Not in the last hour or so – why?'

'I've been looking for her. We came in the same car from the Alpspitze and Harcourt wants us to get back there so we can make a reasonably early start in the morning. I can't see any sign of her.'

'I'm trying to find Hexie; let's look together.'

They found Hexie first. She was performing some wild dance moves with Howard Jack. The Englishman waved to Seb to come and join them, which he declined.

Elena was not so easy to locate. His first thought was that she had disappeared somewhere with Goebbels. That might make sense in light of their relationship. But with his wife present, how would that be possible?

No, they definitely weren't together, for there was Goebbels at a table with the top Olympics men and Werner von Stark. No sign of Elena nearby.

The crowd was beginning to thin slightly, but there were

still dozens of the younger set keen to dance until dawn. Unity was coming off the dance floor hand in hand with a young Englishman.

'Olivia, you simply must meet my old friend Peter Lunn. He's Britain's best skier – and he'll be sure to win the downhill tomorrow.' She was studiously ignoring Seb.

'So long as I beat the bloody Nazis, that's all I care about,' Lunn said.

Unity's gaze turned to Seb and he couldn't help noting the flash of disapproval in her eyes, but she didn't remove her hand from Lunn's. 'Don't listen to him. He's like Howard Jack, always trying to provoke me.'

'No, I'm not. It's nothing to do with you, Bobo. I just can't stand brutal dictatorships.' His voice was deliberately loud. He wanted to be heard by all around him. 'And nor should you.'

'Have you seen Elena?' Olivia interrupted.

'Not recently, but I'm sure she can look after herself.'

Seb and Olivia moved on through the throng. It was easy to lose sight of people here. Perhaps Elena had gone off to powder her nose or to a bedroom with a new lover. Or might she have just found another way back to the Alpspitze Hotel?

Those were the good options, but they didn't ease his fears.

'How do you know Unity Mitford?' Seb asked.

'Elena introduced us when I arrived. She knew about me and I had heard about her. I think she's becoming rather notorious.'

'That's not for me to say.'

'I quite understand. But where is she now? Elena, I mean?'

'She'll turn up.'

'Will she, captain? Are you sure?'

'You sound worried about her.'

'Aren't you?'

He looked at her and saw a hint of fear, the same he had seen in Elena's eyes.

'Is there something I should know, Miss Sands?'

She shook her head. 'Go back to your girl. I'll find Elena.'

Reluctantly, he let her go, his eyes following her into the crowd. His gaze drifted over to the table where Joseph Goebbels held court. Someone must have said something funny, for he was roaring with laughter.

21

Seb and Hexie arrived back at the Waxenstein Guest House at five o'clock in the morning, having still not found Elena Lang.

A hundred and twenty kilometres to the north, Hans Winter was being awakened from an unpleasant night's sleep in Dachau to an even less pleasant morning. The cold had bitten deep: he had heard strange noises, shivered in nightmarish dreams, half awake, half asleep, that took him down dark corridors of the soul.

The gloom from the single low-wattage light bulb made the sight of the man hanging from the rafters even more harrowing. Winter had to ask himself if he was awake now or whether this was yet another horrific dream. Then he realised that the noises in the night had been real. Scuffling, the creak of wood.

'You two,' the SS guard shouted at Winter and Brauer, who just happened to be standing nearest to the suicide, the other men having raced for a hurried turn using the two toilets. 'Cut this thing down and carry it to the infirmary. The rest of you breakfast, shave, then fall in for work detail.' He flung his dagger to the floor. 'Use this.'

The body was naked save for an undershirt. It was hanging from the shredded and knotted remnants of the man's canvas uniform. Winter looked at the corpse in horror. The eyes were open and bulging, the tongue protruding through blue lips. He supposed he must have seen this man the previous evening, but he had no recollection of him.

While Winter stood helplessly, wondering how to go about

this, Brauer had already climbed back to the top bunk and was leaning over, sawing at the taut fabric with the dagger. The body fell to the ground in a heap, the canvas still knotted around the neck.

Brauer jumped down from the bunk and handed the dagger back to the block leader, handle first.

'Get to it. Make it quick.'

'Yes, sir.'

The two men lifted the body, Winter gripping the legs under the knees, Brauer the head and the shoulders. The corpse was light, probably less than fifty kilos.

'Who was he?' Winter asked, as they hurried across the parade ground to the infirmary.

'A man. That's all that matters. A man who could no longer bear the loss of freedom and dignity. He wasn't the first and he won't be the last.'

They left the body in the infirmary for disposal and marched in double time to the eating hall for their porridge. Winter glanced towards the maintenance block and saw a sign painted across the roof: *There is one path to freedom. Its milestones are obedience, honesty, cleanliness, sobriety, hard work, discipline, truthfulness and love of your Fatherland.*

They had forgotten the second path: *death.*

'What work duty will we be on?'

'Something senseless, as always. Carrying stones from one site to another. Tomorrow we'll carry them back again. And so it goes on until we slit our throats with our razors or throw our bodies on to the electric wire. The criminals get the good jobs – cooking, carpentry, repairs. The rest of us? Our tasks are designed to break the soul. There is no way out of here, 7482. None.'

Breakfast was tasteless but filling. Winter saw his two Jews from the previous evening. One looked to be in his twenties

148

with smart, intelligent eyes. The other one was older, and, now that Winter looked closer, he seemed beaten. It had to be the younger man.

Winter wolfed down the last scrapings of his porridge, then made his way across to the Jew. 'Excuse me,' he said. 'You look familiar. Do I know you from outside?'

The man shrugged. 'Perhaps, but do I care?'

Winter thrust out his hand. 'Hans Winter. I'm sure I know you. Where are you from?'

'Schwabing. A short walk from here. Perhaps you'd like to come around for a beer one day.'

It was supposed to be a joke, so Winter affected to laugh. 'And you're in for the crime of being a Jew?'

'No, I'm in for tupping my Gentile girlfriend. Her father heard about it and wasn't very happy, so he called the BPP. He'll be even less happy when he discovers that she's got my child in her belly. A half-Jewish grandchild. How will he like that, eh?'

Above the voices, through the camp loudspeakers, a Beethoven symphony blared. Always Beethoven or Schubert or Haydn, Winter noted. Maybe Mozart. All designed to make you proud of the German-speaking homelands, all designed to throw the cold and pain into sharp relief.

Another bell rang. Work details.

'Can we talk later, maybe at the evening meal? I have a proposal for you. And we might be able to help each other.'

'How? Have you got a pass out of here? That's the only thing that would help me.'

Seb realised he had no option. He had to tell Hexie about the letter. Now that Jurgen knew, there was always the possibility she would find out and that she would be devastated and angry that Seb hadn't told her.

They were both tired from the late night, but they managed to get a good breakfast together at nine thirty. It felt more like a very early lunch: bratwurst with fried potatoes and plenty of coffee.

'There's something I have to tell you, Hexie.' They had finished the meal and she was excited about the day's big events: the women's downhill at eleven o'clock followed by the men's race an hour later. Everyone said the snow at Kreuzjoch was perfect powder – all the way down to the finish line. It could be a great day for the Germans, with Franz Pfnür in the men's race and the brilliant Christl Cranz favourite for the women's.

They weren't individual medals. They also had to race in the two-run slaloms over the weekend, which would be crucial if they were to overcome the Norwegians.

'You've found another woman?'

Seb could tell she wasn't really listening. In her head she was probably somewhere up the mountain, working out the best place to see the race.

'Jurgen's mother has made contact with me,' Seb continued. 'She wrote a letter from Berlin.'

'I'm sorry, what did you just say?'

'Ulrike, Jurgen's mother, wrote to me. She wants to meet her son now that his eighteenth birthday is near.'

Hexie was suddenly in the present. 'That *is* big news. Does Jurgen know yet? Have you written back to her?'

'Yes, Jurgen knows. I told him last night. No, I haven't written back.'

'That must have been quite a shock for the poor boy.'

'That would be an understatement. He doesn't know what to think. He's harboured rage towards her over the years and has taken it out on me, convinced I must have driven her away. But what child doesn't want to know their mother?'

'So is he supposed to get on a train and go to Berlin for a few days? Is that what she's saying?'

'She's coming to Munich. It seems she's an artist now and has an exhibition in a small gallery somewhere in town. She knows nothing about me or my life, but she's clearly full of remorse. She doesn't know about you; she doesn't even know what work I do or whether I have other children.'

'Seb, this really has taken me by surprise. I don't know what to say. Am I supposed to be happy for Jurgen or terrified that you still carry a flame for her? I'm confused.'

'I'm confused, too. I was worried about telling you. You see, I think I have to go with Jurgen to meet her. It seems like the decent thing to do. But I want your advice, Hexie. I need to know how you feel about it.'

'I don't know, Seb. This is all so sudden. I need time to think.'

'Do you want to read the letter?'

'Do *you* want me to read it?'

No, he didn't. Hexie knew he had a romantic history, of course. That was the nature of the world. He had told her about Ulrike and their brief life together, but he had gone to great lengths to make it clear that it was all in the past. A youthful love that had been somehow tragic but wonderful, too, in that it had brought Jurgen into the world.

He had never told Hexie how deeply he had loved Ulrike, because no woman wants to hear that about her man. And the problem with the letter was the intimacy it contained. It was a love story in a single page.

He took the letter from his pocket and handed it to her.

She looked at the envelope for a full minute or two, then smiled and handed it back unopened. 'No, it's nothing to do with me. It's about you and Jurgen and Ulrike. The Gestapo might read other people's letters; I don't.'

He nodded and took the letter, hurriedly placing it back in his pocket.

'But I would very much like to meet her. Anyone you loved can't be all bad.'

Seb drove to Grainau and caught the cogwheel train up through the mountain tunnel towards the top of Zugspitze.

The train was almost empty because all the ski fans were on the far side of the Wetterstein Range to watch the downhill.

Climbing out on to the terrace at the station, he looked around. The film crew was a couple of hundred metres below him, down on the piste. In all about twenty or thirty people. Three cameras were set up at strategic points; actors, two actresses, sound men and others with assorted skills were scattered about. He couldn't miss Alan Harcourt, with his voluminous fur coat and his enormous cigar. He could see Gary Tate, too.

A large, square canvas tent had been set up, probably so the actors could get out of the cold wind while awaiting their takes. Elena was probably in there, having her make-up and hair adjusted.

His boots sinking deep into the snow, he trudged down to the bowl of the mountain, scanning them all the time in the hope of picking her out.

As he arrived, he made a beeline for the director. 'Mr Harcourt,' he said.

Harcourt looked at him without recognition at first, then his expression darkened. 'You're the detective.'

'Yes, sir.'

'So where in buggery is she? Have you found the bloody bitch?'

'Are you talking about Fräulein Lang, sir? I was expecting her to be here.'

'As you can see, she's not. I'm working with damned stand-ins. She's the most unprofessional, useless film actress it has ever been my misfortune to employ. That cripple Goebbels foisted his filthy whore on me; sod the pair of them.'

'I really don't think you should talk about her like that, Mr Harcourt.'

'You don't think so, eh? Well, you can fuck off and find her, because you're just getting in my way. Tell her that if she thinks she's getting the agreed fee for this film, she's very much mistaken.'

22

The body of Elena Lang was found near the entrance to Höllental – *Hell Valley* – the dark, closed-in area beneath the high ridge that ran from the Zugspitze peak down to Brunntal. The corpse was discovered by one of the BPP officers patrolling the slopes to protect the Games from assassins or terrorists.

The officer immediately understood the significance of his find.

Word reached Seb at midday when he called Ruff to update him on the Krieger murder. The news was just as bad as he had feared and his heart sank. He had seen enough death in his time, but this was of a different order: this had been preventable.

Ruff was brisk. 'Get up there, Wolff. Hide the body; tell no one. We'll deal with this when the Olympics are finished.'

'How do I keep the death of Elena Lang quiet? She's making a film.'

'Just do it. You know the consequences for all of us if word gets out.'

'But I have to get her to Munich for autopsy.'

'No, you'll leave the body up there, well hidden. For once in your miserable life, simply do as you're told, Wolff.'

The call ended abruptly.

To Thomas Ruff the death of Elena Lang was an irritation, an inconvenience and a threat to his peace of mind. He believed his career was in jeopardy if this was not handled with the utmost delicacy.

To Seb Wolff the death was heartbreaking. He should have protected her. She had looked to him for help and he failed her.

The BPP officer Martin Sylmann was waiting for him at the Hotel Postillion.

Seb didn't have a lot of time for the Bavarian Political Police. They were Gestapo by another name, brutish men who slung innocent civilians into Dachau without trial and called it 'protective custody'. Not only that: some were also torturers and killers. He knew this because he had encountered such men.

He had never met Sylmann before, but it quickly became clear that there was still a raw innocence to the man; he was an enthusiastic but inexperienced plod. The salutes and introductions over, they headed out with backpacks, driving first in a BPP vehicle to the village of Hammersbach, and then heading out on foot. It was not going to be easy to access the scene: hiking into Höllental required a steep uphill walk of three or four kilometres – not a simple task in this weather, with snow and ice underfoot and treacherous drops into the river valley below.

'And you've spoken to no one?'

'Just Gruppenführer Jena. He liaised with the Police Presidium and told me you would be assigned the case.'

'And you're sure you told no one among your colleagues at the Postillion?'

'No one, I swear it.'

The diligent SS-Gruppenführer had scared Sylmann into complete silence. Jena was punctilious and stern by nature, and it would not do to fall foul of such a man.

Martin Sylmann had got the message. He did not appear to be the most intelligent of men, but at least he was not as coarse or hard-bitten as some of his colleagues, which was a relief, given they were to spend much of the day together.

They followed woodland trails up beside the Hammersbach stream. In springtime, the sound of the rushing rapids would be full of life and promise. But, for the moment, the water was slower and more sinister. The trees, mostly deciduous, were skeletal. The forbidding walls of the valley seemed to tighten around them as they climbed higher.

After almost two hours of trudging knee-deep in snow, they reached the spot, in a forest clearing a little way to the east of the towering sides of the Höllental.

She lay on her side in a snowdrift, still in the beautiful gown she had worn at Schloss Stark the night before. Only her hair was out of place, drenched and lank from the snow.

Seb stood for a few moments, his head bowed in respect and guilt. He had never experienced such an overwhelming sense of remorse and sadness.

His rational brain told him he was not to blame, that he could have done nothing to protect her without her permission. And yet that knowledge could not erase his self-reproach. As a murder detective he was used to dealing with the aftermath of other people's actions. But in this case he had been involved all along.

'She still looks beautiful, Captain Wolff. Just as we have seen her on the screen. I recognised her immediately.'

'Give me the camera.'

Sylmann had brought a BPP-issue Leica in his backpack, which he now handed to Seb.

He took pictures from every angle, including the sheer cliffs above and the town in the distance below. He tried to mark the spot as perfectly as he could. Only then did he turn the body over and take more photographs. There were no marks anywhere, no bullet wounds, no cuts or blood, no bruises to the neck.

How had she died? That would be up to Professor Lindner to deduce when he could eventually examine the body.

And how had she got to this remote spot? Was she killed here or brought here after death? Impossible questions to answer at the moment. There was no blood in the snow, no evident wound.

'We have orders to hide her,' Seb said. 'Are there any caves or overhangs where we could somehow keep her safe from sight?' The body would not deteriorate quickly in this cold, but there was always the danger of wild animals or raptors seeing her as carrion to be gnawed and pulled apart. That must not be allowed to happen.

'There's the gorge. People visit it in summer, but I doubt they do at this time of year.'

It was too much of a risk, too many tourists in town. Someone who wanted a break from the Games might decide to visit the Höllentalklamm.

'Or there's an old hut,' Sylmann said. 'About ten minutes' walk from here. I think it used to be a log store but it doesn't have much of a roof now. I came across it on my patrol.'

They carried her gently and placed her on the soft, leaf-strewn floor in the hut, then covered her in snow both to protect her from marauding carrion hunters and to prevent her from decomposing. They collected fallen branches to fill in the gap where once there had been a door.

'That will have to do,' Seb said at last. 'Come on, Sylmann, we should get back. Somehow I have to find her killer.'

Yet how do you find a killer in such circumstances? Two killers for that matter: there was still the case of Theodor Krieger to be solved. Strange that there should be two killings in such a restricted area within such a short span of time. Only a very poor detective would fail to wonder whether there was a connection between the crimes.

But there were no similarities between the two murder methods and no connection between the social circles in which the two victims had moved.

As for the cause of death, he did not have a pathologist's skill, but as a murder cop he had come across a variety of killings in which no wound was visible, and so he had a few ideas. Poison, drug overdose, smothering.

Or exposure. That was always a possibility in sub-zero temperatures.

But, for exposure to be involved, that raised a whole host of other questions. Why had she come here? Had she been carried while drunk or drugged? She didn't seem to be inebriated when he last saw her at the party.

His one certainty at the moment was that a beautiful woman and a much-loved star lay dead. And, all the while, not far away, thousands of men and women, spectators and athletes, were being enthralled by the spectacle and competition of the peaceful Games.

Hans Winter had never worked so hard. He was not built for physical labour. Brauer had told the truth when he said the work was senseless. They were both assigned to a so-called external commando, which involved marching five kilometres from the camp.

Each of them carried a spade over his shoulder and they sang all the way by order of the guards. At last they came to a snow-covered paddock.

Their task then was to clear the small field of snow. No one bothered to explain the reason for this mad mission and nor did anyone ask. To have done so would have incurred the sting of a bullwhip.

'Makes a change from shifting rocks,' Brauer said under his breath.

'And yet you still insist you wouldn't like to kill whoever denounced you?' It was an effort for Winter to string so many words together, he was panting so heavily. And he was sweating profusely, which had to be some sort of bonus, given the cold.

'If I was interested in having someone killed, I certainly wouldn't tell anyone here. And you should keep your mouth shut, too, Winter. You'll do yourself no favours talking so much.'

'I can't sleep at night, Brauer. I'm consumed by rage.'

'You'll sleep tonight, I promise you.'

Was she really dead? A name as big as Greta Garbo, Marlene Dietrich or Hedy Lamarr. How could she be dead and no one know about it? No one but her killer.

Seb left Sylmann at the Postillion. The BPP man didn't need reminding that not a single word must pass his lips, but Seb drove the point home anyway.

Sylmann might not be clever but he was a fine young man, wasted on an outfit of thugs. Would he be corrupted by the rot that now surrounded him? Was that what was happening to his beloved Germany? Good men hardened by gangsters and subsumed into a world of injustice and savagery? Was that happening to his own son? Jurgen was firmly in the grip of the Hitler Youth, an organisation supposedly dedicated to health and fitness, but in reality training young men for war and their own deaths.

What would Ulrike think when she met him?

Thinking back to the case at hand, Seb's first task was a professional examination of the body. He made his way to the Villa Erika. Using the secure Sicherheitsdienst telephone, he put a call through to the university in Munich and asked to be connected to Professor Lindner.

'Please wait a few moments, Captain Wolff.'

Seb waited. The secretary came back on the line. 'Professor Lindner apologises, but he is too busy to talk to you at the moment.'

'Go back to the professor and tell him that whatever he is presently doing is less important than talking to me.'

'I'm not sure I can do that, sir.'

'Do it.'

Five minutes later Lindner came on the line. He did not try to disguise his anger.

'What do you want, Wolff?'

'You need to come to Garmisch-Partenkirchen as soon as possible.'

'You may not know this, but two planes have crashed in Munich. I'm inundated with work.'

'This is more important.'

'Why?'

'I cannot explain on the phone.'

'Then good day to you, captain.' The line went dead.

Seb cursed and summoned the Untersturmführer who manned the SD office. 'Do you have any idea where I might find Gruppenführer Jena?'

'He's with the propaganda minister. I believe they were due to visit the broadcasting house.'

'Try to get him on the line, would you? This is most urgent.'

Paul Jena's voice was slow, businesslike but not unfriendly. 'What is it, Wolff?'

'I would very much like to have an urgent conversation with you in person, sir.'

'I seem to have become quite popular with you, captain. Can you get to the broadcasting house? We'll be leaving by train for Munich within the next hour.'

'Yes, sir.'

Fifteen minutes later, they were locked away in a private office at the press centre.

'I understand this is difficult for you, Wolff.'

'I'm assailed by major problems, one of which is access. I have no record of Fräulein Lang leaving Schloss Stark, so I need to speak to Herr von Stark and others at the castle to fill in the hours before the discovery of her body.'

'What have you done with it?'

'Herr Ruff ordered me to leave it in the Höllental but concealed. It's in a tumbledown hut not far from where she was found. She's been covered with snow to protect her from wildlife and save the body from decomposition, which brings me to my second problem: we must have the body examined by a pathologist to ascertain cause of death. I have spoken to Professor Lindner, and he's disinclined to come here.'

'So you need a directive from me ordering him to come? And you need me to make it clear to the von Starks that they must agree to be interviewed by you?'

'Indeed. It would be difficult for an ordinary Kripo officer simply to turn up at a place like Schloss Stark and demand cooperation. A telephone call from you could ease my way.'

'I'll call Werner.'

As he was picking up the phone, there was a knock at the door. Seb looked at the Gruppenführer.

'You'd better answer it, Wolff.'

He opened the door and found himself face to face with

Joseph Goebbels. He hobbled into the room, closed the door after him and turned to Jena. 'Is this the Kripo officer?'

'This is Captain of Detectives Wolff.'

For want of anything better to do, Seb gave the propaganda minister a Hitler salute and clicked his heels. 'At your service, Herr Dr Goebbels.'

'All right, all right. We don't need any of that now. Have you found the killer?'

'No, sir. As yet I cannot even determine cause of death. The body is unmarked by any obvious wounds or bruising, and she's still in the evening gown she was wearing at Schloss Stark. Various possibilities come to mind.'

'Where's the pathologist?'

'He's in Munich, sir.'

'You'd better get him down here. You're not going to get very far without a cause of death. Is suicide a possibility?'

'In theory, yes, sir.'

'Very well. Keep me informed. Whatever you may have heard about my association with Elena Lang, you will ignore, but I can tell you that she was a good friend and a fine actress. Her death is a great loss to the German-speaking people and, indeed, the whole world. When the Games are over, we'll have a proper memorial service for her. But I'm sure you understand that for the moment such a thing is impossible. The Führer's orders are clear: nothing is to interfere with the Games.'

'Yes, Herr Minister.'

'I know how difficult this must be for you, captain, and I wish it were not so. But the killer must be found and brought to justice. I'll accept nothing less.' He nodded to Jena. 'Captain Wolff is to be afforded all the assistance he needs, Paul.'

'Of course, minister.'

Goebbels gazed briefly at Seb, then departed.

'That is understood, then, Wolff?' Jena said.

'Yes, Herr Gruppenführer.' His orders were clear, but the character of Joseph Goebbels less so. He had been perfectly polite and civilised, but the coldness was evident to anyone with an interest in the human psyche. This was not about the murder of a woman he loved; it was about the propaganda implications of her death.

23

Seb walked to the Alpspitze Hotel and put a call up to the room of Olivia Sands. She didn't answer and he cursed. What next? He'd have to talk to Harcourt again. He'd also have to go back to Schloss Stark.

As he was leaving, he saw Olivia walking towards him and stopped her.

'I suppose you've heard,' she said.

She couldn't mean that Elena was dead; no one knew that. He nodded. 'I saw Harcourt at the top of Zugspitze. He seemed livid.'

'Understandably so in this case. He's left me down here to find her, but I've looked everywhere and have run out of options. I'm worried, Captain Wolff. Elena is a law unto herself, but this doesn't feel good.'

How could he keep her death secret from this woman? It seemed all wrong. Yet he forged ahead with the fiction demanded of him. 'What will Harcourt do?'

She sighed. 'He thinks he got enough close-ups and middle-distance shots yesterday, so he's using stand-ins for the last of the long-distance work today. He keeps blaming her for ruining his film and sticking a dagger in his reputation. If he could, he'd kill her.'

'Where do *you* think she is?'

'I wish I knew. Harcourt's sure she's with a man, but, if so, which one? I suppose you've heard the rumours.'

'Tell me.'

'Men in high places. Surely word gets around, even in a police state?'

He shrugged. 'Oh, you know.'

She looked puzzled. 'You didn't hear what transpired last night, did you?'

'Go on.'

'You must have been elsewhere at the time. Come inside and I'll tell you. It's too bloody cold out here.'

He accompanied her into the Alpspitze bar, and they found a quiet table. She ordered a Martini and he had a beer.

'Well?' he said.

'I met the Englishman Howard Jack and he told me what he saw. He said Elena was approaching the table where Goebbels was sitting with his wife and the von Starks. You could see Goebbels shrinking, and he's not very big in the first place, is he?'

'When was this?'

'Perhaps an hour before you and I went looking for her. What happened was that Werner von Stark stood up and moved directly towards Elena. He put an arm around her waist. Not violently, but not in a friendly way either. Forceful, Jack said. Werner simply moved her away. She didn't struggle with him but nor did she cooperate. It was all over in a matter of seconds. No shouting, no screaming, no cat fight, but apparently it was very obvious what was happening. A lot of people saw it.'

'What happened then?'

'Nothing.'

'But Elena, where did she go?'

'That's what I'd like to know.'

'And von Stark? Did he return to the table?'

'Again, I don't know. As I said, I heard all this from Howard Jack. You know him, don't you?'

'Indeed.'

'Very witty and indiscreet. The things he was saying about Goebbels and Magda would have been hilarious if I wasn't so concerned about Elena.'

Seb was pretty sure he didn't want to know about that. This was a tough enough conversation as it was – feigning ignorance of Elena's fate. But it was an important conversation: he had to know what happened between Elena approaching Goebbels and being found dead in the Höllental.

Those minutes and hours were crucial.

The enigmatic Werner von Stark had to be a person of interest, a potentially vital witness. Perhaps Howard Jack, too.

'What's your best bet, Miss Sands? Elena must have left the castle.'

'Perhaps she stalked off in a huff and cadged a lift from someone. I did wonder whether she might have been so fed up with Harcourt and Goebbels that she simply fled back to her family in Vienna. But wouldn't she have said something to me? I thought we got on well. And wouldn't she have come back here to get a change of clothes and some luggage? She hasn't been in her hotel room, and the desk staff haven't seen her.'

'Tell me what you know about her. When I talked to her she didn't seem totally in love with her life as a film star.'

Olivia grimaced. 'I hate to say it, but I think she's always been a little troubled. One moment quiet and fearful, the next loud and full of life. I love her dearly, but during the shoot I sometimes feared for her emotional stability. I understand that Harcourt's difficult to work with, but there were times when I wondered whether there was something else – something deeper.'

'Such as?'

'The Goebbels thing, I suppose.'

'I sense you're worried for her safety, Miss Sands.' He

couched his words carefully, but he was beginning to suspect that Olivia Sands knew more than she was letting on.

'Of course I'm worried.'

'That she might be suicidal?' Seb had already just about ruled that out, but then he had met her on only a couple of occasions.

With no marks on her, no warm clothes, was it possible she just walked away from the castle and somehow, perhaps hours later, found herself at the entrance to the Höllental? And then, exhausted, did she lay herself down in the snow to die? She would not have been the first person to choose such an end to their misery and despair.

He had heard that it was a calm, almost comforting way to go.

Olivia shook her head. 'Not that, not suicide. I don't believe it.'

'But you have fears. Can you think of anyone who might wish her harm?'

'Not Alan Harcourt. For all his bluster and insults, he's not a thug.'

'Then who?' There was a silence between them. The hotel bar was busy and noisy, but they were in a world of their own. Seb knew little about this Englishwoman, but he found himself trusting her. A little push, a little indiscretion on his part, might that just help squeeze some more information out of her? It was a risk he had to take; otherwise how was he to solve this murder? He took a breath. 'I'm going to tell you something, Miss Sands, and I would ask you not to repeat it.'

She nodded.

'When I picked Elena up from Schloss Stark, she confided in me that someone was threatening her and that she was scared. I offered her police protection, but she wouldn't accept it.'

'You think some harm has come to her, don't you, captain?'

A thought struck him: perhaps Elena had also confided her fears to Olivia Sands. They were clearly close. He nodded. 'I suspect we share the same concern,' he said. 'But why was she scared? She wouldn't be the first woman to have had an affair with a senior member of a government.'

Olivia Sands gave Seb a hard, angry look, but he knew that her fury was not directed at him. Each grasped that the other was concealing more than they were revealing.

She threw back her Martini. 'This is your country, captain – you know better than I do what goes on here. But I'm not naive. I'm aware there are dark forces at work these days. Her affair with you-know-who must have ruffled feathers. I believe the minister's wife wields power in certain quarters. Maybe that's why Elena was scared.'

He tried to keep his face blank, aware that he had perhaps said more than he should have. 'This gossip you've heard, Miss Sands – might I ask you not to repeat it in public? Such rumours would not be well received by your hosts – and nor would they be fair on Fräulein Lang's reputation.'

'You mean just shut up? Don't disturb the horses? I'm not sure I can do that. Not while there's a chance that I can do something to help my dear friend.'

By the time of the evening meal, Hans Winter was ready to collapse on his bunk and sleep until reveille. But he also needed food for sustenance, and he couldn't be absent from roll-call. Just as importantly, he had to talk to the Jew.

He realised that he didn't know the man's name, only that he came from Schwabing, so in his head that was what he called him. He took his bowl across the eating hall and sat beside the man.

'Hans Winter. We spoke this morning.'

'No, you came over and forced me into a conversation.'

'Forgive me, but I thought you could help me.'

'Why would you think that?'

'Because your star tells me you are a Jew.'

'So what?'

'I have a very good friend who is Jewish, and he is in a bad way, hunted by the Gestapo in Dortmund. He needs to go underground and for that he needs papers – papers which show him as Aryan.'

'And where does he hope to find such a thing?'

'He's struggling. I was wondering whether anyone here might have contacts. Perhaps you know of someone. I have heard of such things being possible, but I don't have the necessary names.'

Schwabing looked at him with scorn. 'I'm happy to be a Jew. I have no intention of hiding who I am – so why would I wish for fake papers declaring me to be something I am not?'

'My friend would not expect such a service for free, but would pay good money – both to you and whoever supplied watertight ID papers and ancestry documents. An Aryan certificate or an Ahnenpass.'

'How do I know you're not a Gestapo spy?'

'You don't. But I promise you I'm not.'

'And what use would such information be if you're stuck here in the Hotel Dachau?'

'I will not be here for long. I have a good lawyer working for my release. There's no evidence against me: just the word of my nephew, a criminal trying to deflect culpability from his own shoulders.'

'How much money are we talking about?'

'A hundred Reichsmarks.'

'Each?'

'Split between you.'

'Your chances might be increased if you doubled that figure. Say a hundred for me and the same for the fixer, if I can find one.'

'You drive a hard bargain.'

'There is no bargain, but I'll ask around for you.'

'Thank you. By the way, I don't know your name.'

'That's because I didn't tell you. And nor will I, Herr Winter 7482. So you go on your way. Perhaps we'll talk again in the morning. Perhaps not.'

And then, just as he slurped down the last of his soup and black bread, the bell went for roll-call and Winter faced another long night in this diabolical place.

The block leader, a smooth brute named Höss, decided to make an example of the Jews.

'All subhumans step forward.'

The Jews knew he was referring to them. They knew, too, that it would be worse for them if they pretended not to understand – and so they stepped forward from their lines.

'Earlier this week, a Jew carried out foul murder on the leader of Switzerland's National Socialist Party, our heroic brother Wilhelm Gustloff. Shot dead by a subhuman. When the Jew attacks us, do we not attack back?'

He made them stand in a line, then other guards gathered around, all carrying their bullwhips and cudgels. They formed themselves into two rows: ten guards lined up on one side, ten on the other, each with weapon raised.

'Now, Jews, you will walk between the guards to the other side. Walk, not run, or you'll be required to go around again. In doing this, you will atone in some small part for the sacred blood of our Aryan brother Wilhelm. March!'

The Jews, about a hundred of them, had no option. The one Winter had approached for help and thought of as

Schwabing caught his eye and smiled ruefully. He held his head high to show that he had no fear, before the blows began to rain down on him as he came between the gauntlet of guards.

Blow after blow, strike after strike, lash after lash. Punches to the face, to the head, kicks to the balls.

For all his unspoken Jewish blood, Winter could only stand and watch. The blows didn't touch him, yet he felt them all the same. He would have closed his eyes and ears, but he couldn't.

Seb wanted to talk to Howard Jack. He seemed to know everyone and go everywhere within the high society of the von Starks and their aristocratic and political friends.

He placed a call from the hotel desk to Schloss Stark, but whoever answered the phone at the castle – some secretary, he imagined – would say only that Herr Jack was not available and nor were the von Starks.

'Does that mean Mr Jack is not there or that he's otherwise engaged?'

'He's not available, sir.'

'Tell him that Captain Wolff called. He can reach me through the Police Presidium number or at the Waxenstein Guest House in Gapa. And tell the von Starks that Gruppenführer Jena wishes them to be interviewed by me.'

'Yes, sir.'

In the meantime, he badly needed to talk to someone he could trust, and that meant Hexie. But she was off somewhere watching the Games or drinking with Carin.

This was a lot to carry on his own shoulders: two murders that could not be publicised under any circumstances. One involved a family of untold wealth, a senior Nazi minister and a major film outfit; the other an SS trooper with potential links to a criminal underworld. Where was he to go from here?

For the first time since they became acquainted, he was almost beginning to wish he had Hans Winter by his side. Shouldn't he be out of Dachau by now? Perhaps he should take control, call the whole thing off and get Winter back.

More than that, he wondered how Winter was getting on. There were dangers; they both knew that. And Winter wasn't the most physically robust of men.

But, with or without his sergeant, there was much to be done. Seb placed another call to Professor Lindner and told him to catch the next train to Garmisch-Partenkirchen.

'Bring stout snow boots and your warmest clothing. And say nothing to anyone.'

'I've had a hell of a week, Wolff. Believe it or not, I was looking forward to an evening with my wife. Can this not wait?'

'No, professor, this can't wait. Personal orders from the minister of propaganda. If you want to argue about it, call Gruppenführer Jena. Oh, and bring your equipment: you'll be performing a post-mortem examination under very trying circumstances.'

24

Hans Winter was so tired, he'd thought he would sleep like a lamb, but unconsciousness wouldn't come. His mind was filled with visions of the beatings that a hundred men had received for the crime of being Jewish. A crime of which he, too, considered himself guilty.

In his head, he heard the harsh sound of leather and wood thudding into flesh and bone; the cries of men reduced to animals on their way to the slaughterhouse.

He had been insane to come here. But this was not just about the murder of Theodor Krieger; this was about his own life and his hopes of a wife and family. If he were to propose to Malwine, he would need expertly produced papers to prove that he was pure Aryan, for her father would never allow her to marry a part-Jew – a *Mischling* – even one baptised and brought up as a Lutheran.

He thought back to his life in Dortmund. His unreasoning hatred of Jews, his belief that they were the cause of all Germany's miseries, that they were Christ killers as preached by Martin Luther, that they cheated and lied and became rich on the backs of decent Germans, that they were responsible for his country's surrender in the Great War.

That was what he had believed about Jews and, yes, he had persecuted them and wanted them driven out of his country.

And then he discovered the old trunk in his parents' attic.

He saw a photograph that didn't make sense to him. A picture of a man in rabbi's shawl and cap. Why would there be such a thing in his house?

He talked to his parents and they laughed. That was his mother's father, Simon Greenbaum, in the days before he and his wife converted to Lutheranism. What, it must be forty years ago now? All that was in the ancient past.

Except it wasn't. Not in the new Germany. It wasn't so easy to escape your ancestry.

That he was now the enemy caused him bewilderment tinged with horror. It was unreal. One moment he was the persecutor, the next the persecuted.

He couldn't tell anyone. He had to escape, get so far away from his family that no one would connect him with them, no one would know. And so he had transferred from the Dortmund Gestapo office to the BPP in Munich.

But that wasn't enough. If Captain Wolff could find out the truth about him, so could others.

Now, watching the brutality visited on the Jews of Dachau, he was wondering whether he really wanted to wipe out his history. He had felt those blows as if they had been meted out to his own body.

To think that it had been the proudest moment of his life when he received his NSDAP membership. That seemed long in the past now.

And then there was the defiance of the man he knew as Schwabing. If he could stand so tall and strong in the face of such brutality, perhaps he, Hans Winter, had been wrong about the Jews all along.

Who wouldn't be proud to have the same blood as prisoner Schwabing?

Why should Winter alter his history? He was who he was.

But, if he *didn't*, how could he marry the woman he loved?

It seemed to Seb that life in Schloss Stark was one long party. Here they were, Unity, Werner and Sophie, Fritz and

Howard, laughing and playing a game which looked very much like boules, in the drawing room where he had met them all before.

'Sebastian Wolff, what an enormous pleasure.' It was Howard Jack, always the warmest and most welcoming. 'You just can't keep away from us.' He waved to one of two liveried servants standing to attention near the door. 'Champagne here for this weary traveller.'

'I won't, but thank you,' Seb said.

'Still got a sore head from last night? No stamina you bloody Germans. And guess where Bobo has been today? Hotfooted to Munich for lunch at the Ost with you-know-who. Cue violins and rose petals.'

Unity stuck out her tongue at Jack.

Werner von Stark approached. He had been amused and light-hearted while he was rolling the ball across the floor, but now his face was grim and hard.

'I'm told you wish to speak to me?'

'All of you, really. I'm looking for Elena Lang.'

'Again? Have the Munich police nothing better to do? Or perhaps you just like coming into my home.'

'You will know, I'm sure, that this is not just me. Your friend Gruppenführer Jena and Minister Goebbels are also taking an interest.'

'Then you had better explain what you hope to achieve by this intrusion.'

'I can find no record of her leaving here last night. I have been told there was an incident: Fräulein Lang approached a table where you were sitting with Herr Goebbels, his wife and one or two others. You jumped up and escorted her away.'

'Jumped up? I did no such thing. I have never jumped up in my life. I got up from my seat, because I understood that

Elena wished to go to the powder room, so I considered that I should point her in the right direction. There was no *incident*.'

'Did you accompany her there?'

'Of course not. I set her on the correct path and handed her into the care of one of my servants to escort her. Is that all? This is becoming tedious.'

'Can you remember which servant? I'd like to talk to him or her.'

Werner frowned, then smiled. 'The White Snake, that was it. The one dressed in the White Snake costume.'

'Perhaps you could find out the person's true identity. It would assist me greatly. After that, when did you next see Elena Lang?'

'I don't know if I did.' He turned to his sister and their guests. 'Did any of you see Elena?'

'I'm sure I saw her dancing,' Unity said. 'But we were all a bit tipsy and there were so many people, so who knows? I had eyes only for my good friend Fritz here.' She batted her eyelashes at her SS shadow. 'Anyway, why do you ask, Wolff? Why are the appearances and disappearances of Elena Lang of so much interest to you? It seems to have become quite an obsession.'

'Once again, she did not arrive for filming. This is hardly ideal when Mr Harcourt and his backers have invested so much money in this film. He's beside himself with fury.'

'Then you had better talk to Mr Harcourt and Miss Sands.'

Her logic – or lack of it – stumped him. 'None of the crew have any idea where she is, and they're worried – as am I. This is why I've come here – it's the last place she was seen.'

Werner was frowning. 'Fritz? Sophie? Howard? Do you know where Elena is?'

'My guess?' Howard Jack said. 'Search all the bedrooms of Gapa. She's bound to be in one of them. Darling Elena has her weaknesses and one of them is men. I know the feeling.'

'I'm sure Howard's right,' Unity said. 'Find the man, find Elena. It's quite straightforward, Wolff. Not a lot of detective work involved.'

As a group, he didn't like these people. As individuals they might be endurable, but all together they reeked of entitlement, sneering at the little people, careless for the welfare of a woman they had entertained as a friend. They were wealthy because their parents were wealthy. Fritz Mannheim was probably the only one among them who had done a day's work in his life. Or perhaps that was being unfair on Howard Jack. Seb knew nothing about him save that he was upperclass English and scratched poetry.

He looked at each one of them in turn, as though some clue might reside in their faces. But there was nothing.

He wanted to tell them that she now lay dead, murdered, her body concealed beneath snow in a mountain valley not far from here. He wanted to say that there was reason to believe that someone here in this castle, or one of their acquaintances, was almost certainly responsible for her death. He wanted to tell these rich, privileged few that he despised them.

Instead, he smiled.

'How many servants were here last night, Herr von Stark?'

'You would have to ask my butler.'

'Is he here at the moment?'

'He's not. Nor are most of the servants, because we bring people in from the surrounding area for such events. If you like, I'll ask him for a list when I see him tomorrow.'

'Thank you.'

'Is that all?'

'For the moment.'

He looked around the room once more, still dissatisfied. He didn't want to leave having gained so little, but he had to meet Professor Lindner. It was going to be a long, hard night. Once more, his eye was drawn to the Klimt painting, and the young, dark-haired woman who looked back at him.

It was an exquisite portrait. There were other fine works in this room, but none compared to this. He was bewitched by its strange familiarity, so alive that one could almost believe she might walk into the room.

25

Lindner was loaded down with a heavy leather bag containing his equipment. Seb asked if he could carry it for him.

'No,' the pathologist said abruptly. 'Let's just get on with this.' He had arrived by train and was kitted out in warm clothes, tough boots and long, thick woollen socks that went over his trouser legs and up to the knees, like knickerbockers.

Seb had thought of taking Sylmann along to assist them but decided that two people would be less conspicuous than three. On arriving back in Gapa from Schloss Stark, he had had a brief and somewhat awkward meeting with Hexie, whose first words were 'Is she in Munich yet?'

She meant Ulrike. 'Perhaps.'

'Hadn't you better go to her?'

'I owe her nothing, so no. Anyway, I have work to do.' He knew he sounded irritable, but this was the last thing he needed. Hexie hadn't been like this when he told her about the letter. What had got into her? Perhaps she had confided in Carin, only to be rewarded with the suggestion that a dose of jealousy was in order.

They took their leave of each other without much warmth. But he'd make it up to her later, perhaps tomorrow if he could find a few spare moments in his gruelling workload.

Seb filled his rucksack with two Thermos flasks of coffee, a small bottle of schnapps, four electric torches and spare batteries. He had borrowed the torches from the BPP bureau at the Postillion, guessing that they'd be using such equipment in their patrols of the slopes every night. He found Sylmann and told him what they were going to do.

'That makes sense, captain,' Sylmann said. 'I would just advise that if you're spotted by our men that you hold up your hands and explain who you are; otherwise they'll shoot you. Should I write you a pass?'

'That might be helpful.'

He joined Lindner in the Lancia and they drove to Hammersbach, parking as close to the track as he could manage. 'We walk from here, I'm afraid.'

'Are you going to tell me what this is about, Wolff? As you've wrecked my evening and probably the whole weekend, the least you can do is tell me why I'm here.'

'Elena Lang has been found dead, most probably murdered – but that's for you to determine.' He kept his voice low, though there was no one in the vicinity to hear.

That stopped Lindner in his tracks. 'Elena Lang the actress?'

'I'm afraid so.'

'Well, that is shocking. Why didn't you tell me before?'

'I couldn't on an open line. This has to be kept secret. Orders of the minister of propaganda.'

'Maintain secrecy? This woman's death is surely an event of worldwide interest.'

'The plan is to keep it out of the public eye until after the Winter Games. The story at the moment is simply that she has gone off somewhere, which she has done before.'

'Tell me, why didn't you think to bring the corpse to me in Munich?'

Seb explained that he had been ordered to leave the body where it was, hidden. Lindner nodded with resignation.

'So be it, then. You lead the way.'

The moon was almost full. Visibility was good. In the

distance behind them the lights of Grainau, Hammersbach and Garmisch-Partenkirchen sprinkled the valley with stardust. The clouds had gone, and the air was becoming more chilly by the moment. Seb guessed it was already minus fifteen and would soon be down to minus twenty or lower. His gloves did little to protect his fingers from the cold.

The two men barely spoke as they hiked ever higher through deep, powdery snow along the path of the Hammersbach river, the incline ever upwards, the cold ever deeper. The mountains on either side snapping in on them like the jaws of a predator.

Both men were physically strong, so they kept up a decent pace. On reaching the hut, Seb tore down the branches that he had constructed as a temporary door, then pointed the beam of a torch at the mound of snow that served as a temporary grave for Elena Lang.

'She's under there.'

Lindner said nothing for a few moments. At last he sighed. 'When you said she was protected from animals in an old hut, I hadn't expected this. You realise the body will be frozen solid. I'll be hard-pressed to make a simple incision.'

'Can you not just examine her externally for signs of injury?'

'I thought you'd already done that. This is impossible, Wolff. Nothing I can do here.'

Seb nodded. 'You're right.' He knew it now: this couldn't be done. This hadn't been thought through by Jena or Goebbels.

'If I tried to do even the minimum work, I would probably lose my fingers to frostbite and I still wouldn't get a result. I can't take samples, can't open her up to look at the internal organs. We have to get the body back to my laboratory in Munich to allow it to thaw. Even that will take some time.'

Seb weighed up the possibilities. She was light. Together they could carry her back to the car. No one would be about at this time of night. Well, almost no one. A BPP patrol could cause them temporary problems, but nothing that couldn't be solved by producing Sylmann's pass.

To hell with orders: this was too important. 'We'll do it your way, professor. I'll carry her.'

'Wrap her in your coat when we approach the car. If we're spotted by villagers we'll tell them that it's a young deer or chamois. Let's avoid awkward questions if we can.'

Seb looked at Elena's poor body with tenderness and sorrow. Whatever faults she might have had, she had done nothing to deserve this.

They began the long walk back to the car.

Midnight. The streets of Munich were still alive with Friday night drinkers and dancers. Seb pulled up outside the university and stayed in the car while Lindner went to talk to the night watchman.

When he returned, they waited until the pavements were clear of revellers for at least a hundred metres in all directions. 'Right, Wolff, let's get her inside. Keep her covered up. We don't want the night porter to see her face.'

Seb didn't need telling. Together they got the corpse to Lindner's pathology department.

Finally, the two men looked at each other in shared dismay. Seb felt complicit in a crime; moving bodies at dead of night did not feel like a proper act for men in a law enforcement agency.

'Coffee?' Seb said, trying to break the spell. 'Schnapps?'

'One small schnapps, then I'm going home to bed and I

suggest you do likewise. Don't expect results from me any time soon. A frozen body takes a good few hours to thaw to the extent that I can deal with it.'

The two men clinked glasses and downed their drinks in one.

'What a night, eh, Wolff. I'm sorry if I sometimes get tetchy with you, because I know you're not to blame. It's just this bloody crew that gets to me. The sooner they're history the better.'

Lindner had never spoken with such openness before. There were times when Seb thought he might have better lines of communication with the dead than the living. 'I couldn't possibly comment, professor.'

'Very wise of you. Keep your head down and try to outlast the bastards.'

His mother was in bed asleep when he arrived home. He tried calling the Waxenstein Guest House in Garmisch-Partenkirchen to give a message to Hexie that he was back home in Munich, but no one answered. So he poured himself a beer and some more schnapps, sat at the kitchen table and tried to make sense of the past few days.

He was aware that he had neglected the murder of Theodor Krieger. It seemed like a case that could be passed on to a less senior detective, but he understood his boss's rationale. This could not be opened up into a full-scale investigation, or there would be leaks.

Perhaps Hans Winter was making some progress with the victim's father-in-law in Dachau, but it seemed a long shot. With luck, he'd be out of the camp soon and file his report.

In his own mind, Seb still didn't consider it likely that Krieger's murder was an act of revenge on behalf of his wife's father. This was something else and it involved a criminal gang, probably the victim's supposed friend Xaver Knorr and the two men with him in the village bar at Liliendorf.

Seb had a lot of experience of bad people; he could smell them.

Knorr and his friends had that stench about them. You wouldn't turn your back on such men. Perhaps that had been Theodor Krieger's fatal error. The question was why? What did their criminal enterprise involve – and why had they fallen out?

The location of the killing had to be relevant. The Scharnitz Pass was almost certainly an ancient trade and smugglers' route: alcohol, stolen cattle, fugitives. At one time or another probably all of these things would have been carried to or from Austria. But what about this year, 1936? That was what he had to find out.

What he needed was one break; one bit of solid evidence against Knorr and his friends and the case would be done. One way or another, Seb badly wanted those three locked up.

He needed to be free to concentrate on the far more important – and complicated – matter of Elena Lang's death.

Hans Winter didn't want to open his eyes when reveille was called at five in the morning. He didn't want to see another corpse hanging from the beams. He didn't want to get out of bed and see more prisoners beaten and whipped within a centimetre of their lives. He didn't want any more of the pointless and backbreaking work that would certainly be inflicted on them today. He didn't want any more of the thin flavourless soup that was supposed to keep them alive.

He opened his eyes and said a word of thanks to God. There was no suicide today.

After a quick wash and shave, he and Friedrich Brauer trotted together to the eating hall. Everything had to be done at double-pace in the camp. No leisurely strolls here. 'Sleep better did you, Winter 7482?'

'Yes, I slept.'

'Hard work does tend to cure insomnia, even in the bitter cold.'

Winter didn't really know what to say to the man. There was no obvious way to delve deeper. If Brauer had arranged the killing of Theodor Krieger, he wasn't going to give anything away. He was far too sly for that. 'The sleep's one thing. The dreams are another matter.'

'They'll go. My advice to you: obey orders, eat every gram you can, do the work, don't get injured and pray to God every day. I was a convinced atheist before I came here; not now. And, believe it or not, people do get out of here eventually, unless they die first.'

At breakfast he saw Schwabing the Jew. His face and head were bloodied and bruised. Once again he went over to him. 'I saw what happened to you and I'm sorry.'

'We were expecting it.' His lip was bloodied and swollen and his voice was indistinct.

'You showed dignity. Courage.'

'That's all you can do with these swine.'

'Have you thought any more about what we discussed?'

'I have an idea, yes.'

'And?'

'It is possible I may be able to help, for the price we mentioned. But tell me about your *friend*.' His emphasis made it plain that he didn't believe Winter was talking on behalf of anyone but himself. 'Why does he need these papers so badly? You said he has to go underground. Tell me more.'

Winter grimaced, as though caught out in a lie. 'Actually, that wasn't completely true. In fact, he's in love with a non-Jew and wants to marry her.'

'Just like me, then. How romantic. I've always enjoyed a love story. And is your *friend* so besotted that he's willing to take a risk? Do a deal with the sort of people who will cut you up without blinking if you give them any sort of problem?'

'I think so, yes.'

Schwabing slipped a scrap of paper into Winter's hand. 'That has two telephone numbers on it. The first one will put you through to my girlfriend. You will say that her man asked you to give her a hundred marks, that's all. No explanation, no names necessary. You will meet her at a café of her choosing in Munich and hand over the money. The second number is the contact who will help you secure an Aryan certificate for your friend.'

'Do you have a name for this contact?'

'Yes, but that's not for me to say. Tell him exactly what you want and he'll arrange it. If you cheat me or him, you'll be killed. Have no doubt about that.'

'I understand.'

'You must memorise the numbers on that piece of paper as quickly as you can, and then eat it. It is written in my blood.' He touched his lip, which was still bleeding from the beating, and held up his scarlet finger.

'Thank you.'

'Don't thank me. This is not an act of friendship, merely a commercial transaction. Pay my girlfriend the agreed sum. She'll need it for the baby.'

'I will. I swear it.'

'So when are these fancy lawyers of yours getting you out of here?'

'Today.'

'I hope your friend and his girl appreciate you.'

26

Seb woke to the smell of coffee. He found his mother in the kitchen preparing breakfast. She was about to cook bacon and eggs for him, the way the English liked it, the way he had often started the day during his years at sea.

'I heard you come in,' she said. 'I never know whether you'll be home or not these days.'

'I'm sorry, Mutti. I didn't mean to wake you. Work is very busy at the moment, what with the Games at Gapa.'

'It's no matter. I'm glad you're home.' She put the frying pan on the hob. 'And are you going to tell me about the letter?'

He was expecting that. His initial thought was that he should say that it was from one of his old war comrades, but she wouldn't believe that for a moment and that would just lead to a futile argument.

'I think you probably know who it's from.'

'And that's all you're going to tell me, is it?'

'She wants to get in touch with Jurgen. She feels guilt and remorse for abandoning him. It seems she's an artist now and she's coming to Munich for a few days because she has a small exhibition here.'

Neither of them used her name. It had rarely been uttered in this apartment since she left all those years ago, and Seb doubted that it would be now.

'But you will have nothing to do with her.'

'You know me better than that, Mutti. I've already spoken to Jurgen and I'm pretty sure he'll want to meet her. It would

be only right and proper for me to accompany him and introduce them in the correct manner.'

'Is that fair on Herta Schuler?'

Seb laughed. 'Since when did you care about Hexie's feelings? You called her a tart and witch.'

'And what about *my* feelings? I've brought up Jurgen as if
he were my own son rather than grandson. Do my feelings
count for nothing? Am I to be cast aside like a worn-out
coat?'

Seb went around the table and took Angela Wolff in his
arms. He had never known his mother to cry and she wasn't
going to start now, but he knew that she was deeply hurt.
Their little family was already breaking up. Jurgen would be
leaving home soon to do his spell with the Reich Labour
Service. Seb was supposed to be marrying Hexie, and they
would hopefully start a family of their own. What was left
for the old woman who had devoted her life to raising two
boys of two generations – first Seb and now Jurgen?

Still holding her, he stood back a little and their eyes met.

'I understand, Mutti, really I do. But you know you'll
always be our first love, don't you? Nothing about this letter
or meeting can possibly change any of that. But I think
we always knew she would get in touch one day. I'm just
surprised it's taken so long. Now, how about that glorious
breakfast?'

'Just don't let her come here. I don't want to see her.
She'll never be welcome in my home. How could a Christian
woman abandon her child? It's unthinkable.'

'Permission to speak, sir,' Winter said to one of the guards as
they moved out to join the work detail.

'What is it?' The guard was twice the size of Hans Winter
and had a perpetual scowl.

'I need to speak with Camp Commandant Deubel, sir. He'll know what it's about.'

The guard, an SS trooper with sharply razored hair at the temples, a thick neck and a face only his mother could love, gazed at Winter like a boy examining an insect he was about to squash. 'Will he indeed? Why would SS-Oberführer Deubel agree to speak with scum like you?'

Winter immediately realised he had made a mistake. He should have found another guard, one more accommodating, if there were such a person in the camp. This one was not going to help him. 'I cannot say, but I swear that if you mention my name to the SS-Oberführer, he will agree to see me.'

The guard hit him around the head with the flat of his massive hand. 'Get in line for the work detail or I'll sling you in the Bunker.'

The blow was hard and unexpected. It knocked Winter's head sideways. His cheek stung and his ear was ringing. He had no option but to obey. If he asked again or begged, he would receive yet worse treatment.

Other prisoners were looking at him. Schwabing had his eyebrows raised and shook his head almost imperceptibly, while Brauer winced and came to his aid as he stumbled away from the guard.

'You bloody fool, Winter, what are you trying to do? Have you any idea what happens to you in the Bunker? For God's sake, Blindorf died in the night.'

'Blindorf?'

'Yes, Blindorf. The man whose bed you now sleep in.'

The sensible thing for Seb to do was to drive back south, continue his investigation and wait for Professor Lindner to call with the result of his autopsy. But he persuaded himself that the best use of his time might be to wait here in Munich for the post-mortem examination.

He drove to the Isarbruck Guest House, just south of the English Garden. That was the easy bit. In the face of the enemy, he did not show fear. He didn't even *feel* it. But this was different. This was Ulrike. He couldn't get out of the car, couldn't walk up to the door and ask the reception desk whether she was there. And so he sat and kept his eyes on the door.

What was he hoping for? That she would come out?

After ten minutes, he steeled himself, climbed out of the Lancia and stepped through the slush to the guest-house entrance. There was no one on the desk, but the register was there and so he turned it around and looked at it.

Ulrike Dahlen. The name was there, clearly written. Except it wasn't her name. She was Ulrike Brandt.

It hadn't occurred to Seb that she would now be married and have taken another name. How foolish of him. Perhaps she'd had more children; perhaps Jurgen had half-siblings. The truth was he knew nothing about her now, except that she was an artist.

He might not even recognise her. People often changed dramatically over the years.

A woman in a smart dirndl appeared. Not Ulrike but the concierge.

'*Grüss Gott*,' she said with a smile, the new salute either forgotten or deliberately shunned. Seb wasn't going to pick her up on it.

'*Grüss Gott*, fräulein. I am looking for Ulrike ... Ulrike Brandt. No, Dahlen.'

'Are you Herr Wolff?'

'Yes.' She didn't need to know that he was a police officer.

'Frau Dahlen said you might call and use her maiden name. I'm afraid she's not here at the moment. She asked me to tell you that she's gone to the gallery.' The woman flicked through papers on the desk. 'Here it is: she's written it for you. The Gallery Braque in Maxvorstadt.'

Seb took the paper. 'Thank you, fräulein. Can you tell me . . . what does she look like? I've not seen her in many years.'

The young woman beamed. 'I would say she is very beautiful, sir. I think you will not be disappointed.'

Seb found himself blushing. She had clearly sensed some emotion in his question, some ancient yearning perhaps. He was angry with himself, for he had made a great effort to exclude Ulrike from his tormented dreams. Hexie was a better woman, far stronger, much more steadfast, just as beautiful in her own way. So why did these raw, untamed feelings for his first love refuse to depart?

His head told him to get back in the Lancia and drive south. His heart took him to the Gallery Braque in a back street of Maxvorstadt, a little way to the west of the Löwenbräukeller beer hall.

Once again he simply sat in the car, the engine ticking over. This time he was able to look through the large glass window that fronted the rather unprepossessing gallery. He could see her clearly and she really hadn't changed a bit. If anything, her beauty had blossomed.

There were three others with her – two women and a man – hanging pictures, standing back now and then to look at them. Was that her husband, Herr Dahlen?

Seb released the handbrake and pulled away.

Had Blindorf died of natural causes in the Dachau punishment block, known familiarly as the Bunker? Or had he been beaten to death? Hans Winter had a horrible feeling it must have been the latter.

Herr Blindorf, about whom he knew nothing, had been sent there so that the bunk next to Brauer would be free and he, Winter, could take it. Blindorf, as far as he knew, was guilty of no infringements of the Dachau rules and now he was dead.

Winter was to blame and he knew it. He was only here because he could think of no other way to find a forger, no other way to marry Malwine Schmidt. In doing so, he had unwittingly sentenced an innocent soul to a cruel, barbaric death.

He barely noticed the work, shifting rocks back and forth, because his mind was elsewhere. Brauer had told him about the Bunker. Punishment for those unfortunate enough to be sent there was exceptionally brutal. Food was restricted to starvation rations; some prisoners were hung up by the wrists with their arms behind their back; others were stripped and tied to a workbench for a fifty-stroke lashing which cut to the bone.

Winter felt worthless. He should end it all now, run at the electrified fence and do the world a favour. Perhaps the SS guards in the watchtowers would gun him down before he even reached the wire. That might be a mercy.

The photo technician was in his darkroom when Seb arrived at the little shop. His assistant – his wife, it seemed – said he would be a while.

'Sergeant Winter of the BPP brought a film here on my behalf. Has it been developed yet?'

'Yes, I have it.'

'How much?'

'Nothing to the BPP. Absolutely free.'

Seb thanked her and accepted the prints and negatives, neatly parcelled in brown paper. He drove to the Café Heck at the corner of the Hofgarten. It was full of Saturday-morning shoppers, but he found a small table and ordered a coffee.

The pictures amounted to nothing. Photographs of furniture and carpets, vases and busts. No human beings in evidence. It was like an antique dealer's inventory, nothing more. Why did Krieger have a roll of such banal pictures in his pocket? He was an SS trooper; did he have a part-time job as a furniture dealer?

Seb sipped the coffee. It was still morning but it had already been a hell of a day. He doubted whether Lindner had even made a start on his post-mortem examination of Elena Lang. Sergeant Winter must still be in Dachau because he had left no word at the Police Presidium. And he, Seb Wolff, was making no progress at all.

At least the coffee was good. Someone had left a copy of the *Völkischer Beobachter* on the table and he idly flicked through it. There was lots of stuff about the Olympics, a picture of Hitler making the official opening declaration, nothing in the first few pages about the air crash that had caused such bloody mayhem in Munich. Nothing about any murder.

Folding the paper, he handed it to the occupant of the next table, who took it with gratitude.

He hailed a waitress, who came to take the pfennigs from him, stuffing them into the leather money bag slung around her waist.

Seb pushed back his chair and was standing up when a thought struck him and he sat down again. He pulled the photographs from the paper wrapping and flicked through them once more. It was like a match striking in his head.

It was so obvious. How had he not seen it before?

27

The day had started clear, but as he drove south towards Liliendorf the cloud cover came down from the mountains and it began to snow again. Good for the Olympics, not so good for driving.

The house named Valhalla looked like a glorious cake, coated in white icing with a perpetual dusting of fine sugar falling softly around the eaves. He knocked at the door and Selma Sachs answered it as before. Still grey, once more dressed all in black as though she were a widow. Perhaps the apparent senility of her husband Moritz, locked away in his study, was a kind of death.

Her face betrayed conflicting emotions. First, she looked horrified to see him, then she smiled with apparent warmth. 'It's Captain Wolff, yes?'

'That's right, Frau Sachs.'

'How nice to see you again. I recall you were looking for our handyman, Xaver Knorr. Did you find him all right?'

'I did. Thank you.'

'And I very much hope he answered all your questions. So how can I help you? Did you not get all you needed from Xaver? He can be a bit withdrawn and taciturn at times.'

'May I come in?'

'I'm sorry, of course you can. And perhaps you would like a cup of something warming. Coffee perhaps? Or we have English tea if you prefer. Winter might have been a while coming, but it's certainly arrived now.'

She was talking too much. Not doing herself any favours.

'Coffee would be very nice.'

As he stepped into the hallway, he saw it in a different light. The empty spaces, as though the house had already been vacated, its residents gone. This was no longer a home.

'How is the Weimar move coming along?'

'Oh, very well. We hope to be there at the end of next week.'

'I'd be grateful if I could have your new address in case I need to contact you after you've gone.'

'It'll be only temporary. A rented property before we find a suitable house to buy.'

'Still, I would like the address.'

Frau Sachs had a smile fixed to her face. Grey-haired and dumpy, she could be anyone's kindly grandmother. Perhaps she was: perhaps her three children had already given her grandchildren. Something about her suggested she might have been quite attractive as a young woman, but those days were long gone. The smile was forced. She was struggling to work out what to say.

'I know I have it somewhere. Perhaps I could call through to your office. Would that be convenient for you, captain?'

He shook his head. His eyes drilled into hers. Did she think him stupid? 'You're not going to Weimar, are you, Frau Sachs? You're leaving Germany. Where are you going? Austria? Switzerland? America?'

She stood, blinking, her fingers gripped on the percolator handle.

Seb reached out and touched her arm. 'Forgive me, Frau Sachs, I know this is difficult for you and that you might be in danger, but I'm not here to give you any grief. I quite understand why you might wish to leave Germany at this time. As a Kripo officer, that is not my business.'

'Then why are you here?'

'I can't say, except that I have reason to believe that your employee, Knorr, might be involved in a crime of a serious nature. As for your hopes of emigrating, I understand why someone in your position might want to remove your belongings from the country.'

Her attention moved back to the percolator, and she placed it on the range.

'As we both know, however,' Seb continued, 'there are draconian laws restricting the removal of wealth from Germany. It is not for me to approve or disapprove of someone's attempt to find a way around such constraints. But, in the present circumstances, I have to bear your actions in mind.'

Her weary eyes and mouth were drawn and tight. 'I don't know what to say.'

'Trust me, if you will. Currency restrictions and customs regulations are not my business, and I very much hope that I won't have cause to discuss these matters with the tax authorities. But I do need your assistance. Xaver Knorr offered to smuggle your goods out of the country in return for payment, did he not?'

She nodded, slowly and sadly. Her lips were tight. 'He did,' she said at last.

'Where to?'

'To Switzerland by way of Austria. He said there was a route through the Scharnitz Pass and that he had friends who could help him, both by van and then handcart through the forests, thus avoiding the customs post.'

'I imagine this would be done over a period of days or weeks.'

She nodded.

'How long has this been going on?'

'Since the beginning of the year – about a month, I suppose. A few things at a time.'

'And who is at the other end to receive the goods?'

'Swiss friends of ours in the Bernese Oberland, at Interlaken. They have a house there which they don't use and would otherwise be empty. They've rented it out to us.'

'And have your possessions arrived safely?'

'Yes. My friends wrote to me to assure me that the first batch of goods was undamaged. And, yes, we have paid Xaver well for his assistance. We understand that it is risky work for him.'

'What about further shipments? Have they all arrived?'

'We haven't heard every time a cargo is despatched. But the arrival of the first one in good order must demonstrate that Xaver has been an honest dealer.'

'Is there not a legal way to get at least some of your money out of Germany? The Haavara Agreement for instance?'

She snorted with derision.

Seb did not understand the ins and outs of Haavara. His knowledge of that treaty was that Jews could sell their effects in Germany and use the credit to buy German-manufactured goods – particularly agricultural equipment – to be exported to Palestine, where the family would then settle.

'We don't want to go to that part of the world,' Frau Sachs said. 'We've never been interested in Zionism. Under Haavara, we would have little access to our wealth anyway – and we would be forced to live in a country of dust. Totally alien to us.'

'I understand.'

'Europe is our home – but it seems not Germany now.'

'These restrictions, I believe they were brought in at the time of the 1931 crisis.'

'Yes, it's ironic that Weimar brought them in. But then the Nazis made them worse. Under the 1931 currency restrictions we're now expected to leave almost everything behind. In just five years the Reich Flight Tax, as it is called, has reached crippling levels. They claim it is sixty-five per cent, which would be bad enough, but we all know that the truth is closer to one hundred per cent once you've been forced to sell off your property at a fraction of its true value.'

Seb nodded. It was indeed grim.

'By the time we arrived in Switzerland we would have been reduced to penury. Believe me, I've looked at this in great detail. It's already happened to other Jews, and it would have been the same for us. Property, savings, jewellery – gone. We've worked hard for our money and treasures over generations and we're not cheats, whatever the local people say. Why should we be forced to give it away to Hitler and his gang?'

'Frau Sachs, you really shouldn't be saying these things to me.'

'Well, it's out in the open now. I speak only the truth.'

Seb had the parcel of photographs in his hand. He began to lay them out for her to see. 'Do you recognise any of the items in these pictures?'

Her eyes opened wide as she studied each in turn. After a couple of minutes of careful perusal, she looked up. 'Yes, yes, there are some of our belongings there,' she said. 'Where did you get these pictures?'

'Are they all your pieces?'

'No, not all, probably a third of them. But tell me about these photographs.'

Seb wanted to put a comforting arm around the woman. Realisation was dawning on her.

'I've a strong suspicion that you're being swindled, Frau Sachs. If I'm correct, these photographs amount to a sales brochure. Some of your treasures might have arrived in Switz-erland, but Knorr and his gang are selling off most of them here. So you're being robbed – and you're paying the robbers to steal from you.'

She recoiled at his words. She was shaking her head. 'No, that can't be.'

'I'm sorry.'

'This can't be true. Not Xaver.'

'Check with your Swiss friends and I suspect you'll find that only a fraction of your property has arrived. You can see it with your own eyes, here in these pictures. If they were straightforward removals men, why would they need photographs of your goods?'

'Are you sure about this, captain?'

'I'm sure.'

She sat down, overcome by the weight of the truth.

'This is terrible. Moritz was right all along. He never trusted him.'

Seb was not sure what he could say.

'And I cannot even testify against Xaver without being hauled before a court for trying to bypass export restrictions.'

'I'm afraid that's almost certainly so, but I'm not an expert. You would have to obtain legal advice on the matter.'

'What do I do, captain?'

He shrugged. This wasn't a problem he could solve. He had no dealings with the Exchange Control Office. He didn't blame these people for trying to remove their wealth from the country that was persecuting them, but nor was he in a position to help.

His only task was to find those who killed Theodor Krieger and bring them to justice, and now he finally had a good start. He could bring Xaver Knorr and his friends in for formal questioning on a number of charges, including theft and illegal export. It gave him a solid reason to hold them while he found a link between them and the murder of Krieger.

'Thank you for your honesty, Frau Sachs.'

'I suppose you'll arrest Xaver for conspiracy to defraud the tax office.'

He nodded. That was exactly what he intended to do.

'And we'll be implicated.'

'It is a serious possibility.'

'Which means we have only one option.'

'I'm sure you'll make the correct decision. But, please, Frau Sachs, it would be better if you did not tell me your plans. I'm a policeman – if I'm questioned, I will tell the truth.'

He knew what he would do in the circumstances – get across the border into Austria or Switzerland by any means possible. And do it today. Don't delay, for there might never be another chance. Put on a pair of stout boots and hike the Scharnitz Pass if necessary.

Poverty in another country was likely to be a great deal more comfortable than imprisonment in Germany.

There was no sign of Knorr or his unpleasant friends, which did not surprise him. They weren't in their favourite bar in Liliendorf, and so he approached the bartender, who clearly remembered his last visit.

'Have you seen Xaver Knorr and his gang?'

'Not today, sir.'

'Where might they be?'

He shrugged. 'I have no idea.'

'You know I'm a Munich police officer?'

'So I understand.'

'And Knorr's friends, what are their names?'

The bartender hesitated.

'Perhaps I should take you to the Presidium for questioning. I'm sure that would jog your memory.'

'Habeck and Paus.'

'Is that all?'

'Georg Habeck and Luther Paus.'

'Tell me more about them.'

'That's all I know, officer. They come in here, drink beer and schnapps, and they go away again. I only know their names from hearing others talking. They're feared locally, that's all I can tell you. People don't like to come into the bar when they're here.'

'Thank you. Where do Habeck and Paus live?'

'With Knorr. They're like a family, I suppose, though not a family I would choose for myself. They live together and drink together and probably commit crimes together.'

Seb walked to Knorr's house. It was locked and dark. Seb wondered whether he had scared him away. He went around the back to look at his outbuildings. He had only to open one door to discover the truth of what he suspected.

It was full of fine furnishings, works of art, Persian carpets, tapestries, even vases and pots of solid silver. A warehouse of astonishing value. Certainly many thousands of Reichs-marks' worth of goods.

This wasn't only about the Sachs family. Nor was it just Xaver Knorr and his two friends. The value involved suggested to Seb that this was a major criminal endeav-our, cheating dozens of wealthy Jewish families of their belongings as they tried to escape persecution – probably throughout Bavaria, maybe even further afield.

The gang would gain the confidence of the desper-ate families by taking some of their property across the Scharnitz Pass. Then they would entrust Knorr and his friends with the truly valuable stuff: the jewels, the gold, the rubies, the diamonds, none of which they would ever see again.

It was robbery on a vast scale.

And seemingly foolproof: none of the victims could ever complain. If they crossed the border and found that their property had not been delivered, who were they going to tell? As far as Knorr and the rest of his gang were concerned, it was the perfect crime.

Seb had other ideas.

28

He placed a call to the Police Presidium and spoke at length to Thomas Ruff.

'Can this be done on the quiet, Wolff?'

'It's a big crime but a small story at the moment. And we can keep it that way. We arrest Knorr and his confederates, then simply hold and interrogate them but make no murder charge. Without that element, the international press won't be interested and the local papers will do what they're told. It won't even make a ripple in the serene waters of the Olympic Games.'

'Still, I don't like it.'

'We have no option. We can't wait until the closing ceremony or we'll miss our chance to clear up Krieger's murder.'

'Don't tell me what options I have, Wolff. We'll do things my way. But I tell you this: I don't like it. And you still haven't told me who killed Krieger or why.'

'Knorr and his gang either did it – or they know the culprit. One of them will crack. Perhaps all of them. Once we have them in the Ettstrasse jail with the certainty of long sentences, someone will try to do a deal. I've seen men like this before. They'll turn on each other. Such lowlifes would slaughter their own families to save their necks.'

Seb could feel Ruff's irritation down the line. He knew he had the deputy president on the ropes.

'You'd better be right about this, Wolff. We're talking about the murder of an SS man here. Don't get sidetracked. No one cares if the Jews are being cheated. Serves them right for trying to evade export taxes.'

'As you say, sir.'

'Very well, I'll accept your assessment and we'll organise a raid. But not just Kripo men – I want representatives of the tax office along, to show we're doing our patriotic duty.'

'Just before dawn, I think. Best chance of their being at home. They'll be armed. And we mustn't involve the local police. Some of them might be in cahoots with Knorr and his friends.'

There was an angry sigh. 'At times, Wolff, you seem to think that you're the deputy president of police and I'm the mere detective.'

'Forgive me, sir. But we're both under pressure.'

'You certainly are – and don't forget it. If this goes wrong, you're done for. You'll lead the raid, Wolff. A senior uni-formed officer will accompany you, but you'll be in charge. Bring these bastards to Ettstrasse and let them stew. A night or two in solitary will prepare them nicely for your interroga-tion. In the meantime, return to Gapa and find Elena Lang's murderer.'

Not a lot to do, then. Find two killers and break a huge racket. Little time for sleep or food.

Garmisch-Partenkirchen was chaotic. Tens of thousands of people were in town for the ski races. He managed to get through at a crawl, then turned eastwards towards Mitten-wald and up into the Scharnitz Pass.

He parked the Lancia Augusta in a layby created by a snowplough. Everywhere else, the new snow was banked up into walls that flanked the road.

This was not going to be as easy as he'd anticipated. When he arrived here before, the Schupo from Mittenwald was waiting for him and guided him towards Krieger's corpse and the woodsman who'd found him. Now Seb had to find his way through dense woodland without assistance and with no landmarks to help him.

It took him almost an hour and he was getting worried that the light would soon be fading, but finally the bark of a dog led him to the woodsman's hut, perched on a narrow ledge of level ground beneath a rocky outcrop.

Seb looked through the only window and saw Hubertus Hirt with his feet up in front of a small pot-stove. The single room was lit by a hurricane lamp. Hirt was smoking a long-stemmed pipe and didn't bother to get up or take the pipe from his mouth when Seb knocked at the door and let himself in. A crucifix decorated the wall behind him, and there were religious figurines on the table: a Madonna and child, Christ on an ass.

The woodsman half turned his head but didn't really look at the newcomer. Seb recalled that about him: he didn't make eye contact.

'Herr Hirt, perhaps you remember me – Captain Wolff of the Munich Police.'

Hirt nodded. 'Yes,' he said without further inquiry or show of interest.

'The body you found.'

'Yes.'

'You might recall that I asked you whether there had been people in these woods late at night on other days. You said you didn't think so, but I noticed that you hesitated.'

Hirt said nothing, but his head edged even further away from Seb. Was the man avoiding his gaze or was that just the way he was?

'Now would be a good time for honesty, Herr Hirt.'

The man's shoulders seemed to be shrinking, tightening.

'I know you're a decent man, Hubertus. You're a Christian; you understand that you must tell the truth at all times, otherwise you'll be in sin. So tell me, how often do men come through these woods late at night?'

'Very often.'

'Every day? Every week?'

'Yes.'

'Which?'

'Every week. Two or three times a week.'

'Always at the same time?'

'After midnight.'

'Have you spoken to them?'

'Yes.'

'And they tell you that you mustn't speak a word about them?'

Hirt nodded.

'Do they threaten you?'

'They threaten Seppy.'

'Seppy? Is that your dog?'

Hirt nodded again. 'They say they'll kill him if I ever say a word about what they do. But Seppy doesn't do them any harm. Why would they kill an innocent dog?'

'And what do they do in the woods, these men?'

'If I tell you, they'll kill Seppy.'

'So long as you tell me everything, I won't let them know what you say.'

'They carry things. Boxes, chairs, pictures. Lots of things. They have handcarts.'

'Would you recognise these men?'

He nodded.

'Was the man you found dead one of them?'

Another nod.

'And do you know any of their names?'

'No. They have guns. Not for birds or rabbits. Different ones. War guns.'

'You mean pistols, rifles, sub-machine guns.'

'They wear black clothes sometimes, like Anselm Tischler but different.'

'Uniforms?' Tischler was the Mittenwald policeman.

'Different to Anselm but like him.'

'Thank you, Hubertus, you're a good man.'

'My father doesn't think so. He says I'm a worthless sod, and he beats me.'

Which was probably the reason Hubertus Hirt had withdrawn from the world, isolating himself like some latter-day hermit up in the woods. Sometimes parents had a lot to answer for.

'Perhaps you would accompany me back down to the road so I don't lose my way.'

The way back was much quicker. He took his leave of Hubertus Hirt and set off on the road back to Gapa. The darkness was closing in. The day's Olympic events must be over by now and all the spectators would be crowding into the bars.

When he arrived, he went straight to the Villa Erika and used their phone to call Gruppenführer Jena in Munich. There was no reply. Seb cursed under his breath. If he had understood what Hubertus Hirt was trying to say about the men wearing uniforms, it was more than possible that Theodor Krieger wasn't the only SS trooper involved in crime.

In which case, he had to maintain Jena's support by keeping him informed, because the SS guarded its reputation with ferocity. They would not take kindly to being investigated by an ordinary detective from the Munich police without their agreement.

No one could afford to make an enemy of the SS.

*

He had one more telephone call to make. Professor Lindner answered almost immediately.

'You just caught me, captain. I've got my coat on and I'm on my way home to have dinner with my family.'

'Did you make any progress with Elena Lang?'

'Oh, yes. Her lungs were full of water. She drowned.'

29

Hans Winter felt sick. His stomach had been churning all day; he was weak and could hardly work. The guards had shouted at him and struck him with clubs, which just made him more feeble. He begged to be allowed to be taken to Commandant Deubel, but they beat him all the more.

Now it was evening. He couldn't face food, but it was the thought of what came after the evening meal that really troubled him: roll-call.

How long would he have to stand for? One, two, three hours? In the bitter cold, desperate to relieve himself, unable to hold it in. Barely able to stand.

Winter remembered his first night here, when a man had collapsed and died at roll-call; and even in death his ordeal hadn't been over, for his corpse was thrashed and kicked. Was that the fate that awaited him this dark, cold evening?

'You don't look well, Winter 7482.'

'I'm sick, Brauer. I can hardly stand, but they just beat me. What can I do?'

'You stick it out. They don't care if you die – it's one less mouth to feed, one less Bolshevik in the Third Reich.'

Winter wanted to weep. Brauer put an arm around his shoulders. 'You're a poor specimen, Winter 7482. Your body has never done physical work and now it's protesting. I will do what I can for you.'

'Thank you, Herr Brauer.'

'Collect your food. If you don't want it, I'll have it. And

dig deep tonight – you have to survive roll-call. I can't help you if you're dead.'

Where was Hexie? The answer was obvious – out drinking with Carin. The only way Seb could find her was by touring the packed bars of the twin towns.

After learning how Elena had died, Wolff had asked Professor Lindner whether drowning could be caused by breathing in snow.

'It's not something I've encountered, but I suppose it might be just about possible if someone was buried in an avalanche – but she wasn't, was she? If I were you, I would consider a stream or lake as a likely murder site. I really must go now, so you'll have to work that one out for yourself. Good luck, Wolff.'

At least now he knew it was murder, and that she had been carried to the spot where she was found. So where exactly did she die? The Hammersbach stream, the Eibsee or Riessersee lakes? Or one of the smaller watercourses that dotted the landscape in these alpine valleys?

There was another possibility: that she was drowned in a bath or a water butt and never left Schloss Stark alive. But how could such a thing be determined? More importantly, how could he penetrate the walls of silence that enclosed the von Stark family and their strange, impenetrable world?

His heart sank when he found Hexie. She and Carin were in the Kandabar and had somehow attached themselves to the last people Wolff wanted to see.

Unity Mitford, still grim-faced. At her side, ever watchful, her myopic SS shadow, Fritz Mannheim.

Mannheim, almost the ideal Aryan specimen, save for the spectacles. Seb found himself wondering about the man. He gave so little away.

Close to them on the far side of a large table were Sophie and Werner von Stark, sitting quietly, listening, smiling, never raising their voices or making themselves at all conspicuous. Closeted in their weird, incestuous bubble.

Their reckless English friend Howard Jack held court as always, saying things about the Nazis that no German dared say. Perhaps he might be Seb's conduit, a way into that exclusive society.

Olivia Sands and Gary Tate were there, too. Laughing, talking too loudly, neither noticeably distressed by the absence of their colleague Elena Lang. Seb knew differently, of course: Olivia was riddled with fear for her friend.

Outweighing all the others, as far as Seb was concerned, was Gruppenführer Paul Jena, back from Munich. He had to talk to him.

First, though, he needed a demi-litre of Augustiner beer.

It was immediately obvious that Hexie and Carin were way ahead of the group in the matter of alcohol consumption.

'Here he is, everyone. It's lover boy Seb. Did you find your darling girl, Sebastian?' Hexie was loud, her voice slurred.

Dear God, she hadn't been telling them all about the letter from Ulrike, had she? That was a private matter.

His beer arrived, and he drank it fast.

Howard Jack, as discerning as ever when it came to emotional nuance, came straight in. 'Hexie Schuler, you are an indiscreet trollop. You will bow down and kiss your man's hand and beg his forgiveness for your injudicious blatherings.'

'It's nothing,' Seb said, his smile a rictus. 'Ancient history.' He turned to Jena. 'Please forgive me for intruding, Herr Gruppenführer, but might I take you aside for a quiet word? I tried calling you earlier.'

'Yes, of course. Where shall we go?'

'Anywhere but here.'

'Outside, then.' The SS-Gruppenführer stood up from the table. He was in uniform and, as he rose to his full height, all eyes turned to him. Such was the power of the sinister black Schutzstaffel livery.

'So, Wolff, is everything under control?'

'Elena Lang drowned, which means it had to be murder, not suicide. The problem is that we have no idea where she was killed. River, lake or –'

'Or in Schloss Stark. Is that what you're trying to say?'

'It has to be considered a remote possibility.'

Jena smiled and shook his head slowly. The SS-Gruppenführer was no taller than Seb, but in his boots and uniform, black against the white of the snow, he cut an imposing figure. 'That's one for the Brothers Grimm and I think you know it.'

'It's no fairytale. I can't rule anything out.'

'So what's your plan? To interrogate everyone at the castle? Werner and Sophie, all the staff, all the hundreds of guests from the party? The athletes, the Olympic Committee?'

'When you put it like that, sir, there are indeed problems.'

'Quite. You need to employ a little subtlety. Work out a motive, then work out who might have had such a motive. But I don't need to tell you this, do I? Because you're the detective.'

Jena was right, but Seb pressed on regardless. 'Point taken, sir. But I wanted to tell you that I've made considerable pro-gress with the murder of SS trooper Krieger. You were correct about his criminality. He was engaged in a large-scale conspiracy.'

'Tell me more.'

Seb told the story up until his second visit to the woods flanking the Scharnitz Pass. Something held him back from mentioning the testimony of the woodsman, Hubertus Hirt. Was it that he'd promised not to involve him, or something deeper and not quite understood? All he said was, 'I have no proof, but I suspect that other SS men are involved in the crime.'

Jena was looking away into the middle distance, but now he turned, and his blue eyes shone. 'You've done well, but there's still something missing. The names of these rogue SS men. How will you get those?'

'We'll get them from Knorr, Habeck and Paus. Herr Ruff has authorised a raid on their house at dawn. We'll bring them back to Munich. At least one of them will break.'

'Perfect. Keep me informed – and let me know when you've identified the SS troopers. I will not have the good name of the SS sullied. I'll see to it personally that anyone incriminated faces the full force of the law.'

'Thank you, sir.'

'No, thank *you*, Wolff. You're doing splendid work. Now back to our beers, eh?'

'Indeed,' he said, but his mind was suddenly elsewhere.

Through the gently falling snow, his eyes had strayed to the far side of the road, where two women and a man were standing in a shop doorway. One of the women was looking straight at him, her eyes wide, her blonde hair round her shoulders, just as she had always worn it.

Ulrike, his first love.

30

They stared at each other for several seconds until, as one, they began to cross the icy street towards each other.

They met in the middle of the road. Their instinct might have been to embrace, but they didn't.

'Seb Wolff.'

'Ulrike Brandt.'

'Did you get my letter?'

'Yes, I did.'

The woman he loved and lost. They had met in 1917 a few weeks before he and his friends went off to the war, Seb to be a killing machine, most of his friends to die.

When they met, she had said she could not allow him to die a virgin and so they spent the warm summer evenings making love, wherever they could but always outdoors. Rain or shine, it made no difference to them. Their bodies were everything.

Later, in the hell of the Western Front where he slaughtered young Englishmen by the score, his MG 08 rattling hot death, he received a letter telling him that she was pregnant. Her father threw her out and his own mother, Angela, took her in. It was disastrous; they never got on.

Seb saw her again in the January of the last year of the war, when she was six months gone, her perfect belly and breasts gently swollen and more glorious than ever.

But when Seb returned to the trenches and the baby came, the relationship between Angela Wolff and Ulrike Brandt became intolerable. And it did not improve when the war ended and Seb returned home.

They had changed, all three of them. The war had hardened Seb. Motherhood had made Ulrike realise how much she was missing in her young life. Angela was full of a resentment, which, as a devout Christian, she should not have felt.

For a few torrid months they all stayed under the same roof, though Ulrike was absent more and more because she wanted to dance and because she could not bear to be in the same room as Seb's mother.

In the summer of 1919, she simply left. Later a letter arrived from Berlin apologising and saying that Jurgen and Seb would both be better off without her. And that was that. No communication between them for sixteen and a half years.

And now here she was, standing in front of him.

'You look just the same,' she said. 'As handsome as ever.'

He wanted to say that she looked even more beautiful than he remembered, but he just smiled and said thank you.

'I suppose you're here for the Olympics,' she said.

'Yes, sort of. You?' It was a trite conversation, the sort of small talk that two vague acquaintances might have when they met in the street by chance.

'I'm visiting an old friend,' she said. 'A wonderful artist named Rolf Cavael. We met in Berlin, but he's living and working here in Gapa, so it made sense to come to visit him for a day or two.' She was gabbling now, talking too much. She flicked her long blonde tresses. 'That's him with the owner of the Gallery Braque, where I'll be showing.' She waved at the man and woman, and they waved back. She looked towards the door to the Kandabar, where Seb had been talking to Jena. 'You seem to have a very important friend, Seb.'

'You mean Gruppenführer Jena? I wouldn't call us friends. We're working together. I'm a police detective now.'

'I hadn't expected that. How exciting.'

She didn't look or sound excited. In fact, she looked a little alarmed.

'And what of Jurgen? Is he with you?'

'He's here in Gapa, but not with me. His Hitler Youth troop are helping usher people around.'

'Oh, Seb, he's not in the Hitler Youth, is he?'

What could he say? *You shouldn't talk like that these days, Ulrike.* Especially not to a man she once loved but now knew to be a police officer. Did she know what she was doing? He tried to make light of it. 'They all are, all his classmates, all his friends. And the girls are all in the League. I take it you don't have any other children approaching that age.'

'No, Jurgen is my only child. Does he know about me? Did you show him my letter?'

Seb nodded. 'I had to.'

'How did he react?'

'I'm not sure. He's harboured a lot of anger towards you over the years, but he was deeply moved by the letter. I really don't know how he feels. I'm not sure he knows himself.'

A car was approaching. 'We really can't talk about all this now, not standing in the middle of the road waiting to be run down. I have to go back to my friends. We have a table booked for dinner. Can we meet, Seb? Just the two of us – or three, perhaps, if Jurgen would agree to come along?'

'Yes, I think he would agree to that. But expect him to be confused. I should also mention that I have a fiancée – Hexie Schuler – she's in the bar with some other friends. I haven't shown her your letter, but I told her about it. I think she would like to meet you one day, but perhaps not yet.'

'Please bring her to my exhibition. I'd love to meet her.'

'And you, Ulrike. I believe you're married, yes?'

'What a good detective you are.'

216

He laughed. 'That was easy – I was in Munich earlier today and called in at your guest house. So where is he, your husband?'

'That's another story. But where can we meet – and when?'

'How long are you staying in Gapa?'

'Just two or three nights, with Rolf, then back to Munich.'

'Give me Rolf's address and I'll try to come by sometime tomorrow. If I can find Jurgen, I'll ask him if he wishes to come, too.'

'I'd like that.'

'If it doesn't work out, we'll catch up with you at the gallery back in Munich.'

'A very beautiful friend you have there, Wolff.' Jena was looking at him keenly. They all were.

'Just an acquaintance from a long time ago, nothing important.'

Hexie looked unhappy. 'Seb?'

'Let's talk about it later. Please, Hexie. I just want another beer, then something to eat and bed. I haven't had a lot of sleep lately.'

It was going to be a long night.

The bell went for roll-call, and Winter wanted to die. He now knew that these events could go on for hours, and his body couldn't take it. He would vomit; he would soil himself. The thought of the humiliation was worse than his fear of death.

Brauer appeared at his side. 'Quick, come with me, Winter.'

'I can't. I really can't do this.' He was freezing and shaking, yet sweating at the same time.

Brauer gripped his arm and pulled him out of the eating hall. A young SS officer, lean and tall, was there. Unsmiling, arms behind his back, looking at him with vague interest.

'This is him, Herr Troop Leader. Winter 7482.'

'Skiver, eh? Trying to get out of roll-call.'

'He's as sick as a dog, sir. Look at him. He won't survive the night without medical help.'

'What's wrong with him?'

'I think it must be food poisoning.'

'Are you suggesting we serve poisonous food?'

'No, sir. Maybe cholera, diphtheria. I'm not a medic, I don't know.'

'You'd better get him to the infirmary, hadn't you? But if the doctor says he's swinging the lead, you'll pay a heavy price. It'll be the Bunker for both of you.'

Brauer pushed him forward, holding him up as he stumbled. 'Come, Winter.'

As they made their way awkwardly towards the sickbay, Brauer whispered in his ear, 'We were lucky. He's the only guard that would have allowed this.'

'Thank you.' He said the words through a mist. He would be able to lie down, sleep, disappear from this world.

Brauer squeezed his shoulder. 'You're right – revenge is sweet for the soul. But first you must stay alive.'

'She was there, wasn't she?' Hexie demanded when they left the bar.

'Purely by chance. She's visiting a friend who lives in Garmisch and we happened to see each other across the road. It wasn't planned.'

'Why didn't you bring her in to introduce us?'

'She was with her friends. They were on their way to dinner. She wants to meet you and insists you come to the gallery. She's a married woman now. You really have nothing to worry about. She means nothing to me. It's all so long ago.'

'Is she still beautiful?'

What could he say to that? 'Yes, she is. You heard Jena.'

'I wouldn't have believed you if you said she wasn't.' Suddenly she clasped his hand. 'Oh, Seb, I'm sorry. I know none of this is your doing and I'm sure I have nothing to worry about. But I can't help it – I do worry about us. We're supposed to be married by now. And why am I not pregnant yet? Is there something wrong with me?'

He put his arms around her and kissed her, snow fluttering about their hair and shoulders. 'Perhaps we're not trying hard enough. Let's see what we can do tonight, Hexie Schuler.' By his reckoning he had three hours to make love, sleep a little and then head off back to Munich to gather the lads for the dawn raid on Liliendorf.

They left Munich in convoy at five in the morning, two and a half hours before sunrise. Seb led the way in his Lancia Augusta, with a uniformed sergeant, his second in command, at his side. Also in the car, in the back seat, was a silent tax officer from the Munich outpost of the Exchange Control Office. He avoided communication, answering Seb's inquiries in monosyllables.

The roads were icy, so he took it slow. They were followed by two police cars, each carrying four men. They all had their Walther PPs, but two of the men also carried submachine guns – one an imported Thompson, the other a new German-made Erma EMP-35.

Dawn seemed to come early at Liliendorf; when they were still a couple of kilometres out, the sky was already bright against the mountains. But it was an unnatural light, glowing yellow and orange, swirling with black-grey clouds.

The smell told Seb the truth. Smoke. The sky was lit by fire, enormous and raging. Seb accelerated. The three vehicles drew to a halt in the centre of the village. Xaver Knorr's house and outbuildings were engulfed in an inferno. Flames leapt into the sky. The houses nearest were also in danger and villagers, mostly in nightclothes, were carrying pails of water in a desperate attempt to prevent the fire from spreading.

No one had any hope of getting into the blazing buildings. If anyone was in there, they were already dead.

Seb turned to the sergeant. 'We'd better help these citizens. Organise your men. Check the fire brigade has been called.'

'Yes, sir.'

'And me?' the tax official demanded.

'There might not be much work for you this morning. But you can help these men if it's not beneath you.'

Seb had other things to do. Were Knorr, Paus and Habeck still around? Or had they fled after setting fire to the house and outbuildings to destroy evidence?

He left the sergeant and his men to deal with the blaze. Seb approached one of the villagers – old, stooped and perhaps a little too frail to be of much help. He was standing back from his neighbours, arms clasped around his chest. 'Where's Xaver Knorr?'

The man shrugged his shoulders. He was huddled in a thick coat and boots, with pyjamas showing at the knees. He wore sheepskin gloves and a hat pulled down over his ears.

'Georg Habeck? Luther Paus?'

'Dead if we're lucky.'

'Has no one seen them?'

'Not this morning. Who are you?'

'Munich police.'

'If you've come for those three criminals, it looks like you might be a little late.'

'Tell me what you know about them?'

'I know nothing and I'm saying nothing.'

'Where's the baker? You have a baker in the village, yes?'

He nodded towards one of the men hurrying with pails. 'That's Grindel.'

Seb went over to the baker and pulled him away from the line. 'You're the village baker?'

'That's me.'

'What time do you start work?'

'Five every morning in winter, four in summer.'

'So you must have seen what happened here?'

'I was working. I heard a car outside the bakery. At first I didn't think much about it, but then I smelt the smoke and came out. It was already a firestorm, so I couldn't get near the house to save anyone. I shouted and banged on the village doors, got everybody up.'

'The car – was it arriving or leaving?'

'Leaving, I'd say. Difficult to tell.'

'You didn't see anyone?'

He shook his head. 'No one. If those bastards were in there, they're goners.'

Seb talked to a couple of women and another man. Each time he got much the same evasive answer. They knew nothing about the fire. The three men who lived in the house were feared and unpopular. If they disappeared forever that would only be good for the village of Liliendorf.

He went round to the back of the blaze. In the distance, the first light was edging the mountains and hills to the east. All the outbuildings were bonfires. They had been packed with wooden furniture and other combustibles, and nothing inside would have survived.

Beyond the smoke he could smell petrol in the air. These buildings had been thoroughly drenched in accelerant to ensure that they would quickly be nothing but smouldering ash.

Seb returned to the village square and spoke with the sergeant. 'I have something else to do. I shouldn't be long. If any of the villagers says anything, listen carefully. We need to know what happened to our three suspects. There must be an outside chance someone saw something. A car left the village – were they in it or was it someone else?'

He climbed into the Lancia and drove to Valhalla. The lights were out in the Sachs house. Had they slept through the fire or were they not in? He rapped at the door but was unsurprised when no one came.

Seb turned the handle and it opened. He stepped inside and called out for Frau Sachs. No answer. He went around the house room by room. In the main bedroom he found the body of Moritz Sachs, tucked up in bed as though he were merely asleep.

On the bedside table there was a brief note.

My husband Moritz Sachs died after lunch today. He came upstairs and collapsed. Whether it was a heart attack or stroke, I do not know, but I am certain it was natural causes. I am leaving fifty Reichsmarks to pay for a decent funeral. Now I must say my farewell to Liliendorf, the village that we loved but which did not love us back.

Frau Selma Sachs

Beside the pathetic note was a small pile of money. Fifty Reichsmarks to bury a man. There would be some left over for a few drinks.

31

Had Selma Sachs started the fire at Xaver Knorr's house? Having discovered that she was being robbed by the man, she had the motive. But Seb's reading of her character did not make it seem likely. For one thing, why would she have hung about until the early hours before leaving the village? Surely she realised that she needed to leave Liliendorf with great urgency; Seb had made that clear to her.

He spent half an hour searching the house. Almost everything of value and small enough to carry had gone, but there were still quite a few interesting items. Beds, lots of clothes, boxes of papers which were probably of no consequence to anyone outside the household.

Someone else would have to deal with all this. Much as he felt sorrow for the family and was disgusted that they were driven out by persecution and ignorant bigotry, Seb didn't have the time or resources to help further. This was not his field of work.

In one of the bottom drawers of the large desk where Moritz Sachs must have sat each day to do his writing, he found a photograph album. Now *that* was worth saving.

He took it with him to the car and drove back to the village, where two fire trucks had arrived. Their crews were finally beginning to get the blaze under some sort of control, though it was clear that there would be nothing left to rescue from the ashes.

'Has anyone said anything of value, sergeant?'

'No, sir. Some of the villagers believe it was started by

the three men who lived there. Others think they might have been targeted by someone else. But these are just theories: no one saw anything. Or so they say.'

'Stay here for a while with a couple of your men and send the others back to Ettstrasse – and take the tax man wherever he wants to go. When the fire is out and the building is safe, I want you to poke through the ashes. See if anything has survived, though I doubt it. And in particular look for charred corpses.'

'Yes, sir.'

'I want your most reliable man to get a message to Deputy President of Police Ruff. Tell him I'll telephone him at the earliest opportunity.'

He returned to the car, and in the early morning light took a few quiet moments to flick through the Sachs family album. He couldn't help but be intrigued by them. Their story was one being repeated throughout Germany.

They were lovely pictures of a well-to-do family – picnics by lakes, costume parties, new babies, Selma young and remarkably pretty, Moritz, mustachioed and dark-haired, friends and relatives with wine and beer, laughing children leaping from wooden jetties into the water. An album of a happy family before the storm, a historical record of a better time. It should be passed down through the generations, not left to rot in an empty house.

One day, perhaps, Selma or one of her children might make contact and he could send it on.

Winter was asleep. The doctor had examined him dispassionately. No warm and friendly bedside manner, no inquiry into his well-being. He ordered him to cough, took his temperature, made him lie down, listened to his chest through a stethoscope, then jabbed a needle into his arm.

Winter vomited and defecated for hours. He felt raw and empty and frail. At last, he slept because he couldn't stay awake, but it was a feverish sleep and did nothing to relax him. As the night wore on, he became increasingly delirious, wondering who and where he was.

One moment he was back in Dortmund with the family he had abandoned; the next he was in the execution chamber at Stadelheim Prison, ankle deep in the blood of a man who had lost his head to the guillotine.

He thrashed and sweated and hallucinated on the thin, unforgiving palliasse that separated his skeletal body from the hard bed springs. His eyes seemed to float, looking down on his own face, hanging somewhere between life and death.

In his moments of relative lucidity, panic surged; he feared that he had been talking wildly, saying things he shouldn't be saying, revealing himself. What had he said? The very thought brought a chill to his tortured bones.

Finally, he slept properly.

Waking in mid-morning, he felt a little cooler. He was still horribly weak, but he had regained control of his bowels and his mind. A male nurse and a doctor were talking to each other a couple of metres away from him.

'Give him soup and some sweet coffee and he can go back to his barrack for the rest of the day,' the doctor said. 'He doesn't need to be here.'

Winter held up his arm. 'Please, doctor, I need to talk to Herr Deubel, the commandant.'

Perhaps his voice was too faint, for neither of the two men looked his way or seemed to have heard him. Perhaps he was still asleep, still dreaming. He couldn't be sure.

'Please . . .'

*

To Seb, the events at Liliendorf seemed almost like an ending. Selma Sachs had gone, hopefully to a better life in a foreign country, and Knorr and his confederates had disappeared. If they were dead, it would be no loss to the world; if alive, then they would be found eventually.

The truth was, however, that Deputy President Thomas Ruff would not see things that way. He would insist that the murder of SS-Scharführer Theodor Krieger be cleared up; someone had to be punished.

For the moment, Seb's overwhelming desire was to find the killer of Elena Lang. To do that, he needed eyes inside Schloss Stark. The secret to her death was somehow hidden behind those high grey castle walls.

There was one person who might help: the English poet Howard Jack.

If anyone knew what had happened inside the impenetrable fortress, it would be Jack – and he clearly loved tittle-tattle, so he might just reveal something.

The exclusive little group had mentioned that they would be skiing up at Kreuzjoch today now that the downhill races were over and the slopes were free for anyone to use. The men's slalom was being run at Gudiberg, close to the Olympic stadium and ski jumps, leaving the rest of the mountain clear.

Seb went to SD headquarters and tried to call both Jena and Ruff, but he couldn't contact either. He returned instead to the Waxenstein Guest House. No sign of Hexie or Carin, so he guessed they were watching the skiing. He found the guest-house proprietor and asked if he had any skis and boots he could borrow.

'Of course, Herr Wolff. We always have equipment for our guests. I'm sure there will be something in your size. Poles and smoked goggles, too, yes?'

'Thank you.'

'Oh, and there was a call for you, Herr Wolff. It sounded rather important. A Professor Lindner from the university, if I recall correctly.'

'May I use your phone?'

'In our private rooms. Follow me, sir.'

'I took another, closer look at Elena Lang,' Lindner said without any small talk introduction. 'I found what looked like a needle mark in her left buttock. I took a blood sample and sent it to the toxicology lab.'

'And?'

'She had a hefty dose of heroin in her system.'

'Enough to kill her?'

'Possibly, but she drowned first. What's clear, though, is that she would have been knocked out by a dose like that so she could have had no idea what was happening to her. Whether she injected herself or had it done to her is for you to determine.'

He collected the borrowed skis and boots and set off towards the lifts that would take him up to the Kreuzjoch. At the top he looked out over the mountains and valleys, all now white as far as he could see. Suddenly he felt new life surging through his exhausted brain.

There was no sign of Howard Jack or the others, so he skied a few runs and felt a new man for it. The smoke from the Liliendorf fire cleared from his lungs, the air was fresh and cold, and he could almost forget the tribulations that beset him on all sides.

But there was something still nagging him: where the hell was Sergeant Winter? Perhaps it was all going brilliantly in Dachau. But, then again, what if it wasn't?

It was a marginal decision whether to put through a call and get him out. Seb didn't want to interfere and ruin his sergeant's investigation. He'd leave it another day but no more.

Half an hour later he found the group from Schloss Stark by the top of the lift at Kreuzjoch.

'Just in time, Sebastian,' Howard Jack said. 'We're about to race. You absolutely must join us.'

Seb looked at the entitled little band: Howard, Unity, Fritz, Werner, Sophie and the other Englishman he had met at Schloss Stark. What was his name? Lunn. Peter Lunn, that was it, the downhill racer. He must have had his slalom race. Well, if he was joining in this little event, it was pretty obvious who was going to win.

Fritz Mannheim read his thoughts. 'Unity and Sophie go first. You, me, Werner and Howard a minute later, and Peter two minutes behind us. Fair, yes?'

'Why not? I'll give it a shot.' Seb had only skied for a couple of days this winter, but he always felt comfortable on the slopes, and he loved nothing more than a schuss through the trees on fresh powder.

'And where is the delightful Hexie today?' It was Howard Jack, the only one of this group who ever showed interest in anyone but themselves.

'Watching some event or other, I think. Maybe the ice-skating.'

'Poor girl, how deathly dull. Anyway, race time. Peter, you say bang and the girls can set off. Last one home buys the champagne.'

'Bang!' Peter Lunn said.

Sophie and Unity stared at each other for a split second, then turned, pointed their skis over the lip and pushed off with their poles. Within thirty seconds they had disappeared. Lunn kept his eyes on his watch for a minute, then said,

'Bang!' again. Werner streaked off into the lead with Mannheim not far behind.

Seb could have kept up, but he had other ideas. He wanted to stay close to Jack, who had clearly not done as much skiing as the others and quickly caught an edge and fell, tumbling down the slope, his skis twisting his body. Seb cruised up behind him.

'Anything broken?'

'My spirit.' He was struggling to untangle his skis, pulling himself to his feet with a helping hand from Seb.

'Let me help. Fritz and Werner can fight it out.'

'No, you go.'

'I've been hoping to talk to you.'

'That sounds a bit ominous.'

'Not at all. I know you make light of everything, but I'm sure you're as worried as I am about Elena. What was going on in Schloss Stark? All that stuff about Werner dragging her away when she tried to approach Herr Goebbels.'

'Oh, I think she must have worked herself up and was about to make a scene. She'd had a few too many drinks. Werner did the decent thing to prevent her embarrassing herself.'

'So it's all true, the rumours about her and the minister of propaganda?'

'Did you ever doubt it? I'm told he has his way with anything he can get his grubby little paws on, but particularly famous actresses. The ones that comply get all the top film parts. Not one of the best-kept secrets in the upper echelons of the Third Reich.'

They were skiing slowly, long turns. Peter Lunn rocketed past without seeming to notice them.

'You don't seem very enamoured of the regime, Howard. Why are you here?'

'Governments come and go. I love this country, particularly Bavaria. Been holidaying here since I was a child, but clearly haven't done as much skiing as the rest of you. But, tell me, you keep on about Elena . . . Do you have cause to think something bad has happened?'

'That's the question I wanted to ask you.'

They were in the trees now. Jack stopped. 'I don't know Elena that well, Seb, but as soon as I met her I felt rather sorry for her. I'm used to people like Unity and the von Starks – I've been around them all my life. They're spoilt brats, full of themselves, scorn the man in the street and yet none of them have done a day's work in their sorry little lives. But Elena, she's new to it all and a little out of her depth. A very serious young woman, I suspect. I know I must seem rather a snob to you – but I'm not really. It's just an affectation. Not so with Unity, Sophie and Werner. They're ghastly, aren't they? And as for Fritz, he's just here to keep Unity intact for the Führer. Ha, ha.'

'What about Peter Lunn?'

'Old friend of the Mitfords. He feels the same way as me about the Nazis. He's the ski team captain but refused to march at the ceremonial opening or attend the banquet. He's a good fellow. But my point is that Elena doesn't really fit in. They latched on to her because of her star status, but to them she's like a curious new beast in a zoological garden. Something to be gazed at before they move on to the next exotic creature.'

'Will you do me a favour?'

Jack frowned. 'Depends what you're asking.'

'Just keep your ears open at Schloss Stark. Who did Elena Lang leave with? And where did she go? Someone has to know. My problem is that the authorities here don't want anything to distract from the Olympics, so I can't even put out a general alert for her.'

'A mystery, eh? I love a mystery. Margery Allingham, darling Agatha, and my favourite of all, Dot Sayers. Count me in, old man. And how about après-ski at the Schloss? Are you coming?'

'Am I invited?'

'You're skiing with us, so you après-ski with us. Those are the rules.'

32

By midday, Hans Winter was still weak, but his thinking was straighter. And that made him panic all the more. He was stuck here in Dachau with no way out.

The agreement with Commandant Deubel was that he would stay in the camp as long as necessary. It hadn't occurred to Winter that it would be impossible to get a message through to Deubel, that the guards were a law unto themselves, and that the prisoners were totally at their mercy. Surely Deubel would be worried about him? And what of Captain Wolff? Was he not concerned?

The nurse came to him and told him he was being discharged. He could spend the rest of the day in his bunk in the barrack-room but then it would be back to normal working.

'I need to talk to Herr Deubel.'

'No one gets to talk to him.'

'But I shouldn't be here.'

'None of us should.'

It dawned on Winter that the nurse was an inmate, too, not on the staff. 'Is the doctor around? Can I not talk to him?'

The nurse put his hands on his hips and stared hard at his patient. 'You need to be careful, Winter 7482. The doctors here are *not* on our side. They're part of the apparatus. If you want to stay alive, your best bet is to get a job in the kitchens. Better food and you won't break your back. What skills have you got?'

Winter shook his head. 'None of any use.'

'How did you earn your bread before you came here?'

'I was a clerk in the city hall in Dortmund.'

'You're right, no value to anyone. You're not going to be sewing or doing carpentry in a hurry. Your only option is to make something up. I told them I was a hospital porter, that's how I got this little number.' His eyes widened as though he had an idea. 'Mind you, there might be an opening in the camp orderly room – registering arrivals, departures, deaths each day. All you need for that is fluent German and legible writing.'

Fine. Except Hans Winter had no intention of staying in this hellhole long enough to be assigned a comfortable berth in the orderly room.

Seb was on his way back to the Waxenstein Guest House when he ran into Jurgen. He was with a group of Hitler Youth friends but broke away when he saw his father, clicking his heels and performing an extravagant straight-arm salute which Seb reluctantly mimicked.

'Still not perfect but you're learning, old man.'

'And I'm honoured that you should deign to come over and talk to me.'

They both managed to laugh. Maybe one day they would achieve a meeting of minds, an agreement to disagree.

'Anyway,' Seb said, 'I'm glad to have found you, because something happened last night. I was walking out of the bar and I saw your mother across the street. She's here in Gapa, visiting an old friend.'

The blood drained from Jurgen's face. 'My mother is here?'

Seb nodded. The confusion in his son's eyes was all too obvious. Seb reached out and touched his shoulder. 'Do you want to go and see her?' The moment he uttered the words, he realised he hadn't thought it through.

'I don't know. I suppose so, yes.' Jurgen winced. 'I'm not sure – what do *you* think?'

'She very much wants to meet you.'

'What's she like?'

'The same as she was.'

Jurgen raised his eyebrows. 'That's not very helpful. I wasn't much more than a year old when she left.'

'I'm sorry, that was a stupid thing to say. Well, where do I start? She looks like you. She's very beautiful. As for her character, she was always strong-willed and opinionated. Very sure of her own mind. Never got along with your grandmother. These things can change as you get older but not always.'

'Are you saying that she's not a National Socialist?'

'I haven't asked her about her politics but given what I know of the old Ulrike, I'd be surprised if she was.'

Jurgen looked at his wristwatch. 'I certainly can't go right now. We have to report back and then we have an hour or two to ourselves. My friends and I already have plans – torchlight tobogganing.'

'Good idea.' Seb was suddenly unsure about the whole thing with Ulrike. 'Perhaps we should leave it until we're back in Munich.'

'Why is that better?'

How could he explain to his son that he was worried about the Hitler Youth uniform that the lad so loved and that Ulrike so obviously loathed? This needed talking through. Both mother and son would have to put politics to one side, and Seb wasn't sure either was capable of that.

'Trust me on this. Much better that you meet her some-where calmer when we're home.'

'You're worried about the uniform, aren't you?'

Seb paused, then nodded. 'I know nothing about her life now, but the Ulrike of old would not have been keen.'

*

Still no sign of Hexie in their room, but she had left a note. *Carin and I have gone to the Kandabar.*

He could join them, but the après-ski party at the castle beckoned. Hexie had been invited, too, but Carin hadn't. Anyway, the truth was he wanted to go alone.

After returning the skis and boots, he made another couple of quick calls. Once again he couldn't get through to Gruppenführer Jena or Thomas Ruff, but he managed to talk to the sergeant who had accompanied him to Liliendorf.

'Three bodies in the house, sir. Charred like badly burnt meat. Unrecognisable.'

Knorr, Paus and Habeck. It had to be.

'Have you removed them for post-mortem examination?'

'Yes, sir.'

'Very good. Leave it with me. I will liaise with the laboratory.'

He placed a last call, to Professor Lindner.

'Very good of you to send me three lumps of charcoal, Wolff. What am I supposed to do with them?'

'Is there any way of identifying them? Their teeth, perhaps?'

'I suppose there's an outside possibility some local dentist would be able to look at them and recall their work.'

'Send over the teeth to Ettstrasse, then. I'll get someone on to it.'

'Oh, and there are the bullets.'

'Bullets?'

'Thirty-two of them in all. Fifteen in one body, ten in the next and seven in the other. They were riddled with machine-gun fire, at a guess.'

'So dead before the fire?'

'I don't think there's much doubt about that.'

'Have you told anyone at Ettstrasse?'

'Only you, Wolff.'

'Don't tell anyone else, professor. Same rule applies – no murders in Bavaria while the Games last.'

The drive up to Schloss Stark was strikingly beautiful, the last of the day's sunshine cresting the lower mountains to the west. The guards had been told to expect him so he was waved through, then quickly escorted to the drawing room, where he was welcomed by a roaring wood fire in the hearth.

A pair of handsome gun-grey Weimaraner dogs with mesmerising eyes sniffed and nuzzled his legs. The heavy metal boules clacked and rang as the assembled guests, all still in ski gear, played a noisy version of pétanque across the carpeted floor.

Everyone was drinking schnapps.

Howard Jack made a beeline to welcome him, while Unity stood at a distance and adopted her customary glare. Seb had a dark sensation that she would destroy him one day, just as his uncle, Christian Weber, had warned.

'Lord Wimsey at your service,' Jack said with a sweep of the arm.

Seb smiled. He understood the reference, having read a couple of Dorothy L. Sayers's books during his years at sea, desperately battling to learn English. 'And where is your valet? Bunting, isn't it?'

'Good try, but no, it's Bunter, not Bunting. Bunting are those little flags strung around village greens on fête days.' Jack looked towards the door. 'What, no Hexie?'

'Otherwise engaged.'

'You're going to lose that girl if you're not careful.'

Seb was beginning to have doubts about asking Jack for help. How much did he know about the man? Yes, he was friendly, good company and intelligent, but that didn't make him innocent or trustworthy. He was, however, Seb's only chance to uncover Elena Lang's missing hours in this castle.

Peter Lunn, the downhill racer, strolled over with Unity. 'How are you at boules or pétanque or whatever this stupid game is?'

'I've never played it,' Seb said. 'You're a remarkable skier, Peter. How did an Englishman get so good?'

'We spent all our winters in Mürren. Still can't believe I skied so tamely in Friday's downhill, though. Didn't take enough risks.'

'Where did you come?'

'I'd rather not say. Nothing to be proud of.'

'Oh, Peter, you were never going to beat the Germans, were you?'

'Of course not, Bobo. They're the master race, aren't they?'

'And you're extremely rude about them. I don't like you at all.'

Lunn grinned. He clearly took great pleasure in baiting Miss Unity Mitford. 'Did you know that Bobo prays to her darling Adolf by her bed each night while giving the Hitler salute?'

'Oh, that's absolute nonsense and you know it.'

'But you told me yourself, Bobo.'

'I was teasing you.'

'I believe it. You Mitfords, you're all as mad as cuckoos.'

Seb listened without comment.

'Anyway, Sebastian,' Lunn continued, 'I'm told you're a policeman and that you're presently looking for the gorgeous Elena Lang, who seems to have bolted.'

'I am looking for her, yes. Do you perhaps have any idea where she might have got to?'

'No, but I would very much like to know. She's a friend of the family, and we want to invite her over to England at Easter. But how can I do that if I can't find her? Perhaps you'd keep me informed?'

'I'll do my best.'

The door opened and all eyes turned. It was Gruppen-führer Paul Jena, accompanied by a pretty young woman with braided fair hair. She looked bored, here under suffer-ance. The Mouse-Frau must be back home in the kitchen, Seb supposed. Time for the mistress to have an outing.

The SS major general was both friendly with the younger people but also a bit distant, rather like a celebrated but aloof uncle. His every glance, smile or nod seemed to be letting them all know who had the power in this room. He was in his SS uniform, standing straight, blue eyes unblinking, as if seeing and noting everything.

He was a hard man to read, but that was the point, wasn't it? He'd been trained well by Reinhard Heydrich. Let every-one know that you are their superior. Intimidate them with the cut of your uniform, your bearing, your cold gaze. Make them fear you and defer to you.

Seb approached him, nodding to the young woman on his arm. 'Good afternoon, fräulein.'

She met his eye briefly but didn't smile. Nor did she ven-ture a name or any other kind of response. Jena did not deign to introduce her.

'Heil Hitler, Herr Gruppenführer.'

'And you, Wolff. You're here again, I see.'

'Yes, sir, I was kindly invited by Mr Jack. I'm sure he told you about our little race today.'

'Ah, yes. Werner beat the English racer. As you'd expect.'

'Indeed, sir.' Seb wasn't going to mention that Werner von Stark had won by less than a metre. 'I'd been hoping to talk to you, Herr Gruppenführer. Have you heard any of the news from Liliendorf?'

'You mean the fire? Yes, I've heard about that. Shocking news. Any idea what's behind it, Wolff?'

'Not as yet, sir, but we're certain it was started deliberately. Might we have a brief word in private?'

'I'm at your service.'

Seb didn't think for a moment that Paul Jena would ever be at his service, but he was being helpful, whether on the orders of Propaganda Minister Goebbels or not. The truth was that Jena was a great deal more easy-going than Seb had anticipated.

They stepped back a few paces, out of earshot of the others.

'There were three bodies found in the smouldering ashes of Knorr's house. Burnt to a cinder. As yet unidentifiable, but most likely Knorr, Habeck and Paus.'

Jena's shoulders stiffened, his eyes widened. 'Good God, how did you let this happen, Wolff?'

'They were murdered.'

'Damn it, man, you were too slow. We needed to hear what these men had to say for themselves. Find out who else was involved. Find the killer of Theodor Krieger. The death of an SS trooper cannot go unpunished.'

'There's more. The fire didn't kill them – they were already dead from a burst of machine-gun fire.'

The idea that Jena was easy-going evaporated. He looked furious. 'Who did this? Why did you wait hours to raise a raid? And why the hell are you here now when you should be rounding up the killers? Who knows about this?'

'Many people know about the fire, but only three people know about the bullet wounds: you, me and Professor Lindner. No one else apart from the killers.'

'Keep it that way. Now get out there and find these dirty murderers.' His voice was quiet and angry, as though Seb were somehow responsible for these shocking events. That was the SS way. Instil fear into your underlings.

Seb could not be intimidated. He sometimes wondered whether it was some psychological flaw in his character, but he had lost his fear in the trenches. Hold a gun to his head and he felt nothing. Death meant nothing, a mere return to the vast emptiness of eternity, the same place you inhabited in the billions of years before you were born.

Yet threaten those he loved, and he would feel unbearable terror and unspeakable rage.

'Herr Gruppenführer, I cannot spend all my time on the incident at Liliendorf. There is still another matter to consider. The death of Elena Lang. We have no sighting for her outside this castle, sir. That is why I'm here. I need to work out her last movements.'

Jena nodded slowly. 'Of course you do. Forgive me, Wolff. Elena Lang's death is just as important – in fact, a great deal more so. People will be shocked and horrified by her murder when the news is eventually released to the public. By contrast, no one will give a damn about the killing of three criminals.'

33

The sky was cloudless, darkness was falling, and the temperature was dropping rapidly. He drove slowly, aware that the roads were icy and dangerous.

His mind was a long way away. The whole time he'd been in the rather modestly titled drawing room at Schloss Stark, he'd barely been able to take his eyes off Gustav Klimt's portrait of the anonymous woman. He now felt almost certain that he had seen that face before.

She was dark-haired, her eyes black but alive, her flawless skin lit by gold leaf and swirls of silver.

There was one person in Garmisch-Partenkirchen who might help him, might somehow confirm his suspicions.

He asked for directions to the house of the artist Rolf Cavael. He found it easily, at the western end of Garmisch. It was an old, twisted farmhouse with darkened wood aged over centuries. It stood at the edge of a landscape of snow-covered fields, a scattering of hay-barns stretching into the foothills of the Alps.

Lights were on in the house, so he knocked at the door. Ulrike answered it. She was dressed casually in a rather Bohemian manner: a long multicoloured skirt with some Asian design, a fine white blouse, hair an uncombed flaxen cascade.

She met his eyes and they looked at each other for a moment, as though the lost years might magically move into the other's mind and all their secrets would be known. She broke the spell. 'I was hoping it might be you.'

He smiled. 'May I come in?'

'Is Jurgen not with you?'

'I told him I saw you but we agreed it would be better to meet up next week when we're all back in Munich.'

'I understand.'

'Do you, Ulrike? Are you sure? The thing is that this could be a very difficult meeting. You were clearly appalled when you heard he was in the Hitler Youth – and he will be appalled if he discovers you are anything other than a fervent supporter of the National Socialist movement. In fact, he already has his suspicions.'

'And you?'

'You didn't seem too happy to learn that I'm a police detective.'

'I meant how do you manage to live with a Nazi son?'

'For all you know, Ulrike, I might be a Nazi, too.'

'But you're not, are you.' It was a statement, not a question.

'Perhaps you're right, but that's my business. My job is not to take political sides, but to try to maintain some semblance of justice in trying times.'

'And at home?'

'At home I do my best. The truth is that Jurgen and I have our disagreements. Blazing rows, actually, but I have to try to find a way to live and let live. It doesn't always work, but we muddle through. He'll go into the Reich Labour Service soon, so he won't have to put up with me for much longer.'

'The labour force? Why not university?'

'My question entirely, but it's a futile argument. His mind is made up.'

She sighed. 'Anyway, come in, please. It's cold on the doorstep.'

'Is your artist friend here?'

'No, he's out with a pal. We have the house to ourselves for an hour or two.'

'What about your husband?'

She shifted uneasily.

'I'm sorry, I shouldn't have asked. It's none of my business.'

'I can't talk about it at the moment. Perhaps next time, in Munich. Let's feel our way first, shall we?'

He followed her through to a warm room, where she offered him a drink. 'We have some wine if you're interested. Or beer?'

'Wine would be a treat. Thank you.'

While she poured, he looked around the room. There were artworks, but on a much smaller scale than the drawing room at Schloss Stark. And these pictures were of a very different nature – not at all figurative. Curious curling shapes and colours. For a moment he seemed to see an eye, then wondered whether it might be an amoeba.

It did not seem the sort of art that would find favour with Hitler, but Seb rather liked it.

'They're all by Rolf. Don't you think they're wonderful?'

'Yes, I like them.'

'My style is not so very different, but you'll see that when you come to my opening.'

They clinked glasses, and he sipped the red wine. 'Believe it or not,' he said, 'I was rather hoping you might be able to help me with some queries of an artistic nature.'

'How very intriguing.'

'Have you heard of Gustav Klimt?'

'What a ridiculous question. Of course I have. He is a god, the Michelangelo of our times. I would kill to be half as good as him.'

Seb produced the photograph album that he had taken

from the house of Selma Sachs at Liliendorf. 'Look through there, take your time and tell me what you see.'

'What is this? Who are these people?'

'A family. A case I'm working on. Just keep an open mind.'

She shrugged. 'All right, then, Herr Mystery.'

For the next five minutes she looked carefully at the thirty or so pages, sometimes with three, sometimes four pictures on each page. The Sachs' home, Valhalla, appeared in quite a few of them, also lakes with mountain backdrops. Lots of children.

Each picture had a handwritten caption in black ink. Names, places, dates.

Ulrike looked at some photographs longer than others. It was obvious to Seb that she was drawn to the lakeside pictures more than the others.

Finally, she looked up, the book open on her lap. Seb could see that she had been staring at a series of pictures dated 1909 with about a dozen people at the edge of a lake. The caption said *Schörfling am Attersee*.

'I've been there,' Ulrike said. 'It's a beautiful lake, about an hour's drive east of Salzburg.'

The caption included a list of names. Ulrike pointed at them. 'You see that? "Gust and Emilie". Those two people in the voluminous robes but a bit blurry, close to the water's edge. The man with the beard and the thinning hair? I would swear that is Gustav Klimt. I've seen many pictures of him. That is Klimt. Seb, where did you get this album? This is incredible. Who are the other people?'

'I can't tell you any more at the moment,' he said. 'Perhaps one day I will.'

He was now certain. The photograph proved that Selma knew Gustav Klimt, and that was enough to dispel Seb's doubts. The woman in the Klimt painting at Schloss Stark was the young and beautiful Selma Sachs, before the war, a quarter of a century ago.

So how had her portrait ended up in the possession of the von Stark family?

That led to an even bigger question: what the hell was he supposed to do with such information, given the extraordinary power of those involved?

34

There was only one answer, and it was not a comfortable one. Xaver Knorr and the rest of his gang had somehow made contact with the von Stark family and sold them the Klimt portrait of Selma.

That the von Starks claimed not to know the identity of the sitter suggested that they did not acquire the painting directly from Selma and Moritz Sachs. So how did a lowlife like Xaver Knorr gain access to Germany's most wealthy family? There had to be an intermediary.

'Another glass of wine, Seb?'

It was too good an offer to turn down. 'Thank you, yes.'

As Ulrike was pouring, he noted that she was looking at him keenly, perhaps trying to find the boy in the man.

'I may be foolish and misguided, but I feel I still know you, Seb. I don't think you've changed that much. Yes, you've had to take on great responsibility and you have to uphold the law, but I get a powerful sense that you've retained your decency and honour.'

'If you say so.'

'Am I wrong?'

'I hope not. But it's for others to make judgements about my character, not me.'

'I want you to know that I'm thinking of moving to Munich. Berlin isn't safe for me any more.'

That took him aback. 'Now that *is* big news, Ulrike.'

'Yes, for me, too. I love Berlin.'

'Why is it unsafe?' Even as he asked the question, suspicions began to form in his mind. 'And why come back to Munich?'

'The second part is easy – my son is here, and I know the city.'

'And the first part?'

'My politics.'

Seb paused. 'You're a Communist.' Even as he said the word, he felt a cold dread.

'Of course I am, as every rational person should be.'

'Then you're in danger.'

'Yes, I am. I wasn't going to talk about my husband, but I think I must. His name is Andreas, and he's in prison. He's been tortured by the Gestapo. They will kill him and I'm scared, Seb – terrified.'

This was bad news, and not just for Ulrike. Simply knowing a Communist in the fourth year of the Third Reich could put you under risk of dawn arrest. Family, friends, workmates – all might be targets.

'And your art exhibition – is this simply a way to come to Munich?'

'No, that was arranged months ago. I've shown my work elsewhere, but it's getting harder. My art isn't appreciated by the Nazis, and I've been banned by the council in several towns and cities.'

'Because they don't like your politics?'

'No, they don't know about my politics; it's because they don't approve of my art. They call it degenerate and say it would corrupt the young.'

'What makes you think anything will be better for you in Munich?'

'I live in hope, that's all. Either I try or I just give in to them. And you are here, and Jurgen. I'm running out of options.'

'Have you considered moving abroad – London, Paris?'

'I can't leave Germany while Andreas is still here. That would be the ultimate betrayal.'

Seb could not help raising a quizzical eyebrow. He had rather thought that abandoning your own baby son might be quite high on the betrayal register.

'I take it you and Andreas are both deeply involved in your cause?'

'Yes. We have suffered greatly. I've been beaten up in the street by the Brownshirt gangs.'

'Has it occurred to you that by bringing yourself back into Jurgen's life you might be endangering *him*? And what if he learns about your politics and denounces you? He wouldn't be the first child in Munich to have a parent or other relative arrested. I've sometimes wondered whether he might be tempted to have a word with the BPP about me.'

'You really think he would denounce me?'

'No, I don't. But I'm not sure that you're going to like each other. I'm worried, Ulrike – your appearance here has come at a difficult time for the boy.'

'I can only hope that we'll be the best of friends. I carried him in me for nine months. My blood flows through his veins. I pray that he'll forgive me for letting him down.'

It was strange, he reflected later when making love to Hexie, how easily the haunted dreams of a lost but unforgotten love could be erased. All it needed was to meet them in the flesh once more and experience the reality, not the fantasy.

Ulrike Brandt, now Dahlen, was even more beautiful than she had been. The years had treated her well. But whatever he had felt for her was now gone. The scales had fallen from his eyes.

She was putting her own interests above those of her child.

*

Hans Winter was taken to his barrack-room and told that he could rest until the evening meal. Then it would be back to normal: roll-call, sleep, breakfast, back-breaking work.

He was weak and could barely stand, but everyone in the infirmary had ignored his protests and refused to listen to his pleas for an interview with the commandant. He had begun to realise that he would never leave this place alive.

In the meantime, he was thinking about Brauer, who had helped him get into the infirmary. Was that the act of a murderer? Winter still wanted to know the truth about the man; officially at least that was the main reason he was here. His instinct was that Brauer must be innocent of his son-in-law's murder, but there was still a nagging doubt in his mind. *Revenge is sweet for the soul,* that was what he had said.

Did that sound like a confession? Not enough for a court of law, surely, and Captain Wolff would not be convinced.

Just before dark a new inmate arrived. He looked in a bad way, his face bruised and bloody. The guard escorting him pointed to a bunk two below Winter's, then clubbed him once more around the head and warned him of the consequences of bad behaviour or attempted escape. Keep clean, shave every day, obey orders, work hard, and you will leave here a decent German. Break the rules and we will break you.

Winter listened without interest. The same words had been used on him.

But his insides were churning again. This time it wasn't food poisoning, but the battered face of the newcomer.

He had seen that face before: had arrested the man himself, for being drunk and dropping litter outside the Wittelsbach Palace just a year earlier. It wasn't really Winter's place as a political police officer to have dealings with such scum, so he had let him off with a stern warning.

But that wasn't the point. The problem was that there was a chance that the man, whose name he had forgotten, might recognise him. All he could hope was that he had been so inebriated that the event – and Winter's face – had slipped from his memory.

The alternative? Word would get around that he was a BPP officer, and that would be extremely bad for his health.

Seb was wondering about the murders of the common criminals Knorr, Paus and Habeck. It seemed to him that they were expendable men who, having come to the notice of the Munich police department, had outlived their usefulness and so had paid the ultimate price.

Safer dead than interrogated.

They would not be missed, and their masters in the SS were secure. Who could touch the untouchables?

Which brought him back to the Klimt portrait of Selma Sachs.

If the SS were involved, it did not take a genius to consider the possibility that the von Starks had bought the painting from one of their officers. And, given Werner and Sophie's status and the rarefied atmosphere in which they lived, the supplier of the great artwork might well be someone with links to their elite circle.

Two names came to mind: Fritz Mannheim and Paul Jena. The von Starks probably knew others, but those were the two Seb was aware of.

Mannheim was supposedly a friend and protector of Hitler's English maiden, but perhaps he had a profitable little business on the side selling on the finest works of art from fleeing Jews.

The same could undoubtedly be said of Jena. Consorting with the wealthiest people in the land, Jena might have been struck by the idea that he would like some riches of his own.

He was a man from humble beginnings. Nazism had brought him immense power, but he would not be the first man to desire wealth, too. An SS officer's salary alone would not make him rich. Selling on looted valuables and works of art certainly would.

And there was something else. Doing favours for one of the great families might just persuade them to admit him to their aristocratic circle. Who could not be impressed that Jena had found such a rare work of art – and probably at a favourable price. Come dine with us, Paul, ski with us, bring your wife, impress your mistress.

It occurred to Seb that he had only spoken to one SS officer about his initial findings at Liliendorf, and that was Jena. Seb had also told him about the planned police raid. Jena had seemed interested and helpful, congratulating Seb on his work.

But then he would, wouldn't he? It gave him time. Time to organise three murders.

An hour before the Munich cops arrived, Knorr and his two comrades were taken out of the game. Riddled with bullets and burned to black ash, they were not going to name names. Very convenient.

As he drove away from the old farmhouse where Ulrike was staying, Jena's face came back to Seb: capable of charm; underneath it, nothing but cold arrogance.

Seb had to play this very carefully. Paul Jena was not the sort of man you competed against with any hope of winning.

If he had ordered the killing of three of his own men simply to prevent their interrogation, he wasn't going to baulk at a small thing like riddling Seb Wolff with bullets. And, if his victim's family happened to get caught in the crossfire, that was just the way things were.

So where now? One police officer against the might of Germany's wealthiest family and the unchallenged power of Himmler's SS.

He couldn't take this to Thomas Ruff. Only one man could help: the Pig.

35

Seb caught up with his uncle, Christian Weber, at the House of Artists in Munich. It was mid-morning, and he was already deep into the brandy, sitting alone in what passed for a meditative mood.

It was the time of day when he did deals. Petitioners approached him as though he were a king. Some begged for investment in their businesses; others had properties to sell or loans which they were struggling to repay. Christian Weber was always open to offers and he drove very hard bargains, which was how he had come to be so rich that he owned half of Munich. Not bad for a former stable boy.

For every thousand Reichsmarks he made, it was said he gained an extra centimetre to his waist. No one except Adolf liked him and everyone called him the Pig, but never to his face.

Every time Seb approached him for assistance of any kind, he felt dirty. But sometimes there was no option.

Weber looked up from a notebook in which he was examining a list of figures.

'Hello, boy, what brings you here?'

'You, uncle. I'm surprised you're not at the Olympics.'

'Can't stand all that ice and snow. Give me the smell of horse shit and the steaming flanks of a thoroughbred. That's where my love lies.'

'And money.'

'And money. How else would I have bought the Riem Racecourse and all my beautiful fillies? Take a seat, boy. Give me the news from Gapa. Did you get into the inner sanctum of the von Starks and find your actress?'

'With your help, uncle, yes. I've been meaning to thank you.'

'Oh, you'll pay me back one day. I do favours for friends; they do favours for me. That's how the world turns. So how can we help each other today?'

'I wanted to ask you about SS-Gruppenführer Paul Jena. I take it you know of him.'

Weber blinked, then lurched forward, his fat fingers gripping the table. 'Are you mad, boy? Keep your damned voice down!' His face strained red. 'We're not alone here.'

Seb simply smiled. He had the Pig's attention.

'Do you have a death wish? Come with me.' Christian raised his great bulk from his throne-like chair and pushed the table forward. 'We're going for a little walk. Just you and me.'

'Very well.'

Weber waved to a waiter. 'I'll be back in ten minutes. If anyone arrives for me, give them a drink and tell them to hang on.'

'Yes, sir.'

Weber thrust a coin into the waiter's palm and lumbered towards the stairs. Seb followed and soon they were out in the cold fresh air on Lenbachplatz, striding along the slushy pavement in the vague direction of the Residenz. When he was sure no one was close enough to hear, Weber stopped and turned his bulging, sausage-chomping face to his nephew.

'What do you know about Jena?' His body stank of cologne, his breath of halitosis and brandy. God alone knew how the dancers and working girls could bear to be close to him, his rancid flesh against their glowing young skin.

'That's exactly what I asked you, uncle.'

'But why – why are you asking? Have you any idea who you're dealing with? Do you really want to cross Paul Jena?'

'He doesn't scare me.'

'He should do. He would cut out your heart and fry it for his supper. You think I'm corrupt, boy? I'm the baby Jesus compared to Paul Jena. He uses the Munich SS as his private army of tax collectors.'

'What if I told you he was stealing works of art and other valuables from Jews trying to get their wealth out of the country? It's a crime on an enormous scale.'

'I would ask you what your point was. Am I supposed to be surprised? I always knew you were naive; I didn't think you were stupid.'

'So there's nothing I can do?'

'There's nothing you can do.'

'And what if there were murders?'

'That would depend on who was killed. Anyone important? God in heaven, boy, what have you got yourself into?'

'I've got myself into nothing. I'm investigating various linked crimes and the evidence is beginning to point in a certain direction. Do I just stop investigating?'

'I can't believe we're having this conversation. Your wonderful mother is my sister. We share the same blood, but then I listen to you and I think, how is that possible? You don't have the sense you were born with. And the answer to your question is, yes, you stop investigating.'

'Then there is to be no justice in the Third Reich. Is that what you signed up for when you chose to follow Adolf Hitler?'

Weber glared at his nephew, then shook his head. 'Who else have you talked to about this?'

'No one.'

'Not even that pathetic, cowering, deputy president of police?'

'Certainly not Jena's part in it, anyway. You may think I'm stupid, uncle, but I promise you I'm not *that* stupid.'

Weber sighed and his enormous belly wobbled. 'What are we going to do with you, boy? It'll break your mother's heart if you get yourself killed.'

'Perhaps you can help in some way?'

'What? And get *myself* killed?'

'With two of us, we might have a chance. You're one of the Führer's oldest and closest friends. Jena wouldn't dare to move against you.'

'You're out of your mind. I have some advice for you. I know you've heard it before, but for your mother's sake you'll listen to it again and act on it: switch to the BPP or leave the police altogether and work for me.'

'Thank you, uncle. You've told me all I need to know.'

'I've told you nothing.'

But he had. He had confirmed Seb's suspicions, told him exactly the sort of man he was dealing with. He had made it clear, too, that it would be almost impossible to bring Paul Jena down. But, one way or another, Seb would do it or die in the attempt.

Winter had survived the roll-call and descended into a peaceful and restorative sleep, undisturbed by dreams. He woke at five with everyone else, washed, shaved and stumbled across to the eating hall for a meagre breakfast of oats and watery coffee.

'You still look like death, Winter 7482.' Friedrich Brauer shook his head.

'I feel it. One night in the infirmary was not enough.'

Winter was losing his grip on the investigation. He had come into Dachau to discover the truth about the murder of Theodor Krieger and, on a personal level, to make contact with the Jewish underground.

He seemed to have succeeded in the second part of his mission but was falling desperately short in the first. Far from being identified as a murderer, Friedrich Brauer had acted as his saviour. Somehow he needed to push further and harder if he was to extract a confession. But, then again, perhaps Brauer was innocent.

In his lucid moments, Winter told himself he was hopelessly inadequate for this task, that he should never have volunteered. And now he was trapped. Even if he could find out the truth about Krieger's murder, would he ever get out of this hellish place?

'But you're alive, so that's a positive sign. We need to get you work in the SS canteen. That's a good number.'

Yet again, words of kindness from the man he was trying to convict.

'I just want to get out of here.'

'As do we all.'

The newcomer – the drunk who Winter had given a severe warning to just a year before – was looking at him from a distance of only five metres. Winter remembered his surname now – Jung – though he couldn't recall the Christian name. Perhaps he had never known it.

Winter turned his face sideways. He couldn't see Jung any more, but he could feel his gaze burning into his cheek.

The bell rang for the end of breakfast. Everyone moved at speed to get on to the parade ground to receive work detail orders. Jung was at Winter's side in seconds.

'I've seen you before,' he said.

'Really? Where?' Winter had no option but to deny this flat out. The truth would get him maimed or killed in this place.

'I don't know, but I've seen you.'

'Must have been Dortmund. Do you come from there? I worked in the town hall until I was denounced by some bastard.'

'No, I'm a Munich man. Never been to Dortmund.'

'Good beer. You should try it if you ever get out of this joint.'

He was shaking his head. His face was bruised, but his eyes were piercing. 'Fuck the beer. It's you I want to know about. I don't forget a face. What's your name?'

'Winter.'

'Means nothing. What are you in for?'

'My politics. You?'

Before he could reply, the block leader arrived with orders for the day. Winter and Jung were put in the same group, bricklaying on a new building at the far end of the camp.

'I'm not wrong. I know I've seen you in Munich. I've got a bad feeling, Herr Winter. I'll be watching you.'

Five murders, four of them linked. But what about the fifth, Elena Lang? Seb couldn't help but wonder whether there was any connection. It didn't seem likely, but there was one common element: the presence of Paul Jena, playing an intrinsic part in both investigations.

But that meant nothing, surely? He was a senior SS officer, a friend of Goebbels, so he had to take an interest in all such cases.

The problem was that Seb didn't believe in coincidences. Murder was a rarity in these parts. Five murders within a few days? It didn't make sense.

Seb had planned to drive to Liliendorf to look through the ashes, talk to the locals. One of the villagers must know something, someone must have heard the rattle of the submachine gun in the early hours of the morning. But instead he was drawn back to Garmisch-Partenkirchen.

He wanted to talk with everyone who knew Elena, however

casually. It did not take him long to discover that Peter Lunn was staying at the Alpenhof Hotel.

The bad news was that Lunn wasn't there. The concierge said that he was out skiing at Hausberg with other racers and friends from various nations. Clearly a different crowd to the Schloss Stark clique.

With daylight dying fast, Seb decided to wait in the front hall of the hotel. Half an hour later the English sportsman appeared with a noisy group of skiers and immediately caught Seb's eye.

Smiling broadly, he came over. 'Sebastian Wolff, are you staying here?'

'Nothing so grand, Mr Lunn. A little guest house nearby with my fiancée.'

'That gorgeous girl you brought to the Stark party?'

'The very same. Actually, I'm here because I was hoping I could talk to you. I didn't have much of a chance with everyone else around at Schloss Stark.'

'Shall we go through to the bar? Thirsty work skiing with those chaps. And, please, call me Peter. If you have no objection I'll call you Seb.'

'No objection at all.'

'Just don't try any of the HH salutes on me, all right.'

They settled down at a small table away from the other athletes, both with demi-litres of Löwenbräu.

'Now, how can I help?'

'It's about Elena Lang. There's still no sign of her. You mentioned that she's an old friend of yours?'

'Yes, we go back a few years.'

'Where do you think she might be?'

Lunn was looking at him with intense eyes. 'Remind me, Seb, who exactly is asking?'

'The Munich police. I'm captain of detectives.'

'Am I under surveillance or something?'

Seb frowned. 'Of course not. What would give you that idea?'

Lunn shrugged and half turned away. 'Oh, nothing. Paranoia, I suppose. I thought I might have upset people by refusing to join the procession in front of AH and absenting myself from the celebration banquet. I can't stomach dictatorships, you see. Which means that they probably can't stomach me.'

'I swear to you, Peter, that if anyone is keeping watch on you, it's certainly not the Munich police. Not our style. We're not political – not on my side of things, anyway. Just an old-fashioned police department much like you'll find in England.'

'Oh, I doubt that. But carry on.'

'As I said, I'm worried about Elena Lang, and I thought you were her friend. It occurred to me you might have an idea where she had gone.'

Lunn was not smiling at all. His mouth was shut in a tight grimace. When he opened it, his teeth were fangs and his eyes were daggers. His voice was cold and angry. 'I think you know as well as I do where she is, Sebastian.'

How to respond to that? 'If you have some information, Peter, I'd very much like to hear it.'

'You know exactly what's happened to poor Elena Lang. She's dead, murdered, and someone in this filthy regime is covering it up.'

The beer mug was halfway between the table and Seb's lips, and it stayed there.

'What?' Lunn continued. 'You think we're all too stupid to see what's been going on?'

Seb replaced the beer on the table. He blinked. 'I'm sorry, Peter, I really can't think where you might have got such an idea from.'

'Bullshit, Seb. I thought better of you. Anyone who's upset Bobo Mitford has my vote, but now you're talking through your bloody swastika. Come on, do the decent thing – be a man.'

'Peter, if you have information about the fate of Elena Lang, you have to tell me now.'

This conversation was mad. They both knew the truth but only one of them could speak the words. But *how* did Lunn know?

Lunn shook his head and took another deep, thirst-quenching draught. He was younger than Seb – only a few years older than Jurgen – but he spoke with maturity, insight and not a little youthful arrogance. 'Perhaps I'm doing you a disservice, Seb.'

'I think you might be. How old are you, Peter?'

'Old enough to fight and die for my country.'

'But inexperienced all the same. I can't help wondering how one as young as you came to believe you know so much about the world.'

'By studying current affairs and history and listening to people. Now let me continue. Assuming for a moment that Elena is dead – and you don't have to say the words, just listen – assuming she's dead, murdered, you're trying to find out why she was killed and by whom, but you're hampered by Herr Propaganda.'

Seb opened his mouth.

'No, Seb, let me speak! My question would then be: do you have the courage to find out? And would you live long enough to bring the killer to justice? Not good odds, I'd suggest. Even slimmer odds would be your chances of surviving the ministrations of the very senior man who ordered the killing. You're in a hole, Seb. And I feel for you.'

'You sound as if you think you know something, Peter. Is there anything you wish to tell me? Any evidence?'

Lunn shrugged. 'If I had evidence, I would give it to you in a flash. No, it's all just simple conjecture. It's about the land you live in. You've allowed the gangsters to take over the government. Heil Capone.'

They were both silent for a few moments. Each understood the other; they both stood for the same things – decency, integrity, honour, justice. But the gap between them was unbridgeable, and it wasn't simply one of age.

'You assume to know a lot about me,' Seb said at last.

Lunn smiled with a hint of despondency. 'It's not an assumption. Bobo has spoken about you in what she considers disparaging terms. Calls you a Jew-loving, Nazi-hating traitor who's alive only because of his family connections, whatever that might mean.'

'My uncle Christian Weber is boss of Munich City Council and an old friend of Adolf. They marched side by side in 1923. He's one of the Old Fighters. I'm not proud of it, but I confess he has helped me on occasion. What about you – how do you know Miss Mitford?'

'That's easy. Our families are old friends, so we speak to each other. I've always enjoyed teasing her and her sisters mercilessly. Not Nancy – she's a good few years older than Bobo and me, and far too sharp. The British upper classes are like that. We all know each other. But Bobo says she'll do anything she can to ruin you. And you *know* she can do it.'

'I agree we don't get on.'

'It's only going to get worse, old man. You should leave the country now. While you still can. The rich Jews know what's going to happen – they're leaving, aren't they?'

'I love my country.'

'Of course you do. And that's the problem, isn't it? The two things get confused. Love of Germany morphs into

262

Love of Hitler – despite the fact that the latter is destroying the former.'

This was not good. They weren't talking loudly, but there were plenty of people in this hotel bar. 'Do you not think that you should keep such thoughts to yourself while you're a guest in this country?'

'I'm safe enough. They're not going to arrest or harm the captain of the British ski team with the great Berlin Olympics on the horizon. Come on, let me get you another beer, old man. I think we both need one.'

'Thank you.'

'You know, Seb, in any other place at any other time, you and I would be the best of friends, but I have a horribly dark thought that we're all going to end up shooting at each other yet again. And that, in my book, is a bloody tragedy. Another generation wasted.'

Seb nodded. It was all he could do. The Englishman might well be right, and it made him want to weep. What did this mean for Jurgen's future?

36

The day was cold and hard. Winter had never done building work before, so he was put on hod-carrying, transferring the bricks from a large pile to the bricklayers, who worked at speed, laying on the mortar with great skill.

None of the workers knew what the building was. They just followed the capo's orders, under the fierce gaze of two SS guards.

Winter had no idea what hit him. The blow came from behind, crunching into the back of his skull, sending him hurtling to the ground, the bricks in his hod spewing forth in an arc across the hard, icy ground.

As he landed, his face caught the edge of one of the scattered bricks, cutting into his cheek and he couldn't help crying out.

One of the two guards moved towards him with unhurried steps. He smacked Winter on the head with his riding crop.

'Careless idiot. Half-rations for you tonight.'

Winter scrabbled to his feet to avoid another blow. His hands and face were bleeding. He was in pain all over, but he had to ignore it. Quickly he picked up the fallen bricks, reloaded the hod and stumbled towards the wall and the bricklayers.

He turned back to collect another hod-load and came face to face with Jung, who had a brick in one hand, clutched like a weapon. The brick that had floored Winter. Jung was grinning through yellow teeth.

'I've remembered who you are, Winter. And by the end of

the day everyone else in this camp will know, too. Consider yourself dead.'

'And I'm the king of Prussia,' the SS guard said. 'Now get in line before we strap you down for a flogging, 7482.'

Winter knew he had to get out. He had pleaded with the guard, insisted that he was a Bavarian Political Police sergeant, working undercover. The commandant, Herr Deubel, knew all about it. Could he please be taken to him? 'I won't survive the night. The other prisoners will kill me – they've found out who I am.'

The guard shrugged. 'That's what comes of being an enemy of the people.' He raised his crop but didn't bring it down.

Everyone was moving into position on the parade ground. Winter might not get another chance of making his case. If he couldn't get a message through to Deubel now, he'd have to stand through roll-call knowing that soon he would be back in his barrack-room with fifty-three other inmates, including Jung.

The chances of him staying alive were zero.

'Take me to the punishment block, the Bunker, I beg you. Anything.'

'Are you serious, 7482? Do you have any idea what that's like?'

'It's my only hope. They'll kill me if I go back to the barrack-room.'

For a moment the guard seemed to have doubts, as though wondering whether this really was a BPP man working undercover, but then he shook his head. 'You're trying to make a fool of me, you bastard. I'll show you who's the fool. Get on your knees and crawl like a worm.'

*

Seb and Peter Lunn managed to remain cordial. They asked about each other's families, Seb's time at sea with the British merchant navy, Lunn's family's history in the travel business. They talked warmly about their mutual love of mountains and skiing.

Finally, Lunn began to move. 'I need a bath before the hot water's all used up, but it was very good to meet you properly, Seb.'

'Likewise. Perhaps we'll ski together in Gapa one day when you return.'

'I'd like that. You weren't really racing before, were you? You wanted to talk to Howard.'

'You should be a detective. But one more thing. I know Unity Mitford hates me and wishes me dead, but do you think there's any chance you could persuade her to meet me for a chat?'

'You *are* mad, aren't you?'

'Probably. But she has access to everybody, doesn't she? She knows Elena Lang well –'

'*Knew.*'

'She counts Elena Lang among her friends, also the von Starks and Howard Jack, Fritz Mannheim and Paul Jena. She probably knew half the people at the party.'

'She knows Adolf, too. Could drip a little poison in his ear about a certain disloyal policeman.'

'I'll take the risk, try to charm her.' God, what was he doing? Hadn't Uncle Christian warned him in strong enough terms? *She is the most dangerous woman in Munich and she can do you much harm. Steer clear of her.*

'It's your neck, Seb.'

'It can't hurt to talk to her, can it? She may discover we actually have one or two things in common. She might be able to help me –'

'You sound desperate.'

'I know what you think of me, but my hands are tied, Peter. It's just possible she might harbour useful information without even realising it.'

'I understand.'

'She doesn't see things the same way as you, does she? I mean about Elena's disappearance?'

'Bobo? Good God, no, she's too stupid to see beyond her nose.'

'And there was me thinking you were friends.'

'I said our *families* are friends. I don't think anyone beyond Bobo's family likes her much, and even those of us who can just about abide her presence struggle with her dull wit and love for AH. My joy comes from provoking her, just as it does for little Howard Jack. Sometimes we join forces against her insane Fascism. She gets so angry it's hilarious.' He paused, seemingly reaching a decision. 'I'll try to fix up something for you, detective, though I wouldn't expect much to come of it.'

'As you said, it's my neck.'

They made Winter crawl on his belly, his fingers frozen as he scraped his way across the hard, icy ground.

Every few metres he was beaten across his back and head, until he made it to the long stone building known as the Bunker.

At last he was slung into a cold, bare cell. From next door, he heard echoing groans, the crack of a lash, a scream, cruel laughter. The heavy door was slammed shut, and the light glared down on a bucket, a thin straw mattress and a wafer-like checked blanket.

It almost made the barrack-room seem luxurious, with its bunk beds, proper toilets, basins, tables and chairs – though never enough to accommodate fifty-four men.

The light bulb in the punishment cell hung from a ragged piece of wire and it never went out, filling the hollow cube of Hans Winter's new home with an unwelcome yellow glare.

He wanted to weep. He thought of Malwine for the first time in two or more days. He was doing this for her. That's why he had come to this terrible place, to find someone who could get him a perfectly forged Aryan pass so that he could marry and have a family.

He wrapped his arms around his chest and shivered. It was one of the coldest nights of the year, and he was discovering, for the first time, that he wasn't afraid of death. He wanted it.

37

It was as he walked along Ludwigstrasse, the historic main street at the Partenkirchen end of Gapa, that Seb realised he was being followed.

The old road was packed with tourists, revellers, people in uniform. Traffic couldn't get through, and officers were trying to direct the crowd to the pavements, but it was all in vain – people simply weren't interested. There was a great deal of laughter and jollity, and no one cared about the cars or the traffic cops.

Every few steps he stopped and looked around, but no shadow was obvious. Many people had skis slung over their shoulders; all were dressed for the cold weather. He began to wonder whether he was imagining things, but his senses were heightened and he knew he was right: someone was tracking him.

He had his Walther police pistol under his jacket and if necessary he would use it. But his first thought was the urgent desire to discover his pursuer, to detain them, question them, find out who had sent them.

Yet again, there was something else itching at his mind: the absence of Sergeant Winter. This undercover operation had been going on a great deal too long now, which meant something had gone wrong. What was Winter still doing there?

Seb's Lancia was parked close to the Villa Erika and it took him a while to get to the Munich road. It was dark now and snowing lightly. He was concerned about fuel, but, if he took it easy, he might just make it back to the city. If not, there were a couple of filling stations en route and they should be open. Didn't want to embarrass the master race by not having enough petrol for tourists and officials.

He had enjoyed the conversation with Peter Lunn, that feeling of potential enemies finding that they have more in common than that which separates them. But it was Lunn's certainty that Elena was dead that really set Seb thinking. How could he keep the lid on this terrible murder? More importantly, how could he find the killer while maintaining this preposterous pretence that she was still alive?

The attack came as he approached Oberau. He had reached the point where the road no longer hugged the Loisach River, edging instead towards the lower part of the wooded hill to the west. High snow walls gave the road a tunnel effect, closing in on him.

The other car's lights weren't lit. It seemed to come out of nowhere, a black, hard-top Mercedes that slewed across in front of his little vehicle.

Seb tried to swerve, but he couldn't control the skid, not on this icy road with balding tyres and no time to think.

But he did react. That's what wars did to you. You reacted to everything, sometimes too many things. Cars backfiring, trains hooting, thunder rumbling, planes flying low. They all did, all the boys who came home from the trenches. They threw themselves to the ground, grabbed for imaginary guns in full daylight and in their dreams.

Mostly it was a curse, but tonight it was a blessing. He had the passenger door open and had rolled out even before the Lancia came to a halt, its nose buried in the snow wall. Instinct had taken over: if he'd got out on the driver's side, he'd have been a sitting target.

The same second in which he twisted his left shoulder

into juddering contact with the icy drift, he moved his right hand into his jacket, pulling out the Walther and slipping off the safety. The only light came from his own car and the dim light of a clouded moon. The door was open, jammed into the snow. He was trapped.

Whispers came from the Mercedes. He couldn't make them out. He expected shots but not yet. They would come.

He slid to his haunches and shuffled towards the rear of the Lancia, desperate for some sort of gap in the wall of snow. But the ploughs had done a good job, banked it up high and vertical. It was less regular, less steep, on the other side of the road. That's where he had to be: the woods. This side of the valley was open, and he was an easy kill.

Run across the road? Smack, smack, you're dead.

That was his first instinct. His second was that he had no option. It was a chance he had to take.

Without covering fire, he had to provide his own. The Walther was fully loaded, seven rounds, but that didn't give much leeway against multiple attackers with heavy weaponry. Worse, the road was like an ice rink and his boots might not grip. If he fell, he was dead.

All these thoughts written down in a police report would seem to cover an age. But in real time, he was calculating in milliseconds. He was crouched behind the Lancia. He could move left or right, but they would expect that. He stood straight up, saw vague shapes and loosed two rapid shots, then ducked back and ran out into the road.

Half hoping to see car lights, he was instantly disappointed. Just him out here, on a dark valley road, snow banks and river on one side, snow and woodland on the other, and that was where he was running. He heard the rattle of a sub-machine gun. It came in one solid burst, a whole magazine emptied out.

He slipped, but got enough purchase to slide forward.

They would have more magazines and they would have more weapons. He couldn't stop to find out. Run in short zigzags – make yourself a difficult target, Wolff – but don't take too long about it. That was what the Kriegerwebel shouted during his brief session of training between call-up and the front line. He'd learnt it then, but it didn't work now, not on the ice-glazed tar.

Somehow – sheer luck – he wasn't hit.

He was at the far side and there was plenty of snow, but it was falling away in places. He had to get through it or over it – any sort of gap.

One incline was a shade lower and he threw himself at it. It was too high, but he would have no second chance. A torch had lit the road. His fingers, cold flesh on the icy steel of the pistol, dug into the top edge of the snow pile and he pulled it down like a miniature avalanche, scrambling, shovelling snow with his left hand.

He managed to haul himself up as a second burst of fire slapped into the snow, carving a heart-height line where his own chest had been just a moment ago.

He was on the other side, tumbling down into the unploughed white. He landed awkwardly, but suppressed a cry as pain coursed up through his thigh.

The snow bank that had previously trapped him now gave him cover. He was able to move unseen, but it wouldn't last long, so he had to make the most of it.

Moving fast, his leg uninjured despite the painful fall, he crossed a virgin strip into the woods. Fir trees laden with white, thick and dense forest: this was what he needed. But there was one problem. A big one. He was making tracks in the pristine snow. Tracks to follow – and there was nothing he could do about it.

Seb needed to find a vantage point and wait for the sweep of a torch or the flash of gunfire in the dark. Take them one round at a time. Five shots left.

It wasn't like this in the war. Five shots was a split-second burst for a machine-gunner. These five shots were all he had. And the Walther PPK was a small pistol, built for ease of carriage and concealability, not accuracy or range. For a hit, you had to let the enemy get close.

His instinct had been right in Ludwigstrasse. He was being followed. Had it been from before his meeting with Peter Lunn or had someone told them he was there?

Them. There was clearly more than one, because a killer doesn't whisper to himself. He guessed there were four, all clad in anonymous coats, which was why they'd been so difficult to spot in the busy street.

His thoughts were coming fast. The tree canopy was high and thick and laden with snow. No starlight or moonlight this evening, just low cloud and no obvious way to go. He continued directly ahead, up the steep slope and into the west and the wilderness of the hills above the Giessenbach Gorge. His alternatives were to turn north – in the direction of Oberau – or south, but he feared there would be less cover there.

All he could do was to make things difficult for the bastards. *Take me down, and I'll take you with me.*

His stride was long and slow and silent in the soft talcum snow. He had to walk with arms outstretched, feeling his way past tree trunks.

He heard voices. Loud and clear now, not whispered. Someone was calling orders to the others. They had his tracks. He looked around and saw flickering lights through the endless pines and foliage. Four hundred metres back, two hundred, one hundred? It was impossible to gauge. But they were coming in the right direction, and they knew it.

He gripped the Walther in both hands and pumped off a single shot towards the light. Slow them down a bit. Let them know their own lives were in the mix.

Four rounds left.

He moved faster, lengthened his stride, took risks in the darkness. One stumble in a hole could result in a twisted ankle; one collision with a tree could cause concussion. Both would stop him or slow him. His breath was coming hard. He was physically fit, but this ascent would be tough for anyone.

The pursuers were fanning out now. The lead man was in the centre, with his torch on the footprint trail, but in separating they could come from all directions and minimise the risk of Seb taking one of them out with a lucky shot.

A small break in the forest appeared, but that would reduce cover, so Seb took a half-turn left and stayed within the edge of the woods. He panted from the exertion as he got higher: he was at least a thousand metres above sea level. In the distance he could make out the dark shadow of a crucifix – black against black – and it drew him on because that meant the summit of this climb and, if he was lucky, new opportunities beyond it.

All these decisions came from the survival mode learnt in the last months of the war. He had lived because he had learnt fast and been lucky. His friends had also learnt fast, but too many of them had been unlucky.

On the battlefield, skill only gave you a small margin. Random chance was the big winner. You couldn't mitigate a shell falling straight into your trench, but you could avoid putting your head above the parapet when you were lighting a smoke.

The first thing you had to reckon with was the chaos. They had marched singing along the lanes of Picardy, the war a distant rumble of big guns. But as they got closer the rumble became a roar, the ground became fetid mud, the trees were broken like matchsticks, and their young bodies began to shake, betraying their fear. They were still behind the lines, but the singing had stopped and the smiling faces were drawn and eyes were wide. If it was like this here, what would it be like in the front trenches, scarcely two hundred metres from the enemy, a thirty-second dash? Their packs and guns and bayonets became heavier by the moment, their stomachs churned, and their throats were dry with a raging thirst. They began to wonder whether it might be wise to don their steel helmets. No one wanted to be first, to betray their fear.

This was war. You were a soldier, a small counter on a big board. If you died, you were a number. If you lost your legs or your eyesight, you were still just a number. A hero to your family and your townsfolk, perhaps, but how did that help you?

A rattle of gunfire came from the right, no more than fifty metres away. It was speculative, but more than close enough to make Seb throw himself to the ground.

He was up immediately, running now, a hunted creature without a lair.

The cross at the peak, perhaps thirteen hundred metres, was calling to him like a siren.

For the first time it occurred to him that there was no way out of this. They would pursue him relentlessly and they would find him, riddle him with bullets as they had done to the three men at Liliendorf, and then they would conceal his body so that it wouldn't be found – at least not until the Games were over and the snow had vanished in the warmth of spring.

This had been their plan all along; they were never going to attack him in the town. This had to be done in the middle of nowhere. Orders from on high – no murders during the Winter Olympics.

If he could reach the high ridge and find his way down to the Giessenbach, the stream that flowed to Oberau, would there be hope there or would it be frozen? He could lose his footprints in a stream, but he needed to be quick; they were gaining on him at an alarming rate.

The last three hundred metres of the ascent were the worst. His thighs burned, his lungs were tortured, but still he ran, and he began to feel he must be distancing himself from the gunmen, if only by a few metres. Their weapons were heavier, the motive to kill less powerful than the desire to live.

The cloud cover suddenly broke as he reached the summit and the moon gave him a clear view of the cross and a sign saying *Schafkopf* – sheep's head. He was the sheep; they were the wolves. Behind him, he saw them, a full hundred and fifty metres back, having closed up their formation. One of them descended to his knee, lifted a rifle to his shoulder, aimed and loosed several shots. The muzzle flash lit the gunmen briefly.

Seb turned away and looked down into the Giessenbach Gorge. It was a difficult descent at this point, almost entirely wooded, with a patch of rocky outcrops down the central way. But there it was at the bottom of the drop – the river. Would the rocks give him enough cover? Only one way to find out.

He fired a round – a toss of the dice for deterrence – then jumped. From a distance he heard a low grunt and what sounded like a curse. Either he had hit one of the swine or someone had twisted their ankle.

Three rounds left.

The descent was steeper and a lot more difficult than the

climb, but he was able to go faster. It was hard on his knees and feet. He stumbled around trees, tripping over fallen branches and raised roots, until after a few minutes he was in the rocks. He heard a couple of shots. Whatever had happened back there hadn't slowed them down much. They were soldiers, he guessed. Was the man who grunted injured? Perhaps not – or perhaps he had been left by his comrades. Gangsters, not soldiers.

The route was difficult, with overhangs and sudden precipices that he had to skirt. He stopped on a ledge. There was an easy way down from here, but this was a good spot to regroup, consider his best option. Three rounds left. One man possibly down – in which case one round for each of the remaining three. That did not leave a lot of room for manoeuvre.

He crouched on the ledge, out of sight behind a long jagged rock, and waited. Calming his breathing. Thinking. He heard them coming and knew he had little time for this. One chance only.

They had fanned out again, clearly unsure of his path through the rocks. For a few seconds, he would be the predator, the wolf. The one in the centre was his prey.

The man, cradling a sub-machine gun, was on the ledge now and was working out his way down, scanning the slope below for his target.

He hadn't seen Seb and he was slow. In two steps Seb was behind him. In his hand, sharp and serrated, he clutched a rock the size of a small melon. The gunman was just about to turn his head as Seb swung his arm and crunched him full on the skull. The man didn't cry out. He fell, his legs crumpling beneath him, hitting his head again as he went down.

Seb didn't need a second blow. He knew the man was at least unconscious, perhaps dead or dying. He didn't really care as long as he was out of action.

Kneeling down, Seb unslung the soldier's EMP sub-machine gun and took the two full magazines from his belt. He had never used the weapon before, but he knew enough about guns.

He knew enough about uniforms, too, to recognise the SS flashes on the jacket collar, almost concealed by a heavy leather overcoat. Well, well, no surprise there.

Slinging the EMP across his chest, he felt its considerable weight. He also had a torch now. The gun and the torch levelled the odds significantly.

The unconscious gunman's friends would soon be wondering about him. He was clearly their lead man, taking the central path that they would follow from the flanks.

Seb could sit and wait for them to come looking. They would be exposed and vulnerable on their approach.

But now there was a new concern: if he survived this encounter – which he now believed he could – did he really want to leave the Giessenbach Gorge littered with the corpses of SS men? This was something for which he would never be forgiven and would not survive. His family would suffer grievously, too, for such organisations took the concept of vengeance seriously.

Which meant he had to stick to the initial plan: simply try to escape these bastards without killing them.

He waited until he heard voices on the hill beneath them. There was a call for *Alex*. No reply, so they called again. Clearly, Alex was stretched out unconscious at Seb's feet. Time to move. Let Alex's friends carry on downhill if they wanted to; Seb would retrace his tracks uphill.

Ascending was going to be tougher.

Even more so when, as he turned to move, his foot released a shower of rocks.

His cover was blown. He began running uphill. The

weather might be dropping to minus ten, but he was dripping with sweat, and every muscle seared with heat and pain.

Having already worked out the sub-machine gun, he sprayed a short, harmless burst into the air. Just to let them know what they faced, just to slow them down to a crawl.

At the top, he stopped to catch his breath. He couldn't get back to the road by the same route because he would probably meet the wounded SS man. Best to go straight downhill towards the village of Farchant and then try to make his way along the road back to the car. He looked at his watch. He had been running for little more than half an hour, but it had felt like half a day.

It was over. He had won.

38

Tiredness cut to the bone. Every organ in his body cried out for rest and regeneration, but Hans Winter couldn't sleep. Nor would he in this icy stone tomb.

All he could do was wrap himself in the thin blanket, shivering and trying to think warm thoughts. He held his hands to his chest, but they were still numb from crawling here. He heard sounds of torment. Terrible sounds of pain and despair. This was where poor Blindorf had died. And this was where Hans Winter would meet his end.

He forced himself to think about Malwine, to recall her warmth and her smile. But all sorts of doubts began to creep in. If he couldn't tell her this most uncomfortable of secrets, the truth about his Jewish ancestry, could they really have a life together?

And why couldn't he tell her? Did he not trust her commitment to him? If that was the case, it could hardly be true that she loved him.

Perhaps he should just give her up. Tell her that no, he didn't love her after all. But that wasn't so simple because he *did* love her.

He heard footsteps in the long corridor outside his cell. Just the guards doing their hourly checks or throwing some other poor soul into this electrically lit purgatory.

The key twisted into the lock and his cell door was pulled open. Three men stood there. One of them was the SS guard; the other two wore prisoner's canvas.

He recognised them instantly, their faces gleaming and expectant in the harsh yellow light: Jung and Brauer.

Jung, the lowlife drunk. Brauer, the possible killer who had demonstrated a charitable side – a show of kindness in a place devoid of decency.

'You've got five minutes,' the guard said. 'But first the money.' He held out his hand and closed it around the coins that Brauer placed there.

'More than long enough,' Jung said.

The two inmates stepped into the cell. The guard closed the door with a clang.

'Time's up, you dirty bastard.' It was Jung speaking again.

Winter saw savagery in his eyes. 'Please, don't do this. I'm on your side. I've seen how you suffer here.'

Brauer laughed. 'You were right. Revenge is sweet for the soul.'

The first punch came from Brauer. Straight into the side of Winter's skull, knocking him to the ground. His head cracked against the stone floor. He was dazed but tried to crawl away. It was hopeless. They were all over him, kicking, punching, biting, gouging. They ripped his jacket from his torso and dragged his trousers down to his ankles.

He was trying to back away against the wall, but there was nowhere to go, no escape. He fought to wrench his head to the side as Jung aimed his gnarled fingers at his eyes. In his other hand he had a razor blade.

Winter was pinioned now. Brauer had somehow forced his way behind him and had his arms in an iron grip.

In front of him, Jung was grinning, his tongue lolling between his teeth like a salivating dog. 'Oh, yes, time's up. We don't like you. The guards don't like you. No one likes you, Winter 7482. The world is going to be a better place without you.'

The blade came scything down and he thought his throat would be slit. Instead, it came to rest gently on his sternum at the base of his collarbone. He could smell Jung's warm, pungent breath. And then he felt the blade. It sliced into his flesh and razored down a few millimetres into his chest. Slowly it was drawn down from his neck to his abdomen, carving a jagged line of blood all along its path.

Jung was slavering. He laid himself flat on Winter's body and licked the blood. Winter could do nothing; these two men were much too powerful for him. Jung didn't raise his face, but his hands went up and found Winter's throat, tightening, his thumbs pressing into his windpipe, strangling him.

He tried to twist his head, loosen the choke hold, but he could do nothing and knew he was dying. He struggled to no avail, couldn't breathe, couldn't move. The light glared down at him from above, but it seemed to be growing dim. This was what death was like. Acceptance. These were the last moments.

Brauer's mouth was at his ear, breathing hot air. 'Of course I had him killed,' he whispered. 'That's why you're here, isn't it? Of course I arranged it. Easiest thing in the world.'

And then he heard something else: the opening of the cell door. Had the guard come to save him or finish him off?

But it wasn't the guard. It was Captain Wolff and, at his side, the camp commandant.

Seb dragged the drooling savage off his sergeant's almost naked body and slammed him against the cell wall. Winter was still held by another man, but the man's eyes were now wide with horror and he was loosening his grip.

Winter's body was smeared with blood, seeping from a central channel. Seb reached out and gently lifted him to his feet. He picked up his canvas jacket and used it to wipe the blood from Winter's chest.

'Let's get you out of here, sergeant.' He turned to Heinrich Deubel. 'This is a disgrace, commandant. I look forward to seeing your full report into this grievous assault and attempted murder. Your guards have a lot to answer for and I expect charges to be brought.'

'I'm as appalled as you are, captain. I will deal with this.' Deubel was stiff, his face a mask. He had brought another SS guard with him, waiting in the corridor. 'My man will take you to the shunt room, where Sergeant Winter can clean himself up and collect his effects.' He nodded to Winter. 'Please accept my apologies, sergeant. It didn't occur to me that my men wouldn't bring you to me when you required it.'

Winter couldn't speak.

'We'll talk later, Herr Deubel,' Seb said.

The commandant hadn't sounded at all appalled or shocked by his men's behaviour. There were those who said Himmler was unhappy with him, considered him too lenient and easy-going. Well, that supposed softness wasn't evident to Seb.

Supporting Winter, he assisted him, hobbling, to the shunt room, where the SS guards looked at him with suspicious, unfriendly eyes. They went through the rigmarole of signatures, stamped cards, provision of wallet, wristwatch and civilian clothes, all in their own time.

Finally, they were out of the camp and safely in Seb's Lancia. It hadn't been badly damaged when it was cut up by the four men in the Mercedes – merely a slight dent to the front bumper. When he'd returned it had still been there, slewed into the snow wall on the side of the road. The Mercedes was there, too, minus driver or passengers. Seb had taken a few moments to examine their vehicle in search of clues.

There was nothing to identify the would-be killers, but he

had a strong feeling that they were the four SS men he had seen outside the entrance to Schloss Stark when he first went there – Jena's men.

They had left the key in the ignition. Seb laughed as he threw it deep into the furthest, most inaccessible snowdrift, then shot out the tyres with the EMP sub-machine gun. As a last act of defiance, he flung the weapon away into the deep snow. Let them sort that out.

It had been a relief to climb into the Lancia and drive north undisturbed. The route to Dachau was easy enough. He was tired but not sleepy. No one could sleep after what he had just been through. The hunted animal had outwitted its predators.

Now here he was with poor bloody Hans Winter outside the grim, grey gatehouse of Dachau concentration camp. Behind the walls, there was only misery. But it didn't end there.

Seb suddenly understood that leaving Dachau didn't really set you free. The whole of Germany had become a concentration camp, and they were all inmates.

For a few moments, the two men sat in the front of the car. Seb reached out with his kerchief and wiped a streak of blood from the sergeant's face. 'I'm sorry, Hans. I should have come sooner.'

'It's not your fault, captain.'

'I should have checked up on you. Anyway, let's get you to the hospital.'

'I don't need a hospital – just sleep.'

'You're going to hospital to have those wounds cleaned with antiseptic and dressed properly. I'll stay with you.'

'You're the boss.'

'And then what? Do you want to go home? If you like, my son's away, so you can use his bed at our apartment, then we

284

can talk some more. We'll work out how to proceed in the morning.'

'I can tell you one thing now: Friedrich Brauer organised the killing of Theodor Krieger – I discovered that much.'

'He confessed to you?'

Winter nodded. 'He said, *Revenge is sweet for the soul*. And then, just before you arrived, he made his guilt clear beyond doubt. *Of course I had him killed*, he said. *Easiest thing in the world*.'

Seb put the car into gear and pulled away. 'Well done. I admit I never thought you could do it.'

'Nor did I, captain.'

'Whether it will convict him, we'll have to wait and see. But his attempt on *your* life certainly will. Brauer and that other creep will not fare well.'

'The strange thing is, though, Friedrich Brauer had been good to me. He helped me and got me to the infirmary. Could I speak on his behalf, to save his neck?'

'We'll talk about that.' Seb smiled at his sergeant, then ran his hand over his head. 'I'm not convinced by your new haircut. What will Malwine think?'

39

Time to pay another visit to Petra Krieger, the woman who loathed her husband and had taken a lover of her own.

But first things first. The body required sustenance and renewal, and that came from food and rest. Having returned home to Ainmüllerstrasse from the hospital, he and Winter shared a beer and warmed-up soup from the tureen.

Mutti came into the kitchen. 'It's you, Sebastian. I thought I heard something.'

'I hope we didn't wake you.'

'No, I was reading.'

'You remember Sergeant Winter, Mutti?'

'Of course.'

'He's had an accident and he's staying the night. Jurgen's still at the Olympics, so I thought Hans could use his room.'

'Indeed. The sheets are clean. You're very welcome, sergeant, and I hope your injuries are not too serious.'

Seb gazed at his sergeant. He'd be all right. A vicious cut down his chest and deep purple bruises. He looked a mess, but nothing too serious. The doctor had given him a precautionary tetanus vaccine and a nurse had cleaned him up.

'I'll be fine, thank you, Frau Wolff.'

'Perhaps you would like coffee and eggs for breakfast?'

'I can think of nothing nicer.'

When she had returned to bed and they had finished their beers, Seb turned to his sergeant. 'You and I have had our differences, Hans, but I want to say something to you. What you've done these past few days has been worthy of the Iron

Cross first class if such a thing were available to a police officer. You've shown courage beyond the call of duty – and you've almost certainly solved a heinous crime.'

'I don't know what to say.'

'Then say nothing. You are a true man, sergeant, but please – don't do anything this stupid again.'

Seb woke early and placed a call to the Alpenhof Hotel. He was quickly put through to Peter Lunn's room.

'Good God, what time do you call this, Seb?'

'I wanted to catch you before you hit the slopes. Just one question: did you get anywhere with that favour I asked of you – a meeting with Miss Mitford?'

'Yes, I was planning to call you. She'll meet you for lunch at the Kandahar. One o'clock. You're buying.'

'Thank you.'

'Good luck, fellow. You'll need it.'

'Enjoy your skiing.'

'No doubt about that.'

Seb let Hans Winter sleep in. He knew Mutti would look after him well and make sure he had plenty of coffee and fresh bread. As a devout Catholic and a mother, she saw it as her God-given purpose to feed anyone who crossed her threshold.

He made a quick call to Hexie, who was the worse for wear from drink, then scribbled a note for Winter suggesting he catch the train to Gapa later or, if he had other ideas, leave a message with Mutti detailing his whereabouts.

On the way south, he tried to make sense of the Theodor Krieger case. Until these last few hours he had been almost certain that the killing was something to do with the gang stealing property from Jews. Thieves turning on each other. Now Sergeant Winter's testimony clearly stated that

Krieger's father-in-law ordered the murder in revenge for being denounced.

Both theories couldn't be right. Or could they? Was it possible that political prisoner Friedrich Brauer had links to the criminal Xaver Knorr and his henchmen? An unlikely partnership, but Seb had to keep an open mind, especially as it was almost certain Krieger knew the man who killed him in the woods.

On the road past Oberau, he was amused to see that the Mercedes was still at the side of the road, its shot-out tyres useless, while a pair of mechanics made themselves busy preparing to lift it on to a flat-bed truck.

He arrived in Farchant, a little way to the north of Gapa, almost two hours after leaving home. Petra Krieger looked alarmed when she opened the door. It seemed to have become a habitual reaction to his visits. What was it about him that disturbed her so much?

Probably the fact that he was a murder cop.

'May I come in, Frau Krieger?'

'I'm very busy, detective.'

'That makes two of us.' He didn't wait, simply stepped past her. He knew this house pretty well now and went straight through to the kitchen. 'Coffee on the go? I'd love some if you have a cup to spare.'

She was staring at his feet. 'You don't even bother to take your shoes off now.'

'Really? How thoughtless of me.'

Reluctantly she poured him half a cup and he sipped it, black. It wasn't bad. He wondered for whom she had made it? Herself? Or was lover boy Horst Feld here?

'I have news for you, Frau Krieger. Bad news, I'm afraid. It seems there's been an altercation at Dachau KZ and your father is almost certain to be charged with either attempted murder or a grievous assault. Either way, he must expect an extremely serious penalty.'

Her eyes widened. 'Papa?'

'I'm sorry to be the bearer of this news.'

'But he wouldn't hurt anyone. He's a man of peace.'

'It seems it was an act of vengeance – he felt that someone, the victim, had betrayed him.'

'Please, detective, tell me this isn't true.'

Seb suddenly softened. 'Sit down, Frau Krieger. Forgive me, I've been too harsh. It may be that there are extenuating circumstances for your father. We'll have to wait and see. Is your friend Herr Feld here perhaps?'

'No, he's at work.'

'Where would that be?'

'He has his own workshop. He's a potter, mostly souvenirs for the tourists.'

'And is that near here?'

She pointed at the front window. 'Just across the road. Why do you want him?'

'I think perhaps you know. Yes?'

She said nothing. She knew. And there was nothing she could do but maintain her guilty silence.

The workshop was an extension to the house on the other side of the street. Seb didn't bother knocking at the door, just turned the handle and walked in.

'Good morning, Herr Feld. I hope you don't mind my barging in on you like this.'

The man was at his workbench, crafting a little figurine from clay. It seemed to be an old farmer with leather shorts, long pipe and a typical alpine hat with a tuft of goat hair. Just the sort of Bavarian souvenir that visitors from northern Germany and other countries would love.

'Captain Wolff, how can I help you, sir?'

He did not seem worried by Seb's arrival – certainly, a lot less concerned than the last time they'd met, when he stepped out of a wardrobe half naked, clutching his clothes.

'Still the same matter. Investigating the murder of Theodor Krieger.' It was pointless pretending to this man that the death had been caused in a car crash, given his relationship to the dead man's widow. 'It occurred to me that you might have had something to do with it.'

He was so overweight, so flabby, that he simply hadn't looked like an assassin. Seb was angry with himself, falling for stereotypes. Why shouldn't a man who dined on double helpings of *Bierwurst* be a killer?

'No, sir, not me.'

'You must realise that you've put yourself in grave danger – not just from the police but also from Krieger's friends in the SS.'

'But I've committed no crime, Captain Wolff.'

'You've been sleeping with his wife.'

'But surely that's not a crime?'

'Krieger's SS comrades might disagree. They might also wonder about your connections to Petra Krieger's father. Is it possible you received a message from him, brought to you out of Dachau?'

'No, sir.'

'My investigations suggest otherwise. Where were you the night Krieger died?'

'Which night would that be?'

'February the fourth or fifth, either side of midnight. I'm sure you remember it well.'

He nodded. 'Of course. And, yes, I do remember it well. I spent the night with Frau Krieger as her pig of a husband was out, either with the English Whore or his criminal friends. It was a wonderful night. We declared our love for each other. As soon as Krieger is buried, we'll be married.'

'How romantic.'

'You're laughing at us.'

'Now why would I do that? Let's get back to the point, Herr Feld. Would anyone else be able to corroborate your alibi for the fourth/fifth?'

'We were in bed. Why would anyone else be there?'

'Just trying to help you, Herr Feld. A loved one or family member is never received in court as a reliable alibi; I'm sure you understand.'

'I can't help that. It's the truth, plain and simple.'

'You're friendly with Frau Krieger's father?'

'Friedrich? Yes, indeed. He's a fine man. But that doesn't mean I would kill on his behalf.'

'And do you share his politics?'

'No, but what has that to do with anything? I'm not a political person, never have been.'

'But you would do anything for him, yes?'

Horst Feld seemed to blink, hesitate. 'Not anything, no. If he asked for a favour, I would consider it, like anyone would for a friend.'

'What sort of gun do you have?'

'I don't have a gun. I never have.'

'But you used firearms during the war?'

'We all did. But I was more than happy to put all that behind me when I came home.' There was a pause. 'Is that all, Captain Wolff?'

Seb nodded. For a few moments he wondered whether to take the man to Munich for a formal interrogation. But on what grounds? He had no evidence. Somehow he would find it, but that was still a way off.

Brauer might have confessed to ordering the death of Krieger, but who pulled the trigger?

Hans Winter woke late and felt dreadful. Every time he moved a sharp pain ran down his bandaged chest where Jung had sliced him with the razor. Blood seeped through. His face, too, was in a bad way where Brauer had punched him. His ribs and back ached from the kicking and clubbing he had received while crawling to the Bunker.

He was an unlovable sight. God, what would Malwine think when she saw him?

'Coffee, Sergeant Winter?'

'Yes, please, Frau Wolff.'

'Do you feel a little better after your sleep?'

'A little.' In fact, the ten hours of sleep had filled him with energy. 'Perhaps I might use your telephone?'

'It is coin-operated – on the landing. Do you have any coins?'

He did, and he went to the phone while Frau Wolff prepared his late breakfast.

His first call was to the girlfriend of the Jew he still knew only as Schwabing. Her number was imprinted on his brain.

'Hello?' she said, not giving her name or her address. 'Who is this, please?'

'I have some money for you, dear lady, one hundred Reichsmarks, from your friend in Dachau. He said there would be no names, that we should meet at a café of your choosing in Munich.'

'Why would you give me money?'

'It's a trade that was made inside the camp – that's all I can tell you.'

'Is this a trick?'

'No trick, I promise you. You'll be perfectly safe, in a

public place. Your friend said you were with child and would need the money.'

She said nothing for a few moments, weighing things up.

'Very well,' she said at last.

'A café, then?'

'Do you know the Isar Café at the Viktualienmarkt?'

'Yes, I do.'

'Can you meet me there at two thirty? I'll be carrying a bright blue bag.'

'I'll be there.'

The second call was more difficult. To start with, no one answered the phone. He tried again half an hour later after his breakfast. Still no reply.

He thanked Angela Wolff for the food and bed, and asked her to tell the captain that he would take the train to Garmisch-Partenkirchen later, as he had a few things to take care of, then he made his way south through the city in the direction of Ettstrasse. First, he called in at BPP headquarters to pick up his pistol and badge from his locker.

A few minutes later he stopped at a public phone booth and once again tried the number Schwabing had given him. He was certain the number was correct. He had a perfectly good memory and, though he had been injured in the attack, he did not think he had suffered any concussion. But, again, no reply.

He slunk into the Presidium. He didn't want to see anyone he knew, because he didn't want to have to explain his injuries and his shaven head. The minutes ticked away and he wished he had agreed to meet Schwabing's girlfriend at an earlier time.

At two o'clock, he left the building and went back to the telephone kiosk and called the second number again. The phone rang for a full minute and he was about to hang up when there was a voice.

'Yes?' A Bavarian accent. Male.

He had rehearsed what he was going to say, but that the phone had finally been answered was so unexpected he became flustered. 'I – I was told you might be able to help me.'

'Who are you?'

'A recently released prisoner from Dachau.'

'Who gave you this number?'

'I don't know his name. A Jewish inmate. He said that for a price you might be able to secure a perfectly forged Aryan certificate for a Jew who wishes to marry a Gentile. Or that you might know someone who could help.' He was babbling.

There was a long pause on the line. 'That would be a very expensive item. It would come with a significant risk. Is there a number I can call you on?'

Winter thought of giving his home number, then thought better of it. 'No.'

'Call me again at midnight. Be in Munich and ready to move at a moment's notice. Have cash, two hundred and fifty Reichsmarks.'

The phone clicked dead.

Winter's heart sank. This sounded like an obvious set-up. A late-night meeting, a bundle of money – far more than Schwabing had intimated – about his person. Only a fool would agree to such a meeting. Or a desperate man.

So what was he? A desperate fool.

For a few moments, he looked helplessly at the phone, then replaced it and walked through the centre of Munich, through Marienplatz and Tal down to the marketplace. The café looked half empty, which was a relief. He was ten minutes early, so he found a table, ordered a coffee and waited, looking closely at the handbags of the women who entered.

She was right on time. A petite, well-dressed young woman. The swell of her belly told him that she was, indeed, with child. Their eyes met and he nodded, then indicated the seat opposite his.

'Would you like a coffee, dear lady?'

He smiled at her; she didn't smile back. Her eyes were dark and nervous. She was looking at his damaged face. He kept his shaven head covered by his tattered old fedora, but it was still obvious something had happened to him.

If for a moment she suspected that he kept a BPP badge about his person, she would probably die of terror.

'No.'

He had collected the money from the bank on the way to Ettstrasse, where he transferred it from his wallet to an envelope. Now, he took this from his inside pocket and slid it across the table to her. He wanted to say, 'I'm the same as your man, you know. I understand how he suffers, how you struggle with him interned.'

But he said nothing and knew that she didn't want to converse with him. Her small hand reached out and took the envelope, slipping it quickly into her blue bag without looking at the contents.

Immediately, she rose without another word and began walking towards the door. Then she stopped and came back. 'My man, is he all right?'

'Yes, ma'am, he's well.' He wasn't going to tell her that he had been beaten almost senseless when all the Jews had to run a gauntlet of whips and cudgels in retaliation for the murder of a Nazi by a Jew in Switzerland. As though they were somehow to blame for the actions of a man they had never met.

'Thank you.' And then she was gone.

'Heil Hitler,' Unity said, thrusting her arm out as though it were a spear. She had just entered the Kandabar.

'Heil Hitler, Miss Mitford.'

'So, Mr Clever Detective, what's all this about?'

'May I get you a drink first? Order you something to eat?'

'Sekt to drink. No, make it champagne, it's not as nice but it's more expensive. And I think a plate of Wiener schnitzel with sautéed potatoes would go down very well.'

Seb summoned the waiter. He ordered two plates of the schnitzel, along with a bottle of champagne to share. God alone knew how he was going to claim expenses for this little junket, but, if he had to pay for it himself, so be it.

'Well?'

'I'm still looking for Fräulein Lang. I'm trying to talk to everyone who knows her.'

'It's plain what's happened. She's embarrassed herself and bolted. Probably gone off somewhere to get away from the humiliation.'

'Why would she feel humiliated?'

'Oh, I'm sure a clever detective like you must have found out what happened at the party – her approaching Joe Goebbels as though she were about to have things out with him in front of darling Magda.'

'I did hear something like that.'

'There you are. Case solved.'

'But I can find no record of her ever having left Schloss Stark. No witness, nothing. Surely someone must have taken her away in their car? As far as I know she didn't have one of her own, and she certainly couldn't have walked far on a night like that.'

'A woman like Elena will always find a man to do whatever she wants. All she had to do was to find some unsuspecting male and whisper in his ear that she had a lovely, perfumed bed back at her hotel. Now tell me, what man is going to turn down such an offer from the world's most beautiful film star?'

'It's a possibility.'

'Case solved again. I thought you were supposed to be the clever detective. I should have your job.'

'And I'm sure you would be very good at it, Miss Mitford.'

Their food and drink arrived.

'You know, Wolff, you don't fool me for a minute. I see you squirm every time you say Heil Hitler. You survive on your uncle's friendship with the Führer. But you should be very careful, because your luck won't last forever.'

'I'm just trying to do my job, Miss Mitford. Bringing killers to justice, locating vanished film stars. There is no political side to me.'

'*Prost*, then,' she said, holding up her champagne flute.

'Cheers.'

They both sipped, then began to eat.

'Just one more thing, though, Miss Mitford.' Seb's fork was halfway between plate and mouth. 'If something untoward *has* happened to Elena Lang, what possible motive could there be?'

'Oh, that's easy. Her loose tongue.'

40

Seb was perplexed. What exactly did Unity mean by that?

'You seem confused, Wolff. I thought you spoke English. Do you not know what a loose tongue implies?'

'Someone who talks too much?'

'That sort of thing. Perhaps you should ask little Howard Jack. I'm sure he knows what I'm talking about. Dangerous things, loose tongues, even more hazardous than loose morals.'

'Are you suggesting she might have upset someone?'

'*Upset* is rather too mild a word for what I'm suggesting.'

This was clearly something to do with Elena's affair with Goebbels. Perhaps she had been scorned and was threatening to make a public scene. Had she been talking about her affair with the wrong people? The foreign press perhaps? Was that why she was moved away so abruptly as she tried to approach his table at Schloss Stark?

It was possible, and yet somehow Seb couldn't visualise it; it seemed out of character. The Elena Lang he had met was in fear of her life, not planning to spread gossip about an untrue lover. No, his instinct wouldn't have it. She was not one to embarrass an ex in public. Far too classy and discreet for that sort of thing.

But that didn't mean that there weren't those who might *fear* she was about to make a scene. Someone protective of the Nazi hierarchy, because it was common knowledge that Magda Goebbels was extremely close to the Führer. In the absence of a wife of his own, Hitler saw her as First Lady of the Reich. A woman above reproach, mother of three beautiful little Aryan children by Goebbels and a fourteen-year-old boy by her first husband. The minister of propaganda's stock would fall like a stone if Hitler discovered he had betrayed such an exemplary woman.

Yes, Joseph Goebbels might well be appalled if his cosy life was threatened with disruption. But was that enough to kill a woman?

'Very good veal. Is this all paid for by the good citizens of Munich?'

'That depends on my boss, Herr Ruff.'

'I'm sure you would never cheat by so much as a pfennig on your expenses.'

Seb ignored her sarcasm. 'Back to Fräulein Lang. You first suggested that she might have found some helpful man to give her a lift from Schloss Stark and next you tell me that her loose tongue might have got her in trouble. Where, pray, do I go from there?'

'As I said, talk to Howard Jack. What do you know about *him*?'

'That he is a poet, that he is not short of money, that he travels wherever the whim takes him, that he has many friends.'

'And?'

'And he can be very amusing in a way that could get him into a lot of trouble if he were a German citizen.'

'Is that it?'

'Yes, but, if there is more, please tell me, Miss Mitford.'

'No, no, that's your job, you're the detective. The *clever* detective. You find out what Howard Jack really is and everything should become clear.'

She pushed her plate away, dropped her napkin on the floor, stood up, smiled at him without any trace of friendliness and strode out.

*

Seb caught up with Hexie in the middle of the afternoon. She had seen the remarkable Sonja Henie going for gold at the figure skating and, almost as remarkably – though duller – her old colleague at the Hoffmann shop, Eva Braun, sitting just a metre behind Adolf Hitler.

The relationship between the Führer and the young shop-girl was, perhaps, the worst-kept secret in Bavaria. Everyone knew but few dared mention it, save at home around the dinner table. Yet here they were in public, together but not together.

'Hitler had a tartan blanket over his knees like an old man. Evie looked so happy. Did the international press have any idea, do you think?'

'It's possible. Some of them are pretty smart.'

'Anyway, Seb, what have you been up to? Have you found the missing film star?'

He wanted to tell her the truth about Elena Lang but he couldn't, not yet. 'We think she's gone home to Vienna,' he lied.

Hexie frowned, clearly unconvinced. 'You're very mysterious these days . . . All these gorgeous women in your life. Talking of which, when are you going to introduce me to the love of your tender years? I can hardly wait.'

He put his hands to her warm cheeks and kissed her on the lips.

She laughed and pulled away. 'Is that supposed to shut me up?'

'I thought it might be worth a try.'

'Then you don't know me as well as you think, Seb Wolff.'

He wasn't convinced that there was any more to be learnt about Howard Jack. That was just Unity Mitford making mischief in retaliation for his rudeness about her Nazi friends. But, then again, perhaps he was worth a visit.

In the early evening, he drove up to the gatehouse at Schloss Stark. The liveried guard asked him if he was expected.

'Probably not but I'm coming in anyway.' He flashed his badge and made sure the gateman caught a glimpse of the Walther pistol nestling in the shoulder holster under his jacket.

'I'll call through for you, sir. Who exactly was it that you wished to see?'

'The Englishman, Howard Jack.'

After a quick call, the guard told Seb to drive up to the main entrance. Howard Jack was there waiting for him, wearing a dinner jacket and bow tie.

'What a pleasant surprise. I heard you had a luncheon with Bobo. Very good of you to accompany her when the Führer's in town with his other woman. Was Bobo a frightful sulk?'

A question that did not require or deserve a reply.

'Are you here alone, Mr Jack?'

'No, we're at dinner. The whole gang and a few others. Bit of a formal affair. Not sure how much more of them I can take, to be honest. A few more days and we'll all be scattered to the wind and it won't be a moment too soon as far as I'm concerned. Are you here about darling Elena?'

'In a way, but it's actually you that I'm interested in.'

'Well, come on in and we can talk.'

'In a moment. First a question, what exactly *are* you?'

'What a wonderfully absurd question.' He was frowning and smiling. 'A man, a poet, a human being, a son, a friend to many. Does that help?'

'Not really. A couple of people have suggested there might be more to you than meets the eye. What would they be referring to, do you think?'

'Is this Bobo talking?'

Seb shrugged.

'Oh dear, oh dear. Bobo has got it into the fluffy little marshmallow that passes for her brain that I'm some sort of secret agent. I ask you, Seb, do I *look* like a spy?'

'I don't know what spies look like. To my knowledge I've never met one.'

'Despite appearances, Bobo can read – and I suspect she has delved into too much Hannay and Ashenden. And there was me thinking I was your Wimsey. Suddenly I am to be re-cast from detective to spy.' He sighed. 'But it's not going to work, Seb – spies have to keep secrets. I never could. Worst gossip in the Western world.'

'She also mentioned that Elena Lang has been loose-tongued. What could she possibly mean by that?'

'I haven't the faintest idea. I've always found sweet Elena to be rather reserved. Look, come on through and we can put these questions to Bobo.'

'I'll come in, but, no, we won't ask her that. I've already questioned her and she simply referred me to you, as though you have an unknown, secret side.'

'Perhaps she's looking at the wrong person. Perhaps *you* are, too.'

'What do you mean?'

'Oh, nothing. My imagination getting the better of me, that's all.' He smiled, almost grinned. 'But come on in. The Starks and chums are all at dinner. I'm sure they'd love to see you.'

'I do have an interesting bit of information for Sophie and Werner.'

'Follow me, dear fellow.'

They were dining at a glittering, candlelit table with a wealth of silver and crystal reflecting the flickering flames: the von Starks, Paul Jena, Fritz Mannheim, Unity Mitford along with four others, two of whom Seb recognised – a powerful industrialist, an opera diva and two other women who might have been mother and daughter.

'Sophie, Werner,' Jack said, 'Captain Wolff says he has some exciting information for you.'

Gruppenführer Jena was looking at him as though he could kill him, as though he should already be dead and buried on a wooded hillside between Farchant and Oberau.

Seb gave an extravagant straight-arm salute, said Heil Hitler, which was received by a bemused silence, and then smiled at them all.

'Yes, captain?' Sophie von Stark said wearily. 'This really isn't a good time. We're just eating, you know.'

He should have bowed his head, apologised for disturbing their meal and walked out, back into the night. That would have been the sensible thing to do. But the sight of them all there, so smug in their wealth and privilege, provoked him. And, most of all, Jena, the man who'd ordered his death, puffed up with power among his wealthy friends.

Seb couldn't stomach it. He had to speak out, provoke Jena back. Instead of making his excuses and leaving, he simply smiled and addressed himself to the von Starks.

'Forgive my intrusion. This won't take a minute and I'm certain you'll be interested. I've been doing a little research on your behalf, you see, and, believe it or not, I've managed to identify the woman in your beautiful little Klimt portrait.'

No one was smiling. No one looked even vaguely pleased. Jena was visibly stiffening. Seb locked eyes with him. He wanted a reaction.

'Her name is Selma Sachs,' Seb said, then let the news sink in.

Jena was shifting in his seat now.

'Isn't that remarkable, Herr Gruppenführer?'

'What are you talking about, Wolff?' His voice angry, lethal.

'Selma Sachs, a Bavarian woman, lives not far from here – little place called Liliendorf. *Lived*, I should say. Perhaps you knew of her, Herr Jena?'

Jena could hold himself in no longer. He rose to his feet. 'How dare you interrupt our meal with such nonsense? If you have something to say, put it in writing and submit it for examination.'

Seb ignored him. 'Selma was a friend of Gustav Klimt, and it seems they even went on holiday together at Attersee, the beautiful Austrian lake. This was all quite a few years ago, before the war. But I thought you would all be delighted to know. No longer is the sitter for the painting anonymous.'

Jena was moving towards him, pushing him in the chest. 'Get out, man. Get out. Your career is over, Wolff.'

Seb held his ground. 'If you still have any doubts, perhaps you might like to look at some old pre-war photographs of Frau Sachs with Herr Klimt, which I can arrange for you. Really, I'm surprised your dealer didn't know all this, as it was very easy for me to find out and I'm but an amateur in such matters.'

Jena had pulled out a pistol and had ranged it at Seb's head. There were gasps from the other diners. Unity simply smirked.

Seb looked at Jena coldly. 'You're not going to murder me here in front of all these witnesses, are you, Herr SS-Gruppenführer? Now that really would ruin everyone's dinner.' He turned his attention back to Werner von Stark. 'But tell me, sir, I would very much like to know who sold you this fine painting, because there's a strong likelihood that it was stolen, and as a police officer I would like to question the dealer.'

'Stolen?' Werner von Stark looked at his sister and they both appeared horrified. 'We bought it in good faith.' Their eyes now were on Jena.

'Anyway, to get back to Selma Sachs. I would have brought her to you in person, but I'm afraid she's left the country in rather a hurry . . . like so many Jews.'

He reached out and, with the back of his hand, pushed Jena's pistol to one side. 'Perhaps you might be able to assist them with some further information, Herr Gruppenführer.'

Seb bowed to them all, clicked his heels, gave another Hitler salute, turned and left.

As he drove away, clutching the wheel, his hands tingled. He had never felt more alive. Their expressions of horror and dismay, the murderous loathing of Jena and Unity, the amusement of little Howard Jack, the curious indifference of Fritz Mannheim, the astonishment of the four strangers.

Never more alive.

And yet he knew for certain that he was now a dead man. He had survived so much in his thirty-five years of life. But not this. The four men pursuing him in the woods and rocks above the Giessenbach Gorge were but the prelude to the real thing. He had pushed Jena way too far.

At midnight, Hans Winter called the number. It rang for a long time, what seemed minutes, but was probably less than thirty seconds. Then it was picked up.

'Yes?'

'You told me to call at midnight.'

'Have you got the money?'

'Yes.'

'Are you armed?'

'No.'

'Are you driving?'

'No. I'm in central Munich, on foot.'

'Good. You know the Augustiner-Keller on Arnulfstrasse?'

'Yes.'

'Be there in half an hour. Have both hands in your trouser pockets. Stand to the west of the main gate. Wear a hat. And wait.'

'Is that it?'

As before, the phone had already gone dead.

To take the gun, concealed, or leave it at the Police Presidium? Every cell in his brain and body told him to take it, fully loaded with the safety off. But the voice on the phone had been clear, and they would undoubtedly search him.

He thought back to the woman in the café. She knew her man was a Jew but still cared about him and stood by him, even at the risk of offending her family. So why did he harbour doubts about Malwine? Why could he not tell her the truth about his ancestry? Why did he fear she would take her parents' side? Why was he not sure about her love?

Yes, he earned a decent-enough living as a sergeant in the Bavarian Political Police, but with his ravaged face and less-than-athletic body he was quite aware that he was not an attractive physical specimen. But then Malwine was in her mid-thirties and was worried that she was getting on, so this might also be her only chance at marriage. Was that why she wanted him? For babies and respectability, not love?

It was the sex imbalance, the preponderance of women over men because of the two million dead in the war. The same reason Petra Krieger had given for marrying her brute of a husband. If women wanted children and a life away from their own parents, they had to take what they could get;

men had all the power. So was that all Winter was? Malwine's last hope of motherhood and a family of her own?

He had already put his life on the line for her by entering Dachau undercover in quest of an Aryan pass. This was a risk of a different order. Walking unarmed into a probable trap while carrying a great deal of money in his pocket – almost a quarter of his hard-earned savings. He would tell anyone else planning such a venture that they were a suicidal fool.

But he had already made his decision. Seb Wolff had called him a true man. That was something worth living up to.

41

The street lamps had been extinguished. The only light came from the occasional shop window or curtainless apartment. The air was a little less cold and the snow of the past few days had turned to drizzle.

Winter huddled into his coat, his fedora tilted forward over his brow, camouflaging the worst of the damage to his face and concealing his shaved head. Standing outside the Augustiner-Keller, hands in pockets, he felt exposed and vulnerable.

Having left the gun and his BPP badge at the Presidium, he had arrived at the beer hall five minutes early. But at least ten minutes had now passed. The man on the phone had told him to wait, so he waited. What else could he do?

Every so often the door to the beer hall opened as another group of drinkers emerged, their revelling finished for the night. He could hear an accordion and a low buzz of chatter. One or two people gave him a sideways glance, but no one spoke to him.

A car drew up. A small, dark green Opel. The driver leant across the passenger seat and wound down the window. 'Get in.'

His legs were like lead, the soles of his shoes glued to the pavement. Was this how it ended, his short life? Stepping into a car and being driven to a brutal robbery and death?

He opened the passenger door and climbed in. At least there was only one man in the car, the driver, so perhaps that gave him a chance.

Winter pulled the car door closed and the driver engaged gear and drove away.

'Where are we going?' Winter asked. He stole a glance at the driver, trying to work out what sort of man he was without staring. In the darkness, he was little more than a silhouette, but he didn't seem large, probably about the same size as Winter. His face was swathed in a woollen scarf.

'Don't talk.'

He was driving west, first in the vague direction of the Nymphenburg Palace, then onwards, towards the outer suburbs. Twenty minutes later, they pulled up in an anonymous street of industrial properties and warehouses.

Without a word, the driver switched off the engine and opened his door. 'Come with me,' he said.

Winter had little option but to do as he was told. He climbed out of the car and followed in the hurried footsteps of the driver. A fine rain fell, the cloud covering the moon. Winter was anticipating going into one of the warehouses, but the driver ducked down a narrow alley.

What followed was a maze-like series of lanes, culs-de-sac and back gardens in which Winter struggled to keep up with his contact and became hopelessly lost and drenched.

The driver stopped at the front entrance to an apartment block with no name or number, looked around to make sure they hadn't been followed, then used a key to enter the front lobby. He ascended the stone stairway to the third and top storey, where he double-rapped a door and stood back.

The door opened. The driver pushed Winter through, then closed it again. Winter was now inside a semi-dark hallway, the driver outside, presumably keeping guard.

'Money?'

At first Winter couldn't see where the voice was coming from. 'I have it.'

Without warning, his arms were grasped from behind and another pair of hands patted him down: shoulders, chest, waist, abdomen, back of his trouser belt, groin, legs, socks.

'He's clear.'

They took him through to a kitchen and switched on a light. Both men were masked.

'First we need the money, then your name,' the taller of the two said.

Winter removed the money from his inside pocket and handed it over. The shorter man counted it, then nodded.

'Now your name?'

Winter hesitated.

'Look, we can't fix you an Aryan pass without your name. We assume you want your real name, yes?'

'Winter. Hans Winter.'

'That's all? No middle name?'

'No middle name.'

'And are you going to give us your ancestry as it presently stands? Place of birth – mother, father, grandparents?'

'No, I don't want that. I want it all new. Say my parents and grandparents are dead. No siblings.'

'That makes sense. But you're obviously not Munich raised. Somewhere in the north-west, given your accent.'

'Let's say Essen. I've never lived there but I know it.'

'And you realise this will be the lesser certificate – should be all right for marriage and most lines of work.'

'Can you not do the greater certificate?'

The man laughed. 'You're a Jew and you want to join the SS?'

'It needs to be good enough for approval by the Race Office. There are complications, that's all. I can't explain.'

'It's a lot more work – we have to establish a family tree

back to 1800 or before, five generations with birth or baptismal certificates, completely free of Jewish blood.'

'I understand.'

'So it will cost more.'

'How much?'

'An extra one fifty. Total four hundred. Can you manage that?'

'I only have two fifty on me.'

'We'll collect the rest from you when we deliver your pass. Such things are not straightforward, so it will be a few days. But you're fortunate in one regard – the name Winter is commonplace and has no Jewish connotations.'

'All right.'

'You realise that your physical appearance will always be held against you?'

He nodded.

'And there is always the danger that the Race Office could implement their own investigation into your history, but that would probably only happen if a complaint was lodged against you. You do understand these possibilities?'

'I do.'

'So we trust each other now, yes?'

'Yes.' He trusted them because if they'd meant him harm, he would be dead by now.

'Call us in three or four days. Then we'll arrange a meeting.'

'Thank you.'

'Be careful, Herr Winter. Be sure to learn your new history thoroughly. One slip and you'll be in a cell so deep you may never see daylight again. Above all, the Nazis are bureaucrats – and there's nothing that enrages them more than being duped by forged documents.'

'I understand.'

'You don't know us and you never will. We would ask

you not to pass on our telephone number to anyone unless you're certain that they are Jewish and in danger. Now give us an approximate date of birth and your address. Then our driver will take you back to the Augustiner.'

And that was that. Unless he was utterly deluded, it seemed these men were on his side.

It was late, too late for a murder cop to make house calls. The Gestapo might like kicking down doors in the middle of the night or just before dawn, but that wasn't Seb's way.

Tonight was different, though. He had exposed the truth about Paul Jena in the most brutal way and he was on edge because there was every chance he wouldn't live out the night. He was worried about Hexie, his mother and Jurgen. All three could be in danger when Jena's men came looking for him, as they surely would.

He needed to protect them, but first he had this call to make.

As he pulled up, he saw a light on in the window and guessed she was awake.

She opened the door almost immediately, cigarette in one hand, small glass of something alcoholic in the other: Traudl Schramm, mistress of the murder victim Theodor Krieger, known as the English Whore.

Behind her, the single room she called home looked smaller and even more chaotic than he recalled. She was alone.

'Good evening, Captain Wolff.' She was speaking English and the voice was more soft and hazy than slurred. She had been drinking but wasn't drunk.

'I'm sorry to call so late.' He continued the language theme. If she wanted to speak English, why not?

'That's all right. I'm a night owl, especially when I'm alone. I never liked the dark. Are you going to join me in a smoke and some schnapps?'

'I'll take a small glass of schnapps.'

'Come into the warm, then, it's nice to have company.' She went to her sideboard. His eyes strayed to a bottle of cognac.

She caught his glance. 'I'm afraid I keep that for special occasions. The choice is Poire Williams or Poire Williams.'

'Then I'll happily take that.'

She selected a small glass and poured a measure for Seb.

'Thank you.' He took a sip.

'So how are your investigations going? Have you nailed the evil witch and her father?'

'I can't discuss my inquiries, but I have a question to put to you. Do you know a man named Horst Feld?'

'Yes. The souvenir maker. Why do you ask?'

'Last time I saw you, I told you that Frau Krieger had a lover of her own, but I didn't mention his name. Horst Feld is that man.'

'Good God, she really is scraping the barrel, isn't she?'

'Why do you say that?'

'Have you seen him?'

'Yes. But tell me, how do you come to know him?'

She had finished her glass and was pouring herself another. The bottle was more than half empty, and Seb suspected that she had already imbibed a great deal of it.

'When tens of thousands of tourists aren't here, this isn't such a big place, detective. Gapa, Grainau, Farchant, Oberau, even Mittenwald and Oberammergau – one big happy family. Well, perhaps not so happy. We know each other or have probably heard of each other. It's a small world – everyone's linked somehow. Marriage, family, hatred, work. Everyone knows me because I'm the English Whore. Everyone knew Theo because he was the war lover and our local SS hero. And Horst Feld? He is the pink snake that slimes through the night.'

313

'Not popular, then?'

'He's a creep.'

'Did you ever have dealings with him?'

'He worked with Theo sometimes. *For* Theo.'

'Doing what?'

She laughed. 'I may not have been entirely honest with you before. I knew that Theo wasn't a saint, that he was up to no good with the likes of Xaver Knorr and others. Everyone needs a sideline. They used Horst Feld, too, when they needed an extra pair of hands. But Theo always spoke of him with utter contempt.'

'Would I be right in thinking that you have heard of certain events in Liliendorf? A house fire . . . three men missing, including Knorr.'

'I did hear a little whisper.'

'And Horst Feld sometimes worked with Theo and these men?'

She nodded and took a large sip.

'Did Theo know Feld was having an affair with his wife?'

'I doubt it. If he had, he'd have told me and we'd have had a good laugh.'

'How did Feld help Theo?'

'Just shifting stuff, I think. From time to time, he would turn up in a bar where we were drinking. He always made me squirm.'

'Do you think he would be capable of killing Theo?'

'Anyone with a gun is capable of killing, aren't they?'

'I'm not sure that's true. It takes a certain nerve and ruthlessness to pull out a gun in a dark wood and shoot a man twice in the back of the head, and then again in the heart.'

'The pink snake could do that. And, from what you're saying, he might have had a motive.'

Seb nodded. He had already worked out that Feld had

powerful motives for murder. One, revenge for Frau Krieger's father being denounced. Two, to get Theo Krieger out of the way so he could marry his widow. Maybe even a third motive – a favour for one of his fellow criminals who wanted Theo out of the way.

'So, will you charge them – the pink snake and the witch?'

'I need some evidence. Solid evidence that will crush their denials in court. At the moment I don't have a single gram of the stuff. How do we even place Horst Feld in the woods at the Scharnitz Pass on the night of the murder? He has an alibi. And motive alone is nothing.'

'But you believe me now? The witch is behind it?'

'I'm leaning that way.'

She was pouring them both more schnapps, the last trickles of the bottle. 'I'm sorry, detective, I wish I could help more.'

'I'll get there.'

She smiled at him as she handed him the drink. She was closer now and he could smell her scent, mingled with the alcohol. 'Would you like to stay the night with me? I really don't like being alone in the dark.'

He smiled back. 'That is a very kind offer, and you're a beautiful young woman, but my fiancée is waiting for me at a guest house near here.'

'Shame.'

'Don't waste yourself, Traudl. You're worth a great deal more than men like Theodor Krieger. Perhaps this town is too small for you.'

'You're probably right. Where do you suggest?'

'Berlin? Or how about London?'

She laughed. 'They'd call me the German Whore there.'

42

Never had Seb felt more frustrated.

He still didn't know who killed Elena Lang. Who drowned her and dumped her body in the snow at the entrance to the Hell Valley? Was it a man or a woman? More than one killer? He didn't even have a motive for her murder, save for the vague suggestion that someone close to Joseph Goebbels wanted her out of the way in case she embarrassed him by going public about their affair.

He knew so much. He knew most of the details of how the goods of fleeing Jews were smuggled out of the country, with the most valuable items stolen. He knew in his own mind that General Paul Jena was at the very top of the criminal tree and that he had sold a Klimt painting cut-price to ingratiate himself with the von Starks.

He knew that Jena and his SS renegades had murdered and burned three associates to prevent their talking to the police.

And he was almost certain that Petra Krieger, Horst Feld and Friedrich Brauer had conspired to murder Petra's husband.

He knew all this, but he had no evidence to show a court.

But what really hurt was that he was nowhere near solving the murder of poor Elena. His failure haunted him.

And there was something else. By humiliating Jena at Schloss Stark, he had ensured not only his own death but also those of his loved ones. Jena was going to come after him with every weapon and man at his disposal, and there was a very good chance that Seb's family and friends would pay the price.

Innocent victims? In the eyes of men like Paul Jena, there was no such thing.

Seb had to act fast to protect his family.

He arrived back at the Waxenstein Guest House at the same time as Hexie and Carin.

'Good evening, ladies.'

'I won't ask you where you've been, Seb.'

Carin blew them a kiss. 'Night, night, children. Don't fight.'

Seb and Hexie were both exhausted, but they managed to make warm, lazy love.

'That was it,' she said, as they lay in each other's arms. 'That's our baby. I could feel your seed connecting with my egg.'

'You might be right. Time will tell.' He wanted to talk to her seriously, to warn her of the danger they were all in, but this wasn't the moment to break the spell.

'I've had enough of Gapa,' she said. 'We've seen some wonderful skiing and skating, and you wouldn't believe the ski jumps, but now I just want to go home to Munich.'

But, then again, he *had* to tell her. It was all too serious to leave her in the dark. 'Something's happened,' he said.

She raised herself on to her elbows and looked down at his unshaven face. 'What?'

'I've done something rather stupid. Me and my oversized mouth. I've managed to make a deadly enemy of an SS general. I'm pretty sure he already tried to kill me once and he's going to try again. This time, he'll succeed.'

'Does he have a name?'

'Paul Jena. He's not going to rest until I'm dead.'

'What are you going to do?'

317

'Try to stay alive. But, more importantly, I'm worried about my loved ones, because Jena won't care who he takes out with me.'

'Assassins might come here tonight and put bullets in us while we're asleep? That's what you're saying?'

'I've locked the door.'

'That will stop a battalion of SS men, won't it? Why don't we just kill ourselves now and be done with it?'

'Perhaps you should go away for a few days, Hex. Stay with a friend in the country somewhere.'

'And lose my job? I'm supposed to be back at work on Friday. You'll need to come up with a better plan than that, Captain of Detectives Wolff.'

'I don't have another plan. No one in the Police Presidium is going to stand with me and take on the SS. That's the reality of the world in 1936.'

'So you just wait to be killed? Sit and wait like a target at the funfair? You know, when I agreed to marry you, I thought rather better of you.'

'I'm trying to protect you and that's the way you speak to me?'

She shrugged.

'So do you have a suggestion?' He was getting angry now. Yes, this was hard news for her to take but a little understanding might not go amiss.

'Yes, I certainly do. Go out there with your trusty little pistol and neutralise Gruppenführer Jena before he neutralises you.'

'Kill him? Are you suggesting murder?'

She shrugged. 'Whatever it takes, Seb Wolff. If it's your life against his, do for him. Better to die with your boots on and a gun in your hand. Take the bastard on – and let the best man win.'

*

When Hans Winter got back to his apartment, his head was pounding. He knew he needed sleep, but the excitement still swirled around him like an electric mist. He had done all this: taken himself into Dachau in search of a Jewish forger.

Not only that, but he had found one – and they hadn't killed him or robbed him, as far as he knew. That was still to be discovered. They had his money, and there was every chance he would never hear from them or see them again, but they had seemed genuine, almost as nervous as he was.

He had taken a terrible risk, but it had paid off.

There were two letters in his postbox and he recognised the handwriting immediately. Both of them were from Malwine. He hadn't seen her for a week, and if she had tried phoning she wouldn't have got through. He had tried to call her before entering Dachau, but there had been no reply.

The thought of the letters made him feel uneasy. He wasn't sure he wanted to read them, but eventually he sat down and slit them both open with a sharp knife.

Malwine had not been impressed by his apartment when he'd shown her where he lived, hoping she might live here, too, if only he could summon the courage to ask for her hand in marriage. She toured his home with a critical eye, telling him how cold and lacking in Bavarian tradition it all was and making suggestions about how each room could be improved.

She hadn't stayed the night, nor had they made love. Not properly. She had allowed him to kiss her lips and stroke her breast, but that was as far as it went. Lovemaking was reserved for the wedding night, when she would give herself to him.

Winter could hardly stand the waiting. A woman of his own, in his bed every night, ready to receive him with warmth and love. Not like the whores in Dortmund, who couldn't wait to bid him farewell with his money in their purses.

With trepidation, he read the two letters in order of date.

My dearest Hansi,

You haven't telephoned me for over two days now. I called by your apartment to see if you were ill in bed, but you weren't at home. I'm worried for you. Please call me or come and see me.

With love, as always,
Your Malwine

The tone of the second letter was rather different.

Dear Hans,

It is five days now and still no word from you. I've spoken to Mama and Papa and they insist that your conduct in ignoring me in this way is unforgivable and that I should call off our friendship forthwith.

But I tell them that you're very busy with important work on behalf of the Reich and that sometimes you're summoned away without notice. And so I will forgive you, if only you will call me. Please do not ignore this letter.

Yours, Malwine

It was too late to call her tonight. He realised that he should have made contact with her during the day while waiting to meet the forgers, but he had been in such a state of agitation that he could think of nothing else. And he had wanted to secure the Aryan pass so that he could make his marriage proposal with confidence.

He looked at the telephone. It was after one o'clock in the

morning. No, he couldn't ring and nor could he go along to where she lived with her parents.

They had met purely by chance at church a couple of weeks before Christmas. They were sitting next to each other, and she smiled at him, which gave him the confidence to say hello.

He could see that she was a few years older and a few centimetres taller and broader than he was, but that meant nothing. They got on well and sought each other out every Sunday, always under the watchful eye of her parents.

At first, they were impressed by the fact that he was in the Bavarian Political Police and that he was interested in their daughter, who had thus far shown no sign of finding a man to give them grandchildren.

But the more he saw of Herr and Frau Schmidt, the less enamoured of him they seemed to be. He knew that they didn't see him as the perfect German husband for their daughter, however desperate they might be to get her married off.

And now these letters. The second one felt very much like an ultimatum. This is your last chance, Hans – no longer the affectionate *Hansi* – one more misstep and you're gone.

'Let's go to Munich now, tonight,' Seb said to Hexie. 'We'll go to your apartment – you'll be safer there, at least in the short term.'

'What about Jurgen?'

'He's with his troop. No reason to think Jena knows anything about him, but he'll have to be warned.'

'You really want to drive through the night to Munich?'

'I think I do.'

'I should tell Carin.'

'I don't think it's in her best interests to be involved. Leave her a note downstairs: say your mother's ill or something. Tell her you're sorry to dash off, but you'll see her at work.'

Even leaving the guest house with their bags seemed fraught with danger. Was anyone out there, waiting for him? Another car on the road to run him into the bank as before? This threat wasn't in his imagination: an attempt had already been made on his life, and others had died.

'Don't you think it's time you filled me in with a few details, Seb?' Hexie said, as they crept out of town along the empty road. 'If I'm going to die, I'd rather like to know why.'

He trusted her, so he told her. The whole sorry tale of the murder of Krieger in the Scharnitz Pass, which then took him to Liliendorf and the unwholesome relationship between Krieger's friend Knorr and the Sachs family.

'What became clear was that this whole enterprise was run by a rogue SS group, either protected or run by a very senior officer.'

'Paul Jena. How did you make the link?'

'The Klimt painting at Schloss Stark. They said it was an anonymous woman, but there was something familiar about her. And then I found an old photograph album in the Sachs' house. There were pictures of a young Selma Sachs at Attersee. She was the woman in the portrait, and Klimt himself was in one of the photographs.'

'That didn't prove the Jena connection.'

'No, but it was becoming clear that the SS were involved in stealing the picture. And to sell it on to a wealthy family, a senior man was required. The von Starks would have dealt with only someone they knew and trusted.'

'Still no proof, though.'

'Not at first, but an idea came to me in a moment of inspiration while I was visiting Howard Jack. Target a man like Jena in front of his upper-class friends and it wouldn't take long for the humiliation to flush him out. There is no doubt in my mind. Paul Jena may be an SS-Gruppenführer, but he's also a common criminal with a taste for murder.'

'He sounds like a very *uncommon* criminal to me.'

Seb smiled. Hexie always did have a way of getting straight to the point.

But there was also the far more troubling matter that he had not discussed with her: the death of Elena Lang. It was a subject he would have to broach, and when Hexie knew the truth – that Elena had been murdered – she might never forgive him.

They arrived at Hexie's apartment at three in the morning. Seb approached with care, scanning the few cars in the road to see whether they were occupied, but all appeared to be empty.

He took her indoors and checked all the rooms. The place was cold after not having been heated for so long, but it seemed secure. 'No intruders.'

'Are you sure?'

'As far as I can be. Have you told anyone at work your new address?'

'Only Carin.'

'No one else?'

'It hasn't come up.'

He hadn't told her that Jena knew about her, knew where she worked, knew that her birth name was Herta, not Hexie. Hopefully, he didn't know about her change of address, but that didn't mean he couldn't find it.

'You go to bed, Hex. I'm heading off to Ainmüllerstrasse. The last thing you need is my car parked anywhere in the vicinity.'

'But they'll know about your apartment – you'd be safer here with me.'

'Mutti's there. And I'm armed.'

He kissed her and held her. The time had come; he could put it off no longer.

'Hexie,' he said. 'There's something I have to tell you.'

'It's about Elena, isn't it?'

He nodded, shamefaced. 'I wanted to tell you before, but I couldn't.'

'Is she dead?'

'She was killed on the night of the party at Schloss Stark. Her body was dumped in the snow up on the Höllental.'

'Was it Jena?'

'Possibly. I don't know. But I intend to find out.'

Hexie fell silent for a moment.

'I know you're angry with me, Hex. I'm angry with myself.'

'Oh, Seb.' She smiled with a terrible sadness. 'I suppose I am, but that won't bring her back, will it?'

43

Nothing happened.

Seb kept the door double-bolted at night. He informed Sergeant Winter of the threat and avoided contacting Hexie in case his calls were bugged, but he was worried for her. On the plus side, he doubted that the SS general would risk harming an employee of Hitler's close friend Heinrich Hoffmann.

To protect his mother, he spoke with his uncle Christian. 'Yes, boy,' he said. 'You've acted very foolishly; Jena is not a man to be crossed. There were others at this little dinner party where he drew a gun on you – and the word is out that he will come for you. There's nothing I can do about it. But I have got word back to him that if anything happens to my sister, I will bring him down.'

Which meant that the attack, when it came, was unlikely to be at home.

When Jurgen returned from Gapa the following Saturday, Seb explained some of the circumstances to him. 'You could be in danger, but it is very slight. That said, you would do well to take extra care when you're outside on the street.'

Jurgen treated the warning as a joke. It was the same casual courage the boys of 1917 displayed when marching off to war with a song and a laugh. They had felt immortal then, the same as his son did now. 'What about you, old man?'

'I'll do my best to stay alive.'

Still nothing happened.

Ninety kilometres away, the Winter Olympics came to a close with a ceremony once again presided over by Adolf Hitler. There had been some remarkable feats: Christl Cranz had won gold in the women's combined skiing, Sonja Henie took the figure skating prize and, against all the odds, Great Britain somehow beat Canada in the ice hockey.

Now the athletes, journalists, Games officials and tourists were on their way home to their various countries with a feeling that, generally speaking, Germany had put on a good show. There had been no trouble, no obvious thuggery meted out by the local Nazis, and the sport had been superb. Roll on the summer Olympics in Berlin.

Munich's deputy president of police Thomas Ruff had rarely been happier. He summoned Seb to his office to congratulate him. 'I don't know how you did it, Wolff, but you managed to keep the lid on things.'

'Thank you, sir, but you do realise that there are still outstanding matters. In particular the murder of Elena Lang.'

'I'm ahead of you. It's clear now that she fell into one of the lakes and drowned. A great deal of alcohol in her system, even a suggestion of heroin. A terrible tragedy but an accident. No one else involved. A press release is presently being prepared for the international media.'

'And you believe all that, do you, Herr Ruff? Her body was found nowhere near a lake.'

'Then a small stream, or even snow breathed into the lungs. It doesn't really matter in the scheme of things. Perhaps wild animals dragged her body away from the stream. So many possibilities. But maybe you have a better idea, captain. If she was murdered, as you seem to imply, who did it and why?'

'I'm still investigating that. And it's almost impossible to believe she walked that far from Schloss Stark.'

'But possible nonetheless.'

'Then there is the murder of Theodor Krieger.'

'Ah yes, a domestic affair, just as I suggested. I read your report. His wife and her lover, yes? A crime of passion exacerbated by the denouncement of Frau Krieger's father, a notorious Bolshevik. Have they been charged?'

'No, because I have no evidence.'

'Bring them in, get confessions. Proper police work, Wolff, that's what's needed. Do things the right way – don't just wait for things to fall into your lap.'

Seb nodded. Let Ruff pretend he understood police work. 'And then there's the matter of three men shot dead and burned to charcoal in Liliendorf.'

'Which is a mystery that might never be solved. And the world will be none the worse for it. They were all criminal elements and will not be missed.'

'You saw my report?'

'Not your finest piece of work, Wolff. Some rot about a Jewish woman and a painting in the home of the von Starks. As I read it, I rather thought you should turn your hand to fiction writing. Your report will not see the light of day, for which you should be extremely grateful.'

Seb smiled. He had known this would be the outcome. Thomas Ruff the coward would never take a stand against wealth or power. 'Do you have no concerns regarding the part played by SS-Gruppenführer Jena?'

'Are you insane, Wolff? Get a grip on yourself.'

'Is that all, Herr Ruff?'

'It is. Now get out there and arrest Krieger's widow and her lover and let's have that confession by nightfall. Put these other matters to the back of your mind where they belong.'

And that was it. Like the catastrophic plane crash over

Munich at the start of the Games, these events would be hushed up and quietly forgotten. In years to come, people would wonder about the great Elena Lang: was her death really an accident, or was it the suicide of a poor desperate woman, scorned in love? It would be one of those mysteries that the newspapers returned to from time to time, without any conclusion.

Seb had never felt such an utter failure.

But he knew it wasn't over.

An unexpected visitor was waiting for him at reception.

'Mr Jack, what a surprise.'

'Howard, please. Do I have to call you Captain Wolff here?'

'Seb will do.'

'Is there somewhere nearby we can go for a drink?'

'The Tirolkeller is just around the corner, but I can't stay long.' He had a pair of arrests to make.

'This won't take more than a few minutes and a beer.'

'Follow me.'

The Tirolkeller was its same old smoky self, filled with alcohol fumes, chatter and laughter. Gudrun the waitress, as gorgeous and sweaty as ever, spotted him instantly and came to take his order. 'Where have you been these past two weeks, detective? I've missed you.'

'Gapa, where else? With the rest of the world. Two beers, and one for yourself.'

As Gudrun wandered off, Howard Jack raised an eyebrow. 'An old flame, Seb?'

'An old friend.'

'I like this place. The true Bavaria. Smells of beer, sex and laughter.'

'Not too touristy. Anyway, what brings you to Munich?'

'The galleries, the Fasching celebrations, the theatre. After all that thrilling sport, I need a bit of culture. And I very much wanted to see you, Seb. Quite an impression you made at Schloss Stark.'

Seb smiled. 'I rather spoilt dinner, didn't I?'

'I should say. Everyone was aghast – and Jena pulling a gun on you! It occurred to me you might like to be brought up to date with the aftermath.'

'Indeed I would.' This was an unexpected development.

'Sophie is absolutely appalled to discover that the Klimt was stolen property. Werner doesn't give two hoots, but Sophie won't have it. She's mortified and is insisting that if they can't find Selma Sachs they should give the painting to a museum, probably in Vienna. She called her parents, who are presently overseas, and they agree. Nothing must tarnish the good name of the von Starks.'

'I'm very glad to hear it, Howard – and pleasantly surprised. I think a great deal better of Sophie now.'

'She and Werner harangued Jena in front of us all, asked him if it was true about Selma Sachs. Asked him why he hadn't mentioned it before when he offered them the painting. He looked like thunder and stalked out. The von Starks can do things like that – their wealth protects them, and Jena knows it. He certainly won't be getting any more invitations to Schloss Stark.'

'Will Sophie testify against him?'

'Not a chance.'

'Then I'm rather short of solid evidence.' That had been the story of his life for the past two weeks.

'Your priority should be your own safety, old boy. Everyone who saw him draw the gun agrees he intends to kill you. I thought you should be warned.'

Seb clinked beer glasses, his face creased with laughter.

'You're so wonderfully English, Howard. Things like this don't happen in the Home Counties, do they?'

'I should hope not. But you don't sound either surprised or worried.'

Seb shrugged. 'I already knew. Anyway, there's not much I can do, is there? Paul Jena is a gangster. He wears a smart uniform with high boots and runic flashes on his collar, but those don't camouflage the lowlife thug within.'

'Then what are you going to do?'

'I'm still working on that one. Bit of a problem. Hexie has her own ideas, but they're not that practical.'

There was silence for a minute, both men knowing the direction of thought of the other. Finally, Jack brought the matter up. 'And then there's Elena Lang. I suppose you've known for a while that she's dead.'

'There are things I can't talk about.'

'But she was murdered, wasn't she? This was no accident or suicide.'

'Why do you say that, Wimsey?'

'Oh, I'm no Wimsey. I just have a certain intuition. And my intuition tells me that Elena was murdered.'

'Interesting.'

'You're keeping your cards very close to your chest, Seb.'

'That's my job. But, say for a moment that you're right, that Elena Lang was taken from the party, drowned and her body dumped, that means that the killer is someone who was at Schloss Stark that night.'

'There were hundreds there, and the servants.'

'I agree any one of them could be involved. But my first thought would be directed to someone in her circle.'

'Which leaves us where?'

'I wish I knew.' He looked at his watch. Sergeant Winter would be waiting for him and getting anxious. He downed his beer. 'Enjoy the art, Howard. If you have time, you might want to pop into the Gallery Braque in Maxvorstadt.'

'It's already on my list. Opening night tomorrow.'

'If I'm still alive, I may very well see you there.'

'I hope so. And bring Hexie.'

'Oh, she wouldn't miss it for the world.' *If only you knew*, he thought.

With the Olympics done, Garmisch-Partenkirchen and the surrounding villages were moving gently back into their normal winter mode. Diehard skiers were here in the week and the Munich day trippers would be coming at the weekends. But it wouldn't last long. It was the second half of February, and the snow would be gone soon.

'What's happening with you and Malwine, sergeant? Have you asked her to marry you yet?'

Winter grimaced. 'It's difficult.'

'Tell me more.'

'She's angry with me because I was out of contact for so long and she didn't know where I was. But the real problem is that her parents despise me. They don't like the look of me, they hate my accent, and as good Bavarians they are appalled at the thought of their daughter marrying someone from Dortmund with a shaven head and a bruised face. The only thing in my favour is that they're desperate for grandchildren.'

'But you're not marrying *them*, you're in love with Malwine. My mother doesn't like Hexie, so I know what the problem's like, but in the end it'll be down to me, not Mutti. The same has to be true of you and Malwine.'

'I went to see her last night, but she just won't let it drop. It's got so bad I no longer know how I feel about her.'

'Have you tried telling her the truth?'

'I can't, you must know that. I'd lose my job and she'd reject me anyway.'

'I didn't mean that. I meant the truth about your undercover work in Dachau. She and her parents might be impressed.'

'I thought about that, but I don't know what I'm trying to prove any more. They should accept me for who I am or not at all.'

They had arrived in Farchant. Seb pulled up outside the Krieger house and looked across the road at Horst Feld's workshop. First things first. He knocked on Petra Krieger's door.

Her face fell when she answered it. 'What is it this time?'

'We would like you to accompany us to Munich to answer some questions,' Seb said.

'I don't want to go to Munich.'

'Let me rephrase that, Frau Krieger. We are arresting you for conspiracy to commit murder and you'll be coming with us to the Police Presidium in Munich. Is that clearer? Do I need to produce my pistol and handcuffs?'

'What about my children?'

'Do you have a friend or neighbour to pick them up from school and look after them?'

'Krista next door, I suppose.' She pointed at the house on the right. 'Our kids play together.'

Seb nodded to Winter. 'Go and ask her, sergeant. Get her details and telephone number.' He turned back to Petra. 'Is Horst Feld here with you?'

'No.'

'Does that mean he's in his workshop?'

'He's gone.'

'Gone where?'

She looked utterly miserable. 'Austria. Innsbruck, he said. He asked me to go with him, but I couldn't leave the boys.'

'When did Feld leave?'

'Two days ago. He'll be there by now.'

Probably through the Scharnitz Pass, close to the spot where he shot Theodor Krieger in the head and heart. 'He guessed he was going to be arrested?'

She nodded pitifully. Seb found himself feeling desperately sorry for the woman. A brutal marriage, her father denounced by her husband, and now abandoned to her fate by the man she believed loved her. And her only thought? Her three young boys. What was to become of them when she was jailed or worse? It didn't bear thinking about.

Justice spread its punishment far and wide.

'Is there anything you want to bring? Or anything you want to leave with your neighbour for your sons?'

'She'll need the door key. Are we going to be a long time?'

'I'm afraid we might well be.'

He followed her indoors as she fetched the key and a few things. She was flustered and couldn't decide what she might need.

'Your purse with money, Frau Krieger, the telephone number and name of any preferred lawyer you might have. Perhaps a change of clothes and your wash things. That will probably be enough.'

He followed her upstairs as she packed a small bag. When they went back down, the neighbour was at the door. Petra handed the key to her without a word, then Seb and Winter led her to the Lancia.

Out of the corner of his eye Seb spotted a black car at the far end of the street, in the direction from which they'd come. It was a Mercedes and there were four men inside.

So this was it.

'We've got company, sergeant. They want me, not you, so you drive Frau Krieger to Munich and I'll try what I can.'

'I can't leave you, captain.'

Seb pushed him forward. 'That's an order, Winter. Go.'

'At least take this.' Winter handed Seb his own Walther.

'Thank you. That might just come in useful.'

Seb stood at the edge of the road as Winter and Petra Krieger climbed into the front seats of his red Lancia Augusta. His eyes were trained down the street at the Mercedes. He wanted them to see that he wasn't in the car, that they had no cause to pursue it.

Winter pulled away from the kerb and managed a three-point turn, then accelerated up the street towards the Munich road. The Mercedes let it pass unhindered. Seb stood and waited. With the Lancia out of sight, the Mercedes began to edge forward.

Crawling, crouched, like a panther stalking prey.

Let them come. He'd take a couple with him.

And then there were *two* black Mercedes. The second one seemed to appear from nowhere and was now on the tail of the first one. They really meant business this time. Four SS men with sub-machine guns were clearly considered not enough to take him down.

He took his own Walther out of its holster, released the safety on both weapons and held one gun in each hand. Like a gunfighter in one of those cowboy films he liked.

An old man, stooped and grey, wearing knee-length lederhosen beneath a thick jacket, walked snail-like along the pavement on the far side of the road. A young mother with a pram was striding towards him. The neighbour, Krista, was standing on her own doorstep. Her arms were folded and she was staring at his pistols, open-mouthed in shock and horror. Things like this didn't happen in her quiet village.

This was bad. He didn't want any innocent bystanders to witness what was about to happen. Even less did he want them injured or killed. This was no place for a shoot-out.

He slipped back to the house. The door was still open, so he went inside and pulled the bolt across. How would they manage this? Break through a window knowing that he, too, was armed? Set fire to the building as they had done at Liliendorf?

Their previous attempt on his life had been carried out under cover of darkness in remote woodland. This attack in a residential street with scores of witnesses was an act of desperation. Or maybe discretion didn't matter now that the Olympics were over.

Not that anyone would ever say a word. Didn't see anything, didn't hear anything. These people knew when to keep their eyes and ears and mouths firmly shut.

He was upstairs now, wondering where he could get to if he went out the back. For the moment he was in the largest bedroom, the marital chamber, looking through the window and down the street towards the first Mercedes. As he did so, something strange happened.

The front-seat passenger from the second of the cars was getting out of the vehicle. His uniform identified him as an officer. Now he was walking towards the other car. The driver's window was wound down. The officer saluted the driver then spoke to him.

This carried on for a full minute, two minutes, then the officer strolled back to his own car.

The men in the first Merc seemed to be having a conversation, then the car began to turn. It mounted the pavement on the far side of the street and completed a full U-turn and lurched forward, racing through the gears as it gathered speed.

The officer in the second Merc watched it go, then climbed back into his own car and drove forward until it slid to a halt outside the Krieger house.

It was Fritz Mannheim, Unity Mitford's SS boyfriend.

44

Mannheim was getting out of the car, alone. There were no firearms in evidence as he walked up the path to Petra Krieger's front door. He rapped lightly with his knuckles.

Seb replaced his own pistol in its leather holster, but kept Winter's gun in his right hand. He walked downstairs and opened the front door, coming face to face with Mannheim, who clicked his heels and gave a sharp little bow of the head.

'Captain Wolff, I was wondering whether I could give you a lift somewhere. It seems your car has gone without you.'

'What's going on, Mannheim? What was all that?'

'You can put the gun away. I'm not going to hurt you.' He was serious but calm. *Disciplined*, that was the word. Whenever Seb had encountered the man, he always seemed disciplined. Fully in control of his emotions. Not hot and cold like Jena, but sure of himself and his authority.

'I'll keep it in my hand for the time being. Are you going to explain?'

Mannheim shrugged with a rare smile. 'Oh, those men in the other Mercedes seemed to have some strange ideas that would not have been good for your health. I explained that there had been a change of plan and that they were to return to base forthwith. They were not happy, but when I explained that I was a junior adjutant in the Führer's bodyguard, they fell into line. Now then, about that lift – Munich, I assume?'

Seb clicked the safety back on and shoved Winter's Walther

into his pocket. 'Thank you, Sturmbannführer Mannheim. I would be delighted to accept your offer.'

'Perhaps we could sit in the back and have a little chat.'

The drive was smooth. There was no sign of the other Mercedes, nor of Seb's Lancia.

'The thing is, Wolff, I have a problem and you might be the only man able to solve it. Assuming you can stay alive long enough.'

'That sounds ominous.'

'I want you to arrest Gruppenführer Jena.'

Seb looked sideways to see if this was some kind of elaborate joke, but Mannheim's eyes gave nothing away. He wasn't joking.

'Tell me more.'

'It's pretty straightforward. He's a criminal and an embarrassment to the SS. Paul Jena does us all a disservice and I see it as my bounden duty to protect the Führer from him and anyone else who would sully the reputation of the Schutzstaffel and the good name of Germany. So you will arrest him in your capacity as a senior police officer.'

'On what charge?'

'Take your pick. Theft, organised crime, murder, attempted murder. Perhaps selling stolen property would be a good holding charge to keep him off the street while we work out how to proceed.'

'You mean the Klimt. Could you persuade the von Starks to testify against him?'

He shook his head. 'The von Starks would never allow themselves to be questioned in public. Their name cannot be mentioned in court. But they could produce a respectable art dealer to testify.'

'You've really thought this through.'

'Paul Jena is a disgrace. He has expensive tastes in wine and women – and he pays for them by criminal means. Perhaps you don't know, but he's been affiliated to the SS-Junker School at Bad Tölz, where he corrupted certain young recruits for his special missions. It has to stop, Captain Wolff. He has no honour – and in the SS honour is everything.'

'How do you propose I go about the physical task of hauling him in? He or his subordinates would shoot me dead before I got within ten metres.'

'Yes, it's not going to be easy.'

'I don't even know where to find him. Where does he live?'

'Grünwald. He has a large villa there. Not bad for the son of an alcoholic mother and a petty criminal father from the back streets of Munich. Just happened to join the Party at the right time.'

'Sounds a bit like my uncle.'

'Oh, Jena only knows brute force – not half as smart as Christian Weber.'

'This villa at Grünwald. Who's there – his wife, I suppose. Any children?'

'No children, but he does have staff – more of a personal protection squad. Elsewhere, there is always at least one SS guard.'

'So where do I arrest him?'

'That's for you to work out. I know you to be a brave man, captain. A little indiscreet at times – your politics or lack of them do not go unnoted. But in the months we've known each other I've seen that you do not lack for courage.'

Seb raised a sceptical eyebrow. He and Sturmbannführer Mannheim had never been friends.

'I know what you're thinking – that the Lady Unity whom I escort might have other ideas about you. But let me tell you something: your remarkable confrontation with Paul

Jena at Schloss Stark was magnificent – and those are not just my words. Unity Mitford was impressed, too. It doesn't mean she'll ever like you, but you've earned a little grudging respect.'

Which was not something Seb particularly wanted.

'And as for Werner and Sophie,' Mannheim continued, 'they had already seen through him and wanted some way to freeze him out. Not so simple with an SS-Gruppenführer.'

'Not easy to arrest him either.'

'But if you do nothing, you'll certainly lose your life.'

'You have a plan of some sort?'

'No, that's your job. But, importantly, you can be sure that you will have my full support once you have him under lock and key.'

'One question: why don't you arrest him yourself?'

'A mere Sturmbannführer take an SS-Gruppenführer into custody? It couldn't happen. This has to be done properly – and you are the official instrument of the law, not me.'

Seb nodded. He was right – and there was nothing to be gained by doing nothing. 'Count me in.'

Mannheim was still looking straight ahead, but now his gaze shifted and he met Seb's eyes. 'And, remember, I'm involved in this now. In protecting you today I've made myself his enemy. You're no longer the only one he'll try to kill.'

Petra Krieger sat at the bare wooden table with her head in her hands. Opposite her, Seb Wolff and Hans Winter exchanged glances. They were in a windowless interview room at the Police Presidium, and for some reason the solitary overhead light bulb was flickering.

'We're going to have to deal with that, sergeant.'

'I'll see if I can find a spare bulb.'

'Be quick about it.'

As Winter hurried from the room, Seb addressed the woman. 'I'm sorry about this, Frau Krieger.'

She was weeping, but there was nothing he could do to comfort her. He needed to get this over with.

'What I have to know is who had the initial idea to kill your husband.'

She didn't answer, just sobbed silently.

'It had to be you, Herr Feld or your father, Friedrich Brauer. The answer to that question could make a difference when the case comes to trial.'

He hated this bit about being a murder cop. Every fibre of his being would love to put someone like Paul Jena away, and if they were taken to the guillotine so be it; such people knew the penalty prescribed by law when they committed their murders.

But this pathetic crime of passion and revenge? Families torn apart, children orphaned, generations devastated – no, this was *not* why he had joined the Murder Team.

Winter returned, proudly clutching a light bulb.

'Where did you find that, sergeant?'

'Your office, captain.'

'Ten out of ten for ingenuity. Nought out of ten for audacity. Now get on your chair and replace it. Try not to electrocute yourself.'

Winter handed Seb a torch. 'I borrowed this. Perhaps you'd do the honours and keep the room lit. Do you, perhaps, have a handkerchief to hold the bulb?'

Seb fished in his pocket and handed his square to Winter. This was becoming farcical, but he didn't really mind. Better to appear a little inept and amateurish than harsh and professional in front of the pitiful woman they were trying to interrogate. They needed to get to some semblance of the truth but not too much. It would help

Petra Krieger's cause if she could be a little circumspect in her testimony.

'I believe you said your husband was brutal to you and the children. Unfaithful, too. Is that correct?'

Suddenly she sobbed out loud, a racking wail that filled the room with despair.

'Perhaps Horst Feld made the decision to shoot Theodor in the woods? Was that how it happened?' Horst Feld, now safely out of the way in Austria and therefore unable to contradict her. 'Did he do it without telling you?'

Winter had replaced the bulb and the new one filled the room with soft, yellow light. He looked at Seb askance and silently mouthed, *Really?*

Seb put a finger to his lips. *Say nothing, sergeant.*

'Perhaps you could describe the sequence of events as you remember them, Frau Krieger.' He paused. 'Would you like a glass of water first?'

She nodded and raised her bloodshot eyes.

'Sergeant?'

Winter shook his head as if to say, *What am I, a waiter?* Seb shrugged, well aware that he had asked him to perform the same service when they broke the news of Theodor Krieger's death to his wife at her home in Farchant. But Winter got the message and disappeared once more in search of water.

'Now then, dear lady,' Seb said, 'you will see that I have kept my notebook closed and my pen is safely stowed in my pocket, so you can talk at will and we can take it from there. How does that sound?'

'He deserved it, the swine. I just wish Horst had killed the English Whore, too.'

None of this was what Seb had intended. She wasn't picking up on his signals. It seemed she had no interest in saving herself, or perhaps she was still so angry that she had no idea of the hole she was digging for herself.

He pushed on. 'I quite understand that you were angry with your husband and Fräulein Schramm, but I ask again, who first suggested the murder? Now think carefully before you answer. You don't have a lawyer present and I must warn you that if you're not clear in your responses there is a grave danger that you will face a murder charge. Think what that would mean for your boys.'

'Why do you mention them? What have they got to do with all this? My children know nothing of these events – I've always protected them.'

'If you are tried and convicted of murder you will no longer be there to look after them. They will have to be adopted, by a relative of yours, a friend or even a stranger.'

'No, I won't allow them to be adopted.'

He had understood when he first met Petra Krieger that she was not endowed with great intelligence or under-standing. But he hadn't realised quite how illogical were the workings of her mind. She clearly had no comprehension of the terrible situation she was in.

'But that is what will happen if you're guilty of murder. You won't have any say in the matter.'

Her face was that of a wounded animal that has been run into a corner and trapped. Her eyes were wild. 'But what are you saying? I don't know what you're saying. I didn't kill him – it was Horst. I don't even know how to fire a gun.'

At last they were beginning to get somewhere, but not quite where Seb wanted to go. She had just admitted that she knew Horst had shot her husband. The next question was crucial. 'I have something else I must ask you, Frau Krieger. Think carefully before you answer, for your life may depend on it if you're asked the same question in court.'

She blinked at him. Her immaculate façade as the perfect hausfrau – spotlessly clean, well-coiffed hair, freshly laundered and pressed clothes – had fallen apart.

'The question is this: did Horst Feld tell you he was going to kill your husband before he did it, or did he confess to you after it was done?'

'Well, both. We both wanted it. Then, when it was done, he came and told me all about it. That was a wonderful moment. I can't tell you what a relief it was to learn that Theo was dead and that never again would he punch me and kick me and stub out his cigarettes on my breast.'

'He did that?'

'And worse. Things so disgusting I cannot speak of them.'

Winter was returning with the water and Seb knew that they could not take this interview any further. There was no hope now of Frau Krieger pleading ignorance and heaping all the blame on her lover.

Her only slight hope was that a court could be persuaded that her crime was not actually *Mord* – murder – but *Totschlag*, a difficult distinction which amounted to killing without consideration of the consequences. A conviction for *Totschlag* could still attract a lengthy prison sentence, but not as severe as that for *Mord*.

Either way, she was not going to be seeing her three sons any time soon.

She needed a good lawyer, and quickly. Germany did not officially recognise the French concept of *crime passionnel*, but if the case was well argued perhaps the judge could be moved by the plight of a woman driven to despair by marital abuse which, Seb guessed, plumbed the depths of degradation.

But that was up to the courts. His own duty as a police officer was clear.

'Frau Krieger,' Seb said. 'I have to tell you that you are to be charged with murder and conspiracy to murder your husband, Theodor Krieger. The precise details of the charge will be put to you in due course. Sergeant Winter, escort the prisoner to the cell block.'

Petra Krieger was looking at them blankly. She still didn't understand what was happening.

45

Seb needed a drink. Beer to quench his thirst and clean the unpleasantness from his throat. Sometimes he hated the world, and this was one of those times.

The senseless shattering of precious lives. What would those three boys be thinking this evening? What would the neighbour say to them? How long would she be prepared to look after them?

He had to focus, think of the work at hand. For two weeks now he had been presented with an impossible task: investigate murders without admitting that any crimes had even been committed. At last he had made some progress and at last the world knew that Elena Lang was dead. It had made big news in the papers, a tragic accident.

Seb knew better.

Hexie was already standing at the bar of the Schelling-Salon, drinking a small beer. 'What is it?' she said.

'A litre of Augustiner, please.'

'No, I mean why the face? You look as though you've just swallowed a bottle of acid.'

'I wish that's all I had done. I could cope with that.'

'What's happened, then?'

'I've just charged a woman with murder.'

'I'm pretty sure that's your job, Seb – what you signed up for.'

'This is different. The woman and her lover killed her husband. He had been brutalising her in the most foul fashion for years, as well as taking at least one mistress, probably more. Now the wife is in a cell at Ettstrasse and she probably won't ever see her three young sons again. The thing is she doesn't understand any of it. She has no idea what's going on or what awaits her.'

'I think some schnapps to bolster the beer, don't you? By the way, am I even safe talking to you?'

'Seriously? No, you're probably not – but you already knew that.'

'I don't understand what's happening, Seb. You're convinced your life's in danger but then nothing.'

'They tried again today.'

'Where?'

'In Farchant. Once again, four SS troopers. Almost certainly the same ones.'

'What happened?'

'Strangely, I was saved by Fritz Mannheim.' He told her the whole story.

'It's all so terrifying, Seb. You just seem to be a sitting target for these bastards.'

What could he say? What could he do? Run away to another town? It wasn't going to happen. But she was right: he *was* a sitting target. He quickly downed a large draught of beer, the refreshing cold biting at the back of his throat.

At last he felt able to smile and managed to laugh. 'Tomorrow night's going to be far more dangerous. Hexie versus Ulrike. How's that going to go?'

She punched him in the arm, hard. 'I'm sure we'll be best friends. We have so much in common – you!'

'I think we should just get married. No wedding, no party, nothing.'

'You and Ulrike?'

He punched her back, softly.

'But I was so looking forward to a hugely expensive dress

with pretty bows and lace and five hundred guests. The whole *Brautstehlen* thing. Didn't the Pig offer to pay for it all and make it the Bavarian event of the year?'

Yes, Uncle Christian had said just that, which was why Seb and Hexie had avoided setting a date.

'Well?'

'God, you're a cheapskate, Wolff.'

'I'll take that as a yes, then. And I'll move in with you. We'll find a decent place together. And in spring we'll marry.'

Hexie allowed herself a smile and, not for the first time, Seb felt that warm glow. She was right. This was the way ahead.

He kissed her and she kissed him back.

'That's settled,' she said.

'You choose the date. But first let me solve the small problem of a senior SS man trying to kill me.'

'Good idea. I really don't want your blood and brains all over my beautiful and extremely expensive wedding gown.'

Seb was only half listening, but the word 'expensive' brought him up short. His mind was suddenly elsewhere: in Traudl Schramm's tiny apartment. What was it Mannheim had said about Jena? *He has expensive tastes in wine and women.*

Why hadn't he thought of it before? The bottle of cognac she kept for 'special occasions'. No one could get hold of French brandy in Germany these days. No one but a powerful man such as Paul Jena.

Hans Winter was on one knee, holding Malwine's hand. They were in the Osteria Bavaria. He had taken her there because he thought Malwine and her parents would be impressed by the gesture. Everyone knew that it was the Führer's favourite restaurant, renowned for its pasta.

Malwine looked at him in horror, trying to free her hand. 'What are you doing, Hansi? Get up. You can't do that here.'

'I want to ask you to marry me, Malwine.'

'Get up, get up. People will see.'

He let go of her hand and stumbled to his feet, then sat down again, mortified. 'I'm sorry . . . I thought . . .'

Malwine's eyes were dancing around the main room of the little restaurant, trying to avoid the gaze of the guests at the other tables. Many people were staring now, wondering what was happening.

'Why did you do that, Hans? I really can't imagine what you were thinking.'

'I thought you would be pleased. I thought it was romantic.'

'If you want to marry me, first you have to ask my father. Everyone's looking at us. I'm so ashamed.'

Ask her father? She was over thirty years old.

Arriving home earlier in the day, he had found the forged Aryan pass and invented family tree in his postbox, along with instructions for paying the outstanding amount. The pass was good. It had created a whole new ancestry for him along with copies of birth certificates. At first sight it looked perfect.

On the spur of the moment, he had decided that this was a sign. His doubts about his feelings for Malwine evaporated. He would propose to her that very evening.

Now the whole thing had gone wrong and they were still only halfway through the meal.

'I'm sorry, Malwine. I really thought this was what you wanted.'

'Then you don't know me very well, Hans Winter.'

'Can you forgive me?'

'I want to go home.'

'Can't we finish the meal?'

She was rising from her chair. 'Take me home. I never want to see you again. My father was right about you. Going away for days on end without telling me where you were. And look at you – your face, your shaven head. You look like a criminal. I can't bear to be seen with you.'

'But I was going to explain that. I was on an important mission, working undercover.'

'Are you going to leave me standing here or are you going to at least do one decent thing and take me home?'

'I'll have to get the bill first.' He was looking around for a waiter or the maître d', but there was no one. Should he stand up or remain sitting? He had not dined at many restaurants in his thirty-one years, and he wasn't certain of the correct form in such an exclusive establishment.

He was sweating, his heart pounding with the humiliation.

'God in heaven, I'm going to call my father to come and get me.'

The waiter arrived. 'Is everything all right, sir? Madame?'

'Fräulein Schmidt has to get home in a hurry. I need the reckoning.'

'Yes, sir. One minute if you will.'

'And I would like to use your telephone,' Malwine said.

'Come with me, madame.'

Winter simply stood there while she followed the waiter. When he first met her, she had been so friendly. Perhaps she was not the most beautiful woman in Munich, but he had found her very attractive. She was warm. She made him long to take her to bed.

Now he wished never to see her again.

'The project, Seb.'

'Ah, the project. You mean the baby project?'

'Of course. Have you got your car? We can go to my place.'

He looked at his watch. He needed to get to a phone and call Hans Winter, then go home and prepare Jurgen for tomorrow's meeting with Ulrike. But there was enough time for both matters surely?

It was a quick drive to Stiglmaierplatz, only a few minutes, but he took great care. Before leaving Schellingstrasse, he checked under the car for explosive devices, then scanned the street for suspicious cars. And when they set off, he kept glancing in the rearview mirror in case they were followed. Always keenly aware of the gun nestling against his body.

Parking outside her apartment block, he left the engine running as he once more looked out for any car or person who shouldn't be there.

'Everything all right, Seb?'

He applied the handbrake and switched off the engine. 'I'll go first; keep close behind me.'

The way in was secure. Her door had not been tampered with. He looked in the cupboards, beneath the bed. Nothing had been touched.

'You're making me paranoid, Seb.'

'Just keeping you safe.'

'You didn't warn me about this side of your life when we got together.'

'I'm sure I did.'

'I thought you were joking. Let's go to bed and make that baby.'

'First, I need to use your phone.'

He got through to Hans Winter immediately. His sergeant sounded despondent, but Seb didn't have time for kind words. 'Get your arse to Garmisch, Winter. You're about to learn all about surveillance.'

Seb spent all of three minutes explaining to Winter exactly what he was supposed to do, how to make himself inconspicuous as he followed Traudl Schramm – and what to look for. He put down the phone less in expectation of results than hope.

He turned to Hexie, who had been watching him make the call.

'I'm glad you're finally doing something, Seb Wolff. But before you dash off into the night –'

'It's lucky I love you, Hexie Schuler, because you can be very demanding and very difficult.'

'Coming from you, that's a bit rich. Come on, get on with it. Trousers off – or do we have to do the deed with you fully clothed?'

Suddenly they were both laughing, and then they were on the bed ripping each other's clothes off.

Afterwards, they lay together, panting.

'Surely that *must* have made a baby,' she said.

'Twins. Perhaps triplets.'

She elbowed him in the ribs. 'Go on then, get back to Ainmüllerstrasse and give Jurgen his pep talk.'

He clambered off the bed and searched for his scattered clothes. 'I'll pick you up at six thirty.'

'I can't wait. In the meantime, try to stay alive.'

When he arrived home, Mutti was already getting ready for bed and Jurgen was still out. Half an hour later, the door opened and there he was, in his Hitler Youth uniform, ceremonial dagger lodged proudly in his belt.

'Hello, old man.'

'Good evening, Jurgen. Come and sit with me in the kitchen.'

They sat down facing each other. 'Is this about my mother?'

'It's important to me that everything is right between you.'

'You mean you don't want me wearing the uniform?'

'I think it could well be difficult on both sides. I fear you're not going to like each other's politics.'

'I don't like your politics, old man, but we manage to live together.'

'This is worse.'

'Are you suggesting she's a Bolshevik or something?'

Seb shrugged. What could he say? Yes, she was a Bolshevik, but he couldn't tell Jurgen that. 'Let's just say she is not keen on the National Socialists. I fear that some of her opinions might be verging on dangerous. But she's here in Munich as an artist and we'll be going to the opening of her exhibition, so let's just try to talk about art and life – and avoid politics. Can you do that?'

'I'll try. You know I've been thinking about this meeting every hour of every day since I saw the letter. I still don't quite understand my feelings. She abandoned me and I know that I should hate her and have nothing to do with her. But something in me says the opposite. She's my mother. The other boys I know, they would die for their mothers. You would yourself, old man. You would die for your Mutti.'

'I understand, Jurgen, truly I do. I very much want you to accept your mother and love her, but it won't be easy.'

The boy laughed, tears in his eyes. Suddenly the toughness inculcated in him by the Hitler Youth had vanished, and he was a small boy bereft of a mother's affection. 'Then I shall avoid the salute.'

'That would be good.'

Jurgen was blinking away tears. 'And what about you? You must have loved her once? How do you feel now?'

Seb smiled, surprised and pleased to hear such perceptive words from his son. 'A little confused, just like you, Jurgen.'

'What do I call her? How can I call her Mama or Mutti?'

'You can call her Ulrike if you like. It's up to you. See what she says – and how you feel.'

'Is Hexie coming, too?'

'She is. I'm sure they'll be fine. They're both made of stern stuff.'

46

Seb was fast asleep, but somewhere in the distance he heard a ringing. Constant ringing, but it was just a dream. No one used the telephone in the middle of the night.

And then came a hammering at the door. That wasn't part of the dream. He leapt from his bed and ran barefoot to the front door. Jurgen was just ahead of him.

'Don't open it,' Seb said.

Jurgen stepped back, and Seb edged his way to the door. 'Who's there?'

'It's me, Frau Miedler.'

Their neighbour. He opened the door and glanced out into the hallway. The phone was hanging off the hook and Frau Miedler was standing there, bleary-eyed, arms crossed, in her dressing gown and slippers.

'Didn't you hear the telephone, Herr Wolff? Someone wants to talk to you and it sounds urgent.'

'Thank you, Frau Miedler, I'm sorry you were woken.'

She grunted, then shuffled off back to her own apartment. It really was time that he acquired a phone inside the apartment. He was captain of detectives. He could be needed at a moment's notice. But then he wouldn't be here much longer, would he? He was moving out, to be with Hexie.

He picked up the dangling phone. 'Hello?'

'It's Winter here. Something's happened.'

'Go on.'

'I drove to Gapa and waited outside her apartment. The lights were on, so I was sure she was there. Within an hour, a black Mercedes arrived. It just had a driver; no sign of Jena. She came down with him, got in the back of the car and drove off.'

'And? Get on with it, Winter!'

'I followed them back to Munich. The car dropped her off at an expensive apartment block. Ten minutes later, he arrived in the same car.'

'He?'

'Jena. I've never met him, but I'm sure it was him. Jena and his driver, or guard, or whoever he is. They're at Vagenstrasse 18 now. Second floor, I think; I saw the lights.'

'Stay there. I'll be with you in a few minutes.'

Seb looked at his watch. Two thirty in the morning. He really hadn't been expecting such quick results. This was not going to be easy. Paul Jena was a strong, athletic man and he had a guard. Armed or unarmed, they'd put up a fight.

Vagenstrasse was five minutes away. No one was outside the building except Winter, which meant the guard had to be upstairs, directly outside the apartment door.

'We have one chance at this. The guard will almost certainly recognise me, so you're going up first. Second floor, you say? You have a simple story. You live in this block, you're drunk, you're struggling to find your key.'

'And then?'

'You disarm him and you don't let him make a sound. There must be no shouts, no gunshots or we're done for. Got it?'

'I've never done anything like this, captain.'

'First time for everything. I'll be right behind you.'

Winter was almost paralysed with fear. In the past couple of weeks he had been incarcerated in Dachau, beaten up and almost killed, as well as dumped by the woman he had wanted to marry. All that was bad enough, but this was the limit.

He removed his shoes and crept silently up the stone staircase to the second floor of the well-appointed and expensive block. He did not switch on the lights. He could hear his heartbeat, feel the blood rushing, his head throbbing. Wolff was a few steps behind him, also shoeless, also silent.

They both had Walther semi-automatics. The captain's was in his right hand; Winter's was in his pocket.

He peered around the corner. The light was on up here, a very low-wattage bulb giving an orange glow. Next to a door at the end of the corridor, the guard stood with his back to the wall.

Suddenly Winter felt himself pushed from behind and stumbled to the floor. Wolff hadn't warned him, but Winter understood and played along. He staggered to his feet, swaying like the drunks he had seen over the years.

The guard had his pistol out and was aiming it down the corridor at him, but Winter was committed now. He tripped again, crawled a couple of metres, then dragged himself up, holding on to the wall as if he would fall again if it wasn't there.

'Can't find my key.' He was patting his pockets. 'Is this the third floor?'

Slurring his words, blinking, moving his head awkwardly.

'Fuck off before I shoot you like a dog.'

'I need a piss. Open the door, pal. Let me in.'

'I told you, fuck off. This is the second floor.' He pointed irritably towards the ceiling. 'You want up there.'

'But I need a piss. Don't know where my key is. You don't know where it is, do you, pal?'

The guard was a good head taller than Winter. He had

moved away from the door now, shoving his pistol into his belt to free up his hands. He grabbed Winter by the collar and turned him around to kick him away.

'I've got gin. Want a swig?'

Winter's hand was in his own pocket now, fishing for his Walther. The guard sensed something was wrong. His hand went back to his belt for his own gun, but Winter was ahead of him. He lurched forward and wrenched the guard's weapon from his hand just as he removed his own pistol.

As if from nowhere, Winter was standing face to face with the tall SS guard, gun in each hand, both pointed up at the man's face.

'Not a sound or you're dead.'

Seb was moments behind his sergeant. And then there they both were, their weapons trained on the hapless guard.

'Hands behind your head; get down on your knees,' Seb said.

Reluctantly, slowly, the uniformed SS man obeyed.

'Now flat on the ground, arms outstretched.'

'You'll die for this,' the man muttered.

'Very possibly, but I'll take you with me. Where's the key?'

'I don't have a key.'

Seb knelt down beside the guard and pulled his hands behind his back. In a quick, expert move polished over his years of police work, he removed his handcuffs from his belt and snapped them on to the guard's wrists, tightening them until he couldn't move his arms.

'Does that hurt?'

'Fuck you.'

'There will be worse if you make a noise.' He patted Winter on the shoulder. 'Good work, sergeant. Keep him there like that, put your foot on his back and train both guns on his head. Any sound, any movement, shoot.'

'My pleasure, captain.'

Seb tried the door handle, just in case. It turned, and the door swung open.

Half the rooms were lit and he could see that this was a beautiful apartment. Polished wood panelling, expensive rugs.

He heard sounds from the room directly in front of him. The door was closed, but a sliver of light was visible at the base. The main bedroom – it had to be.

That's where they were: SS-Gruppenführer Paul Jena and Traudl Schramm, one of his mistresses.

It was a shame to interrupt their night of passion, but someone had to do it.

From outside, silence. The guard wasn't moving. Seb took short steps forward, his stockinged feet soundless on the Persian rugs.

He hesitated momentarily at the door to the room. The noises of lovemaking were becoming more and more intense.

The romantic in him wondered whether he should let them bring their ecstasy to a climax. Would that be the decent thing to do? The murder cop thought otherwise, turned the handle sharply and pushed his way in.

47

Traudl was on top. She was naked, her breasts hanging over his face, riding him like a jockey at the Riem Racecourse, low in the saddle in a tight finish. And then she stopped, realising they were no longer alone.

They turned to Seb and his pistol.

Jena was wide-eyed and flushed.

'I'm sorry,' Seb said. 'Did I disturb something?'

Jena was pushing at her, struggling to free himself.

Seb took a step forward, the pistol now pointing directly at the man's panting chest. 'Herr Gruppenführer Jena, I am arresting you for receiving and selling stolen goods, namely a painting by the renowned Austrian artist Gustav Klimt. Further charges are almost certain to follow.'

'Get out, damn you.'

'Put your clothes on. We're taking you to the Police Presidium for questioning. If you resist in any way, you'll be shot. I trust I make myself clear.'

He was already off the bed, struggling to get into his undergarments. Seb spotted Jena's pistol on the bedside table. 'Don't even think about it,' he said.

Traudl, her skin a pale sheen of perspiration, was hunched up against the pillows, clutching the bedclothes to her chest. Seb nodded to her. 'Just stay there, Fräulein Schramm. This doesn't concern you for the moment.'

Jena pulled on his trousers. He stood there, tall, pushing out his bare chest, full of anger and power, trying to control the situation.

'You've crossed a line, Wolff. You have never known such pain as I'll inflict on you.'

'I can hardly wait.'

'I'll take you down. You and your family. All of you.'

'That sounds very like a threat to commit murder. Let's add that to the charge list, shall we? Now, are you going to put on socks, shoes, shirt, jacket? Or perhaps you want to come like that. Either way is fine by me.'

'I'll do this in my own time.' Slowly and with great care, he put on his socks, his shirt, his tie. They were civilian clothes, very expensive. Finally, he got to his polished shoes, then he patted himself down and ran his fingers through his hair while looking in the mirror.

'Let's go. Take it slow. No sudden movements.'

'I promise you one thing. I'll be out within hours and you'll be lucky to see daylight ever again.' He threw a last look at Traudl. 'Call Brühne at home. You have his number.'

Seb knew Brühne. Supposedly Munich's finest lawyer.

'Move. My sergeant is outside with your guard and his trigger finger is getting shaky, as is mine.' Seb moved forward and pushed at Jena's jacket with the muzzle.

Jena recoiled from the touch, his body stiff, his eyes hard, then stepped towards the open doorway. Seb prodded him in the back, smiling at the woman on the bed.

'A pleasure to see you again, fräulein. I'll expect you at the Police Presidium at ten in the morning. That's a requirement, not a polite request.'

Traudl Schramm, the English Whore. Mistress of the late SS-Scharführer Theodor Krieger. So she was over her heartbreak and on to pastures new. A busy young woman. A keeper of secrets, perhaps.

*

The situation at the Presidium was not easy. The desk man had never before had to deal with the arrest of such a senior person and insisted on putting a call through to the deputy president of police.

Thomas Ruff was furious at being woken and demanded to speak to Seb.

'What is this insanity, Wolff?'

'I'll explain all when you arrive in the morning, Herr Ruff.'

'You'll explain it now.'

'Very well. SS-Gruppenführer Jena is involved in multiple crimes, including attempts on my own life and the murders of at least three men. His arrest was requested by Sturmbannführer Mannheim of Hitler's personal bodyguard. Is that enough to be going on with?'

'Yes, yes, I know exactly who Mannheim is. But I don't like it.'

'What do you suggest, sir?'

'Can you not release Jena and ask him to attend for interview at a convenient time?'

'No, he's too dangerous.'

'Put him in a cell, then. And stay in close proximity.'

'That's exactly what I intend to do.'

'And don't ever call me at this time again.'

Seb sent Winter home to get some much-needed sleep, then personally marched Jena to one of the better cells in the prison section of the Presidium. He did not argue and made no more threats, just stood by the low bench that was supposed to serve as a bed and folded his arms.

'I'll be just outside,' Seb said.

'Bring Brühne to me as soon as he arrives.'

'He won't be given access to you until daylight. Feel free to go to sleep.'

Seb stepped outside. The jailer with the keys slammed the heavy metal door shut and locked it, then grinned at Seb. 'You've gone and done it this time, captain.'

Seb couldn't help grinning back. 'It certainly looks like it.'

'Can I bring you a coffee? I reckon you need it.'

'You're a gentleman and a junker.'

'And one for the prisoner?'

'Why not? One for him, too.'

It was a difficult morning. Seb was exhausted from lack of sleep and found himself firefighting on several fronts. Hermann Brühne, the lawyer, had arrived first thing, having already tried to call in favours from every senior man he knew, including both Gauleiter Wagner and council boss Weber.

Brühne was a small man with a big voice and an even greater opinion of himself. He had stormed into the Presidium with two juniors trailing in his wake and demanded to see the captain of detectives.

Seb managed to avoid him for an hour but eventually capitulated and allowed him into his office.

'How can I help, Herr Brühne?' he asked wearily, sitting on the edge of his desk facing the lawyer and his two rather larger assistants.

'Captain Wolff,' he boomed. 'You will release my client forthwith. He is an innocent man and the victim of wrongful arrest.'

Seb shook his head slowly. 'No.'

'What do you mean *no*?'

It wasn't worth replying.

'This could be bad for you, Wolff. Very bad. I can ensure that you face such charges that your career will never recover. Indeed, I'll see to it that you yourself will end up incarcerated for a long time. I have powerful friends, as does SS-Gruppenführer Jena.'

Seb smiled at the lawyer. 'I believe you've been talking to my uncle Christian.'

'What do you mean? Do I know this man?'

'Weber. Christian Weber. He phoned me soon after you called him. I explained everything to him and he told me to carry on the good work.'

'Christian Weber is your uncle?'

'You seem to be catching on. Perhaps you should call Sturmbannführer Mannheim of the Führer's bodyguard. He knows a lot about the case.'

The lawyer's eyes were glowering, his juniors were shifting uncomfortably.

'You don't seem well, Herr Brühne. Perhaps you'd like to sit down for a moment?'

'This is intolerable.'

'For once in your life you seem to have found yourself on the wrong side, I'm afraid. Your reputation is on the line. I'm sure you wouldn't want to lose a client like Uncle Christian. Nor would a sane man wish to antagonise a family like the von Starks.'

The blood drained from Brühne's red face. 'Why do you mention the von Starks?'

'Ah, you seem not to be fully aware of the facts here. Your client stole a valuable painting and sold it to Sophie von Stark as though it had been acquired legally. She and her family are beside themselves with anger. They want blood.'

Brühne blinked rapidly. His teeth were grinding. For a few moments he looked at Seb with bewilderment and loathing. He had walked into a trap that he couldn't get out of. And then, without another word, he turned on his heel and left the office.

It was obvious that Brühne knew he was beaten: threatening a murder cop was one thing; going up against the power and wealth of Christian Weber and the von Starks was quite another. Not to mention the dark influence of Hitler's bodyguard.

Seb was happy to see him go, but his problems were far from over.

The question now was how to proceed. He closed the door behind Brühne and sat down with his head in his hands.

There was possibly enough to convict Jena if Sophie von Stark could come up with an art dealer with a convincing story. But it would be a great deal more secure if Sophie would make a statement of her own testifying that she had bought the Klimt painting from Jena in good faith. That should be enough for any court.

But Mannheim had been adamant: Sophie von Stark would not appear in court.

Half an hour later, Seb was summoned to the fifth floor. Thomas Ruff was pacing. Other men might have a facial tic; Ruff just walked back and forth, back and forth, like an animal in a zoo.

'You called, boss.'

Ruff stopped. 'God damn it, Wolff, you've turned the Presidium upside down! And to think I was congratulating you not long ago. What is the matter with you – why do you insist on reducing gold to dust?'

'My nature, boss. I suppose I like truth and justice. Not very fashionable concepts these days.'

'Don't you dare talk to me like that. I believe in justice as much as you do. But there are ways and means to achieve it, political considerations. And now I'm told you're trying to involve the von Starks!'

'I take it Brühne has been talking to you.'

'He wants your head on a plate. You can't afford to alienate people like that, and you certainly can't demand help from the richest family in Germany.'

'I need someone to testify against Jena. Sophie von Stark is the person to do it.'

'That's not going to happen, Wolff, and you know it.'

'Mannheim says that the von Starks will have their private art dealer testify.'

'It's not enough.'

'I'll have to interrogate Paul Jena, then – and either find a hole in his testimony or acquire a confession from him.' Or one of his gang of SS thugs. Could they be turned? Not a hope; they were all up to their necks in this. They knew what happened to those who threatened Paul Jena because they had seen it happen to Knorr, Paus and Habeck. They were the ones firing the sub-machine guns, pouring the petrol, striking the match.

As for Jena himself, nothing. Such a man would never confess to anything, whatever pressure was applied.

So if Jena would answer no questions, what then?

Thomas Ruff was pacing again, his hands clenched behind his back.

'Is that all, boss?'

'Get out of here – and sort this mess out.'

48

Shortly before ten thirty, Traudl Schramm arrived and was brought up to Seb's office. They sat facing each other.

'You're late,' Seb said.

'But I'm here. Should I have a lawyer?'

'Only if you have something to hide, fräulein.'

'Perhaps I do.'

'Do you have a lawyer? Do you even have enough money to pay for one?'

'I'm worried about what will happen to me if I tell you certain things.'

'That will very much depend on what you tell me. Are there matters that might incriminate you?'

'I don't know.' She had switched languages. 'Can we speak English, please? I would feel safer. People say these walls have ears.'

'English is fine. So what do you want to say?'

'Is there any chance that Paul will get out of here?'

Seb held his hands up. 'Courts decide such matters, not cops.'

'Because if I speak to you and he *does* get out of here, I'm dead.'

'We all are. And the truth is that I really don't know how this is all going to turn out. As a cop, I must tell you that you should do the right thing. If you have evidence of criminality by Paul Jena, it's your duty as a citizen to testify against him. But do I understand your trepidation? Of course. Jena would not hesitate to have you killed if he thought you had betrayed him.'

'You're not offering me much comfort, Captain Wolff.'

'I'm giving you the truth as I see it, nothing more.'

'Can you protect me? He has influence way beyond these walls.'

Seb wasn't even sure he could protect his own family. He softened his voice. 'I could try. I could certainly make suggestions which might make you safer.'

'But no guarantees?'

He shook his head. He wanted to keep this gentle, seek out some possible evidence. 'Are you comfortable, Fräulein Schramm? Perhaps something from the canteen?'

'No, thank you.'

'Well, at the moment I can assure you that you're in no trouble. So why don't we go back to the beginning of the story and take it from there? For instance, how long have you been involved with the general?'

'Eighteen months.'

That was a surprise. He had imagined this was something new, post-Krieger. 'So you began this affair when you were already seeing Theodor?'

She nodded. 'Yes. My affair with Theo began in the summer of 1932. What's that? Nearly four years ago. I liked his strength. I've always been drawn to fighting men.'

'And Jena? How did that begin?'

'Theo was working for him.'

'You mean he was his commanding officer in the SS?'

'Yes, but that's not what I'm talking about. I think you know what they were doing together on the side. If I say the words it will make me sound complicit, as if I was part of it all – but I wasn't. I just heard things, pieced things together. They thought it was hilarious, cheating Jews, smuggling stuff out of the country, keeping the good things for themselves.'

'So you knew what was going on but had no part in their criminal activities?'

She nodded. 'Essentially, that's correct.'

'At this point I must warn you that it is possible to be charged if you know that an offence is being committed but do nothing to prevent it. That said, your cooperation today will be very much in your favour. If you give evidence against certain perpetrators, I will do everything in my power to ensure you do not face prosecution. Anyway, put that aside for the moment. You were explaining about your relationship with Jena. Did Krieger introduce you to him?'

She smiled wryly. 'Yes, he did, the fool. He was proud that he had a girl on the side and wanted to show me off. Jena liked what he saw and decided he wanted me for himself.'

'He fell in love with you?'

'There was no love.' Her voice was suddenly bitter. 'Let's just say that he was a difficult man to turn down.'

'Because of his power and status?'

'Yes. But mainly because of his brute strength and his refusal to take no for an answer. He is powerful both physically and psychologically. He gets his own way in all things.'

'You say he wouldn't take no for an answer. That doesn't sound as if you welcomed his advances. Did he rape you?' Seb could see that she was uncomfortable. 'I'm sorry, that's a harsh word – but it implies no criticism of you.'

'Yes, it was rape. At first, anyway. I just didn't know how to stop him. He was so strong and he overwhelmed me. Could I report it as a crime? What do you think, captain? No one would take my word against that of a senior SS officer.'

'But that wasn't the end of it. It wasn't just the one time?'

'No, it turned into something else. What could I do? I didn't want to leave Theo – and I didn't wish to leave my home town, so I just gave in to Paul Jena until he became part of my life. Something I accepted when he wanted me, because I had no option, like an occasional dose of flu. Now and then he gave me things – little bits of jewellery he probably stole from Jews.' She snorted with something like self-loathing. 'That makes it sound as though I were being paid for services rendered. I suppose all the gossips are correct – I *am* a whore. Traudl Schramm, the English Whore.'

'That's not the word I would use. You were abused by this man, and he assumed control over you.'

'You're very kind, Captain Wolff.'

No, I'm not, he was thinking. *There's still every chance that I will have to charge you as an accessory to some serious crimes, fräulein.*

'Did Krieger know about this?'

'He found out, but what could he do?'

'How did he get on with Jena after that?'

She said nothing.

'Well?'

'I suppose he was resentful.'

'How did his resentment manifest itself?'

'I don't know what you mean.'

'Did he take it out on you? His wife has told me that he could be brutal with her and their children. I wondered if he ever beat you or mistreated you in any way?'

She shrugged. 'No more than any other man I've been involved with over the years. It's what my father did to my mother. Men drink beer, then beat their wives or girlfriends.'

'I'm sorry to hear that, fräulein. You've suffered grievously, I know. But you must tell me how Krieger's resentment played out against Jena.'

That made her smile and her face lit up. She was a lovely woman when she smiled. Briefly Seb thought back to her little room in Garmisch-Partenkirchen when she asked him to stay with her. Anyone would have been tempted,

370

and Seb knew that he was no more immune to lust than the next man.

'I know what you're getting at,' she said. 'You're wondering whether Paul might have had cause to kill Theo.'

The death of Theodor Krieger was now an open-and-shut case. Horst Feld and Krieger's wife had conspired to kill him. The interview with Petra Krieger had made that indisputable. But could there have been another element? Did Jena authorise the killing of Krieger?

After all, very little happened in this den of thieves without his say-so.

'Was Krieger unhappy about Jena's relationship with you?'

'Not just the relationship. Theo was always complaining: Jena was making himself rich; Theo did all the work but Paul took the lion's share. There was a lot of bad blood.'

'So Krieger started skimming for himself?'

She shrugged. 'Neither of them was a saint.'

'That would give Jena a motive for killing Theo Krieger.'

'There you are, then.'

'So not Petra, her father and her lover?'

'I don't know.'

'You seemed pretty sure before.'

'Well, I hate the bitch.'

'Did you perhaps know that Theo Krieger had been killed before I told you?'

'I guessed. I didn't know. Just something Paul said.'

'Go on.'

She sighed, the weight of the world upon her.

Seb could see that she hadn't intended going down this path, but he wasn't going to let her off the hook, not now.

'Fräulein Schramm?'

'The night of the killing. I told you that Theo left while I was asleep.'

'Yes.'

'I knew he would be going but I expected him back sometime before dawn. That was the way it had been on other occasions. Instead it was Paul Jena who turned up – sometime after seven in the morning, as I recall. He saw the surprise on my face when I opened the door of my room in Gapa. "Expecting someone else, were you?" he said. I didn't reply. "Don't worry," he said. "He won't disturb us." '

'Meaning Krieger?'

'Yes.'

'Meaning Jena had killed him?'

'That was my conclusion. Or someone had done it for him.'

Seb's mind was spinning. He had already solved this case. Horst Feld had killed Hans Krieger. It was a crime of passion and revenge. Now Traudl Schramm was saying something else – that SS-Gruppenführer Paul Jena was the murderer. A falling-out of criminals – hatred based on a dispute over money and a woman.

Could both stories be true? It was just possible – if Horst Feld was working on Jena's orders.

'One more thing, Fräulein Schramm – did Jena ever mention the actress Elena Lang?'

She laughed. 'All the time. He loved boasting about his high and mighty friends at Schloss Stark.'

'And do you think he could have caused her harm?'

'Paul Jena could cause *anyone* harm.'

'Do you have any reason to believe he might have been involved in her death?'

'None at all, but nor would I be surprised.'

The guard outside the door of the Vagenstrasse apartment had been brought to the Presidium at the same time as Jena, slung in a cell and largely forgotten. Seb decided there was nothing to be lost by talking to him.

Seb went to the cell and asked the guard to leave. The man moved, limping, across the tiny room to sit on what passed for a bed.

'Name?'

'Ambach, Alois.'

'What's happened to your leg?'

'Twisted my ankle while hiking.'

'Near the Giessenbach Gorge by any chance?'

'As a matter of fact, yes. It's a nice place for a walk. Had my dogs with me – they like to hunt rats.'

'A comedian, eh? You won't be laughing soon, Ambach, you're in big trouble.'

'Why? What have I done?'

'You tell me. What does Jena demand of you? A few killings, a little robbery?'

'I'm a soldier; I merely obey orders. I was told to stand guard outside Jena's little love nest, so that is what I did – and then I was attacked.'

'Not quick enough, were you? Fell for the oldest trick in the book – the staggering drunk.'

He looked bored.

'Jena isn't going to be very pleased with you if he secures his release from here. You let him down badly. I wouldn't want to be in your shoes.'

Seb was looking at him closely. The drift of Ambach's eyes spoke of indifference.

'Then again, if you were to help us in our prosecution of Herr Jena, it would do your career in the SS no harm at all. The Gruppenführer has become an embarrassment, and other senior officers wish him eradicated like the rat he is.'

'He was just having his way with the English Whore. No crime in that.'

'What about the murders and the torched house at Lilien-dorf? I have a description from villagers of a man with your features and height.' No harm in a little lie. 'Tall guy with an EMP sub-machine gun.'

'Bollocks. You think I'm a fool?'

'That's certainly not in doubt. Only a fool would throw in his lot with a man like Paul Jena. So are you going to help me and save your skin – or are you intent on going down with your boss? Your choice.'

'Go fuck your mother, Wolff.'

Seb turned to leave. That had been a waste of time. Jena's men were more scared of him than they were of the law.

He had nothing to hold him on. Seb held the cell door open for him. 'Good luck, Herr Ambach. I'll tell Herr Jena what valuable assistance you've given me.'

For the first time he thought he noted a hint of concern in Ambach's eyes. But then Ambach snorted, 'If you survive long enough, Wolff.'

He let Jena sweat in his cell until after lunch, then had him brought to his office. Winter had arrived and Brühne was still hanging around the Presidium, so he invited them both in.

'Take a seat, Herr Gruppenführer, and you, Herr Brühne. Sergeant, you can remain standing and take notes.'

'I demand you either charge my client or release him,' Brühne said.

'Yes, yes, I think we've been through all that. But I'm afraid things have taken a turn for the worse for Herr Jena. I have evidence of his direct involvement in the murder of SS-Scharführer Theodor Krieger.'

'I must protest!' It was Brühne again.

Jena turned to the lawyer and glared. 'Is this what I pay you for, Brühne? You are like a clown. Keep your mouth shut unless you have a point of law to address.'

Winter was clutching a stub of pencil, scribbling away in his notebook.

Seb glanced at Jena and then Brühne. 'Have you two stopped fighting? Good, then I can tell you, Herr Jena, that, in the first instance, I am charging you with selling stolen goods for gain.'

'I bought that Klimt painting in good faith.'

'Then I look forward to inspecting the paperwork. And I'll be interested to discover how you came to be making a deal with Selma Sachs. And why you didn't mention its provenance to the von Starks.'

'I concealed that to save the von Starks' feelings. I thought they wouldn't wish to know that the subject of the portrait was a Jewess.'

'Not very convincing, I'm afraid. Sophie von Stark wants you to face the full force of the law, so we'll leave it for the courts to decide.'

He snorted with scorn. 'Such a charge wouldn't last five minutes at trial and you know it, Wolff.'

'It'll do for the moment. Do you have anything more to say, Herr Jena? The murder of Scharführer Krieger? The smuggling and theft of taxable goods? A fire and three murders in Liliendorf?'

'I protest my innocence.'

'And what do you know about the death of Elena Lang?'

'Elena? What has that got to do with me?'

'You and Herr Goebbels took a great interest in her disappearance.'

'Because she was a friend of the minister. I did my duty. This is an outrage. I refuse to say another word.' He turned to his lawyer and glared at his impotence.

Seb shrugged. 'Then it's back to your cell.'

After Jena and Brühne had gone, Seb's phone rang. He was about to leave the office himself, but he picked up the receiver. 'Hello,' he said irritably.

'Captain Wolff?' It was a woman's voice.

'Yes.'

'Please hold the line.'

He wanted to get away – why should he hold the line? Finally another voice came on, a man's. One he had heard before, both on the radio and in the flesh at the broadcasting house at Garmisch-Partenkirchen.

Joseph Goebbels. The minister of propaganda.

'Heil Hitler, Captain Wolff.' He didn't bother to introduce himself.

'Heil Hitler, Herr Minister.'

'I'm told your inquiry into the tragic death of Elena Lang is concluded. I wished to thank you for your diligence and discretion. Your efforts helped to secure the success of the Games and settled the matter of poor, dear Elena. I have already passed on my gratitude to Herr Ruff, but I wished to speak to you in person. Keep up the good work, detective. Germany needs men like you.'

And that was it. The line went dead before Seb could think of anything to say.

49

'Will this do?' Jurgen had appeared at his father's bedroom door. He was wearing his long school trousers, a plain white shirt, grey pullover, no tie, black shoes. 'Not too military?'

'You look just right, a fine young man.'

'And do you want me to check *your* attire? Make sure you don't look like a plain-clothes cop?'

'What does a plain-clothes cop look like?'

'Oh, you're always very visible, you and your colleagues. The bulge under the jacket for one thing, the general air of seediness. I'd see one of your lot coming from a kilometre away.'

'So tell me, what should I wear to a gallery opening?'

'I've no idea. I've never been to one.'

Seb laughed. 'Nor me.'

Whether it was the impending meeting between Jurgen and Ulrike, he didn't know. But the dark spell of hostility between father and son seemed to have been broken, at least for the moment.

The problem now was Seb's mother. She had given most of the last eighteen years to Jurgen, and she felt pushed aside. Seb had tried to smooth things over. 'It was always going to happen one day, Mutti. Jurgen still loves you the way he always did. We both do.'

'She'll lure him away from us. Artist indeed! She had talent for nothing save making mischief.'

'No one will ever lure Jurgen away from you, Mutti. You'll always be his number one.' He looked at his watch. 'Come on, Jurgen, time to go.'

Seb drove to the Gallery Braque. It wasn't far, just a few minutes, and they arrived early, as he'd hoped. The gallery was almost empty, but Seb saw Ulrike through the large front window, talking to the man he had seen with her across the street in Garmisch-Partenkirchen.

'Is that her?'

'That's her.'

'I can't bear it, old man. What do I say?'

'Just be yourself, and try to smile, answer her questions. I'll introduce you, then leave you to talk together. She's not a monster, you know. I loved her once and something good came out of it – you.'

Ulrike had seen Seb's car and was opening the gallery door. She stood on the pavement, wearing a long dress and a colourful waistcoat.

'Quickly,' she said, 'come in. It's freezing out here.'

They followed her into the gallery. It was not a large space, deep rather than wide, with about twenty-five or thirty pictures on the walls.

'And you must be Jurgen.' She smiled nervously and held out her hand to shake his.

For a moment, Seb thought he would ignore the hand and thrust out his right arm in the Hitler salute, but instead something remarkable happened: he took his mother in his arms and held her.

She held him in return, and there was no more for Seb to say, so he just moved away and began to examine the works of art.

He was looking at a strange, almost abstract painting that seemed to have the form of a woman, but wasn't. His eyes were fixed to it, mesmerised.

A man was standing at his shoulder. 'You won't see a finer picture this evening,' the man said.

'It's certainly interesting,' Seb said.

The man grinned. 'No, not the one on the wall – that one over there. Mother and son in each other's arms.'

Seb turned and looked at Jurgen and Ulrike, and couldn't speak. Who was this man at his side? He couldn't weep in front of a stranger.

'Rolf Cavael,' the man said, putting out his hand. 'You came to my house in Garmisch while I was out. And you're Sebastian Wolff, yes?'

'Yes.'

The man was about Seb's age, mid-thirties, perhaps a little older, his hair thinning on top, his expression serious. Cavael put a comforting hand on Seb's shoulder. 'It's all right, Herr Wolff. I'm welling up inside, too.'

Seb rubbed his sleeve across his eyes.

'They are so alike. No one could mistake them for anything other than mother and son.'

Seb laughed, but it sounded like a spluttering engine as he choked back the emotion. 'He was lucky – got her looks, not mine.'

'I'm sure he got plenty of good things from you, too.'

'You're very kind. I've been dreading this. I didn't know how it was going to go.'

'Ulrike was terrified, too. Come on, leave them to it. They have a lot of catching up to do. Let's find you a glass of wine and I'll talk you through her pictures. She's rather a good artist, you know.'

Guests were arriving, and soon the windows were steamed up and the chatter was loud and insistent. Seb felt a bit lost; this was not his world. He and Ulrike had drifted far apart in every aspect of their lives.

Then Hexie appeared, and he waved her over.

'How's it all going?' she asked.

He nodded to the far side of the gallery. 'They're over there. They seem to have hit it off. Jurgen was wonderful. I'm very proud of him.'

Hexie followed the direction of Seb's gaze, then raised an eyebrow. 'That's her, the famous Ulrike?'

Seb nodded. 'Looks just like Jurgen.'

'I'm not sure you told me how gorgeous she was.'

'I only go for the beautiful ones; you should know that by now.'

She nudged him with her elbow. 'You're a smooth-talking so-and-so, aren't you, Herr Wolff? Time for you to introduce us.'

The crowd seemed to drift apart to allow their passage. Ulrike and Jurgen saw them coming and moved towards them.

'Seb, this young man is magnificent. What a job you have done as a parent.'

'Oh, more Mutti than me.'

'Angela, then, but I'm sure you played your part. And is this your wife?'

'This is Hexie Schuler, my fiancée. Hexie, this is Ulrike Dahlen, Jurgen's mother.'

'It's very nice to meet you, Frau Dahlen.'

'Please call me Ulrike. May I call you Hexie?'

'Of course.'

'And I know that I don't really have the right to be referred to as this young man's mother, having deserted him and the family home so many years ago. I won't try to make excuses for my behaviour.'

Jurgen shook his head decisively. 'She *is* my mother and I want the world to know of her.'

'You may think differently when you come to know me better,' she laughed. 'But for the moment I'm touched and honoured.'

They talked about art and inconsequentials and ignored difficult subjects such as politics and the problems of long ago. Seb could tell that his son was besotted by Ulrike, but he wasn't sure that Hexie was so smitten.

Nor could Seb remove the thought that Ulrike might be a dangerous person to know in the Third Reich. There had been no mention of her new family so far. How would Jurgen feel when he learnt that her husband had been targeted by the Gestapo?

These were serious matters, out of kilter with this happy family reunion.

'And now,' Ulrike said at last, 'I must circulate and talk to other people – hopefully buyers of my paintings. And Rolf Cavael will be making a little speech. But we'll all meet again soon, yes? There is so much I want to know about you, Jurgen.'

They went their separate ways. Seb kept looking at his watch, wanting the evening to be over, but Hexie seemed to have found friends and Jurgen was talking to a schoolfriend, a girl, whom he had spotted.

'What a surprise to see you here, Captain Wolff.' It was Olivia Sands. 'Though you do look rather bored . . .'

'Hello, Miss Sands. What a delight. I thought you might have gone home.'

'Oh, a week or two more.' Her smile and slightly glazed eyes told Seb that she had had a few drinks.

'You know, captain, I wasn't expecting to find you at a gallery. Very narrow of me, but I didn't have you down as an art lover.'

'Not so narrow, Miss Sands. I'm only here because the artist is the mother of my son.'

'And what do you think?'

'There's a lot to like. I haven't seen Ulrike in sixteen years, so this is all new to me. What about you? How did you get an invitation?'

'Oh, I saw it advertised and just came along. I think the work is magnificent.'

'And Alan Harcourt's back in England?'

'He left clasping the reels a few days ago. Doesn't like them to be out of his sight. I'm pleased to have a break from him. To be honest he's strong meat. I'm not sure I can work with him again.'

'Then make your own films.'

She shrugged. 'Actually, I think I might have rather more important things to do with my life. Awfully trivial, the silver screen.'

'I hope you're enjoying your time in Munich.'

'Lots of alcohol to dull the pain,' she said, confirming his suspicions. 'The wine's rather good. The pictures are good, too. But I'm not enjoying myself at all. The murder of the wonderful Elena Lang has quite knocked the stuffing out of me.'

'Murder? That's not the official conclusion.'

'But that's what you get in a totalitarian state, isn't it? Uncomfortable facts are simply hushed up or brushed under the carpet. Anyway, it's unbearable. She was so brave. An extraordinary human being and I shall miss her forever.'

'*Brave*, Miss Sands? Why do you use that word?'

'You mean you haven't worked it out yet? I'm surprised at you, Herr Wolff, captain of detectives.'

'Tell me more.'

'She knew they'd kill her – and yet she stayed. The sad

thing is it will probably all have been in vain. She warned the world, but they really didn't want to know.'

'Miss Sands, you're talking in riddles.'

She gave him a look of ineffable sadness. 'I'm talking too much.'

'I think you need to tell me what you know, Miss Sands.'

'You'll know soon enough. On the seventh of March you'll know everything.'

'What's happening on the seventh of March?'

She touched his arm and her face betrayed her inner desperation. 'I'm going home.'

'Is that all?'

She gave him another of her enigmatic smiles. 'It's just the drink talking. Don't listen to me. It's not good for your health.'

'Miss Sands, if you know something about the death of Elena Lang, it's imperative that you tell me.'

Her lingering smile suggested she understood everything and he knew nothing. As though she had known all along that Elena Lang had been murdered. 'Goodbye, Captain Wolff. It's been a pleasure knowing you. Germany needs more men like you.'

And then she was gone.

50

Could he arrest Olivia Sands, interrogate her? It seemed impossible, given the delicacy of German-Anglo relations. The evening continued. Guests came and went; a couple of paintings were sold. Howard Jack turned up, seemed unimpressed by the pictures, exchanged a few inconsequential words with Seb and bade him farewell. 'The rest of the world beckons and I'm heading for Prague,' he said.

'Perhaps we'll meet again, Herr Jack.'

'Not for a while, I'm afraid. I'd rather cut my own throat than spend any more time with Sophie and Werner. They really are the most dreary people. You were the high point, Seb – you and Hexie. And Paul Jena's gun, of course. Now that was fun.'

Seb eventually managed to round up Hexie and Jurgen and head for home. He was exhausted, having had no rest the night before, but delighted that Hexie and Ulrike had managed to hit it off, on the surface at least.

He slept late and, when he finally emerged, his mother was eager to engage him in conversation.

'Are you going to tell me about it, Sebastian?'

'Mutti, whatever you want to know. There are no secrets.'

'What is she like now?'

'Much the same. A little older and more confident.'

'Did they get on well?'

'Ulrike and Jurgen? Yes, they did, but it might be more difficult in the long term. Their politics do not align.'

'I suppose she's a Bolshevik.'

'Something like that, perhaps.'

'That doesn't surprise me. I never liked her.'

The feeling had been mutual. But this was ground that really didn't need going over again.

'I tried to talk to Jurgen at breakfast,' she said, clearly smarting, 'but he just muttered a few words. He's in a strange mood.'

'He's growing up, that's all. I'm sure I was much the same when I was his age.'

'Oh, you were much worse. At first you couldn't wait to get to the war, and then you took up with her. And you changed so much I hardly knew who you were.'

'I'm glad Jurgen's not as bad as me yet. But give him time.'

She handed him a cup of coffee. 'Perhaps you would like bread and eggs?'

'Thank you, yes.'

'Oh, and there is a message for you. Herr Mannheim. I think he mentioned some sort of SS rank.'

'Did he leave a number?'

'He said he would meet you at the Police Presidium this afternoon, at two thirty.'

'Thank you, Mutti. And, just before I go, there is something I have to tell you. I'll be moving out to set up home with Hexie. I'll ensure you're provided for and we won't be far away, but I think it's time. Perhaps we could talk more about it later?'

He said the words over his shoulder and quickly moved to the door because he really didn't want to hear her response, or see the disappointment in her eyes.

His words had been brutal, but there was no other way. His future lay with Hexie Schuler.

Sturmbannführer Fritz Mannheim was in full SS uniform when he arrived at Ettstrasse. They went through the Hitler salute ritual and then got straight down to business.

'Has he confessed yet?'

Seb shook his head. 'He'll never confess.'

'This can't carry on. Questions are being asked.'

And who might be asking them, wondered Seb. Various names came to mind. Himmler? Heydrich? Goebbels? 'I'm holding him on the stolen-goods charge. I'm not sure that will stick, though. And it is very little compared with his murders and his use of SS men as gangsters. Nor will his gang turn against him.'

'Then we must force him to confess.'

'Short of torture, I can't work out how to do that.'

Mannheim pushed his spectacles up his nose. He looked almost intellectual and he really was very smooth. Not for the first time, Seb wondered whether there actually was a physical spark between him and Unity Mitford, or whether he was simply her designated escort.

'I'm going to talk to him man to man,' Mannheim said. 'Officer to officer. Appeal to his better nature.'

'He has no better nature, so good luck with that.'

'Would you take me to his cell, please, Captain Wolff?'

'I can have him brought here to my office if you like.'

'No. I prefer his cell. Keep him where he belongs.'

'Follow me.'

The warder began to open the heavy cell door. Jena was sitting on the bed, gazing up at the small barred window. Still in his smart Bavarian jacket, he was smoking a cigarette and did not bother to turn around and see who his visitors were.

Seb stepped forward, but Mannheim blocked him with his arm. 'No, captain, you wait out here. I'll discuss this with Gruppenführer Jena alone.'

'As you wish.'

'And close the hatch. This is a private conversation.'

The door closed with a clang. Seb slid the viewing hatch across and stood with his back to the wall.

'How has he been?' he asked the warder.

'Demanding. Not one of the better prisoners. Thinks he's a cut above us all, which doesn't make him popular. He threatens us, says that when he gets out he'll make our lives hell.'

'I'm sorry, but can't say I'm surprised.'

'I've had plenty of threats from prisoners before. They can try it on with me if they like, but they'll always come off second best.'

There was no more to be said. They stood in silence. Seb couldn't believe that Mannheim would make any progress.

The seconds ticked away, then the minutes. Four minutes, five . . .

The silence didn't last.

A loud but muffled crack shook the air. A gunshot.

Seb pulled his own Walther from under his jacket and told the warder to open up the cell.

The door opened.

Jena was lying on the floor. A blood-red flower bloomed on his jacket where the bullet had entered and pierced his heart.

Mannheim was holding his smoking pistol dangling by his side, his finger still on the trigger.

'He made a grab for my gun, tried to wrest it from me . . . I had no option.'

It was as good a story as any.

'But he had already confessed everything to me. The murders of the three men in the burnt-out house at Liliendorf, the large-scale crime network he was running, offering Jews a way of moving their wealth abroad, then simply stealing the best of it, the murder of Theodor Krieger.'

Seb didn't believe for a moment that he had confessed, but it was a convenient lie. The whole case would be wrapped up by the end of the day. There would be no trial; the SS would not be scandalised. Fritz Mannheim had protected their reputation and none of it would be laid at the door of Adolf Hitler.

'It is good that he's dead,' Mannheim continued. 'He would not even have been considered for membership of the SS these days, but he was one of the old ones, one of Herr Himmler's first recruits, one of those selected because they were tough and were obviously Aryan. He looked the part – as Aryan as they come – but he never understood the word *honour*.'

That word again.

Seb said nothing. These rats were fighting among themselves; he found it difficult to care when one of them died. One rat fewer was hardly a tragedy for the world.

He understood something else, too. This had never been about stealing from Jews. That wasn't a crime for people like Mannheim. No, this was about cheating the Reich tax office, which would have raked in all the Sachs treasure had Jena not got there first. That was the real felony, the one Hitler and his henchmen could never forgive.

Mannheim droned on. 'As Reichsführer Himmler said, the SS are a knightly order from which one cannot withdraw, to which one is recruited by blood and within which one remains with body and soul so long as one lives. So Jena had to go and the only way was death. He brought it on himself and we must think of it as a fortunate cleansing.'

Fritz Mannheim, the faithful servant. Explaining himself. Willing to do anything for the leader and the movement. The glasses might have given him a slightly academic air, but he was as ruthless as Paul Jena. Perhaps even more so.

Seb turned to the warder. 'We'll leave you to clear up this mess.'

'Of course, captain. It'll be a pleasure.'

The question now was what to do with Petra Krieger. Traudl Schramm had made it clear that she believed Jena had killed Theodor Krieger because he was carving off profit for himself. He had, she said, admitted it in so many words.

Perhaps not a confession that would stand up in court, but it didn't need to now. Especially as Mannheim would testify that Jena had confessed as much to him.

Jena hadn't made any confession to Mannheim, and they both knew it. But that didn't matter. Perhaps Jena had ordered Horst Feld to kill Krieger. So what? One was dead; the other had fled.

The important thing was what it meant for Petra Krieger. A way out.

He had her summoned from her cell.

Her head hung low as she entered the room. Her hands were clasped together and she made no attempt to meet his eye. Just stood there, looking down at the ground, hair lank.

'Frau Krieger, it seems there has been a grave error. I believe you did not fully understand the questions I put to you.'

She said nothing, as if she had lost all will to live.

'I interpreted your answers as a confession to having conspired to kill your husband. I now realise that, although you did wish him dead because of the brutal treatment he had visited upon you over the years and were pleased when you learnt of his death, you did not in fact do or say anything that led to his murder.'

No response.

'So I'm releasing you without charge, which means you can return home to your three sons today.'

Her eyes rose slowly to meet his, the understanding finally entering her befuddled brain.

'My boys?'

'Yes, I'll organise your return to Farchant. You'll be able to cook supper for your three boys this evening.'

'I can see them?'

'You can see them and be with them, prepare their breakfasts and take them to school as usual. You will no longer have to be in a cell and you won't be appearing in court.'

'Thank you, sir. I love my boys.'

Seb smiled at her and squeezed her hand. It really didn't matter who had pulled the trigger in the woods by the Scharnitz Pass. Nor who knew about it. The case was closed, and the world had lost nothing with the death of Theodor Krieger.

51

On the seventh of March, Seb drove towards the centre of the city from his new home near Stiglmaierplatz. He was living with Hexie in her apartment while they searched for something better.

A few minutes later, he arrived at the Vier Jahreszeiten Hotel. He had come here on the off-chance that he might find Olivia Sands, and he was in luck. She was sitting in the lobby, small and almost insignificant save for the fur that enveloped her. At her side were two suitcases.

'So this is the day we say goodbye, Miss Sands.'

'Cab's on its way. I'll be up in the air on my way to dear old Blighty within the hour.'

'When we saw each other a couple of weeks ago, you seemed to mention the seventh of March in some other context. I was wondering what you meant by it.'

'Did I say that? To be honest I don't recall much of that evening at the gallery. I think I was just letting you know when I was going home.'

'Nothing else? Have you heard this morning's big news by any chance?'

'You know, I do believe I have. Hitler has sent thousands of troops into the Rhineland, and it sounds as if they are being welcomed with open arms. The British and French, meanwhile, are doing nothing to stop them.'

'Indeed, that's exactly what I was referring to.'

She looked him in the eye. 'Are you accusing me of something, Herr Wolff?'

'Should I be?'

'Do you always answer questions with questions?'

He laughed. 'Do you mind if I sit with you while you're waiting?'

'Another question. But, no, I don't mind. In fact, I'd be delighted to have your company.' She patted the seat at her side and he sat down.

'So what do you make of this news, Miss Sands?'

'Quite a gamble by your glorious leader. I imagine he'll be emboldened now. He'll believe he can march across any border and no one will try to stop him. If only the British and French had known what he was planning, eh, Herr Wolff?'

Seb wasn't going to reply to such a loaded question. There were other people in this lobby.

'Then again, perhaps they *did* know,' she said, 'but didn't have the stomach to stand against your stormtroopers.'

'How could the British have known?'

'Oh, a spy maybe? Perhaps a Mata Hari – some woman sleeping with a senior member of the regime. Maybe she inadvertently heard something about these plans.'

'Elena Lang . . .'

Olivia answered with a sphinx-like smile.

'And she might have passed on this information to an English friend?' Seb said.

'Indeed she might. And that would not be treason, because she was Austrian – which is no more German than me.'

Howard Jack had come to mind as Elena's English contact, because Unity Mitford had suggested he was some sort of spy. But it wasn't him, was it? That was clear now. 'I suppose if she was passing on secrets it would explain why she was scared for her life.'

'Yes,' Olivia Sands said. 'Yes, it would. And she would have known there was nowhere to hide – not Vienna, not

London, not New York. This regime's reach is very long – and she wouldn't have wanted her family or friends caught in the middle.'

His brow creased. 'Miss Sands, you seem to know an awful lot about this.'

'Do I?'

'And do you have any idea who might have killed her?' This was why he was here. He had already worked out the motive for her murder; now he wanted the name of the killer.

'Oh, I think that's rather obvious, don't you? One of those strutting SS fellows. They're the ones who swear allegiance unto death; they're the ones who would do anything for Hitler and his gruesome chums; they're the untouchables.'

Paul Jena? Surely that was what she was saying. Seb lowered his voice; this was dangerous talk for both of them. 'You realise he's now dead? So not so untouchable –'

'Dead? Really? When?' She sounded genuinely surprised.

'The day after the gallery opening. Died in a cell in the Police Presidium.'

Olivia frowned. 'That's nonsense. I saw him with Bobo Mitford in the bar here, just last night, peering at me through those very non-SS spectacles as though I were a fly to be swatted. I promise you, he was very much alive.'

'Ah.'

Fritz Mannheim, then. So urbane, intellectual, personable, almost civilised.

But there was his other, darker side. He had shot Jena in cold blood just to clear up one little problem for his masters.

So why not another special task for the Third Reich? Killing a courageous young woman who had outlived her usefulness as a bedmate for Goebbels and knew too much, had spoken too much, was suspected of passing on pillow talk to a foreign agent.

A cold vision came to him. Mannheim escorting Elena Lang from Schloss Stark, bundling her into a car, drugging her into unconsciousness. Holding her beautiful body beneath the icy waters of the Eibsee or the Hammersbach River, carrying her lifeless corpse up into the lower reaches of the Höllental and casting her adrift in the snow.

Seb could see it all so clearly now. He had thought Jena was the ruthless one, but he was just a street thug. Mannheim was the professional.

And the English spy? That was Olivia. Sweet, efficient Olivia Sands.

'Do you have any evidence that Mannheim was the killer?'

'Only the word of a dead woman. Elena warned me on the night of the party before she disappeared. It had suddenly occurred to her that he was the one. The way he looked at her. She told me not to cross him.'

'And the incident when she tried to approach Goebbels?'

'A sudden panic. It was her last hope. Time was running out for her and she wanted to plead for her life. But she couldn't get close to him. She was pushed away by Werner von Stark. Reprieve denied.'

'So what was his role?'

She shrugged. 'Werner? At a not-so-wild guess, I'd suggest Werner helped Mannheim dispose of poor Elena. A family like the von Starks don't keep their wealth for five hundred years without doing a few favours for whoever is in charge.'

The entitlement Seb had found so objectionable now extended to murder. 'Miss Sands, I promise you this: I will make it my business to bring down Sturmbannführer Mannheim and Werner Freiherr von Stark. It may not be this month or even this year, but I will do it.'

One of the hotel desk jockeys was approaching. 'Your taxi is here, Miss Sands.'

'Thank you, I'll just be a moment. Perhaps you'd take my bags.' She stood up and turned to Seb with a wan smile. 'I know you will. But, God, what a waste of a life. She was more than just a wonderful actress; she was a beautiful human being.'

'I would like to have known her better. I would like to have saved her. But I will bring her justice.'

She moved closer to him, kissed him lightly on both cheeks. 'If you want to arrest me, this is your last chance.'

'I don't want to arrest you.'

She put a finger to her lips. A mutual pact of silence. 'You know I rather suspect you're one of the good Germans, Herr Wolff. Perhaps our paths will cross again one day.'

Perhaps. It was dawning on him that the quiet, unassuming Olivia Sands was also a remarkable human being. Just like Elena Lang but rather more dangerous.

Author's Note

Almost all historical fiction includes a few real characters. Some are obvious – for instance, Adolf Hitler and Joseph Goebbels – but some less so. Here are four real people from *Evil in High Places* whose lives – both good and bad – are worth a mention.

Peter Lunn

He was a hero of James Bond proportions. A member of the famous Lunn travel company family, Peter was captain of the British ski team at the 1936 Winter Olympics in Garmisch-Partenkirchen. He was disappointed that he came only twelfth, saying he was 'much too cautious'.

His love of skiing was bound to happen. His father was ski pioneer Arnold Lunn and his grandfather was Henry Lunn, who founded the tour company that bore their name and carried thousands of British ski fans to the slopes.

Peter, who was born in 1914, spent much of his childhood in the Swiss Alps. By the age of nine he was climbing mountains, ski-racing against adults and even teaching skiing.

As a young man in the 1930s, he came to hate the authoritarian regimes that seemed to be taking over the world, and he refused to march in front of Hitler at the Olympics opening ceremony. He was also well-known to Unity Mitford, whose Fascist politics he despised, and in April 1936 he went on a cruise around the Mediterranean with her and other members of their families. While at sea they seemed to have teased each other mercilessly over politics and Unity's passion for Hitler (whether Peter and Unity liked each other on a personal level is not clear).

The rest of Lunn's long life was equally remarkable. In 1939 he joined an artillery regiment and was soon recruited to MI6. He despised Communism every bit as much as he loathed Nazism, and after the war he went to Hamburg with the secret intelligence service to do his bit in the Cold War. Next stop was Vienna, where he had the brilliant idea of digging a tunnel into the Soviet sector to spy on the Russians via wire taps. Later, he went to Bern in Switzerland, then in 1953 he was made head of the MI6 Berlin Station, where he organised more tunnelling on an even larger scale: the idea was to create an early-warning system against a Soviet attack.

He always found time to continue his love of skiing and was still competing in the famous Inferno ski race in his nineties. He also wrote several books, including ski manuals, and – in 1947 – a thriller called *Evil in High Places*, a book title I am proud to share.

Peter Lunn died aged ninety-seven in 2011.

Rolf Cavael

Like many so-called 'degenerate' artists, Cavael suffered financially and artistically under the Nazis. Unlike most of them, he was actually sent to Dachau concentration camp – from December 1936 to April 1937 – for defiantly continuing to make art and for telling the world what he thought of Hitler and his crew. While in Dachau, the SS employed his skills by forcing him to draw architectural plans for various structures. On the plus side, this activity gave him access to pencils and paper and he was able to create drawings of his own, which he managed to smuggle out at the end of his term.

Rolf had been targeted by the Nazis because they didn't like his abstract art – despite enjoying great success during the 1920s with the likes of his close friend Kandinsky and the Bauhaus Movement.

He tried to continue his work in Berlin, but his shows were closed down, and eventually he headed south to escape the Nazis, settling in the ski resort of Garmisch-Partenkirchen, where he was less well-known. That didn't save him, and he was denounced. The Gestapo arrested him and locked him up.

But Rolf Cavael, who had been born and brought up in northern Germany, survived the Nazis and continued to work in secret. After the war, he found success again, winning several big prizes around the world and teaching art in Munich and Hamburg. His work was shown at important international exhibitions such as the Venice Biennale.

He died aged eighty-one in 1979.

Heinrich Deubel

He was that rarity, a concentration camp commandant who lost his job for being too lenient. Having been put in charge of Dachau in May 1934, he fell foul of Himmler because he was seen as too soft and undisciplined, and was replaced in April 1936.

Deubel, who was born in 1890, had spent much of the First World War in a British PoW camp. He became a Nazi in the early 1920s while working as a civil servant and went on to join the SS. When he was replaced at Dachau because of his 'liberal' regime, he was put in charge of Columbia concentration camp in Berlin. But that prison was soon closed to make way for the expansion of the nearby Tempelhof Airport. Deubel quit the SS and went back to work as a customs officer.

After the war he was interned for three years but was never brought to court. He lived out his life in a small town near Munich, dying aged seventy-two in 1962.

Rudolf Höss

By comparison with Commandant Deubel, Block Leader Rudolf Höss thrived in Dachau. He learnt his disgusting trade so well that he went on to be commandant at Auschwitz, introducing the gas chambers and turning the camp into a murder machine.

The son of a former army officer, Höss was originally marked down for the priesthood. Instead, at the age of fourteen, he joined the German Army and was almost immediately engaged in a series of First World War battles, where he was said to have fought bravely. After the war, he joined the Nazis in 1922 and committed his first murder on their behalf in 1923, serving five years in jail.

On his release, he worked with horses, then joined the SS. He came to Himmler's attention and was recruited as a guard at Dachau. In his memoir *Death Dealer* (written while awaiting trial and execution in 1947), he spoke of his horror at watching men being flogged. But that didn't stop him working his way up the concentration-camp ladder, culminating with his command at Auschwitz – which he turned into a death camp, killing a million men, women and children.

At the end of the war, he went into hiding but was caught, handed over to the Polish authorities and hanged, aged forty-five. Just before the end, he confessed his crimes and returned to the Catholic Church in which he had been born.

Acknowledgements

My heartfelt thanks go to Rosa Schierenberg for her diligent and brilliant editing of this book. She has been a joy to work with and has helped me to make *Evil in High Places* the novel I always wanted it to be. I must also say a big thank-you to the rest of the fabulous team at Viking Penguin, my new publishing home. In particular I would like to mention the superb copy-editor Donna Poppy for correcting my errors. As always, my agent, Teresa Chris, has been steady at my side, that calm voice of wisdom when things may not be going quite to plan. But, most of all, of course, there is my wife, Naomi, whose help, advice and love are simply invaluable.